Web
of
Obsessions

Carol W. Hazelwood

aventine
press

Published by Aventine Press
55 East Emerson St.
Chula Vista CA, 91911
www.aventinepress.com

ISBN: 1-59330-840-X

Cover by Arthur A. Hazelwood

Visit his website
www.arthazelwood.com

Also by Carol W. Hazelwood

Fiction
Coyoacan Hill (out of print)
Assume Nothing
Dark Legacy
Twilight in the Garden
Beastly Island Murder
Rising Mist
Treasures of the Heart - ebook only

Non Fiction
A View from the Jury Box
Co-author of Tiger in a Cage, The Memoir of Wu Tek Ying

Visit her website
www.carolhazelwood.com

Acknowledgements

My thanks and appreciation to Jim Harder, Dorran Nadeau, Adele Kopecky, Janice Clark, Nancy Poss-Hatchl, Tom McCranie, Joan Blue and Sonja Lagon for their comments and encouragement.

Facts concerning Operation Morning Light can be found in C.A. Morrison's book, Voyage into the Unknown.

The names of the rivers, lakes and towns are real. The scenes of the area are as I remembered them when I canoed on the Thelon River near the Cosmos 954 crash. All characters are the product of the author's imagination.

"The earth does not belong to man, man belongs to the earth. All things are connected like the blood that unites us all. Man did not weave the web of life, he is merely a strand in it. Whatever he does to the web, he does to himself."

Chief Seattle, Chief of the Suquamish Indians

Chapter 1

Summer 1994

Henri Deforte strode along the rock-strewn bank above the Thelon River, his old Winchester balanced in the cup of his right palm. Like a father taking pride in his son, he scanned the vast hills, carpeted with dwarf trees, grasses and stunted brush. Lifting his swarthy face toward the sky, Henri sniffed the air. Thunderheads gathered far off, threatening to sweep across the Barrenlands of Canada's Northwest Territory. The first hint of a breeze brushed the land, and a deep rumble shook the air. The Arctic's summer sun nursed its hold in the sky against the onslaught of the storm. A peregrine falcon darted earthward toward its prey on the opposite riverbank.

Henri scratched his thick eyebrows, then swung the rifle onto his shoulder. Like the wolves he hunted, he loped over the ground, covering distances quickly, despite his stocky-bowed legs. Ice-heaved rocks crunched and rolled under his heavy boots as he traversed the terrain that was as familiar to him as his own lined and weathered face.

Despite the beauty around him, his mood was as foul as the distant brooding clouds. He'd separated from his trapping partner in predawn's gray light after a bitter argument. For several years he and Erich had trekked across the land and canoed the rivers checking and setting trap lines, but this trip Erich had insisted upon venturing close to the boundary of the Thelon River Sanctuary. Grudgingly Henri had agreed, but with each passing day, his anger had built. Although wolf dens were nearby, Henri had shied away from the area since '78.

After spending a fruitless day reconnoitering the area for future traplines, Henri headed toward the canoes. He spotted Erich dragging a large limb of a white birch tree, his tall frame hunched with the effort. Erich disappeared in a dip of the land, then reemerged. Glints of sunlight reflected off metal objects. With deep foreboding, Henri leaped from rock to turf, his wolf hide vest flapping like beetle wings against his thick sides.

Erich waved. "I found it." His voice carried across the distance separating them.

Sweat dribbled down Henri's broad face. His stomach churned. He set his rifle aside, wiped his forehead with his shirtsleeve and waited.

Erich's thin face held a grin that split his parched lips. "After all these years, pieces of the satellite. Back there." He swung his skinny arm toward the esker behind him. "About a mile in, buried deep in the sand. How could I have missed it all these years?" He threw back his shaggy gray-haired head and yelled, "I found it!" He pounded Henri's shoulder. "Everyone thought I was crazy. Help me retrieve my box from the canoe." His laugh sounded strange. "You made fun of my lead-lined box, but see, it's important. He pointed to a long metal object. "This is a beryllium rod. It could still be radioactive. We must be careful how we handle it." He held out his hands in front of him. "See? I'm wearing my special gloves. Come on." He gestured to Henri to follow him to the canoe.

Henri stood his ground, arms folded across his chest, quivering with rage. His mouth curled downward. "What do you do with this stuff?" He nodded toward the metal with a sneer.

"Take it to Yellowknife, of course. The Mounties will want to see this debris from Cosmos 954. I...you and I will be heroes."

Henri's eyes narrowed. "The Mounties, they'll search this area, no?"

"Of course." Erich's eyes gleamed as if he'd discovered gold. "There may be more pieces scattered about. One part of my search is successful and I'm closer to the other. Closer than I've been in years. Geology doesn't lie. I thought I might die before—"

"No!" Henri's lips trembled; his head spun with disbelief and rage. "Leave the stuff. Take it back."

"Are you crazy? The government needs to know." Erich stared at his treasures.

"Screw the government. Hide the stuff." Henri grabbed the sleeve of Erich's khaki shirt.

"Are you nuts?" Erich brushed aside Henri's hand. "Why do you think I've been out here for seventeen years? I've been searching for pieces of that damn Russian spy satellite ever since it went down. If my geological calculations are correct, I may have stumbled onto another find. Stick with me and you'll be rich."

Henri shoved Erich hard, sending the taller man backward. "Don't feed me shit. Operation *Morning Light* fini. What they find? Not much, but my land got scars. No one, no government screws with my wilderness."

"Your land? Your wilderness? You crazy half-breed. This material is radioactive. You know what that means?"

Henri stuck his pug face forward; his forehead touched Erich's bearded chin. "Don't call me half-breed you dumb kraut. Shove the junk in your lead box and hide it. Nobody need know."

"If you're so stubborn, I'll handle this myself." Erich turned away.

Henri snatched his arm, spinning him around. "No. You can't." He spat out the words and followed them with a menacing growl, more wolf than human. "You fuckin' government brown nose." Henri's spittle narrowly missed Erich's face. "Once a sergeant, always a sergeant." He let go of Erich's shirt and shoved him away.

"And proud of it." Erich launched himself at Henri.

The little man stepped aside, tripped Erich and caught the man's shoulder on his thigh. Reaching down, Henri trapped Erich's head under his armpit and clamped down. Erich thrust his boot behind Henri's heel, tumbling him backward. They fell to the ground in a heap with Erich on top. A rock gouged into Henri's spine, sending a spasm of pain through his body. Erich reared back, straddled Henri's body and pummeled Henri. Under Erich's weight, Henri writhed, feeling the skin on his face split.

The quiet of the tundra echoed with angry sounds as if two bull caribou had collided.

"Radiation," Erich said, as he hammered Henri's head with his gloved fists, "is not going away."

With one hand, Henri tried to ward off the stinging blows, while his left hand clawed at the scrabble earth for a weapon. He clutched a rock and swung it at Erich, once, twice. Erich sagged. Henri struck again and heard a hollow thud. Erich fell to one side and Henri straddled his opponent.

Gasping for air, Henri said, "Not in my land. Never. You never take that stuff out." Henri slumped over Erich's chest. With the stillness of his partner under him, his anger seeped away. He leaned back to gulp air and nudged Erich's chest with one hand. "Hey, big man, good fight. Hey, *mon ami*. I got you this time."

Blood poured from Erich's ears; his eyes, like marbles, stared at the vast sky. The round granite rock still nestled in Henri's callused hand. The rock slipped from his fingers and tumbled down the stony slope into the wide churning Thelon River.

Henri shook Erich's shoulders. "Hey, you. Come on. Don't fool me." He tapped the man's cheek. "No!" He didn't want to believe what he knew was true. Although it was Erich beneath him, he saw the image of another, the prospector, the old man he'd killed in '78. How could this happen again? Forcing his eyes away from the body beneath him, he searched the horizon as if the answers lay out in the stunted tundra.

He squinted at a far knoll where a lone bull caribou stood motionless, framed against the blue beyond. The rolling plains of the Barrenlands stretched out in all directions, hiding an endless seam of eskers, rivers and lakes. Only muskoxen, caribou, grizzlies and wolves inhabited this area. Dwarf shrub, moss, lichen, stubbly grass, and sedge enveloped the jade green land. Except for the roiling river, silence surrounded Henri. A wolf howl broke the stillness, and he thought of his wolf traps set deep in the taiga.

Suddenly aware of the inert body between his knees, he rolled off, stumbled to his feet and staggered a few yards away. His breath came in raspy gasps; he rubbed his hands down the side of his stained wolf-hide vest. Despite the heat, he shivered. Although he knew there was not a soul within hundreds of miles, he glanced around, then wiped his bruised mouth with the back of his gnarled hand.

"You dumb kraut," he shouted. "Why you have to find goddamn wreckage? What's it worth to you now?" He stared at the large jagged piece of metal, the small cylinder and other odds and ends that lay like serpents strapped to the dead birch limb.

He sniffed and pawed at his cheeks as tears sliced through the lines on his craggy face. "Hey, Erich, the wilderness is all I got. I didn't mean to kill you. Remember, I told you this was an evil place. No good. Now look what's happened."

He sank to his knees by Erich's body. "This is crazy." He leaned over and grabbed Erich's shoulders, shaking him. "Come on. Come on. You live." Erich's head lolled backwards. Henri laid hm back down and rested next to him. He hadn't cried since his mother died, but now his wide shoulders convulsed in hard sobs.

After a time, he quieted and stood. A keen wind ruffled his clothing, keeping the persistent blackflies at bay. Temporarily, only temporarily. The tiny, carnivorous flies would soon descend upon Erich's bearded face. In early August the flies were at their peak.

Piss on uranium, Henry thought. What did he care about Uranium 235? After listening night after night to Erich's talk about Russian Cosmos 954's disintegration over the Northwest Territory, the story had become a fairy tale to Henri.

He stumbled off through the scruffy vegetation and wandered down the rocky embankment to the shore. He sat with his short legs crossed Indian fashion and stared across the flowing ash-colored water. Clumps of caribou fur, silent evidence of the herd's massive crossing somewhere to the North, clung to the river's edge. The great movement of the herd would continue on through the years, following their natural instincts. Wolves were predators just as Henri was theirs. He made nature's cycle complete. The Thelon River and the wild lands surrounding it were all that he loved. "Everything at peace in the wilderness," he murmured. "Nobody, not you, Erich, not shitty government, not anyone, can harm my land. I tell you over and over. You knew I spoke truth. The government must never know. Nobody destroys the peace of the tundra."

His eyes searched the distant slope for the mantled head of the caribou, but the bull had vanished. Henri's breath came in one long rasping sigh and he shook his head as if to dispel all thoughts of what had just occurred. It was then that he thought of Leah, which he often did when away from Fort Smith for long periods of time. "Leah," he whispered her name. "You always say my temper is too quick." Had her Inuit blood given her second sight?

His hands fell limp in his lap. It was an accident. Who would believe him? They all knew he had a temper. Should he leave the body here? It would be safe from the animals in the esker. Would the Mounties want to see the body? Why? He had to report the death. Use his short-wave radio? No. It was an accident, men stumble, fall. He pondered a dangerous place where a man could fall and hit his head on a rock, visualizing the river and its tributaries. He knew the exact place and formulated his plan.

The permafrost of the North had no place to bury a man, but near his cabin was a proper burial site and he'd be thanked for taking Erich there. The Mounties would believe his story of how Erich died, wouldn't they?

He stood, picked up his rifle and headed toward the canoes, stashed above the waterline. Reaching into Erich's canoe he pulled out a tent and thought of the irony of its use—protection in life and now in death. His hand brushed against Erich's load of furs. As far as he knew, Erich had no relatives, so the profit from the furs belonged to him. His gaze fell on Erich's personal pack. The man was never satisfied with maps and carried a Nautical Almanac and a sextant. He'd even talked about getting one of those Global Positioning System gadgets. *Merde. I always knew where we were.*

When the summer sun rotated at the edge of the horizon, allowing a short time of darkness, the wind would died. He had to bundle the body before the carnivorous blackflies and mosquitos fed upon the body.

From his vest pocket, Henri yanked out his head net and pulled it over his battered wide-rimmed canvas hat. With the tent slung over his broad shoulders, he trudged back up the rocky incline and stared at the body. Although he told himself there was little difference in death between one species and another, he felt a stirring in his chest and wondered what it was.

Vaguely he remembered his Catholic upbringing. He shrugged off the dim memory, for he found no hope in pious words, priests, nuns and other do-gooders. Born a bastard from an Inuit mother and her French lover, he had faced the world alone: unloved, unwanted and unfettered. The wild land of the tundra had become his home.

He knelt next to Erich and fanned the flies away from the face before pulling the tent's cover sack over the head. He cinched the drawstring tight around the neck, knowing that even then flies would crawl inside. Resettling himself, he squatted with the toes of his heavy boots nudging up against Erich's torso. Methodically, he examined the man's pockets and laid the items on the matted grass.

He unpacked the tent, unzipped the opening and spread it out next to the body. Erich's arms and legs flopped unceremoniously as Henri rolled the body onto the canvas. Like stuffing sausage into a casing, Henri pushed and jerked Erich's long frame into the tent. *"Mon Dieu,"* he muttered as he finished his task and lashed the package with rope. Breathing heavily, he stretched and belched. With the summer heat, the stench of the dead would draw bears and wolves. The journey homeward would have to be fast, but against the current it would take him at least three days even if he paddled day and night.

Moving away from the wrapped body, he looked down the slope and glanced at the canoes some distance away. He shrugged, bent and shoved, watching the bundle bounce over the rocks and come to rest at the edge of the river. In short order he settled the body in the bottom of Erich's canoe. After going back up the slope, he retrieved the items from Erich's pockets—pencil, spiral notebook, wallet, pocket watch, a handkerchief wrapped around an odd looking rock, a knife, and a harmonica. Fingering the harmonica, he realized how much he'd miss the music. The haunting tune *Aura Lee* echoed through his head. Irritated with the thought, he stuffed the items into his pockets.

He slapped his hands on his thighs to rid himself of the annoying insects and pulled on his leather gloves. Now he would handle the scraps from Cosmos 954. What had Erich said? Radioactivity could last hundreds of years. Were these pieces really radioactive? Erich had thought so. What did this mean to the land? He'd hide the pieces and no one ever need know of their existence.

He wrestled Erich's lead-lined box from Erich's canoe, grunting as he carried it up the slope. Erich had been particularly worried about the long rod. He'd handled it with his special gloves. *Merde.* The gloves were still on Erich's hands. He leather gloves will be enough protection, he thought. He lifted the rod and fit it into the rectangular box, then gathered up the rest of the fragments and dropped them inside as well. He closed the lid and snapped the hasp shut. Studying the ground, he scratched his face under the head net, then jerked his head back and studied his gloves. They looked okay. The stuff had been stuck in the earth for seventeen years. What harm could it do?

Hiding the box was a problem. The permafrost would prevent burying it anywhere but deep in the eskers. In the distance a wolf howled. He smiled. The wolves would be the sentinels of the box.

Chapter 2

Five days later in the drab hours before dusk, Henri paddled to the gravel shore below his cabin on Lake Damant. He got out of his canoe, dragged it high onto the shore, then grabbed the line connected to Erich's boat and towed it to high ground. The smell of rotting flesh hung heavy in the still air as hordes of blackflies buzzed over the tent-shrouded body. Feeling the ache of exhaustion, he escaped up the incline to his cabin.

Inside his dimly lit hovel, he flung off his head net, gloves and vest. His palms itched. The bottle of Canadian Club whiskey half-hidden on a shelf behind a yellow cloth was his main objective. As he grabbed the bottle, the gold lettering on the black label winked at him in the misty light. He unscrewed the cap and tilted the bottle with its amber-colored liquor to his lips. He couldn't afford to get drunk; not yet, but he couldn't remember when he'd wanted a drink so badly. In the wilderness he never brought liquor with him. Yet, these last five days he would have given every piece of wolf hide he owned for the gulp of whiskey that now swirled in his mouth. He swallowed, shuddered and wiped his parched lips with the back of his gnarled hand. The burning whiskey in his gut doubled him over.

When he straightened, he gazed numbly around the stark interior. A calendar, displaying a nude girl for May, hung on the wall above a wood hand-hewn table. He'd been gone from the cabin over two months. The mattress spread over wood planks on the far side of the cabin drew him like a siren. In three long steps, he collapsed onto the bed.

He slept for four hours and awoke to a cloudy dawn. With a surreptitious glance at the whiskey bottle on the table, he heaved himself off the bed and grabbed his head net, vest and gloves. Outside, the air was cooler, but no breeze stirred the air. He hurried to the outhouse one hundred yards from the cabin. Afterward, he stood for a few moments looking down at the beached canoes. The task needed to be done.

Later as he stood over Erich's grave, he reviewed the lie he would tell of his partner's death, because his story to the Mounties would have to be perfect, but not too perfect. Perfection of a tale could get him into trouble. He'd tell the Mounties they'd lost their radios shooting the rapids.

Back in the cabin, he took out the items he'd found in Erich's pockets, placed them on the table and drew up the only chair with its wolf hide seat. With the bottle of whiskey, a tin of hardtack and a packet of beef jerky next to him, he began to examine each item in between bites of food and swallows of whiskey. The pocket watch was Erich's most valuable possession—gold-plated, with an eagle engraved on the front cover. Henri's thick fingers worked to open it, but his fingernails, bitten to their quick, were no match for the slick metal. He picked up Erich's Swiss army knife, inserted one of the small blades into the gap and pried it open. The cover popped up, revealing a snapshot of four young men in uniforms. He peered at it with bleary eyes, then took it out and looked on the back. Erich Mann, Phil West, Boris Sweet, Cal Sterling.

He replaced the photo, snapped the watch shut and set it aside. Erich's small wallet contained business cards and a few bills. After taking another swig from the bottle, he stared at the harmonica. With his forefinger, he pushed tentatively at the engraved instrument. He clasped his hands to his ears as if to stop the music that persisted in his head. Grabbing the bottle, he took a large gulp.

Only later did he reach for Erich's notebook. The writing was in German, handwritten. He remembered Erich talking about the enjoyment of writing in German script, but thought nothing of it until now. He could only read the name, Phil West, and an address. Frowning, he wondered about this man that Erich had never mentioned. The rest of the scribbled text appeared to be numbers, lists, then paragraphs of illegible words. He tossed the book aside and fingered the handkerchief. A seemingly innocent rock rolled onto the table. Why had Erich wrapped up a rock? Carefully, he picked it up and turned it over in his hand. *"Merde!"* Encrusted in the rock were sparkling flecks—diamonds. Where and when had his partner found this? Henri tried to remember Erich's words right before their fight, but his head was foggy with sleep and liquor. If the source of these diamonds was near where Erich found the debris, then it was good Erich had been silenced.

He thought of the old prospector so many years before. *Why must evil haunt me?* Feeling justified about what he had done, he stumbled to his mattress with the whisky bottle clutched in his hand.

A week later Henri stood on the shoreline in front of his lakeside cabin, gloved hands shading his eyes from the noon sun as he watched the Twin Otter seaplane arch across the far bluff before it descended. Grant McDuffy was on schedule with his latest canoe tour. Henri glanced up the embankment where McDuffy had stored the guide's five green-hulled canoes. The jack pines stood tall above the esker's beach, and if you didn't know where to look, you'd miss the canoes stashed in the thicket of stunted willows, fireweed and white spruce.

Henri paced back and forth from his battered canvas bag to the dwarf spruce snag at the far end of the gravel shoreline. It seemed he spent his life waiting. Although he knew his lie explaining Erich's death, he continued to review it.

The hum of the engine grew louder. The plane settled on the lake like a duck coming home. When it taxied close to shore, Henri waved to Chip, the Loon Air charter pilot, and got a grin and a wave in return. Chip cut the engines, and Grant opened the door under the wing.

After jumping onto shore to secure a rope attached to one of the pontoons, Grant said, "Surprised to see you here, Henri."

Henri gingerly caught another rope Chip swung to him, and clumsily fastened it to a dead log.

"What's wrong with your hands, Henri?" Grant asked.

"Blisters. Can you believe that with all the paddling I do? Never happened before."

A group of seven men began to disembark from the plane, chattering, joking and staring at their surroundings as they lugged their gear onto shore. "Will you look at that," one middle-aged man said, pointing to the outhouse door that swung open on sagging hinges. "Shocking pink! You takin' us to some kinda far out whorehouse, Grant?"

"Meet Henri. He's the wolf trapper who owns this cabin." Grant gave a sweeping gesture toward the shabby plywood cabin. The men smiled, and two gave mock salutes.

"No *belle*," Henri admitted, noticing the men's skeptical glances. "It's strong, not bad in winter."

Grant arched an eyebrow and gave a lopsided grin. "Only if you like it cold and icy."

"It's not what I expected," one of the younger men said. "Those plywood sheets can't give much protection. Is the inside insulated? Don't mean to be disparaging. It's just that I'm in the construction business. Looks stable though. Solid roof." He glanced at Henri. "A hard life out here."

"I'm no southern white man." Henri turned and spat to emphasize his disdain for those who lived south of the Arctic Circle. "It's, how you say, insulated, and I got a new pellet burning stove. Chip brings supplies." Disgusted, he pointed. "See on the point? Good view of Thelon River where you paddle. My outhouse," he said with a grin, "last chance at civilization." Henri turned and walked over to Chip, who was busy checking out his plane's new blue paint job.

"Damned if I didn't get another dent," Chip said more to himself than to Henri. "Must have happened at dockside."

"I need ride to Fort Smith. Okay?"

"Sure. What're you doing here anyway? Thought you and Erich would be out trapping in the backcountry."

"Ran into trouble on the Hanbury River, near Helen Falls."

"Hey, Chip," Grant called out. "Could you check to see if I left my map folder in the cockpit?"

"Right." Chip jumped onto the pontoon and entered his plane.

Henri watched Grant and the men organize their equipment. *Useless in the wild.* He thought of the word used for such men: greenhorns. Most of Grant's clients couldn't even paddle, and none could survive a day in the interior without Grant. Henri shook his head. Grant never took a rifle with him, something Henri never understood. With grizzlies, you don't take chances. Oh sure, Grant knew the wilderness, and he knew wolves, studied them, liked them, while Henri made money on their pelts. Long ago they'd made peace with each others profession regarding wolves.

Henri spoke to Grant with the ease of a longtime acquaintance. "Before you go, I need to talk." He didn't look up at the tall angular man, but kept his eyes locked on the bag he'd placed between his feet.

Grant continued counting duffels, making notes about the equipment. "Yeah. I'm listening."

"It's Erich." Henri removed his battered hat and pawed at his thick black hair. "He had accident. Dead."

Grant stopped checking equipment. "How did it happen?" Grant squinted as if he were in pain.

Henri felt the man's steel cold stare. "At Helen Falls," Henri tried to meet Grant's eyes. "He fell. Hit his head. Quick end."

"What did you do with the body?"

"Buried him deep, up there." Henri pointed to the top of an esker half a mile away. "Plenty of sand and rocks."

"That's a hell of a long way to paddle with a dead man. Why didn't you radio?"

"Radios lost." Henri looked into the distance.

"The Mounties will want a full accounting."

"That's why I go with Chip to Fort Smith." Henri hesitated, then looked up at Grant's lean, tan face. He never had been able to read those quiet gray-blue eyes. "You think Mounties will dig up Erich?"

"I don't know. Never had anyone die on me out here. I have no idea what the policy is. Would it matter?"

"It would to Erich."

"Why would Erich care? He's dead."

"He was Catholic."

Grant raised an eyebrow, but remained quiet.

"You knew we got along, good friends, partners."

Grant snorted. "You guys fought like mad dogs."

"*Oui,* but we liked each other. We were friends. You know that. You known me longtime now."

Grant's eyes followed his clients as they roamed over the hill chatting in good humor. "What're you driving at, Henri? I've got a two week tout with those dudes up there and have to get going."

"I need a witness, how do you say...character witness. Would you do that?"

Grant stared out across the lake. "I'd say exactly the truth, nothing less, nothing more. You aren't the most lovable guy I know, but you've always been honest with me. I'd tell anyone that. You trade in wolf pelts, and I don't like that, but every man's got to make a living the best way he can. I've never begrudged you that. The trouble is you're the best damn wolf trapper around. I'd tell 'em that. I know Erich and you were close despite your quarrels." Grant studied Henri, then continued, "Yeah. If you need a character witness, I'll do it."

"Merci. My reputation in Fort Smith is, well…you know." Henri thought how Leah always tried to keep him from drinking at the Road End Bar. *Sacré bleu. I'm not going to change just for her.* Henri reached down, grabbed his bag and started toward the Twin Otter.

"Hey." Grant grabbed Henri's khaki sleeve. "Erich never did find that uranium, did he?"

"What?" Henri felt the color drain from his face.

"I was just thinking it's too bad Erich spent so much time looking for wreckage that doesn't exist. He wasted his life on a dream. Most of that satellite burned up on reentry, and he was too stubborn to believe it." Grant shrugged and then seemed to reconsider. "Maybe we all have crazy dreams we strive for. I shouldn't short him his."

Henri stared at Grant without flinching.

"Never did figure why the two of you took up together. You weren't into that Cosmos satellite stuff."

"You're right, *mon ami.* It was Erich's dream, not mine."

Chip jogged up with a packet of plastic covered maps and handed them to Grant. "You're getting forgetful in your old age."

Grant swatted Chip's shoulder with the packet. "Don't tell my wife. She'd never let me hear the end of it."

"She's too darn good-looking for you anyway." Chip grinned, his dark eyes danced with mischief. "How you caught such a young filly, I'll never know."

"Karen would have your head if she heard you called her a filly," Grant said.

"I know. All that newfangled feminism is lost on me." Chip glanced at the pile of furs Henri wanted to take with him. He lifted them on his shoulder and tossed them into the plane. "Come on, Henri. I got a business to run."

"Coming." Henri started to follow the charter pilot, then stopped and turned back to Grant. "The wolves in sector three left their dens. Big litter at Hornby Point."

"Odd, sector three has been a hardy pack for a long time. Wonder what would have made them move on?"

"Caribou migration's early. Wolves needed to roam farther afield to feed that large litter they had last year. Come winter, I'll see 'em down this way," Henri said.

Grant nodded. "Hope not. Thanks for the tip."

"See you in Fort Smith, *mon ami.*"

"Right. Mounties will probably keep you talking until I get back."

"Think so?" Henri licked his upper lip.

"Don't worry. It's the way they do things. Paper work and all." Grant touched a finger to his forehead as a parting gesture.

"*Sacré bleu.* I don't like talking," Henri said out loud as he untied a line to the plane. "Waiting and talking. Waiting and talking."

Chip, who stood on a pontoon, overheard his muttering. "What're you mumbling about, Henri? Missing your girlfriend?"

"I miss Leah when I'm away, I just can't stand her when I'm with her." Henri threw his bag into the aircraft. "Let's go. I got much to do before I head back here to set my trap line. Winter sneaks in too soon." He followed Chip through the empty fuselage.

"So where's Erich?" Chip asked as he settled into the pilot's seat.

Henri took off his gloves and picked at the blisters on his chin.

"Still in the backcountry?" Chip asked.

"In a way. He had an accident. Buried him back there." He motioned with his head toward the land above his cabin as he wiggled into the copi-lot's seat.

Chip's mouth gaped. "Damn. I liked the guy. Really sorry to hear it. So that's why you have to go to Fort Smith. Grant know?" Chip stroked the end of a pencil along his temple.

Henri looked out the window at the group gathered around Grant. "I got to take Erich's stuff to the Mounties." *And see a doctor about my blisters.*

Chip began to run through his preflight checklist and noted offhand, "Looks like they're going to get rain on their first campsite. Weather's head-ed in."

"Tough for greenhorns," Henri said.

"Grant's groups are tougher than they look." Before Chip pulled out the throttle and started the engines, he asked, "Did Erich have family or friends in the Boston area?"

"Don't think so." Henri glanced at Chip with a wary eye. "Why?"

"Thought he might. He sent letters there." Chip met Henri's stare with a sheepish look. "I wasn't meddling. He asked me to take letters out when I had a charter to Edmonton. You'll probably come across the guy's name. Ask his housekeeper. She might know. She kept Erich's Fort Smith house in tiptop shape. If you have to go through Erich's stuff, you'll have to cross her path."

"I know her. She's okay." Henri rubbed his whiskers with his knuckles and thought about the names on the photo. "Erich never talked about family and friends. Remember the names on the letters? If I get their addresses, I let them know about Erich."

"Most of the time I don't pay attention, but the letters were frequent to one fellow. West, Philip West. You might want to let him know what happened to Erich." Chip revved up the engine, coasted along the lake and lifted off into the mounting wind.

"*Oui*. That would be the thing to do." What could be the harm? He stared out the small cockpit window at the earth below and watched the view of his cabin get smaller and smaller.

Chip climbed to 1000 feet and set his course for Fort Smith. Over the engine's din, he shouted, "Maybe Erich's death will end all this rubbish about pieces of uranium floating down the Thelon. Do you remember what happened when that satellite went down? Jesus, I thought we'd have three-headed fish coming out of Slave Lake. Poor Erich. He spent years wandering through the wilderness and never found a scrap of the stuff. Funny, isn't it."

"*Oui*, funny."

Chapter 3

Phil West hurried up the wood steps to his bachelor apartment, located behind a refurbished Colonial in Cambridge, Massachusetts. The carriage house had been remodeled into a small, modern unit. Away from prying eyes, this rental allowed him to relax away from students, faculty, and nosy acquaintances. He'd asked few guests over—the price of his clandestine life.

He retrieved his mail from a slim metal box attached to the gray shingles on the porch, stuck the contents under his arm and put his key in the lock. The door creaked then banged shut behind him. He'd been meaning to fix the hinge ever since he'd moved in three years ago.

Slinging his Irish fedora onto the peg next to the hall mirror, he glanced at himself and grimaced at the loss of his once wavy brown hair. So much for aging, he grumped, knowing his baldness made him look older than thirty-eight. Only a fringe of dark brown hair surrounded his shiny dome, and even that had gray thatches. Hats were his friends—caps in summer, fedoras in winter.

This cool September brought the flood of new students onto the campus and into his Northeastern University biology classroom. If his real employer had found a position for him at Harvard, it would have been a coup. When he walked through Harvard's campus, he sometimes reminisced about the could-have-been, but government agencies set limitations for their agents. His undercover assignment was marred only by Nancy Plowright's activist antinuclear group, *Cure the World*. But then, that's why he was here.

Tonight he had a meeting with her concerning the semester's agenda for the organization. He reflected on this as he went to the refrigerator, pulled out a bottle of Sam Adams and retreated to his teakwood-furnished living room. Setting the beer on a side table, he lounged in a rust-colored chair and sorted through the mail piled on his lap—bills, bills, advertisements, LL Bean catalog. A letter from Erich. He pushed his horn-rimmed glasses farther up the bridge of his nose. The letter was postmarked Edmonton, Canada, but it wasn't Erich's handwriting. He slit the back of the white business envelope with an ivory letter opener and took out the slim sheet of paper. The scrawled handwriting was childish.

"I learned Erich wrote you for long time. I'm sorry to tell you Erich died in accident in the wilderness. I was Erich's friend and fellow trapper. His lawyer says Erich's books are yours. Erich was a good man. I am at the address below. Sincerely, Henri Deforte."

Phil's hand slid down to his lap with the letter between his thumb and first finger. His gaze wandered across the oriental rug and up the wall to a photo at the left of the entryway. The snowy landscape reflected the beauty of the Thelon River in winter.

January 1978. Every time he recalled his first helicopter ride over the frozen territory, he smiled. Pieces of *Cosmos 954* had been located, but the area had to be marked for the ground personnel. As part of the recovery team sent from the states to help the Canadians, he'd been handed boxes containing thousands of condoms and a gallon of red dye. Canadian Sergeant Erich Mann ordered him and two others to inject the dye into the condoms and drop them on the targeted area. To this day, every time he used a condom, he had flashes of small balloons falling onto white snow and exploding in bright red swatches.

He began to laugh out loud as tears streamed down his cheeks. Operation *Morning Light*. God, how he missed the camaraderie of those days and the quiet of that wild land. The secret he shared with the others remained a bond. When they'd discovered the old prospector's body with a haversack containing rocks flecked with raw diamonds, they vowed to find their source. Erich became the wanderer in the wilderness, while Phil and the other two financed his search. The partnership remained in tact all these years.

When the Bureau enlisted Erich's help to ensure that any debris of Cosmos would be reported to them, Phil had become Erich's official contact and his notebooks had arrived like clockwork every three months. Longitude and latitude of every spot the man had searched for fragments of *Cosmos 954* were written in detail. Erich wrote in German script—a language Phil had studied diligently under his grandfather's tutelage. Phil passed Erich's information on to his superiors, and the information was squirreled away in a government file. Would the map grids ever be of use to the government?

Unknown to Phil's employer, Erich had mapped more than his search for *Cosmos* debris. Included in Erich's notes were the geology of each map grid for the benefit of his partners. Diamonds spark greed in everyone.

Phil grabbed a tissue, blew his nose, then rose and walked to his overflowing bookcase at the far side of the room. He pawed through magazines and rifled through piles of books on the bottom shelf before he found the worn album. Flipping it open, he moved to the window to let the afternoon sun shine on old snapshots while he thumbed through the pages. He found the black and white photo taken long ago, removed it and tossed the album down on top of the magazines now scattered on the floor. Written on the back of the photo—*Erich Mann, Cal Sterling, Boris Sweet, Philip West*. Phil had become the accountant for the group, delivering funds to Erich. As each year passed, the search seemed like an exercise in futility. Then six months ago Erich reported finding Epicontinental conglomerate, sandstone and potassic volcanic rock that contained micro-diamonds. He was getting close. Now he was dead. Had the dream of finding the diamond lode died with him?

Phil wanted to know more about Erich's death. Had the search for radiation fragments been in vain? Where was Erich's most recent notebook? With several large mining concerns actively pursuing sites above the Arctic Circle, Phil and Erich had felt a greater urgency to find the source of the diamonds.

Phil returned to his chair, sipped his beer and leaned back. Over the years Erich had written to him about Henri Deforte, a fiery half-breed. A feeling of apprehension came over him, and his curiosity was tweaked. How much did Henri know about Erich?

Phil's first duty must be to his employer. Ever since he'd joined the Bureau, he'd never wavered in his loyalty. Yet, if they were ever successful in their diamond search, he could quit. Would he?

He walked to the phone in an alcove off the living room. A window to the left of the desk overlooked the yard between the Colonial home and his carriage house. Every year he watched as the maple tree went through its fabulous color change, but now he focused on the phone as he punched in the memorized number. He sat in his swivel chair, then moved closer to his desk when the voice answered.

"Phil here. I've lost a friend in Canada. Could I come visit you?"

The reply came quickly. "We've heard rumblings. I'll be at the Copley Plaza, usual room, tomorrow at six."

Phil hung up, glanced at the old Bavarian wall clock ticking, and realized he'd be late for tonight's meeting with Nancy. "Damn!"

Nancy lived in a brownstone house in Boston's Back Bay just off Dartmouth Street. She'd come from wealth bequeathed to her by an Irish immigrant grandfather. Born to a scholarly professor and a musician mother, Nancy's upbringing ran heavily to academic philosophy, which Phil thought had little bearing on the real world. She wanted desperately to be a savior and her cause became the antinuclear movement. Although Phil could see the merit in restraining government from doing foolish things—he knew his government was not above doing foolish things—he disliked causes that professed the end to justify the means. Perhaps that's why he maintained his cover without tremendous sacrifice to his character. At least that's what he told himself.

As he bounded up the gray steps to the brownstone house, he glanced at his watch. He was a half hour late, having grabbed a quick dinner before he left home. Eating one of Nancy's well-meant, yet unpalatable vegetarian meals was not an option. She was a recovering alcoholic, and had taken another step into fitness—vegetarianism. Nancy attracted "isms" and obsessions like a magnet did iron.

"Thought you'd forgotten," she said as she opened the heavy wood door. She held her Beatle's era reading glasses and a copy of Anne Lamott's *Operating Instructions* in her slim hand.

"Thinking of having kids?" Phil asked, as he followed her into the living room, dropped his hat on a nearby hassock and removed his chocolate brown corduroy jacket.

"Guiding teens through their first year of college is as bad as raising a seven year old," she said. "I sometimes wonder about the younger generation."

"Whoa. You're a bit depressed." He sat in the only armchair he found comfortable in a room full of art deco furniture. She tucked her long black skirt under her as she settled onto the couch behind an glass coffee table with stacks of pamphlets, notebooks and papers. As she leaned forward, her V-neck white blouse drooped open, revealing the top of her small pointed breasts. It was a game she played. One he had, so far, avoided. Her olive-complexioned beauty was stark, hard. He liked a softer, vulnerable look. Immediately, he thought of Laura and chastised himself for letting his thoughts roam.

"You said you'd eaten. Care for a soda or a cup of tea?" she asked, while looking through papers. A tall glass of iced tea sat on the carpeted floor by her slippered feet.

He declined. Their meetings started off in a routine, which she apparently found relaxing, and he found amusing. She reached for a cigarette, lit it, and settled back with a silver-lined glass ashtray next to her on the cushion.

"This is only my fourth one today. I'm getting better." Her pale brown eyes gazed out from an intelligent yet narrow face that seemed to ask for approval.

"The only way to kick the habit is an abrupt end," he said.

"You would. Do you have any bad habits, Phil? I have yet to discover your soft underbelly." She inhaled deeply and let the smoke drift out through her nose.

"Hey. What you see is what you get. I'm not complicated." He crossed his legs and leaned back. Her sexual overtones always left him feeling off balance.

"Scientists seem to have that trait. Not one I like very much." She glanced at her cigarette. "I can't kick all my bad habits at once. I'd have nothing to strive for." Nancy moved forward on the couch, put the ashtray back on the table and tapped a small stack of papers with her nicotine-stained index finger. "Your stack."

He grabbed the papers, settled back into his chair and began flipping through them. "Quite a few goals you've set for the organization this semester."

"We're losing memberships. Can't imagine where the young people are putting their energy these days. I've gone through the incoming class. You'll see a list of possible candidates for *Cure the World*. We can't recruit members if we don't have a big agenda. Stir up the masses; get their adrenaline flowing."

"Get them while they still want to rebel against their parents," he chimed in.

She laughed, her voice husky. "You got it. I'd like us to join forces with the Sierra Club. They plan to disrupt the Cassini space probe to Saturn."

His antennae went up. "Do you know how?" He tried to sound nonchalant.

"No, I'm not sure they've formulated all their plans yet. At the moment they're doing research and will disseminate information after that. I've got a contact there."

"Want me to take that on?"

"No. My contact is a bit skittish of new faces. Just keep giving me info you get from your connections." Nancy brushed back brown wisps of hair that straggled down her temple. Although she wore her hair in a ponytail, she never seemed to capture all of her heavy mane. Phil envied her abundant locks.

"What I want to do is educate others about the amount of deadly plutonium that's not only going to be sent into space, but the amounts." She put out her cigarette. "It's a crime what they're doing to our environment in the name of space exploration. There's absolutely no excuse." She started to reach for another cigarette, hesitated, and looked at him as if she were a child caught stealing a cookie.

He smiled, acknowledging her glance, but remained silent.

"Oh, hell!" She took another cigarette. However, instead of lighting it, she held it between her fingers and continued outlining her plans. "Our first meeting on campus will be on the 12th of October in my classroom, seven o'clock. I'll have posters put up around campus. I cross-referenced names and found three are taking your biology class. Those should be easy pickings for you, although I can't say you're my best recruiter. New prospects seem to slip through your fingers like jelly. Why is that?"

He shrugged. "My batting average isn't too good, is it?"

"No, it isn't. Some are beginning to question me about you."

He felt a flush creep up his neck, but there wasn't a thing he could do about it.

"Oh, don't look so sheepish. I told them you more than made up for your lack of recruiting skills with your ability for getting information to me about other nuclear projects around the country."

"We can't all have your magnetic personality. Besides, your English majors are more susceptible."

"Flattery will not save you, only information. Anything to report?"

"I'm getting in touch with several people: Dr. Michio Kaku, nuclear physics professor at the City University of New York, Dr. John Gofman at the University of Berkeley and John Pike, head of space policy at the Federation of American Scientists. I'm asking them if they'd address the subject of nuclear material in space." He hesitated. "They're probably going to want to speak to the entire campus and not just *Cure the World*."

Nancy frowned, but after a second, smiled. "We can work that to our benefit when the time comes with rallies before and after their speeches. Schedule their appearances throughout the semester. Check with my secretary."

The meeting continued with Nancy going over details. She was a list freak. In the end, Phil knew this would be her undoing. Her files were lengthy, and if she ever crossed the line from mere radical activist to criminal activity, they'd have her cold. He hoped she'd never cross the line, but as NASA reached farther and farther into space, she became more vocal and adamant about what should be done to those involved with putting nuclear waste into the atmosphere.

When the grandfather clock in the hall chimed nine, Phil shuffled his papers. "That about it?"

"Just about." She swigged her tea down and chewed on the last remnants of ice.

I bet she wishes it were booze in that glass, he thought. "If there's anything new, I'll be seeing you on campus before the twelfth."

"There's one piece of information that's just come to me." She eyed him. "I have my sources too, you know."

Indeed, he did know, but he'd never been able to track who her sources were. "You're incredibly well-connected. I admire that in you."

"Thank you." She smoothed out her skirt. "You were in on that incident in Canada, the Cosmos 954."

Of course she knew that; he had told her because it gave him credibility. Why bring it up now? "Lord, that's been over with for, what—sixteen, seventeen years?"

"The crash, yes, but both the Canadians and our government covered up the details of the nuclear fallout and wreckage. They collected only one percent of that spy satellite. How long did they spend? January through October." She flung one arm across the back of the sofa and stabbed at the air with the other. "They walked away, leaving all that plutonium debris in the Northwest Territory's wilderness. Their reports were a complete hoax."

"You must know something new or you wouldn't have brought it up." His mouth felt like cotton.

"Rumblings, only rumblings. But if more of the wreckage has been found, we need to get that information out to the public." She leaned forward, eagerness shining in her face. "It would be quite a coup."

"It certainly would. How strong are the rumblings?"

"I'll know more soon. The Canadian government has its hands full with the demands of the mining industry in the area. If new pieces of Cosmos have been found, it'll cause a wave of anxiety that we can use to our advantage. Something's going on around Fort Smith. A doctor reported a case of possible radiation burns to a wolf trapper. See what you can find out."

"Got a name?"

"Henri Deforte."

Phil dropped a sheet of paper on the floor and reached to pick it up. He felt a nervous tic in his left eye. "I don't know anyone in Fort Smith anymore," he said, straightening the papers in his lap. "Heck, I was just a young man in '78, didn't know pee from squat."

"Well, you do now. So dig a little. No. I take that back. Dig a lot."

"Yes, ma'am." He rose and bowed.

"Oh, don't be facetious." She got up and walked around the coffee table to stand in front of him, an arm's reach away. "You and I have worked well together on *Cure the World*. It's a shame you and I never got together…you know what I mean."

"Nancy, has anyone ever told you that you are one scary lady?"

"How sweet. You called me a lady."

He turned and picked up his jacket and hat. "We're friends. I think we should keep it that way."

She crossed her arms and scrutinized him. "It's not that I'm older than you is it? Four years. That's not much."

"You've studied my personnel file."

"Prerogative of a mentor. After all, I stuck out my neck for you your first year here. You needed to learn how to teach."

He raised his eyebrows and cocked his head. "I've thanked you many times."

"I do love it when you get that puppy look." She moved closer to him, and he backed away a step. "I often wonder," she said, then hesitated, "if it hadn't been for your romantic fling with that girl last spring, I'd think you were gay. What was her name? Ah, yes, I remember, Laura."

"Next time I'll be more discrete about confiding about my…my vacations."

"Don't be angry. I loved hearing about Costa Rica, but the fact you fell for a woman made it most delicious."

The conversation was headed in a direction Phil wanted to avoid. He was usually circumspect about his private life, but his affair with Laura had hit him hard. "I don't play around with anyone on campus. I have my ethics. And I'm not gay. Would it matter if I was?"

She smiled with a hint of mischief in her dark eyes. "No, but it would soothe my ego."

He walked toward the front door with her close at his side. "Your ego doesn't need soothing. You exude confidence. That's why you're good at what you do—a first-rate recruiter for saving the world." He leaned over and gave her a peck on the cheek. "Nite, Nancy."

"Nite, Phil. Keep *Cosmos 954* in your thoughts."

"Right." He fled out the door, down the steps and on to tree-lined Commonwealth Avenue. His thoughts dwelled on *Cosmos,* Erich and Henri Deforte as he hurried toward the train station that would take him back to Cambridge. What really happened in the wilderness? Had Erich finally found parts of the wreckage? Why else would Henri have radiation burns...if they were radiation burns?

Chapter 4

The Arctic autumn light streamed through the far window and spilled across the long wooden dining table where Grant sat. Papers and notes he'd made the night before lay stacked in neat piles in front of him. Two wildlife photos, one of wolves, the other of muskoxen, graced the cream-colored walls. The sideboard contained no bric-a-brac, and the overhead light was simple and functional.

Karen hummed a tune as she worked in the kitchen just out of sight through the half-opened door. Saturdays she spent cooking as relaxation from teaching Fort Smith's high schoolers German and Latin.

During the three years of their marriage, he had come to appreciate her youthful exuberance as she threaded their lives into a harmonious pattern. Her unobtrusive style had crept into every corner of his house as well as his life. Subtle changes occurred without his noticing for days or weeks. Sometimes when he returned home from the wilderness, he'd find an entire room transformed, yet aware of his desire for a pristine environment, her redecorating was always understated.

For Grant, late autumn meant cleaning and repairing equipment, checking inventory, and stowing canoes and camp gear away for the winter. Since he ran a canoe guiding enterprise from his home, it was easy to divide his time between the business and his passion for writing about the wild. In past winters he'd holed up and written, but his winter monk-like existence had ended when he'd met Karen.

The soft swish on the front steps meant the *Northern News* had been delivered. Grant padded on slippered feet through the living room and retrieved the paper from the brick steps. Normally, he'd have placed it on the table next to his favorite chair, but a headline caught his eye: *Wood Bison Wildlife Researcher Retires.*

He scanned the article. "Karen," he said as he walked into the kitchen. "Have you heard about this? Howell is leaving his position with the Department of Resources. He never said a word when I saw him last week. He's joining an environmental firm to supervise the Environmental Impact Report for that proposed diamond mine outside the Thelon Sanctuary." He put the paper on the counter in front of Karen. As she bent over to read the article he pointed to, he put his arm around her shoulder.

"Another one going to the dark side," she said, pushing up the sleeves of her denim shirt. A frown creased her freckled brow as she pointed to another headline. *Lac de Gras May Be Drained.* "That lake's fifty kilometers long, and all for diamond mining. It's such a shame."

They stood close together, her light brown hair falling against his shoulder, her slight body leaning against him, as if she were unaware the effect she had on him. The scent of her lavender perfume gave him a heady feeling. For a moment, he forgot the headlines.

Her voice broke the spell. "The town is shifting into two camps. It's not good, Grant. Even the high school kids are taking sides."

He didn't need to see her face. The worry was in her voice. "I know. Jobs versus the environment and jobs are winning." He shoved the newspaper aside and returned to the other room to continue working through the neat stacks of letters, envelopes and brochures.

Karen watched him from the doorway. "I thought the meeting the other night would defuse the situation."

He shook his head. "When that public relations fellow from De Beers said, 'We don't trust anybody' and then went on to assure us that nobody is more ingenious than a diamond thief, I thought the Dene Nation Chief would erupt like a rocket."

"He wasn't the only one who was angry." She came forward, kissed his forehead and sank into the chair next to him. "Your face was flaming red."

"Even the local RCMP plan to help with security for the diamond mines," he said.

She sighed as she reached across the table to cover his hand with hers. "People need jobs, particularly the native population. Times are changing. We're going to have to change, too."

"You mean I'm going to have to change." He looked up at the wolf photo. "His range is being cut down, and so is mine. No wonder Henri Deforte is glum these days."

"Glum is hardly the word," Karen said. "Leah is furious with his drinking. She knows he's angry and wants to get back into the wilderness, but she feels something else is eating at him. Did you know Sergeant Michael plans to retrieve Erich's body? Something about regulations."

"I'm not surprised. Too many loose ends. Any mystery will send our good constables to investigate." Grant moved an old brochure aside. "I'm not sure Henri is telling the entire story. The doctor thought Henri's blisters could be radiation burns. Henri claims that's impossible."

"Maybe he doesn't know how he got the burns. Maybe Erich had something or touched something."

"Exactly. That's why the sergeant plans to exhume the body."

"Leah's worried Henri might get some long-term illness." Karen's brown eyes swelled with sympathy. "But the doctor assured Henri that his burns would heal in about three months, and he shouldn't have any lasting effect." Karen's knuckles shone white as she clasped her long slim hands together. "Leah thinks if Henri could get back to trapping, he'd be okay. The wilderness is where he's happiest."

"I can relate."

Karen eyed him skeptically, and she wrinkled her snub nose. "I thought I'd changed your viewpoint."

He smiled, reached over and ruffled her glossy hair. "I have the best of both worlds." Karen sniffed the air. "The carrot cake!" She dashed into the kitchen.

Grant smiled and tried to turn his attention back to the paperwork, but his mind drifted to Karen. She made both the civilized world and the wilderness more exciting and meaningful for him. The fifteen years difference in their ages seemed nonexistent, at least to him. From the very first, he'd marveled at how someone so slender could have such endurance. She'd taken one of his tours, and instead of going home to Seattle, she'd stayed on in Fort Smith. They were married when the summer season was over.

Karen came out of the kitchen, smiling. "Just in time. The cake will survive." She placed the newspaper on the table. "Isn't there anything we can do to slow down the government's intrusions?"

"Letter writing helped last time, but some who helped before don't think that will have much effect this time. Maybe you're right. Change is coming. We'll have to bend." He hesitated and stared out the window. "God, for the sake of the wilderness, I hope not too much."

The thought of the mining interests and the government conspiring to invade the Thelon Sanctuary scared him. He viewed all the interested parties, the fur association, the mining interests and the anti-everything groups with skepticism. Each had its agenda, but if they didn't begin to work together, people and the environment were going to be hurt. He wasn't sure what he could do. For the moment, he planned to keep his head out of the line of fire and conduct business as usual. He didn't tell Karen that. Instead he smiled up at her, hoping he looked brave and convincing. She returned his smile, but her eyes were clouded in doubt.

He sighed and began to outline his new brochure for next year's canoe trips.

Chapter 5

Chip's plane swooped down to land on Lake Damant. Sergeant Michael of the Royal Canadian Mounted Police sat in the copilot's seat. In the fuselage, Henri and two constables huddled in cold discomfort behind a wood casket.

Although it was only the first of October, ice had begun to form at the lake's edge. Since daylight hours this time of year waned quickly, they'd waited for good weather and had taken off when the sun offered its first glow. In another month the ground would be frozen and the sergeant could not dig up the body, Henri thought. *Timing is everything, and mine's terrible.*

Henri's mind continued to twist. If only he hadn't gone to the doctor about his blisters. If only he hadn't gotten drunk and talked too much one night at the Road End Bar. But it was Erich's fault for finding the damn stuff. The Mounties knew nothing about the debris, only about Erich's accident. But then there were his damn blisters. His mistake had been in going to the doctor. *Sacré bleu.* Blisters were blisters, weren't they? But this part of the Northwest Territory had once been contaminated by radioactive fallout, so all medical personnel watched for burns that had no known cause. Henri comforted himself with the thought that at least he wasn't going to die from them. He sat scrunched up in the rear of Chip's plane, waiting to land on Lake Damant so they could dig up Erich. He looked down and spotted his cabin, and a warm feeling swept over him.

When could he get back to set his trap lines? Paperwork. That's what the sergeant said. Paperwork was just government folderol to deny people their rights. He had a permit to hunt. Besides, he wasn't like those companies that used snowmobiles and helicopters to hunt wolves. He did it with cunning. *Mon Dieu,* a man had to earn a living.

Erich's lawyer said Henri was mentioned in Erich's will, but until the cause of death was determined the will couldn't be processed. If Erich had money stashed away, he hadn't mentioned it to Henri.

As usual Chip set his plane down like he was brushing lint from his trousers, smooth and easy. After the plane stopped close to shore, a constable jumped off the pontoon and fastened the lines to tree snags on shore, while the other man snatched up the casket in his brawny arms and carried it onto the gravel beach. Henri watched, feeling like a guest in front of his own cabin.

No matter how cooperative he'd been, Sergeant Michael had pushed for more details, about Erich's fall, about where they'd been and what they'd seen. *Merde!* Enough. He wasn't going to be so goddamned helpful anymore. Hadn't he turned in Erich's effects? Of course, he'd kept the notebook with the German writing and the picture. Had Erich written about him, about radioactive debris or about diamonds? So many questions. The notebook, the rock and the picture remained at his cabin. He'd get them now and hang onto them.

Chip patted the dashboard and stretched his long legs over the seat next to him. "I'll stay put."

Sergeant Michael moved out from the cockpit and motioned for Henri to disembark, then followed Henri onto shore. Like mourners, the four men stood around the wooden casket with its rubber lining. The sergeant stared at Henri. "Well, show us the way."

"Oui." Henri set off at a rapid pace up the embankment toward his cabin. "I show you the grave, then I get my stuff."

"We could use your help," the sergeant said.

"Not part of the bargain. I came of my own free will, didn't I? I show you the grave, that's it."

They followed Henri past his cabin and into the taiga beyond with the two constables trailing the sergeant as they carried the casket between them.

"It's not right to move a body once it's been buried," Henri said in a loud voice over his shoulder.

"We have a court order, Henri," the sergeant replied.

"Oui. Still, not right." Henri hurried on. The crisp air filled his starved lungs. During the past months in Fort Smith, Henri felt smothered. The town had 2,500 people—a crowd. On a drinking binge he'd mentioned

Cosmos 954 and his world had caved in. Although Henri denied knowing anything about debris, the Mounties began to ask questions.

On top of the esker were a few straggly dwarf spruce. Henri stopped and pointed to a mound with a crude cross. The constables moved forward, set the casket aside, took out shovels they'd packed inside it and began the ghoulish job of unearthing Erich.

"I go to my cabin. This…this sacrilegious." Henri blurted out.

"Okay, Henri," the sergeant said. "You've made your point. Go back to your cabin or wait in the plane. We'll be along shortly."

With a curt nod, Henri headed to his cabin, gathered the two packs of furs he'd left behind and hauled them to the plane.

"It's okay? I don't have to pay?" he asked Chip, as he stowed the furs in the back.

Chip was reading a book in the cockpit. "No matter to me," he said over his shoulder. "We're not carrying that much weight. Hell, I could have brought some of your winter rations if they'd let me, but they contracted for the plane, and it's government work. Can't see as they should mind a few loads of furs though."

"I got more things to get." Henri ducked out of the plane. Just as he got back to his cabin door, Sergeant Michael came through the scrub bush and headed in his direction. The constables followed a short distance behind him carrying the casket. The funereal scene gave Henri a chill.

"We'll go now. Are you ready?" the sergeant called out.

Henri waved his hand and went into his cabin, pulled out a sack and began stuffing some clothes into it. The door opened and the sergeant stepped in as if he owned the place. Wandering about the small hut, he looked on shelves and poked at Henri's things in a corner cupboard. Henri broke out in a sweat. The sergeant walked over to where Erich's photo and notebook lay on the far side of the table. The diamond-flecked rock he'd stashed in an old cigar box. Why hadn't he hidden Erich's things?

"You look for something?" Henri asked.

The sergeant toyed with the top of the notebook. His hand strayed to the picture. He glanced at it. "Friends of yours?"

"What do you think? Of course, friends. Long time ago." Henri moved to the table, took the photo and stuck it in his pocket and jammed the cigar box and the notebook into his sack. Was the contents of Erich's notebook meaningless scribbles? Somehow he'd have to find out.

The sergeant remained passive. "If you have your personal belongings, we'll leave. We have what we came for."

Henri nodded, followed the man out and closed the door behind him, throwing the outside bolt.

"I don't lock against men," Henri explained, "but against animals."

The sergeant shrugged.

"Men are welcome to use my cabin if they get stuck out here, but animals make big mess."

By the time they got to the shore, the casket had been loaded and already daylight had begun to fade. Everyone boarded the seaplane, and Chip closed the cargo door.

"Weather's coming in," Chip said as he made his way to the cockpit. "I'm swinging farther east than my flight plan called for and I'll come in over the east arm of Great Slave Lake."

The cloud cover forced Chip to fly at nine hundred feet. The land below had endless polygons and other odd geometric shapes where frost had heaved up the tundra. The land below had a million lakes, or was it a sea with a million islands? Yellow liquid dribbled across Henri's window, and he knew Chip had pissed out his window. He leaned his head back against his sack of pelts and nodded off, lulled by the Otter's banging pistons.

He woke with a start to a high-pitched squeal. The plane's right wing dropped precipitously. Henri was thrown against the metal side of the fuselage. The casket broke from its straps and careened across the floor, bashing into one of the constables. The plane's nose headed toward earth. Henri's stomach lurched as he grabbed for anything solid to hold onto. Chip yelled profanities. Henri prayed. A roar of a jet engulfed them. As quickly as the sound had come, it disappeared. Chip righted his plane.

Henri stared out the window at a fading gray fighter jet doing a barrel roll. *"Mon Dieu,* we are attacked by our own Air Force."

"Not our Air Force," Chip screamed back. "It's those goddamn diamond mining people." Henri watched Chip through the open cockpit door twiddling the radio dials to the standard frequency 126.7 to call the pilot of the jet. No response.

Sergeant Michael sat next to Chip, transfixed and ashen. "What the hell you going to do about this?" Chip asked the shaken sergeant. "That damn mining company has been in our hair for the last two years and now this."

"I'll report the incident to headquarters in Yellowknife," Sergeant Michael said.

"Yeah," Chip said. "And the politicians will sweep it under the rug. They don't give a damn about the area. Diamonds mean money in their pockets. If we don't keep fighting to keep this land a sanctuary, it's doomed to be overrun by engineers, miners and jet jockeys." Chip turned toward the men in the rear of the plane, his brown eyes glinting with black anger.

"The government must protect all rights, not just yours, Chip," the sergeant said.

"Well, it seems to me you and the government boys are bending too much in their direction."

"I have my orders," the sergeant said.

Henri shook his head, sneered at how the sergeant pimped for the shitty government and the fuckin' miners.

Flashes of the old miner's death in '78 came to mind. Henri thought of him all too often lately. People who harm my land pay the price. The new threats to his Barrenlands came from all sides. Mining interests were pushing into the Thelon Sanctuary, but he never thought they'd buzz a private plane. A great heaviness fell upon him. So many problems for his beloved land. Where could he turn for help?

Who loves the Thelon area as much as I do? Passion alone was not enough. Action was the answer. Money-grubbers cared nothing about keeping the wilds pristine. These people were his enemies. Like Erich, they didn't understand. Anyone who tampered with his wilderness deserved Erich's fate just like the old miner. No exceptions.

Chapter 6

Laura Boswell reached for one of the bottles of nutritional supplements in front of her on the breakfast table. Zinc. Absolutely essential. Having downed her other supplements, she swilled down her glass of algae mixed with orange juice that turned the liquid green. Even after two years of living like a Buddhist health monk, she shuddered at the taste, but she was determined to be the healthiest thirty-three-year old in the world.

If her father had followed her present healthy regime, perhaps he'd still be alive. Oh, Dad, why didn't I take better care of you, she thought, almost uttering the thought out loud. Ever since he'd shot himself, she'd been on a fast pace to nowhere. The memory of his bloody face haunted her.

This morning, the day of her big interview, she'd risen extra early, meditated for an hour and run two miles. Instead of feeling energized, as she usually did, she felt lethargic and nervous. Wasn't she supposed to always have energy with her new vegetarian diet and exercise program?

She walked through the archway to her airy living room and gazed out her second story window. Twenty-ninth Avenue in San Francisco's Sunset District had expensive two-story homes with adjoining walls. The November air was clear, crisp, with no fog, not even near the Presidio. Her attention turned to the photographs of exotic animals she'd taken in Costa Rica last March she'd propped up on chairs and the long couch. The Costa Rica trip had been one of her better adventure travels for photographic work. Thoughts of Phil West brushed her mind. *Forget him.*

"Who am I kidding?" she said out loud, picking up a pencil and throwing it onto the emerald green couch. She paced around the room, her black pumps a stark contrast to the white carpets. *Maybe I should wear my black pantsuit instead of this skirt. No, showing a little knee won't hurt. If I end up sitting down, it means I've got a contract.*

She didn't need the money, but she wanted affirmation of her work. Since her father's death, she'd become financially independent with the house and a tidy inheritance. But he'd also left her with a load of guilt. She knew he'd been in pain from liver damage, but suicide had never entered her mind. Looking back, she could detect the warning signs. Why had she been so blind? She gazed about her. Even after two years, she'd kept everything that belonged to him, except his guns. Those she'd disposed of immediately.

Laura gathered up her photographs and put them into a large portfolio case. Parking downtown would be a problem, but taking the bus was out of the question with her portfolio and briefcase in tow. Laden with her cases, she thrust the heavy door open and let it slam behind her as she walked down the slippery terrazzo stairs to the garage.

Friday morning's rush hour traffic frayed her nerves. Sleep had evaded her last night and left her exhausted in the morning. Maybe she should go to the health food store and get some ginseng. Was she getting enough iron? Perhaps she wasn't exercising enough. That's it. She'd run a few miles in the evening. The more she ran, the fewer nightmares.

She parked her black Honda in the underground parking lot near the new Embarcadero buildings. In her haste to exit her car, she clipped her knee on the edge of the door, snagging her hose. As she walked between parked cars, she brushed up against a grimy sedan. Why don't people keep their cars clean? The day was not starting out well—a sign? She also noted creases across the lap area of her linen skirt. "Damn!"

Five minutes to nine she stood in the reception area outside Mr. Kenall's office. His secretary buzzed him and immediately motioned for Laura to enter his office. Without a moment to gather her composure or comb her hair, Laura entered the sanctified office of one of the most important magazine publishers on the West Coast. Her mind went blank. So much for her rehearsed speech. The maroon carpet felt soft underfoot; the dark red cherry wood walls glistened; the windows overlooking San Francisco Bay were enormous. Her breathing came in shallow spurts. Her knees felt as if she'd been running through sand. Did her expression show confidence?

"Miss Boswell." The gray-haired George Kenall rose from behind his desk. "Glad to see you're punctual." He walked toward her, shook her hand and introduced her to Marv Jensen, editor for picture books.

Marv Jensen's hand felt flabby and moist. The chubby man's smile didn't reach his eyes. The vibes in the spacious room felt wrong. Defeat grabbed at her like a black-mantled villain.

Kenall turned to someone in the corner of the room. "I'd like you to meet Cal Sterling, publisher of *Earth's Attractions*. Do you know the magazine?" Kenall didn't wait for her reply. "Cal happened to drop by. You don't mind him looking at your work, too, do you?"

Cal Sterling? Her best friend's husband? What was he doing here? He came forward out of the shadows, revealing his tall, angular frame. He nodded in her direction. "Nice to meet you, Miss Boswell." He did not offer to shake her hand.

"Ah, yes. Nice to meet you," she said, completely at a loss. She wanted to say something more, but he looked away and stared out the window, ignoring her. Why did he pretend not to know her? What game was he playing?

"Please, set your work up over there." Kenall gestured to a wall with a low shelf on which to place artwork.

Perspiration dampened her face. Thank God, I don't wear pancake makeup, she thought as she began to set up her photos—ten in all. She'd thought of bringing more, but had decided these were the best. If Kenall and Jensen wanted to see more, she had slides as well as 4 x 6 photos in her briefcase. She'd meticulously guided the photos through the entire developing process. Now they sat in a publisher's office matted, ready to be judged. She stood aside to watch and wait. The gold charms on her bracelet clinked from her trembling arms. In the quiet room, they sounded like gongs. She clasped her hands together in front of her.

The three men took their time studying each photograph. Laura scrutinized Cal. His slick black hair shone in the ceiling's spotlight. She hoped he'd give her a nod or some indication of what he was up to, but instead, he studied the photo of the howler monkey and acted as if she didn't exist.

Jensen studied the two wildcat pictures. The margay was a favorite of Laura's. The sunlight flickered off the reddish fur and spotlighted the black streaks and spots.

"Ocelot?" Jensen asked.

"No. A margay. They do look similar," Laura assured him, "but the margay is a little smaller and has a longer tail."

"Not sure our writers have anything on it." Jensen shook his head, making his jowls quiver.

"Not too much has been written about them," she said. "Readers will be interested to learn about them."

"Maybe," Jensen said. "But it would lead to research. That takes time." He glanced in Kenall's direction.

George Kenall walked back to his desk and sat down. "That one looks like a weasel." He pointed to a wildcat photo at the end of the lineup. "Don't need pictures of them."

"Ah, sir, it's not a weasel. It's a jaguarundi." Neither man seemed to know anything about tropical forest animals. Where were their writers? "This animal is in the cat family. Although you're right, it doesn't look much like a wildcat."

"I've seen the work you did on African wildlife," Kenall said. "Good work. Didn't care for the text, but that wasn't your department." He looked down at a letter on his desk. "You said your work was on tropical forest animals." He pointed at a picture of a quetzal bird. "Hardly an animal."

"I wanted to show you the diversity of my work," Laura began.

Kenall cut her off. "I see. Your shots are rare, maybe too rare for what we're looking for. A book needs a theme."

"I have other photographs."

"I know. I saw your slides. If I hadn't liked them, you wouldn't be here now. However, I'm not sure this is what we're looking for." He looked at Jensen, who stood across the room next to the photos with a blank expression on his round face.

"Our writers already have copy written," Jensen said. "Some of these photos aren't what we had in mind."

"I was told you wanted exotic wildlife shot on location the tropical forest." Laura tried not to raise her voice. "I was led to believe you wanted photos to complement articles on each animal." She stood statue-like. "I have other photos of less exotic animals." She realized her words weren't going to change Mr. Kenall's decision and Jensen seemed to take his cues from Kenall. She was going to lose the argument and the assignment.

"George," Cal said, as he stood on the opposite side of the photos from where Laura stood. "Do you know how difficult it is to take a picture of a Quetzal bird in a rain forest?" He walked in front of the picture. "Where did you take this, Miss Boswell?"

"Monte Verde Rain Forest, Costa Rica," she said, knowing he didn't need to ask. He knew all about her trip with his wife.

He pointed to another photo. "Were the howler monkeys also in the rain forest?"

Laura moved in front of the photo to stand next to him. "There were some there, but this one was shot on an island on the Pacific Coast side of Costa Rica."

Cal took her elbow and moved her aside, so Kenall had an unobstructed view of the photos. "Go on."

"I was sea kayaking. These particular monkeys were a few hundred yards from our campsite."

"You aren't afraid to travel to difficult areas to get good shots," Cal turned toward Kenall. "Many animal photographers use animals in the zoo." He walked over next to the large windows that outlined the sparkling bay in the background. "Wildlife books are plentiful, but truly exotic animals taken on location are harder to come by."

"Harder to sell, too," Jensen said.

"Are you sure?" Cal said. "I did an offbeat piece in my magazine on exotic animal sculptures. Got a great response from our readers. Thought your company had first rate marketing." Cal looked at Kenall, then at Jensen and back to Kenall. "It's easy to go with the usual. George, you've done well because you're willing to take risks." He strolled over to stand in front of the photos again. "Timing is everything, and exotic is definitely in."

Kenall smiled. "Cal's got an eye for talent," he said, looking at Laura. "He's also competitive for talent. If I don't snap you up, he might." He looked at Cal, hesitated, then returned his gaze to Laura. "Tell you what. Leave your work. Jensen will meet with the writers." He nodded to Jensen, who, in turn, nodded back. "We should be able to get some good research from those writers," he said, staring at Jensen. "We're paying them enough." Kenall rose from behind his desk. "If our writers can come up with good text for some of these more exotic photos, we'll use them. Otherwise, we'll do a standard contract for some of your animal photos. Jensen will get back to you. Say two to three weeks." He nodded to Jensen. "Schedule it."

She hesitated. Should she leave her work? She'd heard stories about publishing houses ripping off artists. Could she trust the man?

He noted her hesitation. "I'll have my secretary give you a receipt for your work. Thank you for coming." The interview had ended rather abruptly she thought, but he'd made a decision in her favor.

She thanked him, picked up her cases and shook hands with him and Jensen. Cal gave her an aloof good-bye nod. Surprised at Kenall's fast turn around, she made her exit from his office with her head held high.

Later when she left the building with a receipt and a signed letter from Kenall, she felt excited, but she wondered why Cal had helped her. He'd never bought any of her work. As she walked down the street gripping her two cases, the fumes from the traffic engulfed her. She needed to sit down and gather her thoughts before returning home. A small Chinese teashop across the street beckoned.

"Laura," someone shouted from behind her.

She turned and spotted Cal jogging toward her through the crowd with a wide grin on his face. Upon reaching her, he seized her shoulders with his immaculately manicured hands. "What do you think?" His flushed face was close to hers.

"I'm dumbfounded. What were you doing there? I appreciate your help, but why did you do it?"

He threw back his head, laughed. "God, that was fun."

"Fun? Is that what the meeting was to you?" She tried to pull away, but he held her fast.

"Come on, there should be a cafe nearby where we can talk and I'll explain."

She pointed to the tearoom.

"A café would be better."

She gave him a quick discouraged glance, and his dark eyes flashed with understanding.   "I forgot. Okay. Tearoom it is." He took her briefcase in one arm and latched onto her other arm as they crossed at the signal. When they were sitting together at a small wrought iron table, she asked, "Deirdre sent you, didn't she?"

His gangly legs stuck out into the aisle, blocking the passage of the Chinese waitress. "In a way." He smiled in an offhanded manner and glanced out the window. "The wind has kicked up. See those whitecaps on the bay?"

The elderly waitress moved around another table and waited while Laura ordered cinnamon flavored herb tea. When Cal asked for coffee, he received a smile and a no. He settled for regular black tea.

"Caffeine isn't good for you." Laura bit her lower lip. "Sorry. I didn't mean to sound like a fishwife."

"Since you're not my wife, I'll accept your apology." He straightened his red and white striped silk tie and brushed a piece of lint off the sleeve of his gray herringbone jacket.

Deirdre and Cal were a perfect pair, like Siamese cats, beautifully groomed, but deadly when cornered. They remained together, yet couldn't breach the void that had engulfed them since the death of their baby. If only they could communicate like they used to, she thought as she asked, "Why were you in Kenall's office?"

"Would you believe it was fate?"

"No." She leaned back in the rigid iron chair, brushed back a blonde lock that had fallen across her forehead and scrutinized him. "I should thank you. Kenall and that wretched fat Jensen were about to discard my work. You rescued me from that fate, but that hasn't been your usual tactic. What do you want?"

"Women. Never satisfied."

"Don't say that to Deirdre." She sipped her tea, enjoying its spicy taste and warmth. "Just joking."

"I was coming to San Francisco on business, and Deirdre knew of your appointment with Kenall. She suggested I stick my nose into the interview."

"More likely she insisted."

"Well, you know Deirdre. I never have been able to say no to her."

"She has that effect on people." Laura watched as he stirred half a pitcher of cream into his tea. "Are you going to drink it or drown it in cholesterol?"

He gave her a heavy-hearted look. "Let the rest of us be," Cal said in measured tones.   "Sorry." She gazed into her teacup, thinking how she wanted others to conform to her way of life. Is that why Phil had ditched her?

"Look, Laura." His intake of breath was audible. "Deirdre and I care about what happens to you. Ever since your dad's death, you've been in a, I don't know what to call it, a funk. He loved life; lived it to the hilt. Can't you do the same?"

"He'd be alive now if I'd watched over him better." She could feel the tears and tried to stifle them, but they rolled down her cheeks.

"Yeah, maybe. Would he have been happy living your way?" Cal stared at her.

"He drank too much. Ate too much," she said.

"Sure, he did. Was he happy?"

"A happy drunk, you mean? It chewed up his liver till he had no choice but to do what he did." Other customers looked her way as her voice rose.

"Cut it out. Everyone makes choices. You couldn't have done anything to stop him. And for the record, I don't think he drank that much."

"I appreciate your concern, but that's not why you showed up today."

He sighed. "Okay. Deirdre warned me not to nag you." He held up his hand. "But you drive yourself too hard. Can't you lighten up? You used to be such fun."

"Who are you to lecture? We all change. Look at you and Deirdre." She hated verbal battles. "Sorry. That was a low blow."

He slumped back in his chair. "Me too. I'm always saying the wrong thing to you." He hesitated, pushing at his teacup. "Sometimes friends can be too frank." He smiled in his boyish disarming way.

She regrouped her thoughts. "Why did you help me with Kenall? You've never offered to help me before."

He shrugged and looked uncomfortable. "I didn't lie about anything in Kenall's office. If I had, he'd have smelled it. He's no dummy. I was right, and he knows it. You'll get the job."

"What's in it for you?"

"There's a trip Deirdre wants to go on this summer."

"So? She loves to travel."

"But this time I don't want her to go. If I say no, she'll dig in her heels. Besides, ever since we lost Brian, I can't say no to her. I want you to talk her out of it."

"Why?" She leaned forward.

"That's my affair."

"Why don't you go with her? It might bring you closer together."

He bit at his thin lower lip. "It's a trip I have to take, and I don't know yet what it might entail. It might be dangerous."

"Traveling together would be good for you both. You reneged on the Costa Rica trip even after you planned to meet your friend." She couldn't bring herself to say Phil's name.

He cocked his head. "From what I heard, nobody missed me. You and Phil hit it off, didn't you?"

She felt her cheeks flush. "That's beside the point. You always leave Deirdre in the lurch. She needs you."

"Let's not go into my married life. I'm trying to point out that this trip could be dangerous. If I tell her that, she'll really want to go. She adores adventure travel, but this trip is business for me and she mustn't go."

For a split second he seemed vulnerable, worried, an attitude she'd seldom seen. "Why is it dangerous?"

He squirmed and perspiration beaded his bronze brow. "I did you a favor. Won't you reciprocate?"

"Ah, tit for tat. I knew you wanted something."

"Will you?" He seemed puzzled as if saying, 'that's how the game is played.'

"If her mind is set on going, I don't think I can talk her out of it," Laura said.

"Will you try? Deirdre wants you to visit for Thanksgiving. It would be the perfect time to nix this trip idea."

"Thanksgiving is out." Why did she say that? She wasn't doing anything Thanksgiving, but Deirdre would line up men for her to meet. She didn't want to deal with that.

"Christmas then? Deirdre's request."

How often could she say no? Besides, the past two Christmas holidays had been dreadful. "All right. Christmas."

"Good. You and Deirdre can work out the details." He gave her his salesman's grin. "I'd love to chat more, but I've got a noon plane back to Los Angeles."

As they were about to leave the teashop, she asked, "By the way, where is this place you plan to visit without Deirdre?"

"Canada. Northwest Territory, Thelon River Sanctuary."

Chapter 7

Like a musician fingering his instrument, Boris Sweet moved his hand along the spines of the books as he walked through the stacks of his used bookstore. Christmas time in his Berkeley store held a different tempo than when the students were on campus. Now, the professors and teaching assistants came in to catch up on their pleasure reading among the neat, clean rows of ten-foot-high shelves. Sweet Bookstore on Telegraph Avenue had the usual Christmas decorations in the window—lights, a small tree, artificial snow, but inside, instead of *Rudolph the Red-Nosed Reindeer,* Handel's *Messiah* played softly in the background, reflecting Boris's classical tastes.

He took the day's mail and relaxed in a leather lounging chair set in one of the many small alcoves on the perimeter of the tidy book stacks. He preferred this setting to his cramped back office. Adjusting the reading light above him, he thumbed through the letters. A Massachusetts postmark with Phil's return address caught his eye. What could he want? He'd paid his quarterly dues to Erich's funds. He sliced the business envelope with his letter-opener, but he hesitated before removing its contents.

A chill crept over him, and he shrugged as if trying to dispel a sense of foreboding. He looked around the store, but his customers were too busy browsing and reading to bother with him. When he unfolded the crisp white sheet of paper, a faded photo fell onto his lap. For a moment, he studied it, recognizing himself as well as the three other young men in uniforms. He grunted and smiled. He'd been a gawky, skinny recruit then. Time had allowed his large brown eyes, broad forehead, Roman nose and square chin to form into a reasonably handsome man. Back then, he'd looked like the farm boy he'd been. Seventeen years ago. Checking the other side of the snapshot, he read the names printed there: Erich Mann, Boris Sweet, Cal Sterling, Phil West. Boris hadn't seen any of them since, nor had he any desire to do so now, unless Erich had found the mother lode. Phil's assignment had been to keep vigil over Erich, be the accountant for the funds, and keep the rest of them posted as to his progress. After all these years, Boris had given up on Erich's search, but out of a sense of obligation he had continued to mail in his dues. He remembered the day the photo was taken. Had Phil kept track of the Canadian soldier who'd taken the photo? Boris tried to recall the fellow's name, a little Canadian guy with acne—Gilbert Tupper—that was it.

Putting down the photo, he read the letter. *Erich Mann is dead. His search for Cosmos 954 debris may have come to something. Henri Deforte, his wolf trapping friend, had radiation burns, and Erich's last note indicated he was close to our objective. The Canadian government has stopped all unauthorized visits into the Thelon area. Entrance is by permit only. I'm taking Grant McDuffy's July canoe tour into the Thelon River Sanctuary. Check out the December issue of Earth's Attractions for his ad. McDuffy's trip travels near Erich's last geological find and where we found the prospector's grave. I plan to investigate the area. I expect you to come with me.*

Meanwhile, I hope to get Erich's last journal. Make your reservation. I have contacted Cal Sterling. We will not acknowledge we know each other. I'm in contact with Henri Deforte; however, I'm not certain about his reliability. I shall see you in Fort Smith in July to finish our project from long ago. Yours, Phil West.

Boris laid the paper down on his lap and rubbed his eyes. Phil had stated his case and expected Boris to respond. If he didn't, all the years of supporting Erich's search were for naught. To get involved again was ludicrous. He had a safe life, a quiet life. Why take the risk? He knew the answer, and it irked him. Nothing comes cheap, and you reap what you sow, his Iowa mother used to say.

He sighed, rose and went to his office to sort through the rest of the mail. Anxiety, or was it fear, began to burn slow, but grew white hot. Thank God, tonight's activity would keep his mind off his dilemma. After picking up his fencing gear, he stuffed the picture and Phil's letter into the pocket of his tweed jacket.

When he walked back through the store, he noticed old professor Dalbin hunkered down in a chair. Despite his pent up emotions, Boris grinned, knowing the old fellow was happiest when surrounded by books, a feeling Boris could relate to.

His newest assistant looked up as he reached the front desk. "Professor Dalbin's in the last cubicle," he said to her. "Check on him before you close tonight. Can't have him locked inside again."

She nodded with a dimpled smile. "Don't worry. I'll make the rounds before closing."

Boris hesitated by the magazine rack at the right of the counter. "I saw a copy of a magazine called *Earth's Attractions* with a cover story about the Northwest Territory. Must have come in last week. Do we still have a copy?

She leaned over and rummaged through the magazines, pulled out a copy and handed it to him. "Is this the one?"

He stared at the cover. "Yes, I've never read it before. I'll take it with me."

"Are you off to your bridge club or is it astronomy tonight?"

He held up his odd shaped bag that held his suit, mask, and epee. "Thursday night is fencing club. I'm walking. My Audi's got transmission problems."

She raised her eyebrows and shook her head. "Seems like you always have car trouble. Why don't you get a new one?"

"Haven't had the time or the inclination. I'll get a ride home with Professor Jerome. See you tomorrow."

The old-fashioned bell above the door jingled softly as Boris walked out and closed the door behind him. He transferred his canvas bag to his right shoulder and strode up Telegraph Avenue toward the campus.

The cold damp night refreshed him. Traffic whooshed over the pavement, wet from an earlier rain shower. A different kind of cold than the Arctic, he thought, as he hunched his solid six-foot frame forward against the brisk night air.

By the time he got to the gym, his jacket smelled of wet wool. He should have taken an umbrella or put on a topcoat, but felt both labeled him as part of the older generation. Not that thirty-five was old, but lately he'd begun to feel middle aged.

A sigh escaped him as he laid down his canvas bag, opened a locker and began to dress in his new fencing outfit. His girth had expanded during the past year, another sign of aging, and he'd gotten tired of stuffing himself into a suit that restricted his movements.

"Evening, Boris," Jerome said as he came around the corner. "New whites?"

"It was either a new suit or lose weight, and I can't seem to do the latter." Boris gazed at Jerome's lanky figure, topped by a head of white hair. "My genes betray me."

"Something to that. You have to be careful who you pick to be your parents." Jerome patted his waist as he finished dressing. "I've got fifteen years on you, but look at me."

"I've seen your appetite. I exercise all the time, too. It has to be genes." When Boris placed his street clothes into his locker, his magazine fell to the floor.

Jerome picked it up and glanced at the front cover. "Wolves, caribou, muskoxen," he read out loud and thumbed through the pages. "Look at this." He stuck his finger on an adventure travel article. "That's what you need to do and get away from that store of yours," he said and handed the magazine back to Boris.

The two men joined the other fencing members in the gym and warmed up fencing each other., although their match was more ritual than fight, but they worked up a sweat. Jerome made the final winning touch, but Boris felt no dejection, since fencing each other was like eating pudding. It slid down easily. After they saluted and took off their masks, Jerome put his arm on Boris's shoulder. "You seem distracted tonight. Are you going to your family this Christmas?"

Boris glanced at his friend. "Too much family at Christmas time. They're farmers, talk farming. It's a good life for them, but I hated it when I was growing up and I haven't changed my mind about farming."

"Black sheep, is that it?" Jerome asked, straightening his epee.

"I love 'em and they love me, but Christmas isn't a good time to visit."

"How about joining me and my family for Christmas dinner?" Jerome wiped the sweat from his brow.

"Thanks. Good of you to think of me, but I've got plans," he lied, even though he knew Christmas would be lonely as hell.

"When's the last time you took a trip? You never get away. Even at Christmas time, you hole up here in Berkeley."

"The store doesn't operate on its own." Boris nodded to a member he was scheduled to fence. "Be with you in a minute," he called out then turned back to Jerome. "Time to work off a few pounds."

"If you want to get away this summer, I'll be glad to help out."

"What would your wife say to your moonlighting in a used bookstore?"

"Well, she and I have always been curious how you live so well on the income from that store of yours."

"Ah, the gossip mongers of the faculty wives are at work."

"Wouldn't hurt you to have a wife."

"Easier said than done. The right woman hasn't come along."

Jerome grinned. "I'd try to change that if I were you."

Boris shook his head and walked to the mat for his next match.

After several bouts and a shower, Jerome and Boris trudged across the dark campus with the wind whipping their jackets and their bags full of fencing gear.

"Clear night," Boris said, looking up. "You can see Jupiter and Venus even with the glare from the city. Have you ever seen the northern lights? They're spectacular this time of year in the Arctic."

"Humph, too damn bitter cold for me. I don't do winters anymore. This dampness is bad enough on my arthritis." Jerome got into his car with Boris in the passenger seat. He eased the car into traffic, drove up the winding hilly street, turned right onto Grizzly Peak Road and pulled into the narrow driveway of a house partially concealed with overgrown shrubbery.

Boris got out and walked to the trunk as Jerome clicked it open from the driver's seat. After retrieving his bag, he slammed the trunk closed and came abreast of the driver's window.

He leaned down and peered in. "I might take a trip this summer after all. Give you a chance to see how my store operates."

"It'd be a change for me," Jerome said. "I could give you a month."

"Appreciate your offer. Thanks for the ride." Boris waved and headed toward his front door. Inside, he tossed his bag on the floor, then leaned down to remove the magazine. At the small den on his left, he flipped on the overhead light, lowered himself into a swivel chair and placed the magazine together with the letter and photo on the desk in front of him.

Erich Mann—dead. *Cosmos 954*—Thelon River Sanctuary—canoe tour—Grant McDuffy's July—Henri Deforte. The words spun out in front of him, and he rubbed his eyes.

After opening the magazine, he studied the table of contents, the authors and publisher—Cal Sterling, main office, Los Angeles. He rubbed the back of his neck. He'd never kept in touch with Cal. Was this Phil's way of telling him where Cal was? Perhaps he should find out what Cal intended to do, but he didn't want to call him. A drive to Los Angeles over Christmas might be pleasant. That way he could meet Cal face to face.

He rose and walked through his house and out onto the patio. Across the Bay, San Francisco's lights twinkled. Above, the stars glittered, brilliant as diamonds. *Diamonds. How could I forget? They've given me a good life.*

Back at his desk, he thumbed through the magazine, found Grant McDuffy's ad, picked up his pen and began to write.

Chapter 8

Snow laced downward, spreading a mantle of white over the usual dingy gray of Copley Square. Phil walked out of the Copley Plaza Hotel, ignored the white fluff that landed on his shoulders and to hail a cab. Hunched inside his overcoat with his fedora pulled low on his brow, he shrugged in annoyance as he waited on the corner. His undercover work always got to him during the Christmas holidays.

His latest briefing with his FBI contact hadn't gone well. Due to the Canadian political unrest caused by French separatists, the United States reacted with caution to Canada's "no comment" regarding any radioactive findings, and Canadian officials were leery of foreign inquiries. Phil's orders were to continue to monitor Nancy and her *Cure the World* organization and stay out of Canadian affairs.

A cab stopped and he gave the driver directions to Nancy's house, then sat back and thought about Erich's missing notebook. Had it been lost or taken? Until proven otherwise, he presumed Henri or the Mounties had it. How discrete had Erich been about secreting his notes concerning Operation *Morning Light?* Phil needed to find out if his, Boris's, and Cal's names were in Erich's files. A visit to Fort Smith was in order.

He had the taxi drop him at a flower shop three blocks from Nancy's house. Having forgotten to buy her a Christmas gift, flowers were essential. He chose a large bouquet of roses, yellow, not red. Keeping their relationship on a friends only basis was essential.

Normally, he enjoyed Nancy's faculty Christmas bash, but tonight he was in no mood for socializing. When he arrived, the party had been in full swing for two hours. Nancy greeted him with open arms and a kiss, and he noted she hadn't had a drink. Her dark green dress draped off her shoulders and loose folds of soft material billowed about her slim hips.

"I thought you'd forgotten my party," she said in a pretend pout.

"The snow threw off my timing." He presented her with the flowers.

"How sweet." She placed them in the crook of her left arm.

He took off his overcoat and hat, hung them in the front foyer and whisked off his glasses to wipe off the condensation.

"You do look sharp tonight." She ran her hand along the lapel of his navy cashmere jacket. "You shouldn't wear cashmere unless you want women to paw you."

"What a delightful idea. Mother always knows what to buy me."

She eyed him and laughed. "Your mother? Good taste. I must meet the woman someday." She took his arm with her free hand and pulled him into the living room.

Looking at the crowd and hearing the bedlam, he realized Nancy was probably the only sober person present other than himself.

As if she were reading his mind, she said, "Odd, isn't it? Everyone's having such a smashing good time, but no one has made one intelligent statement. It's odd to see brilliant people make asses of themselves and I can't even enjoy it. That's what sobriety has done for me."

The group around a piano player made *White Christmas* sound like a jazz session run amok. Nancy handed the flowers to a maid she'd hired for the occasion. When a waiter came by with a tray of glasses brimming with champagne, Phil took one and said to Nancy, "I'm proud of you. It must be tough to have liquor flowing around you and not indulge. I'm surprised you're serving alcohol."

"Only Champagne. The service I employed brings the stuff, serves it and takes it away. I've had enough ginger ale tonight to explode in one gaseous bubble." She looked about the room as if she were a queen ruling over her subjects and, in a way, she was the queen of this particular group of faculty.

Nancy led Phil to the food-laden dining table. "I've got to be witty with Professor Jackson. He's got a connection in Canada I want to use. Don't leave the party until I've had a chance to talk with you. Promise?"

Nodding, he watched her wade into the undulating crowd, then helped himself to an assortment of dishes: caviar, smoked salmon, brie on crisp crackers and seafood tidbits. People whirled by, snatched food, greeted him with glowing, grinning faces, and indulged in nonsensical conversation. Wanda, from the language department, gave him a hug. She was a shy, big woman, who seemed to have been reborn, thanks to Champagne. For a moment, he felt as if he were in the grasp of a dragon.

Eventually, Phil joined a quieter group by the fireplace, only to realize they had passed through the boisterous stage into tedious incoherence. He glimpsed Nancy making the rounds of her guests in effortless grace, and admired her ability to maintain sober equanimity surrounded by such a bacchanal.

The woman next to him leaned over and asked in a bleary voice, "Are there still lobsters in Maine?" She pointed to his plate with its smattering of lobster. "I heard they were all gone. Pollution. Destroys everything."

He had no idea what to reply, so he just nodded. This seemed to satisfy her, and she sashayed to the person across from her to blurt out another question. Phil observed, ate and sipped his champagne. He caught words and pieces of gossip, listened politely, and nodded his head at the appropriate time, wishing he could leave.

Someone tugged the sleeve of his jacket. Turning, he found Nancy's frowning face close to his. "You're not into the Christmas spirit, I see."

"Sorry. Thinking of home."

"You're going home for Christmas?"

"Thought I would. Driving to Philadelphia tomorrow."

"Then you and I need to talk tonight." She took his hand and led him toward the stairs.

He dropped off his plate and glass on a nearby table.

"My bedroom is the safest place," she said, walking up the stairs. "I've been warned I'm under federal scrutiny."

"What?" Phil almost stumbled at the landing. "Who told you that?"

"A source." She opened her bedroom door and ushered him in.

"You and your sources. Perhaps you should be more worried about gossip."

She smiled. "My guests are too busy enjoying themselves. Besides, the right kind of gossip couldn't hurt."

He surveyed the frilly feminine decor with its large blue and yellow flower print pillows heaped in abundance on a white-laced bedspread, and the canopy above the bed swaged with lace.

Nancy asked, "Do you like it?"

"Unexpected. It's quite different from the rest of the house."

"You've found out my secret."

He raised his eyebrows, thinking he was about to learn some intimate detail.

"I'm not just a hard-bitten, environmental activist. This," she said, twirling about with her arms outstretched, "is my true and happy self. The real inner me."

"I'm glad," he said, and meant it. "Now, what is it you need to talk about before I leave town?"

"God, Phil." She flounced down on the bed and stared at him. "Can't you ever lighten up? You always want to come to the point. Are you this way with everything? How about in bed? Don't you enjoy foreplay?"

He stood in the center of her bedroom unable to think of a decent reply. They looked at each other. Neither spoke. Finally, she turned her head away and stared at the far wall. "I always scare you."

"Yeah, but this time, I deserve it. Christmas isn't my favorite time of year."

"Mine either."

He sat next to her and took her thin hand in his. "You're doing a great job tonight. It's your first party since you stopped drinking, isn't it?"

She nodded, gave a small sniff and smiled at him. "I am doing well, aren't I?"

"You're very brave, but you still scare me."

She started to laugh. "That's good. Gives me some power. But you see, I'm the one who's scared. If the Feds are watching me, what does that mean and who could it be?"

He swallowed hard. "Who told you such a story?"

"I can't answer that."

"Okay. Do you want to tell me what's bothering you? About the organization, I mean?"

She rose, walked to a table in the far corner and picked up a cigarette. After she lit it, she turned toward him. "My organization is losing members every semester. The slump started about three years ago."

"About the time I came on board." It was better he stated the fact.

"I'm not blaming you. I have to do something to perk things up, get young people motivated. I've got to do something extraordinary. I thought the Cassini project with the Sierra Club might do the trick, but it isn't enough. With the new *Cosmos* discovery in Canada, the environment effect of radiation is back in the news. I thought we could collaborate with a

Canadian group. I have a connection to Pierre Giraud."

"You can't be serious." He stood and glared at her. "He's a known terrorist. Even the French separatists have avoided him and his group."

"You don't approve."

"Not at all. Have you spoken to other board members?"

"No. But they'll agree with me."

He was truly shaken and wasn't sure how to continue. His worst fear that Nancy would reach out to the violent side of activism might come true. "Do you remember what happened three years ago?" He waited, then, not getting a response, continued, "One of your members got it in his head to bomb the Maine Yankee Atomic Power Station at Wiscasset. The newspapers played it up. Thank God, he didn't succeed."

"That facility falsified computer data to get a higher power rating." Her chin jutted out.

"Did that justify bombing the facility?"

She looked away and nervously puffed on her cigarette.

"You know it didn't. You don't want to hurt people or destroy property. At least that's what you tell your recruits."

"Maybe it's time to change."

"Why? Groups like yours are forcing the government to wake up. You said enrollment in *Cure the World* is down. When did it start to drop? I'll tell you when. Right after that nut tried to blow Maine Yankee. It's taken all this time to recover from that black eye. Now you want to connect with a known terrorist?"

"I'm losing ground."

"*You're* losing ground?"

"I mean, *Cure the World*. Haven't you noticed how unimportant our meetings seem to have become? Publicity is down. Newspapers ignore us. I haven't been able to get any new members from Harvard or MIT. I, ah... we used to."

Her continual use of 'I' bothered Phil. In the larger scope of the antinuclear movement, Nancy felt less influential. Of course, she was right. That had been his objective, and he'd succeeded.

She frowned, took a last drag on her cigarette and stubbed it out in a porcelain ashtray. "Perhaps you're right about Pierre, but it's an opening I plan to explore." She held up her hand when he began to speak. "I won't commit to anything, but I'm making the connection."

He shook his head. "I don't like it."

"I'm head of the organization," she said, then softened her stance. "I won't do anything until the fall semester. Does that suit you?"

"Me? Ask your fellow members. They're in this with you. You started the organization, but it doesn't belong solely to you any more."

"True, but I guide them. We'll discuss my connection with Pierre as a group in the fall. All right?"

"Just connecting with that fellow is trouble. If the Feds are watching you, what do you think they'll think?"

"I don't give a damn what they think."

He raised his eyebrows and stared at her. "Earlier you said you were scared."

"Phil, you can be impossible. You twist everything I say and throw it back at me. Aren't you with me?"

"On this? No."

"I'll wait until I learn more about the recent uranium findings. In July I'm going on a guided canoe trip into the Thelon River Sanctuary."

Chapter 9

On Christmas Eve Laura's cab pulled up in front of the Sterlings' Brentwood home. A heavy overcast huddled the southern California landscape blurring the neighborhood's Christmas lights. After tipping the driver, Laura grasped her suitcase, threw the strap of her large travel purse over her shoulder and walked up the brick path to the front door. Before she could knock, the door swung open, and Deirdre welcomed her with open arms.

"Laura. Glad you made it. I'm sorry neither Cal nor I could meet you at the airport. You know how it is getting ready for a family Christmas dinner. Tons of details to look after, and Cal's been in a blue funk lately. He's no help."

Laura hugged her dear friend. "Getting a cab was easy."

They stood in the small round entrance hall gazing at each other before simultaneously launching into conversation. Deirdre laughed. "Just like always. We're on the same wavelength. I'm so pleased you came. I haven't had a good laugh since the last time we were together."

Deirdre's merriment was catching, and Laura smiled. "Your home is beautiful." She looked at the pine boughs laced with berries hanging above each archway and peeked into the living room at the massive blue spruce Christmas tree, shining with elegant decorations. "You're a genius. Nobody can decorate for the holidays the way you can."

"Wait till you see the guest cottage." Deirdre's shoulder length auburn hair fell forward as she picked up Laura's suitcase.

Laura followed her friend down the long hall, past the master bedroom and out across a garden with its small recirculating waterfall. Once inside the mother-in-law cottage, Laura closed the door, muffling the rhythmic bubbling from the courtyard. Like a department store showroom,

Christmas decorations festooned every table and window. Holly draped the mantlepiece above a cozy fireplace where artificial logs glowed from gas-fed flames. Stocky white and red candles graced the red cloth draped over the table set between two large white-upholstered chairs. Every picture had a pine garland around the frames, and the queen-sized bed had a white bedspread laden with a red quilt and matching pillows. Two large stuffed toys, a white lion and a toy soldier, stared from a window seat. Laura felt smothered by the decor, but said, "As usual, you've outdone yourself." Half-joking, she added, "I suppose even the bathroom has holly and red and white towels."

"Of course." Deirdre broke into a broad smile. "I've had such fun getting ready for Christmas. Wait till you see the toy band on the buffet. It's precious." She collapsed her long slim frame into one of the chairs. "Go ahead and unpack. I'll watch." Her ice-blue eyes squinted in a query. "What are you going to wear tonight? Something elegant I hope."

"You said it was just family, nothing elaborate." Laura opened her suitcase.

"That didn't mean you shouldn't buy a new dress."

Laura paused then lifted out the dress she'd bought last week in Chinatown. She was a bit apprehensive about Deirdre's reaction. As she pulled out the silk dress and held it up, folds of tissue paper whispered onto the floor.

"Oh, Laura, it's smashing. Only you could wear a red dress with a high collar and make it look sexy."

"I'm glad you like it. I fell in love with it the minute I saw it. A bit expensive, but I couldn't resist." She took a hanger from the closet. "What about you? What are you going to wear?"

"Won't tell. You'll have to wait and see."

"That's not fair. You can't have everything a surprise."

"This Christmas I have lots of surprises." Deirdre leaned back with a smug smile and crossed her elegant legs.

"When have you ever been able to keep a secret?" Laura raised an eyebrow.

"From you, seldom, from Cal, always."

"So give." Laura sat on the bed to face Deirdre.

"You'll never guess. It's about the Arctic."

"The Thelon trip? But Cal doesn't want you to go."

"I've got all the information. All your negative talk isn't going to prevent me from going with him, even if you refuse to go with us."

"It seems so far away and foreboding, too." Laura thought of her promise to Cal. "You complained about the camping conditions in Costa Rica. This Thelon trip will be worse."

Deirdre walked to the window seat, grabbed the stuffed lion and hugged it to her. "Whose friend are you anyway, Cal's or mine?" She didn't wait for Laura to answer. "I'll get my way. The trip would be perfect for you, for your photography. Think, all those wolves and grizzly bears and things. Cal could publish your work."

Didn't Deirdre know that Cal's magazine had recently done a piece on the Arctic? "Why is Cal going to the Thelon?"

Still hugging the lion, Deirdre walked to the large overstuffed chair and curled up in it. "He was there when he was in the Air Force, but never said much about the place. His stay there remains one big mystery. Now, he says he has to go to Fort Smith on business and then canoe into the wilderness. It's not like him. I want to go with him, but he's being so stubborn."

Laura laughed. "And of course, you're not." She looked at her friend affectionately.

Deirdre slouched in the chair and played with the lion's large red bow. "Why can't he see it? We don't have fun together anymore. Nothing I do is enough. He's always too busy."

"You're both still hurting from baby Brian's death." Letting Deirdre talk about her baby had seemed to help her get through her grief, so Laura had become Deirdre's sympathetic listener.

"It'll be three years on January fifth. If I've gotten over it, why can't he? It wasn't my fault." Deirdre struggled to keep back tears, but her eyes brimmed.

Laura hurried to Deirdre's side, knelt and took her hand. "It wasn't anyone's fault. Things happen we can't comprehend. You and Cal love each other."

"Then why doesn't he show it?" Deirdre hid her face in the stuffed lion. "I do so much for him. He closes me out."

"Is he still seeing the psychologist?"

Deirdre sniffled. "He quit going and so did I. It wasn't helping."

Laura didn't know what else she could say or do. She had traveled with Deirdre for the past three years, all the while knowing their adventure travels were escapes for Deirdre. She stood, but remained by the chair and stroked her friend's hair.

"So tell me," Laura finally said, breaking the silence, "what's your other surprise?"

Deirdre looked up, wiped her eyes with a handkerchief, careful to avoid smearing her mascara. "You are a good friend." She sighed heavily. "Stupid to get all maudlin at Christmas time. I'll let you settle in. I've got to talk to Cook. She's in a bit of a tizzy over the dinner tonight."

"Oh no you don't! You aren't going to leave me here wondering about your surprise."

Deirdre's smile, albeit a small one, returned. "I have a special guest coming for dinner. I haven't told anyone, especially not Cal. A man he knew in the service up in the Arctic. Hey, he isn't married or anything. Maybe you and he will hit it off."

Laura shook her head in resignation and disgust. "You didn't ask this man to dinner to meet me, I hope."

"Of course not. I'm going to surprise Cal with his old Air Force buddy, Boris Sweet. Isn't that a delightful name?"

"How did you find out about him?"

"That's the kick. He called and said he'd just learned Cal was the publisher of *Earth's Attractions.* He was going to be in town for a few days over Christmas and wanted to look him up. So I invited him to Christmas Eve dinner."

"Do you know anything more about him, other than he was in the military with Cal?" Laura thought of Phil, another old military buddy of Cal's. If Phil had spoken of a Boris Sweet, she would have remembered the name, but it sounded familiar.

Deirdre rose, put the lion down and walked toward the door. "That's why it's exciting. I don't know a thing about him. Maybe he'll turn out as intriguing as Phil."

Laura cringed, but before she could hide her emotions, Deirdre apologized. "That was insensitive of me." She came over and put an arm around Laura's shoulders. "Phil turned out to be a cad, leaving you the way he did."

Laura moved away from Deirdre and raised her chin. "We never made promises to each other. It was just one of those vacation romances. Fun while it lasted."

Deirdre nodded. "Right. Whatever you say. Forget the guy and find another. You deserve better." She moved toward the door. "At least this

Christmas should be exciting with Cal meeting an old buddy, and of course, there's my extra surprise for Cal."

Boris began to have second thoughts about his visit with the Sterlings. How would Cal react? Phil had instructed them to pretend they didn't know each other when they got to Fort Smith. Hell, he thought, I don't even know if Cal's going. Boris shifted the Audi into second and drove through winding streets following Deirdre Sterling's directions. Darkness had fallen, and Christmas lights twinkled through the evening fog. Spotting the address, he parked, shut off the motor and checked himself in the mirror. The years had been kind to him, but he didn't look anything like the skinny lad Cal had known. Would they recognize each other?

Boris gripped the leather binding around his steering wheel, surprised at his hesitation. Something in Deirdre Sterling's voice had put him on edge. She had wanted his visit to be a surprise. Nothing wrong in that, yet her tone and the clip of her words had sparked his wariness. A cozy Christmas Eve dinner party is how she'd put it. Well, it beat being alone.

A Mercedes turned into the long driveway and drove to the back garage. He caught a glimpse of the man driving—slick hair, dark complexion. It had to be Cal.

Boris got out with the box of chocolates he'd bought from a small store on San Vicente Boulevard. Not much of an offering, but he figured it was the thought that counted. Smoothing his navy blue blazer, he walked to the front door and rang the bell.

After a moment the door swung wide, and he gazed into the face of a tall, slim woman with ash blonde hair offset by a striking high-collared red dress. Her large blue eyes made him want to move closer.

"Mrs. Sterling? I'm—"

"Boris Sweet. Come in." When the woman smiled, Boris felt as if he were drowning. Cal was a lucky man.

"I'm Deirdre's friend, Laura Boswell." The heavenly apparition motioned for him to enter.

He grinned and felt like a kid going to his first prom. "Merry Christmas." He fumbled with the box of chocolates and handed it to her. "A little offering for the hostess. I feel a bit awkward stumbling into the Sterlings' home on Christmas, but Mrs. Sterling insisted."

"Deirdre will be along in a minute. Some last minute chores in the kitchen with the cook. Cal just got home."

Boris followed Laura into the living room where a giant Christmas tree dripped with clusters of ornaments, lights and tinsel. She must have noticed his look of awe, for she commented, "Beautiful, isn't it? Deirdre loves to decorate."

They stood next to each other gazing at the tree. He could feel her warmth and smell her perfume. What was it? He felt lightheaded. "My appearance is supposed to be a surprise for Cal."

"Yes, I know. Deirdre told me you and Cal were in the military together. In the Arctic, wasn't it?"

"Yes. About seventeen years ago. I'm not sure Cal will remember me, nor am I sure my visit will be a good surprise."

"You had little choice. Deirdre loves excitement, and your arrival has given her a wonderful lift."

"Does she need a lift? I thought Christmas was uplifting by itself."

Laura looked sideways at him. "Deirdre lives for thrills. This Christmas you are the added attraction."

"I'm not sure I like being the center of attention."

"Your appearance may solve some of Deirdre's questions about Cal's past," Laura said.

Boris felt his collar tighten. "I'm beginning to feel very apprehensive."

Laura turned and looked him in the eye. "I have the impression you're quite able to handle yourself in any situation."

He felt a soft glow surround him, yet managed to ask, "Where did you come by such a feeling?"

Laura smiled, but the doorbell rang, stopping her reply. They stood waiting for someone to open the door, but no one came.

"Cal," Deirdre yelled from the kitchen. "Answer the door. I've got cheese all over my hands."

"Can't," came the yell back. "I haven't finished changing."

"Laura," Deirdre called out.

"Yes," Laura answered with a cheerful voice. "I'll get it." She turned quickly to Boris. "It'll be Deirdre's parents. Don't fret. They're easygoing."

Boris waited by the fireplace, while Laura answered the door. He'd been hoping he and Cal could meet before other guests assembled. Cal would be at a disadvantage, but Boris remembered how Cal had taken everything in

stride during Operation *Morning Light,* following directions, never balk-
ing at orders the way Boris had. Even when they got lost and found the
diamonds on the old miner, Cal had maintained control of his emotions.
Boris often wished he could develop that trait.

Laura walked back into the room and introduced George and Sylvia
Turner, Deirdre's parents. Soon Deirdre swept into the room. Her long
Christmas maroon velvet skirt fell in soft folds from her hips. The scooped
neckline of her blouse shimmered with gold sequins. She embraced her
parents. Her mother oohed with enthusiasm over Deirdre's dress.

Boris had never seen such an ostentatious gown. He watched a startled
look flit across Laura's face.

When she commented, "You've outdone yourself, Deirdre. Your
dress is definitely in the Christmas tradition." He smiled at Laura's clever
understatement.

"I'm so glad you like it." Deirdre whirled around and then without
missing a beat, she took up the reins of hostess and turned to Boris.

"Boris Sweet." She took hold of his hands as if they'd known each other
for ages. "I'm delighted to meet you after all these years. Cal will be thrilled.
He doesn't talk about the old days, but I know they must be precious to
him. His Air Force friends are somewhat of a mystery. Do you know Phil
West?"

Without waiting for Boris to respond, Deirdre continued her sweeping
flow of thoughts. "How marvelous—another mystery man has come forward." Deirdre dropped his hands and continued, "You will, won't you?"

"I'm sorry," he said. "I don't quite follow you."

"She wants you to tell her all about your time in the Arctic with Cal,"
Laura said.

"Not too much to tell. It was a long time ago."

"We'd love to hear about it," Sylvia Turner said. "Cal's always been
closed-mouthed about that part of his life. When he became a civilian, he
started the magazine."

"Made a damn good career for himself," George Turner said. "Got a
loan just like that." George snapped his fingers. "Not many fellows out of
the military could have talked a bank into that. He's a real breadwinner."

Boris smiled at the proud father-in-law, knowing Cal got his start the
way he had—Diamonds.

"Merry Christmas everyone," Cal said as he walked in with a tray full of
glasses of champagne. "Time to celebrate." Concentrating on not spilling,

he placed the tray on the coffee table, then straightened up to greet his in-laws and Laura. He turned to Deirdre, and then Boris. "Who's our guest?"

Cal's face paled, and beads of sweat flecked his upper lip as he shook hands. "Boris?" He moved close and whispered, "Did he send you?"

Knowing Cal meant Phil, he mouthed back, no. As the two drew back from each other, Boris said in too loud a voice, "Didn't mean to give you a start, but your wife insisted."

They stood eyeing each other until Cal moved to Boris's side and put his arm around his shoulders, grasping him tightly. "You son-of-a-gun. What in the hell are you doing here?" He pounded Boris on the back.

Boris played the game. "Found out you were publisher of *Earth's Attractions* and since I was in town, I thought I'd look you up."

Everyone chatted about how wonderful it was to have Boris as a surprise guest, while Cal retrieved another glass and passed out the Champagne. "Here's a toast to good friends, family and," he nodded toward Boris, "old buddies."

"Hear. Hear." George Turner said.

While Deirdre passed the caviar and crackers, Cal sidled next to Boris and quietly whispered. "We'll talk later. Watch what you say." Cal moved away, retaining a set smile.

"Do get comfortable," Deirdre said, motioning to the chairs. Boris found a seat in a chair opposite Laura and Deirdre, while the Turners sat on a couch to his right. Cal stood stiffly at the fireplace overlooking the group.

"Boris, tell us about your stint in the Air Force with Cal," Deirdre said, setting her drink aside and folding her hands on her lap as if she were awaiting some startling news.

"You don't want to hear that," Cal said, staring at Boris.

"Yes, I do." Deirdre kept her eyes on Boris. "Cal never talks about his military life. When did you meet?"

"We served in the Arctic together," Boris said. "A short stint in '78. We separated after that when I was sent to California." He glanced at Cal. "I made Airman First Class before I was discharged. How about you?"

"They wanted me to go to Officer's Candidate School, but after the Arctic tour, I got out. Thought you were from Iowa. Where are you now?"

"I opened a bookstore in Berkeley."

"Sweet's Book Store," Laura said. "I've heard of it. The only place to go if you want to find a treasured old book."

"You live in the Bay area, too?" Boris became more intrigued with Laura. "Thanks for the compliment. You should visit soon, and I'll show you around the store."

"Oh, pooh," Deirdre interrupted. "What did you do in the Arctic? Cal simply won't say."   "It's no secret," Cal offered. "I've told you dozens of times, honey. Operation *Morning Light* was designed to find fragments of the Russian spy satellite that broke up over the Northwest Territory of Canada."

"What was it like?" Laura chimed in, trying to take some of the heat off her friend. "Deirdre wants to visit the Thelon River Sanctuary this summer with Cal."

Boris glanced at Deirdre, then Cal and cleared his throat that felt like sandpaper. "We were there through the winter. So cold it could freeze your nose off. We had to mark the debris the Canadians located." He looked up at Cal who remained statue-like by the hearth. "Did you tell them the condom story?"

George Turner chuckled, "Yeah, we heard that story, several times."

"Tell us something about you and your friends," Deirdre said.

Boris looked about the expectant room. "We did get lost once. Did you tell them that story?"

Cal stiffened. "Hardly worth telling."

Boris warmed to his audience. "In the spring we were told to check out a certain area. Our helicopter crashed, burned, the pilot died. We lost most of our equipment and couldn't contact base. Bad weather set in. Our Canadian sergeant, and our U.S. sergeant, Phil West, Cal and I plodded around for days. One day we came across a grizzly." He glanced at Cal. "I don't know about you, but I was scared. That beast was the biggest, shaggiest thing I'd ever seen. Iowa doesn't have creatures that big, fast and fierce. The only scary thing in Iowa is a farmer who's had his farm sold out from under him." He caught Laura's grin, which egged him on. "Well, that creature took one look at the four of us, roared and raised up on his hind legs. We backed up real quick." Boris pointed to the large Christmas tree. "He was as tall as that. Someone yelled, 'shoot,' but nobody did. We had orders not to harm the wildlife and that included grizzlies. Sarge ordered a retreat back to the lake behind us. Thinking back, we probably looked like a comedy team. Left our gear and backed up real slow. When we were out of that old bear's sight, we hightailed it to the lake. Before I jumped in, I turned and saw old grizzly bearing down on us. The quickest monster I've ever seen. Cal, you were already in the water, when I leaped in next to you. Damn, but that water was icy, but none of us was about to move toward shore, not with that bear glaring at us. He was weaving his head back and forth while the four of us stood in freezing water up to our arm pits. If he'd have come in after us, I was ready to swim to China. Finally it waddled off. When I got out of the water, I was shaking bad, and I couldn't figure out if it was from the cold or the scare the bear had given me."

Deirdre turned to Cal. "Why didn't you ever tell me?"

Cal shrugged. "Didn't seem important. The place was a hellhole. I try not to think about it."

Boris realized Cal never had admitted being scared even when the rest of them had joked about how terrified they'd been. Couldn't Cal ever admit to being less than super?

"How did you get back to your base?" George Turner asked.

"That was tough. The bear slashed our gear and ate what rations we had left. For two weeks we floundered around until a rescue plane spotted us."

"If your food was gone, what did you eat?" Deirdre asked.

"Caught a few fish, found patches of berries, made tea from pine bark." Boris glanced at Cal. "What were those berries called? Do you remember?"

"I only remember they were barely edible." Cal gazed at his long fingers with a look of boredom.

"Couldn't you shoot a deer or something?" Sylvia Turner asked.

"Didn't come across anything we could shoot. The barrenlands that time of year are wildlife sparse." Boris leaned back. "That old bear was mighty mean. We were lucky he didn't chew us up and spit us out just for fun."

"The male grizzly can be a terror even toward cubs," Laura said. "You really have to watch out for the sow if you get between her and her cubs."

Cal's face remained taut as he said, "As bad as the grizzly was, Boris didn't tell you how bad the black flies and mosquitoes were, nor how isolated the area is and how lonely it makes you feel."

Everyone began talking at once until Deirdre held up her hand and asked for quiet. "I have a special Christmas gift for Cal." With great ceremony, she pulled an envelope out of a pocket in her voluminous skirt. Her bright red manicured nails contrasted sharply against the white paper.

Boris felt a chill. Her nails reminded him of drops of blood. Silly, he thought and shook off his foreboding.

"Merry Christmas." She held out the envelope to Cal.

He leaned over, gave her a kiss on the cheek. The room fell silent as Cal ripped the envelope open. His face paled as he read the contents. Deirdre hugged her husband and said, "It'll be such fun."

"Darling," Sylvia asked, "what did you give him?"

"Cal, tell them," Deirdre said, encircling his waist with her arm, a smug expression on her face.

Cal's eyes narrowed as he scowled at Laura over Deirdre's head. Then he glanced at Boris. His voice broke as he read, "Two reservations in July on McDuffy's canoe trip on the Thelon River for Deirdre and Cal Sterling."

Chapter 10

The soft sun of late March streamed across the side of Boris's Audi as he parked near the beach at Point Reyes National Seashore, north of San Francisco. Stepping out of the car, Laura stretched. "What a heavenly day. Perfect for taking pictures."

"Are you going to lug all this photo equipment?" Boris asked before reaching into the trunk. "I'll take the lunch pack, more dear to my heart than your equipment, but I'll be a gentleman and carry your tripod."

Laura chuckled and grabbed her pack. "No, I'll strap it to my pack. This time I've whittled down my equipment." She thought of their outing to Big Sur when she'd brought several long range lenses and two cameras, and he'd helped carry it through a cloudburst. "I notice your picnic goodies have grown."

"I made avocado and portabello mushroom sandwiches on that seven-grain bread you like."

"You're spoiling me." Teasing him was such fun. Their relationship sparkled with happiness, something she hadn't indulged in since…Phil.

"A gesture to reward your artistic talent." He gave a mock bow, then patted his pack. "Besides, I filled the extra space with a book."

"A book?" She poked at his bulging pack. "I bet you've got two or three squirreled away in there."

He grinned. "They keep me content while you're taking photos. You must have taken over two thousand slides since we met." His brown eyes twinkled under his bushy eyebrows.

They donned their packs, perused the map and started down a narrow trail that led around a wetland. Despite the crisp morning air, they wore hiking shorts and T-shirts, knowing they'd warm up from hiking under the midday sun. Boris strode ahead in a pace that matched her own. His gray canvas hat placed jauntily on his head revealed wisps of brown hair from under the brim. He always seemed in need of a haircut. She smiled at how this bear of a man could be comforting and intellectually interesting. Binoculars bounced against his wide chest as he ducked under an overhanging bush and held it for her.

As she bent under the same bush, she grabbed the camera hanging from her neck. Stepping over a log, her foot landed in Boris's imprint, creating an image which caused an odd sensation. How did she really feel about him? He was all she could want and yet she had no intention of slipping into a sexual relationship as easily as she had with Phil.

Everything about Boris spoke of steadiness, responsibility and goodness. What was there to find fault? Too adoring? Her dad had told her the man should be more in love than the woman. Of course, that was the other thing about Boris; he was like her father.

Boris stopped and pointed through the tall grass toward the lake. At the edge of the water ten yards away, a great blue heron fed. Laura checked her camera, set the aperture and clicked. The heron's red eye gleamed. She clicked again. With a jarring, yet royal gait, the bird moved deeper into the foliage until it was no longer visible.

Laura put her hand on Boris's shoulder and whispered, "Good eye."

With a bashful wink, he stepped closer, leaned over and brushed his lips against her cheek, then turned and walked on. His simple gesture made her tingle.

They continued the circuit around the wetland, stopping occasionally to view either the birds or the vegetation. After a while they walked across a road, then through tall headland grasses to the ocean with its cool breeze. From time to time Laura stopped and photographed a scene, while Boris scanned the area with his binoculars. Each in turn pointed out a sight the other found interesting. Eventually, they hiked down to the shoreline and found they were alone.

Lines splintered around Boris's eyes as he squinted at the sun. "Time for lunch." He pointed toward rocks jutting into the ocean about a half-mile down the beach. "How about there for a picnic spot?"

"I vote for something softer." She pointed to the mossy cliff. "It shouldn't take us too long to get up there."

"Slave driver." He studied the terrain. "We'll have to cut along that rocky ledge to the slope above, but it's doable."

"It'll make a much nicer picnic area, and you'll be happier to settle in with your books while I wander around looking for photo ops." She strode off, and Boris followed.

He admired her energy, her zest for life. Whenever they'd spent a day with nature, Laura was at her best. He knew she enjoyed the nights they went to the theater, the opera and ethnic restaurants, but on days like today, she blossomed. As much as he relished these times with her, he wanted her to enjoy his favorite outings as much. He had the impression this was not the case. Still, he hadn't been as content with anyone in years. Would sex change their easy-going relationship? How should he take the next step? He wished he were more sophisticated in the art of romance.

By the time they reached the top of the grassy butte, both were breathing hard and perspiring. In a meadow of clover and early spring flowers, they slid off their packs. Boris spread a plaid blanket, kneeled down and pulled out neatly wrapped sandwiches, sliced apples and pears and a thermos of fruit juice.

Laura gazed around and held out her arms as if she were beckoning the gods to approve of her. "The aura of this place trembles with good vibes."

Boris looked up to see the sun behind Laura shimmering like a halo. A nearby tree stretched its limbs toward the sky, and he reflected on her grace as she walked through the slashes of sunlight and shadow. When she again stood above him, he wanted desperately to take her in his arms and smother her with kisses. Instead he said, "The trembling you hear may be an earthquake. We are directly above the San Andreas Fault."

She collapsed on the blanket, threw her arms about his shoulders, shoved his hat off and ruffled his hair. "Spoil sport." Her cerulean eyes glinted with laughter.

He drew her to him and kissed her awkwardly. Her lips were tentative, yet not uninviting. With pent up longing, he pulled her closer. Abruptly she pulled away and a bubble of nervous laughter escaped her lips. He felt part of himself peel away.

"You're right," he said in a choked voice. "The place does have wonderful vibes." He attempted to kiss her again, but she shoved at his chest.

"I love your humor, Boris."

"But not the kiss?"

"I didn't mean it that way." She sat up and ran her fingers through her short blonde hair. "We have an audience," she said as a seagull alighted nearby.

Her reaction to his advance frustrated him, yet he took heed of the stormy color in her eyes. He reached out and smoothed back a blonde lock from her forehead. "We've had such good times together. I care for you very much."

She bit her lower lip, glanced away then turned to gaze at him. "I care for you, too." She patted his hand, but the motherliness of her action felt like a sting of rebuke. He pulled his hand away. Perhaps realizing she'd hurt him, she said, "I'm comfortable with you, and I do love your sense of humor."

A sense of humor is the other face of despair, he thought.

"I enjoy being with you. But…."

There's always a but, he thought, and picked at a blade of grass.

"We've become good friends in a short period. Let's take the next step slower," she said.

At least she sees a next step for us. "You've been hurt." When she stiffened, he knew he'd assumed correctly. "You'll never have to doubt my loyalty."

She looked away. "I need time."

They sat, feeling the breeze, not speaking. Her shoulder touched his, her scent encircled him, and he was lost to her whims and decisions. Did he dare ask: how much time?

Suddenly, she turned to him with a distracting grin and put her arm across his wide shoulders. "I've decided to go on the Arctic trip. I called Grant McDuffy, and he seemed to want another person with canoeing experience. And—"

"When did you decide? When I mentioned I was going, you said you weren't." He wasn't sure if he should be elated or scared. He wanted her with him, but had concerns for her safety. The Canadian trip might be more than a paddle on a river above the Arctic Circle.

"Deirdre talked me into it." Laura's eyes sparkled. "The wildlife should be spectacular." She hesitated and peered at him with a speculative rise of her eyebrows. "Are you unhappy with my decision?"

"No, of course not. I'm delighted you're going." He studied her, trying to determine her motives. Was she going because of him or in spite of him? Facing her, he took her hands and noted the curl of her fingers, delicate, yet strong. "Why did you keep it a secret?"

She moved away from him and gazed out at the meadow with her arms around her knees, then turned toward him. "I get the feeling there's more to this trip than you and Cal wanting to pay your respects to a former Air Force friend."

Boris knew he was a lousy liar, so he told her part of the truth. "When you go through a life threatening experience with men, there's an emotional link that binds you forever. I want to see how Erich lived and how he died."

Laura's eyes misted. "I should have understood. It's all right that I'm going, isn't it? I mean I wouldn't interfere—"

"We could go as a couple." His hopes soared.

"I'm not ready, Boris. Ever since my dad died, I've been…I need to find my equilibrium again." She reached out and her fingers intertwined with his.

His heart beat faster. How young and shy and wonderful she was. Her words washed over him, and for the moment he was content to just be there with her and for her.

"You've given me back something I'd lost," she murmured in a hushed voice. "But I'm frightened of…I don't know how to say this, but the future seems scary. I'm not sure what I want." She scanned his face. "Can you wait?"

He reached up and gently traced the outline of her face with his forefinger. She didn't pull away, and that warmed him. "How can I do otherwise?"

She smiled and scrambled to her feet.

He began to arrange the food on the blanket, pretending nothing new had passed between them. "We'll have a fine time." His voice came out with less affirmation than he'd intended. "I'm a very good woodsman."

She knelt, hugging him from the back with her soft cheek against the side of his face. "It'll be grand being in the wilderness."

If she'd added, with you, he'd have been happier, but she'd asked for time, and he'd honor her request. However, despite Laura's outdoor experiences, the Barrenlands might be more than she anticipated, but he'd protect her from whatever came.

Chapter 11

Spring in Fort Smith was difficult for anyone, but for Henri, it was worse, now that he lived in Erich's house. It had been willed to him, together with a small income to maintain the place. From the grave Erich had reached out to sentence Henri to prison by saddling him with his house in civilization. It baffled Henri how Erich could have afforded this house and have money left over. Trapping in the outback all these years brought in little, and Erich's military pension had been minimal.

A storm had lashed Fort Smith for three days. Icy sleet crackled against the windows, causing the timbers of Erich's squat house to creak from the buffeting wind. Moans from the stressed wood made Henri's skin crawl and convinced him that Erich's spirit dwelt in every corner. To Henri, even the forest across the meadow from the house emitted a feeling of chaos as the trees arched and swayed with each gust.

When Henri had moved into Erich's house, Leah came with him. She was ecstatic at the prospect of living in a well-built home off the main road outside of Fort Smith. Her humble apartment was all she'd known as an adult. The dark skin from her mixed blood marked her by society to live among the native Dene population and suffer their poverty. Once settled in the house, she'd dismissed the housekeeper and taken over the chores with glee, and her exertion from dusting and scrubbing made her full cheeks shine. With her usual practical sense, Leah refused to sell any of the furnishings, not even Erich's bed that she and Henri now slept in.

With Henri's permission, Leah meted out Erich's clothes to her needy fellow Denes. Henri knew Leah's friends had often told her to leave him, saying he was no good and his temper would lead to trouble. Despite his feelings about Erich's house, its ownership proved to those who spoke ill of him that he was a good provider to Leah.

This should have made Henri happy, but despair gripped him as he sat at Erich's desk, holding his head in his hands. His trapping and hunting permit had been pulled. "Temporarily," the authorities had said. He squirmed at the word. The Mounties refused to tell him how long temporarily would be. Without a permit to trap, he remained confined to Erich's house.

He had spent his days wallowing in drink and pondering the German script of Erich's notebook. For months he'd tried to decipher the scribbling using a German dictionary and grammar book. On a separate pad of paper, he wrote names, dates, and places he could interpret. The first page was the last logged entry; the date before Erich's death, followed by long unreadable rambling paragraphs. After thumbing through the rest of the notebook, Henri realized each place of Erich's travels had been logged with detailed descriptions of the geology, as well as longitudes and latitudes. He'd gotten the gist of the material, but little else. Erich's interest in geology would have surprised him if he hadn't found the diamond-flecked rock in Erich's things. He stared at the books on the desk before him. The letters blurred.

Leah's soft moccasins whispered on the hardwood floor as she glided to the entrance of the small den. "When are you going to finish packing those books?" She stood with her fists resting on her ample hips.

He frowned and glared at the bookshelves that yawned like a gaping mouth filled with books instead of teeth. Six cartons, half-filled with books, made a minefield of the room. "I haven't finished."

"It's been two weeks since the estate was settled," she harped. "The books don't belong to you. I saw the letter that man wrote you. He wants the books right away."

"*Merde*, woman!" He slammed his meaty fist down on the desk. "I do it my way. I look through them first."

"Not supposed to. The lawyer said…." Leah stopped and changed her attack. "They're just books. You can get them anywhere."

"If you had education, you'd know books like these are important."

"How do you know? You aren't any more educated than me. When was the last time you read a book?" She walked up to his desk. "Karen McDuffy can help you with that book." She put her hand out as if to take the notebook.

He moved it out of her reach. "I do it myself."

"Well, you've been at it ever since you came back last summer. Seems a waste of time to me."

"No wonder I never marry you," he yelled. *"Mon Dieu,* you're more a fishwife, than a real wife. Go clean somewhere." He turned his back to her and faced the window to look out on weather that was as nasty as the emotions seething within him. Henri felt suffocated by Leah, by his confinement, by Erich's indecipherable notes.

Is she right? Am I worrying about a harmless notebook and Erich's papers? Why would he write in German unless he had something to hide? His head ached, and he rubbed his eyes. He heard the front doorbell and Leah's shuffled steps to answer it. Curious, he turned away from the window. From the chatter, he presumed it was one of her Dene friends, but Leah came in with Karen McDuffy at her side.

"We have a guest," Leah said of the obvious. "I asked her to come talk about the books."

The intrusion was almost more than he could stand. He grasped the stone paperweight on the desk, thinking to throw it at the women. Instead, he stood rigidly behind the desk, forced himself to take a few deep breaths and wiped the beaded sweat from his brow.

"I don't want to interfere," Karen said, "but when Leah mentioned the books, I had to come see you. Perhaps you don't know, but the high school is in need of quality literature. There isn't enough money to buy good books. The faculty and the students would be very grateful if some of Erich's books could be donated to the school library. I thought perhaps you and I might persuade the man who owns the books to donate some of them."

Henri sat with a thud. This was not what he'd expected. He motioned toward the cartons. "I've been getting them ready to send to Massachusetts where Phil West lives. He's the fellow who gets them."

Karen wove her way through the boxes, glancing at the titles. *"Moby Dick, Red Badge of Courage.* Hemingway, Campbell, Tolkien. What treasures! Perfect for high school students." She stood in front of his desk. "Have you talked to Phil West?"

"Oui."

"May I call him, put my offer to him and see what he says?"

"Oui," Henri said, not knowing why he should give any other answer. Once he had all Erich's scribbled papers out of the books, he had no interest in the collection. "I don't care, but you may have to talk to the lawyer."

"Don't worry," Karen said. "If I can get the books, I'll take care of any legal documentation that might be needed." She looked at her watch. "With the time difference, he may be home now. Do you have his number? I can phone from here using my calling card."

He couldn't think of a way to dissuade her and gave her the number. While Karen put in the call, Henri walked to the half-empty bookshelves. Leah and Karen shocked him. Where had all the obedient women gone?

Once Karen had Phil on the line, Henri listened intently. She presented her case without mincing words, without letting the man get a word in. *Smart woman.* Finally, she was quiet, listening to the man.

"Yes, I'm Grant McDuffy's wife. No, I didn't realize you're going on Grant's tour this summer. I haven't seen the list."

She listened, her lips pursed, her fingers toying with the edge of Erich's notebook that had been left open on the desk. When she looked down, Henri moved forward. Did she notice the script or was her mind far away, visualizing Phil West on the other end of the line?

"Would you really do that? Wait, let me ask him." She held one hand over the phone. "He'll fly up this weekend and go through them. He'll let me have the books he doesn't want. Would that be all right with you?"

"It'd save money." *Why is everyone in a hurry?*

Karen relayed Henri's acceptance. "You've made my day, Mr. West," she said. "Grant and I would like you to have dinner with us when you're here."

After she hung up, she raised her hands in the air. "YES! The high school will get some of the books. Isn't that wonderful? Henri, you're an angel."

He didn't feel like an angel, but he felt better than when Karen had first arrived.

"He's a teacher, too," Karen said. "I know he'll be generous. Isn't it thrilling?"

Leah, who had remained standing by the door, looked at Henri, a big grin on her wide face. "Now you can concentrate on getting your hunting license back instead of trying to read that stupid notebook." She pointed to the book on the desk in front of Karen.

Karen picked it up before Henri could grab it. "Is this part of the collection?" she asked as she studied the contents.

"Yes," Leah said.

"Not exactly," Henri said.

Karen looked from one to the other.

"Erich had it with him. It's only a notebook, not a book like the others." He held his hand out for the spiral notebook.

Instead of handing it over, Karen continued to study it. "Wonderful old German script. Erich loved writing and reading in his mother tongue. When Erich was in town he'd visit me, and we'd talk German together. I really miss those talks. Do you mind if I read a little?" Without waiting for his reply, she read the opened page. "What a lovely description. Very thorough."

Henri didn't want to raise her suspicions, but felt as if he were burning. "The notes tell about where we went during our trips together. I pieced that together."

"Maybe you should sit in on my German classes," Karen said with a smile that showed off her dimples. "If you want the notes translated, I'd be glad to help." She closed the notebook and handed it to Henri who gripped it tightly against his side.

"I'm almost through with it," he lied. "You said Phil is a teacher. Does he teach languages?"

"Math and biology is what he said."

Henri wondered what Erich had in common with a math teacher. They'd been in the military together. That much Henri knew from the picture. After traveling in the backcountry together for years, Henri had begun to realize how little he knew about his former trapping friend.

"This Phil West is going on Grant's trip this summer?" Henri rubbed his bearded chin.

"So it seems. Interesting, isn't it." Karen's gaze drifted to the books. "If you'll pack the rest of the books, Grant can pick them up. Is the day after tomorrow all right?" Karen moved toward the door.

"Why take them to your house? West can come here for them."

"I thought it would be easier, since the books he doesn't want will stay with me until I can catalog them for the school."

Henri nodded dumbly, thinking that if the books were out of the house, he would think less about Erich. *Were Erich's notes only his love to write German and nothing more?*

"I've got to be going. The weather's getting worse. Thanks again," Karen said as she followed Leah out of the room.

Henri sighed and listened as Leah and Karen chatted in the hall while Karen put on her boots. "It's so exciting," he heard her say. "It'll be wonderful to meet one of our tour guests before the trip. I get butterflies when I'm not sure what our group will be like. This fellow was very pleasant on the phone. I think I'll like him."

"What about the notebook Henri keeps reading?" Leah asked.

"Lovely description of the country. Very detailed. It might make a wonderful book for research purposes. Perhaps when Henri's finished, he could lend it to me, so I could translate it. It's great he has so much interest in it. What a pleasure for him."

"Pleasure? It's driving him nuts." Leah said in a loud voice.

On the day Grant came by in his truck the ground had turned to mud. The night before, Henri had left the books scattered around the room after stuffing the remaining loose papers he'd found into a desk drawer. The Road End Bar had beckoned, and he'd slipped out of the house, leaving the book packing to Leah.

Today Henri's head pounded, and he longed for a drink. Sitting on a chair in front of the empty bookshelves, he watched Grant heft box after box and carry them to his truck. He made no attempt to help.

"Karen's thrilled," Grant said, passing the seated Henri. "Even if this guy decides on taking the bulk of the books, she figures the school will get a few."

"This Phil West? He's a client of yours this summer. Has he been here before?"

"He didn't say." Grant stood in front of Henri with a box in his arms.

Henri shrugged. "Many coincidences, no?"

"He wants to see the area where his friend spent much of his life. Nothing strange in that." Grant walked out with the last box. Leah smiled and shut the door firmly.

Later that night after returning from another visit to the Road End Bar, Henri collapsed in the desk chair, stared at the empty shelves and opened the top drawer to get the notebook. Empty pinewood gleamed at him. He bent down, ran his hand throughout the drawer as if he were blind, then slammed it shut. Fumbling, he wrenched open each drawer and jammed it shut again. All bare.

He screamed. "Leah!" Nobody answered. "Leah!" he yelled, again. "Where's the notebook? Where are the papers?"

She sidled into the room, her face wary, her dark eyes defiant. "I packed them with the books."

Henri lunged across the room and yanked her forward, pinning her in the corner against the empty bookcase and struck her repeatedly with his open palm. His hand was heavy, hard, and coarse, and the sounds echoed through the otherwise silent room. The sound and the feel gave him pleasure—a release of his coiled emotions.

With her hands covering her head, Leah slipped to the floor. Henri leaned over her, panting, his arms heavy, drained of energy by his angry explosion.

Leah cowed into a round ball, but she remained adamant. "An evil book. Bad omen. It possessed you."

Henri staggered away. Her words pounded through his liquor-dulled brain. He whirled and went into the kitchen to get a beer. Flinging open the refrigerator door, he glanced back and spotted Leah crawling out of the den. A vision of Erich appeared and stood over her, helping her, smiling. Henri's stomach rebelled and bile rose in his throat. He swallowed hard and rubbed his eyes. Had he gone insane? Erich's ghost vanished. The house was haunted. The notebook was bad luck. He never wanted to see it again. To hell with Erich's writings.

He sank onto a stool and stared at the kitchen wall with the beer bottle clutched in his beefy hand. *I'm cursed.* He took a long pull on the beer, swirling it around in his mouth before swallowing. He needed to get back to his Barrenlands, to trap, to live without guilt. *There I'll be safe.* Drops of beer spilled onto the floor and twinkled in the light from the open refrigerator door. His laughter sounded insane even to him. *I must go to the river, to my hut, to my traps, to my wolves.* Wolves and Grant mixed in his mind. His head nodded forward, and he sprawled across the kitchen table in a drunken sleep.

Chapter 12

Phil's stomach lurched as the wings of Chip's plane dipped and the earth fell away. Had he made a mistake grabbing Chip's charter to Fort Smith? What did he know about the fellow's flying abilities or safety record? When the Cessna's wings leveled off, and the engines settled into a rhythmic sync, Phil relaxed in the copilot's seat. Without another passenger, Chip had insisted Phil join him in the cockpit.

"Good of you to contact me about taking your charter," Phil said over the noisy propellers. He looked down at the disappearing houses of Edmonton. "You were right. The airline connection was lousy, especially since I only have two days."

"Thought as much." Chip tapped his altimeter. "Weather's been nasty, but I can fly under the clouds. It might get a wee rough, but an old Air Force guy like you should be able to handle it."

Phil stared at Chip. *How did he know I'd been in the Air Force? I'll have to be careful with this fellow.* "Did the McDuffys give you a heads up on my plans?"

"Grant?" Chip smiled. "No. Henri Deforte told me. You know, Erich's wolf trapping friend."

"Interesting," Phil said. "What did Henri tell you?"

"Your plans to fly up this weekend."

"Henri told you I'd served in the Air Force?"

"Right." Chip scanned the horizon and his hands twisted dials off and on. "Erich must have been a real good friend for you to come all this way."

Phil wondered what else Henri knew about him, and what else he'd passed on to Chip. "Erich talked about me?"

"Hell, I've been taking correspondence from Erich to Edmonton ever since I started my charter company."

"Must be an interesting job," Phil said as Chip pulled the plane's nose up, "hauling mail and knowing everyone's troubles and contacts. Kind of like a bartender people tell their troubles."

"Never thought of it that way." Chip glanced at Phil. "You've known Erich since 1978, right?"

Without answering directly, Phil said, "Erich didn't mention you in his letters. Were you a good friend?"

"I ferried him back and forth from Fort Smith to Henri's cabin on Lake Damant. Everyone in Fort Smith knew he'd served his stint during Operation *Morning Light*. That's why he was so screwed up, looking for pieces of that Russian satellite. Shame he never found any wreckage." Chip pulled out a map and put it on his lap.

The plane bumped dramatically, and Phil reached up to the top of the cabin, thinking he'd hit his head despite his seat belt. The cold metal against his palms did not reassure him. He pushed his glasses firmly in place. When the plane settled again, he said, "The Canadians must have been upset about the radiation scare back then. How are things now?"

"Fouled up in Fort Smith and in the Thelon Sanctuary. Mounties have curtailed all backcountry expeditions, no trapping, no fishing and no guided trips without special permission. But guess who gets to go about business as usual?" He waited as if he expected Phil to answer. "Guys from De Beers, that's who. Stinks of politics. Killing my business and all the rest of the people who depend on the tourist trade. Normally, I'd make runs up north to the Thelon Sanctuary and land supplies for the guides. Now I'm sitting on my can in Fort Smith like everyone else."

"I'm expecting to go on a canoe trip with Grant in July. Haven't heard his trip's been canceled." Phil pulled his safety belt tighter as the plane pitched again.

Chip concentrated on his flying and stared out the cockpit window at the darkening clouds. "Bet I'm the last plane into Fort Smith." He dropped the nose of the plane until the altimeter read 600 feet. Chip pointed to the instrument panel. "They can't nurse those big jets low enough. Bet they cancel the flight to Fort Smith."

Phil let the conversation dwindle as Chip guided the plane through the turbulence. Lightning streaked off to the north, and menacing black thunderheads embraced the area where they were headed.

Phil's breath came in short gasps.

Chip smiled. "Rough ride makes for some sporty times. I haven't cracked up yet in this country, and I don't intend to now. I'm lucky. Pays to be lucky, but smart's better."

Phil didn't say anything. He was too busy gritting his teeth, trying to prevent himself from heaving up the greasy lunch he'd grabbed at the Edmonton airport.

"If you gotta puke, slide the window open, lean out and down. Don't want the stuff coming back into the cockpit." Chip's voice held a note of merriment, as he slid his window open a crack, allowing cold fresh air to pour into the cabin. Phil gulped deep breaths.

For the next hour, Phil hung on in desperation. He wasn't particularly subject to airsickness but the noise, fumes, the rolling and lunch played havoc with his head and stomach. By the time Fort Smith's airstrip came into view, he felt as green as a toad in heat. Chip landed the plane with one bounce on the slick runway. As they taxied toward a building away from the small terminal, Phil slid his window open wide, thankful for the blast of cold air that washed over him.

When Chip brought the plane to a stop and turned off the engine, the quiet engulfed Phil like a comforting shroud. Chip slapped him on the back. "Nice going. Not many could have gotten through that trip without losing their cookies."

"I might've been in the Air Force, but I wasn't flying." Phil managed a weak smile. Once on the tarmac with his canvas bag in hand, he felt better. Chip pointed to the building, and side-by-side they ran toward it to get out of the pelting rain.

"Can I rent a car at the terminal?" Phil looked at the terrain of open land edged by a forest of jack pines and spruce in the distance.

"You don't need a car unless you want to see the countryside. I can give you a ride into town and you can walk just about anywhere. Where you staying? Pelican Rapids Inn?"

"How'd you know?"

"Grant tells everyone to stay there. The Inn is near the center of town and has a reasonably good restaurant." Chip waved his clipboard. "First, I have to stop and file my flight report. That won't take long."

Twenty minutes later they were in Chip's Ford pickup bouncing along the main road into town past bare poplar trees that had yet to leaf out. After a time Chip pointed to a house set back away from the road. "Erich's place is over there. He left it to Henri."

"Henri must be pleased."

Chip chortled. "Hell, Henri thinks the house is prison, haunted or some such. Spends most of his time at the Road End Bar."

"Why doesn't he sell it?"

Chip shrugged. "Where would he live? Like I said, Mounties are keeping everyone close to home." Chip glanced at him and hesitated before he said, "Erich's body held traces of uranium. Mounties are looking for answers, but you know what I think? I think they're letting the mining companies explore the Thelon Sanctuary and are hiding that from us."

"Hope our summer tour doesn't get canceled."

"The Mounties are letting a few guides have permits. Grant's been doing business for years. He'll be okay. Discriminatory I'd say, but I'll get some business from Grant." Chip pulled his truck into the parking area next to The Pelican Rapids Inn. "That's it." He nodded toward a chocolate-brown building. "I'll pick you up at six a.m. Monday for your return flight."

Phil hauled his canvas overnight bag out from behind the seat, slammed the door shut behind him and waved as the pilot drove off. For a moment he watched the truck and wondered how much Chip knew about Erich.

After settling into his room, he called Karen. She offered to pick him up, but Phil said he needed to stretch his legs. The rain abated, making his walk pleasurable and, except for paved roads and a few more buildings, not much had changed since '78. Several inebriated Inuits hung around the grocery store to buy cheap liquor. Employment was obviously still a problem.

He noted where the RCMP office was located since he planned to visit it before he left town. After wandering through a park, he made his way down to the Slave River, a magnificent sight in early May as the ice broke up. Except in winter, the Slave was a roaring, cruel river, a reminder that nature was the master.

After a time, he turned away and followed Karen's directions to their home. She responded to his rap on the front door and ushered him into a small mudroom. Her enthusiastic smile gave him a lift. After removing his overboots, he followed her into the living area where he met Grant. As they shook hands, Phil read a careful piercing appraisal by his gray eyes.

"It's nice to meet one of our summer clients before the trip," Karen said, motioning Phil to a slipcovered sofa. "We're delighted you came. I thought you'd like to have dinner before you see the book collection."

"Fine with me. The trip up was a little dicey in Chip's plane."

"Chip flew you in?" Grant asked. "I was wondering. The regular scheduled flight is delayed."

"Henri put him on to me. Apparently, business is slow right now."

"More so than usual." Grant stood behind a chair, the top of his head a few inches below the room's wood support beam. "Would you like a glass of wine or a beer before dinner?"

"Beer. Thanks." Phil turned to Karen. "Hope you haven't gone to any trouble, but I appreciate your hospitality."

"That's the least we could do," Karen said. "I hope we can agree about some of the books." A blush flamed her cheeks. "Besides, we're glad to meet you," she hurriedly continued. "I haven't read your correspondence with Grant. He always likes to know as much about his clients as possible to get an idea of their expectations for the trip."

"And to find out my clients' paddling and outdoor skills," Grant added, as he came back into the room and handed an icy glass of beer to Phil. "Molson, Canadian. Hope you like it."

Karen excused herself to look after dinner and Grant sat down in a rocking chair across from the sofa. "Glad Chip gave you a lift. I use him to ferry my canoes and supplies into the backcountry."

"You wrote we'd pick up the canoes on a lake where a wolf trapper has a cabin. Would that be Henri Deforte's place?"

"It would. Any special reason you ask?" Grant took a sip of his beer and studied Phil as he rocked.

"Chip said Henri has Erich's house, but he doesn't like it much."

"Wouldn't know about that. Chip and Henri meet at the Road End Bar. I'm married. It's not a place I frequent anymore."

Karen came in and announced dinner and further conversation about Henri slid away through a pleasant conversation about the Thelon River Sanctuary. Phil never admitted he'd been to Fort Smith before and avoided saying when he'd become acquainted with Erich. Although he thought he'd gotten around the subject nicely, Grant had looked pointedly at him several times.

After dinner, Karen took Phil to a paneled room in the basement and showed him six boxes of books. "Grant keeps his tour supplies down here as well."

Each peg on the wall was labeled, ropes were strung in perfect alignment, paddles stacked according to size, and numbered cupboards glistened with new paint. "It's good to know my tour leader is an exacting man," Phil said.

"He is that," Karen said. "I'll leave you to it then, unless you'd like me to stay and help."

"Let me have a look, and then I'll call you." He glanced about the room. "I don't want to make a mess. Perhaps if you gave me an empty box, I could transfer the books I don't want into it."

"Good idea." Karen brought a sturdy cardboard box from a closet and set it next to him.

When she left, he knelt and set about going through the books. After opening the first box, he pulled out each book, leafed through the pages and put it into the extra box. Although he was fast and efficient, each box caused his anxiety to rise. It wasn't until the fourth carton that he found the notebook. As he hefted it in one hand and scanned the pages, he smiled in relief—Erich's last report. In the same box, Phil found a stack of loose papers. He'd always suspected Erich had kept some information about his geological findings from him, but now the papers were his. When he translated them, he should be able to pinpoint not only Erich's last position, but also his last reference to the diamond lode Phil hoped existed.

Sweat broke out on Phil's brow and guilt gnawed at him. Phil's FBI supervisor believed Erich's journal could pinpoint where and how Erich had encountered uranium. Phil's duty was to the Bureau, to his government, to the oath he'd taken. He wiped his mouth with the back of his hand. The diamonds had remained a secret between himself, Erich, Cal and Boris. "Damn. They're separate issues," he muttered. The government doesn't need to know everything. He stuffed the papers into an empty box along with the notebook.

Tempted as he was not to open the other boxes, he had to make it look as if he'd gone through all the books and wanted more than just the notebook and papers. He sorted through the rest of the boxes, removed geology and navigational books, put them in the same box with the papers and notebook, closed the top, then called Karen.

When she came into the room, he said, "There are only a few books I want. You can have the others."

"You're kidding." She clasped her hands together. "This will be great for the high school. Do you want a receipt for tax purposes?"

He smiled and wiped his brow. "No. That's not necessary."

"The students will send you a thank you letter."

"That won't be necessary either."

"It's good for students to know how generous people are."

"Tell you what. Put a small plaque in the library honoring Erich Mann for his book donation. After all, they were his books."

"If that's what you want." She moved closer and looked at the box he intended to take. "What books did you keep?"

"Ah, a few geology and navigational books." He leaned over and picked up his carton.

"Did you find the notebook?"

He almost dropped the box. "Notebook?"

"It was in German. Henri was going to keep it, but Leah put it in the box because she thought he'd become obsessed with it."

"Leah?"

"Oh, sorry. Leah is Henri's girlfriend. He got extremely angry with her when he found out she'd packed it. She wondered if you'd take it."

He nodded and looked down at the box. "I did."

"You can read German script, then?"

"Yes."

They stood in the neat cellar staring at each other, then he nodded to the other boxes. "Erich would be pleased to have the books put to good use."

"You've been more than generous." Her blue eyes sparkled with questions. "Is there something important about the notebook? I noticed it had descriptions about places."

What could he say? Or more to the point, what would she believe? "Erich wrote to me about the geology of the area. The notebook will be a great help in my research."

"I thought you taught math and biology."

"It's a hobby gone amuck. I'd like to write a book on the area," Phil added hastily.

Karen nodded. "Research material. That's what I thought."

"That's also why I wanted to go on this canoe trip." His lie began to flow. "I've been wanting to make such a trip for some time. Timing is strange, isn't it?"

"It is." She trailed him up the stairs and into the dining area where Grant sat at the table with papers before him.

"You don't want to haul that box through the streets," she said and turned to Grant. "Hon, will you drive Phil to the Inn?"

Grant stood and swept a packet of papers into an envelope. "Sure. I wrote letters about what equipment to bring and a list of names and addresses of the trip's participants. Since you're here, I'll give you yours now."

Phil put his carton on the table and took the envelope. "Thanks. I've been wondering who else is going."

Chapter 13

Back in his hotel room Phil tucked the box of books beside the bed, tossed his parka on top of it and sat on the wood chair by the window. He grasped Grant's envelope in one hand, rapped it on its edge and tore off the end, letting the papers slide onto the tiny table. After scanning the letter of introduction and the equipment list, he read the participant list. The first name stopped him.

Laura Boswell.

"Damn." A heavy sigh escaped his lips, he slumped in the chair and swallowed hard. The paper remained in his hand as her image swirled in his mind. He'd been tempted to throw his career aside for her. If he found the diamond lode, he might do just that. Would he? All his relationships seemed to hang between duty and desire.

Why would she come on this trip? He picked up the paper and when he read Deirdre's name next to Cal's, he had his answer. What possessed Cal to bring his high-strung wife along? She hadn't enjoyed the camping in Costa Rica, so why would she come on a seventeen-day wilderness trip? Was Laura coming because she knew he'd be on it?

"Cal, you stupid bastard." Phil rose and paced, thinking he should have known Cal would screw things up. But he had to ask him, didn't he? We had a bargain. He's part of the financial team. Could he depend on Boris and Cal? What could he do about Laura?

He walked to the window, scratched at his day-old whiskers and stared at the rain sliding down the panes. A few lights blinked in the distance blurred by rivulets of water. He folded Grant's information and stuffed it back in the envelope.

Laura would get the list, too, so if she didn't know he was going before, she soon would. Maybe she wouldn't come. Would she want to see him? Could they start over? If they did, where would it lead? He shook his head.

"Shit." Scooping up his parka, he walked out of the room and slammed the door behind him. It took five minutes of fast walking to get to the Road End Bar. Removing his wet parka, he entered a large pine room that echoed with loud voices from bleary-eyed customers. Smoke hung like a smog belt above the men and women seated at tables. A broad-hipped woman with a mane of black hair cascading over her partner's shoulder grinned at him as he passed their table.

He continued threading his way between the crowded tables to the bar that spanned the length of the room. Two sweating bartenders drew beer and poured drinks as they listened to customers. After ordering a Molson, he turned to watch the crowd, as thoughts of the complications of the July trip swarmed in his head.

He felt a hand on his shoulder. "Hey, pal, taking in the night spots of the greater downtown?" Chip stood next to him, one thin hand holding a large frosted beer mug.

Phil glanced at Chip, swung back to face the bar and noted their reflections in the mirror behind the bartenders. "Couldn't sleep."

"Did you get what you came for?"

"The McDuffys were very hospitable. I was able to give the local high school most of Erich's books."

"So, mission accomplished?"

"You might say that."

"If you want to meet Henri, he's over there in the corner. See?" Chip pointed to the far end of the room. Phil spotted a black-haired, wide-shouldered man gesturing wildly to another fellow whose back was to them. "Come on." Chip pulled at Phil's sleeve. "I'll introduce you."

This was a meeting Phil wanted, yet he didn't like the setting or Chip's insistent manner. Chip's stumbling movements indicated he'd had too much to drink, so Phil allowed himself to be propelled along.

"Hey, Henri. This is Phil West, the collector of Erich's books." Chip collapsed into the chair between Henri and another man.

Henri's eyes were unfocused and red; his mouth agape. "Ah. The mystery man."

Phil ignored the comment and acknowledged the introduction. "Glad to met you, Henri. After all these years of Erich's letters, I feel I know you."

"Well, I don't know you," Henri blurted out. "Erich never speak of you. Why he give you his goddamn books?" Henri brought his sweat-beaded glass to his mouth.

"I'm a teacher." Phil kept his voice low, hoping Henri would mellow.

"Why you come here, eh? Why you go with Grant McDuffy this summer?" Henri barked out his questions, slurring his words.

"I've always been interested in the Arctic. After Erich's death, I wanted to visit the country he knew."

"You're a damn liar," the other man at the table said.

Taken aback, Phil glared at the man. "I don't believe we've met."

The man laughed, throwing his head back to expose gold-filled teeth. His longish brown hair fell away from his high forehead. "We've met. A long time ago. Do I look so different?"

When Phil said nothing, the man continued. "Gilbert Tupper's the name. Ring a bell, Sarge?"

Gilbert's pasty face was not one Phil should have forgotten. His thin nose and deep-set eyes gave him a lecherous appearance and his acne-scarred skin added a cruel dimension.

Phil remained standing and although anxiety dug at him, he said in an easy manner, "Sorry, I didn't recognize you, but we met only briefly many years ago."

"Yeah. You look a lot different. Glasses are a new addition." Gilbert waved his hand over the top of his head. "You've lost a lot on top."

Phil grimaced. "We all grow older, but not all grow wiser."

Chip flung out his arm and motioned to the extra chair. "Sit down. Old friends got to get reacquainted."

Phil's stomach tightened, but he joined them, and the chair scraped the planked wood floor as he moved it forward under his weight. "I thought you had plans to leave Canada, Gilbert. What are you doing these days?"

Gilbert shrugged. "I'm a newspaper reporter. Work out of Yellowknife. Getting Henri's story about his last trip with Erich."

"Nobody listens to me," Henri said. "Erich dies, and Mounties think I'm bad guy. Can't go to my cabin. Can't trap wolves. Can't do goddamn thing!" Henri pounded his fist on the table, slopping beer out of his glass.

Chip leaned forward, nodded at Phil and said to Gilbert, "How do you know this guy?"

"Operation *Morning Light*. I was a photographer in the Canadian army. Phil here, Erich and some other soldier boys got lost for three weeks in the backcountry. They'd been given up for dead, when one of our helicopters spotted them. I snapped their picture when they got back. A sorry bunch of young airmen, happy to be hauled out and returned to their unit. I've never forgotten the names. Erich Mann, Phil West, Boris Sweet and Cal Sterling."

"Surprised you'd remember such a small incident," Phil said.

"It wasn't a small thing back then. Besides, there was something about you four." He gazed steadily at Phil. "You were tired and hungry and looked like hell, but each of you had a glint in your eye, something indefinable. I wanted to catch that look. I also wanted to know what the hell caused it." Gilbert hesitated, then added, "You brought back a dead guy as I remember. An old miner, I think."

Henri's eyes shifted and narrowed as he glared at Phil, then scowled and stared into his beer glass.

"Were you really glad to be back in the arms of the military?" Gilbert asked.

"We were glad to be rescued." Phil turned to Henri. "I'd like to hear about your trips with Erich. Could you tell me how his accident happened?"

"I tell Mounties. I tell this man." He pointed to Gilbert. "How many times I tell the story?"

"Sorry. I guess it's been rough on you. Erich was a good friend. I'd feel better about his death if I heard exactly how it happened."

Henri sighed, shrugged and leaned back in his chair. *"Oui,* why not. Get me another beer, and I tell you, too."

Phil was about to get up when Chip put his hand on Phil's arm. "You buying all the way around?"

Phil hesitated, then said, "Sure."

"Okay. Give me the dough, and I'll get the drinks. What's your poison?"

"Molson." Phil handed a few bills to Chip and watched him walk through the crowd toward the bar, steadier now than he'd appeared before. *He got sober quick.* Phil turned back to Henri and smiled. Soon Henri retold his story of the last days of Erich's life, ignoring Chip when he eased into his chair with the drinks. Henri sipped his new beer, then continued his tale. Gilbert listened quietly, taking notes, something Phil wanted to do, but knew it wouldn't be appropriate.

When Henri finished, Phil said, "Helen Falls are on the Hanbury. That's a long way from Lake Damant. How long did it take? You must have been exhausted when you got back."

"Oui." Henri took a slug of beer. "It took two, three days and nights. I don't remember. Erich stunk. I buried him, but stupid Mounties dug him up, and for what? Trouble." He peered bleary-eyed at Phil. "How you know my cabin on Damant?"

"Grant told me." Phil leaned forward, close enough to smell Henri's foul breath. "They say Erich had uranium traces on his clothes."

"So? He dug all over the place. He could have got, how you say, contaminated, any place. Now Mounties make life stink. Business stink, too." Henri stared at Chip. "Isn't that so, *mon ami?*"

Chip shrugged and Henri turned his attention to Gilbert. "Hey, you write true story. Get people mad at government. Stop them acting like goddamn kings. Their new rules hurt native people. Leah plenty mad."

"It's the diamond miners' fault," Chip said. "They've got the Mounties in their hip pocket. Who's still flying over the Thelon? De Beers' jets. Who buzzes charter planes? De Beers." Chip stabbed his finger on the table in front of Gilbert. "You put that in your paper."

"If I wrote that, I'd be fired," Gilbert said, then shifted his eyes toward Phil. "Okay, Phil. Give me the real scoop. What's the deal? Why did you lie to Chip about not being up here before?"

"Just like a newspaper man, trying to cause trouble." Phil rubbed his moist palms together, then traced a line on his sweating glass. "I didn't say I'd never been here before. I said I wanted to see the country Erich had lived in these past years."

Phil could feel Henri and Chip's eyes locked on him. When Gilbert found out Cal and Boris were on Grant's trip, he'd have more questions. The little fellow would ferret out information and insinuate the worst and Phil couldn't think of a way to divert him.

Henri rolled his tongue around his heavy lips. "Perhaps, I take the trip with Grant, too." Chip laughed. "Jesus, Henri, why would Grant take you along?"

Henri shrugged and waggled his finger. *"Mon ami,* you never know. We'll see. A woodsman is always needed. You fly Grant's group to my cabin, and I'll be there to welcome them, Mounties' permit or no."

Chapter 14

After a restless night and a light breakfast, Phil walked over to the Royal Canadian Mounted Police office. The rain had let up, but the skies remained sullen, matching Phil's mood. A new storm was brewing and he hoped his trip out of Fort Smith would be smoother than the flight in, but from the looks of the sky, he wasn't going to be that lucky.

Inside the small wood-framed building, he found a young constable writing reports and answering phones. The office held none of the hurly-burly activity of a city police department. Pristine white walls, a well-scrubbed wood floor and several tidy desks emitted a military aura. A quiet Sunday in a small town seemed to be easy duty.

Phil's boots scraped on the wood floor, and the young constable looked up. "What can I do for you, sir?"

"I'm a friend of Erich Mann. Came up this weekend to receive a few items from his estate."

"It was a sad thing. I'm sorry for your loss."

"Thanks." Phil moved closer. "Too bad there's such a mystery around his death."

"Mystery?" The young man frowned. "You're mistaken. There's no mystery about his death."

Phil smiled. "Perhaps you can clarify some points for me. My friends in the states don't understand the fuss about his burial, his unearthing, the autopsy and then his reburial. Is he buried in Yellowknife?"

"Why, of course. We checked to see if there were any papers recording his wishes. None could be found. Everything was done properly."

"I'm not saying otherwise but I'd like to know the circumstances of his death." Phil glanced about the empty room. "Is there someone else I should ask about this?"

"No, sir. I can tell you everything you need to know. We've interviewed Henri Deforte at great length and have no doubt that Erich Mann's death was an accident." The constable stared at Phil. "Do you have cause to believe otherwise?"

"Could I see the autopsy report?"

"That could only come from Sergeant Michael, and he's gone for the week."

"Can you tell me the cause of death?"

"His skull was crushed. We believe death was instantaneous."

"And the uranium traces? Were they found only on his clothes or on his hands as well?"

"You're asking a lot of questions, sir. The case is closed."

"Could you look up the autopsy report and clarify this one item for me? I've come a long way. I'd rest easier, if I had a clear picture in my mind of Erich's last day. You see, not being able to say good-bye is hard. Knowing details will help me deal with his death."

"Good friends are hard to come by, sir." The constable walked back to a cabinet and pulled out a file. "Perhaps this will help." He glanced at the report in his hand. "Traces of uranium 235 were found on his jacket, front of his pants and on his shoes. The largest amounts were found on his gloves. These were made of special material that protected his hands from exposure to uranium."

"His gloves were on his hands?"

"Yes."

Phil wondered, but didn't ask why Erich would he be wearing special gloves at the time of his death if he hadn't found something? "He was looking for pieces of the Russian satellite, Cosmos 954. Did you know that?"

"Of course, we were aware of this and that's why we've stopped all traffic into the backcountry. If Erich found radioactive fragments, we'd have to haul them out. Our job is to protect the public and the environment." He hesitated, studying Phil's face. "How do you know he was searching for parts of *Cosmos 954*?"

"Everyone knew. It wasn't a secret." Phil thumbed through the visitor's book on the desk. "Can you tell me anything else?"

The constable referred to the file. "His skull was cracked on the right side as a result of a fall."

Phil pondered this evidence, then said, "The locals are upset about your office setting restrictions on their entering the Thelon area."

The constable's back straightened to an even more erect posture. "We are quite aware of the discomfort we've caused by putting the Thelon Sanctuary and nearby areas off limits. Sergeant Michael made the decision on the advice from his superiors. We understand the strain it's put on those whose livelihoods depend upon access to the wilderness. It's a short term precaution."

"It's good to know the Mounties care about the people and the environment. I'll tell my friends back home of your courtesy."

"Thank you, sir." He tapped the visitor's book. "Fill in the information, please. We keep a tally of visitors to our office."

Phil signed and under the column marked business, he wrote, "Erich Mann."

"If Sergeant Michael comes in before you leave town, he might want to talk with you," the constable said.

"I'm leaving in the morning, but I'll be back in July. Taking one of Grant's canoe tours. Mighty glad he got a permit."

"We have to be very thorough these days," the constable said, as Phil turned to leave. "Every tourist on Grant McDuffy's list will be checked out by security."

Phil nodded. "Interesting." As he walked out, he wondered what they'd find out about Nancy and him.

Chapter 15

Grant's July tour group flew aboard a commercial flight from Edmonton to Fort Smith. Laura slipped past Phil while he was conversing with a woman. She and Boris sat in the back of the plane. The woman had to be Nancy Plowright from Boston. It had been fifteen months since Costa Rica. Apparently, Phil had moved on to greener pastures. Well, so had she. She squared her shoulders and squirmed in her seat.

When Laura had learned Phil was one of the participants, she'd almost reneged. Phil was no longer important to her. How could she still feel anything for him when he'd ignored her letters and never called? What kind of man does that? The two-timing kind.

"Shouldn't be too much longer." Boris glanced out the window.

Laura tried to concentrate on a crossword puzzle, but instead, she thought about her coming meeting with Phil. She'd have to sound confident, or the trip would be a calamity. Anguish seeped through every pore.

Laura's eyes rested on Boris's broad, strong hands as he held his GPS instruction manual. Hands told a lot about people; Boris's were square, nails trimmed, no hangnails, calluses or cuts, yet they were powerful and firm.

Boris shifted his gaze to her and in his quiet shy nod, she knew how much he cared for her. He was an easy man to read and comfortable to be with, so why did she keep putting him off? She knew Phil wasn't the only reason for her go-slow strategy. Sometimes she wondered if any man could make her happy. Her independence was important. The thought of committing matrimony sounded like committing suicide.

She looked across the aisle at Deirdre and Cal asleep facing each other. For all their carping, they needed each other. With this trip to Canada, Deirdre was convinced their marital trouble would cease, as if their personalities would molt. Laura sensed Cal had given in to Deirdre's demand to come to avoid a confrontation. Perhaps this adventure would mend the breach between them. Unlikely therapy, but maybe it would work.

The pilot announced their descent into Fort Smith. As the plane decreased its altitude, Laura leaned across Boris and peered through the window and spotted the small town bordering Slave River in the distance.

Boris put his book and GPS in his carryon.

Laura said, "I know your passion for technical gadgets, but isn't your GPS overkill? We'll have a guide."

"It's interesting to use. The future of technology is going to amaze us. The GPS calculates my position and stores a location, so I can find my way back."

"Well, I know who to stick with in case we get lost."

"I hope you'll stick close to me in any case."

Laura smiled at how transparent he was. He'd never make a spy.

Cal and Deirdre awoke and began to fuss with their seats, magazines and earphones. Deirdre pulled out her lipstick and studied herself in her compact mirror. Although Laura felt rumpled in her denim blouse and khaki pants, Deirdre's starched white blouse remained immaculate. How did she manage? Laura had followed Grant's 'what to bring' list exactly, including sewing Velcro between buttons to keep out blackflies and mosquitoes. Deirdre had laughed at the meticulous instructions and said that Grant was a control freak. No one dictated to her what she should wear.

When Laura disembarked down the plane's metal ramp, the sun's brightness stunned her. On the tarmac, she stood aside to allow others to pass, while she fumbled for her dark glasses.

Boris stood next to her. "Can't say it's changed much."

"Really?" Laura studied the squat wood and metal terminal building. "It does seem a little primitive, but I like that. Sort of third-world looking."

"The Canadians would hit the ceiling if they heard you," Cal said as he and Deirdre stood nearby.

"Let's go," Deirdre said. "I can't wait to get to the hotel and freshen up."

"You might as well enjoy civilization," Cal said. "You won't have it much longer."

They moved into the terminal, but were stopped by a Canadian Mountie waiting inside the entry door. Although they'd gone through customs in Edmonton, this constable scrutinized their passports and waved Laura and Deirdre through, but asked Boris and Cal to step into a side room.

"We'll meet you at baggage claim." Cal handed his baggage stubs to Deirdre. "Don't worry, probably some snafu."

Boris placed his baggage stubs into Laura's outstretched hand, and followed Cal and the constable.

"What do you suppose that's all about?" Laura shifted her camera case to her other hand, watched the men enter a side room and caught sight of Phil and his woman companion already there. Momentarily Phil's eyes flickered across Laura's face, then the door shut.

"Phooey, Canada," Deirdre said. "If they think Boris or Cal are carrying drugs, they have the wrong men. Come on, let's get the luggage. I thought Grant would meet us."

"He made reservations for us at the Pelican Rapids Inn and leave us a message." Laura said.

Baggage handlers threw luggage from a cart and each piece hit the linoleum-covered floor with a bang that echoed off the steel-sheeted walls. After picking out their bags, Deirdre looked about skeptically. "Hope there's a cab in this burg."

A tall slim man stepped forward. "Can I be of service? The name's Chip. I pilot the charter plane Grant uses."

"It was good of Grant to send you," Deirdre said. "Our men seem to be having some difficulty with the local authorities."

Chip smiled. "Sergeant Michael's a careful man these days. We've been having some disagreement about entry into the backcountry. Not everyone is welcome, since we had a scare about uranium." He lifted up two of the larger bags. "I'll take these out to the truck and be right back."

Laura eyed him, then turned to Deirdre. "You stay here, and I'll follow him." She picked up her duffel bag, shouldered her carryon and followed Chip to his truck. "Not enough room for all of us to fit in your pickup," she said.

"Right you are. You take a cab." He pointed to a taxi stand. "There are six of you, right? Figured I'd take the luggage; taxi can take the human cargo."

"Interesting way of putting it." He took her duffel and swung it into the truck bed, then reached for her carryon, but she hung on to it. "My photo equipment and I stay together."

He leaned against the side of his truck and shoved his baseball cap back off his forehead. "Just trying to be helpful."

"I'll wait here while you fetch the rest of the gear."

He grinned, pushed away from his truck and ambled back to the terminal. His swagger annoyed her. He hadn't said Grant sent him. Deirdre had jumped to that conclusion. Laura's skeptical antenna always rose when she traveled. *How do I know he's who he says he is? And what did his remark about uranium mean?*

While she pondered these questions, the rest of the group emerged from the terminal with Chip toting a few of their bags. He stowed them into his pickup truck.

"I don't believe we've met." Deirdre extended her hand to the woman who'd been questioned by the constables along with the men. "You must be Nancy Plowright from Boston." Deirdre, playing hostess, continued to introduce everyone else.

Phil glanced at Laura, then asked Boris to hustle up a taxi.

Boris hesitated, shrugged and said, "Sure. I'll be right back."

"It's good to meet you Laura," Nancy said. "I've heard so much about you from Phil. This trip has brought old friends together."

After an awkward silence, Deirdre took hold of Cal's arm. "All one happy family." She looked at her husband. "What did the police want?"

"They're called constables, hon. He knew we'd been here before." Cal nodded to Boris and Phil. "Wanted to chat, but he was especially interested in Phil."

"I came up a few months ago to collect books from a friend." Phil cracked his knuckles, a nervous gesture Laura knew well.

"The authorities detained you too, Nancy. What was the problem?" Laura asked.

"Too many cigarette cartons." Nancy shrugged. "Guess I'll have to buy a supply here."

"Didn't customs in Edmonton catch that?" Cal asked.

"I guess they're more thorough here." Nancy glanced over at the taxi where Boris stood talking to the driver. "I don't know about the rest of you, but I'm for settling in and getting my bearings." She walked toward the waiting cab, and Cal and Deirdre followed, while Phil, Laura and Chip remained standing by the truck.

For a moment, Laura thought Phil was going to hug her, but he dropped his hands to his side. "It's good to see you, Laura."

"Phil, you riding with me?" Chip asked.

"Hmm. A tight squeeze in that cab. Maybe I'd better." He looked at Laura. "Would you like to ride with Chip?"

"No. I'll join the others." She gave a sidelong glance at Chip. "I gather you know Chip, so I guess he's okay. I'll see you at the inn."

"Laura." Phil put his hand on her arm. "We need to talk."

"You've had over a year to talk."

"Hey, if you two want some privacy, I'll make myself scarce," Chip said.

"That won't be necessary." Laura turned toward the waiting cab, but Phil held her arm.

"Don't put me off," he said. "We're going to be together for over two weeks. We need to talk...so...."

"So everything will be peachy keen." She bit her lip, then sighed, letting her anger ebb. "You're right. What happened is past. I won't cause you and your girlfriend a problem, I assure you."

"Girlfriend?" Phil looked over at Nancy and chuckled. "You're way off track. She's my boss and several years older if you hadn't noticed."

She had, but didn't want to admit it. "Okay, I'm wrong, but our relationship is finished."

"Is it?" He continued to hold her arm. "Not for me. There were and are reasons I didn't get in touch with you."

Laura glared at him. "It's been too long. I'd forgotten all about you. We'll talk and we'll be cordial, but don't expect me to run after you like a puppy dog."

"I wouldn't love you if you did."

"Careful how you bandy that word around." They stood toe to toe, and Laura momentarily wondered what Boris must think of this scene. "I'd better go."

"Give me a moment. We can get back together. I haven't forgotten anything about you."

"Oh, stop with the line, Phil. Do I have to keep reminding you that it's been over a year? I'm with Boris." She was surprised and pleased at her defiance.

"You and Boris?" He sneered. "He's not your type."

"Well, obviously I'm not yours."

While they talked, Chip had stepped into his truck and pretended not to listen, yet she knew he heard every word.

Phil watched Laura get into the taxi with the others. He'd wanted to take her in his arms and explain everything, but couldn't. Honesty wasn't in his job description. "Damn." He turned on his heels, strode around the front of the truck and got in next to Chip, slamming the door after him.

"She kinda got to you, didn't she?" Chip said. "A real looker and independent. A sure combination to boil a man's blood."

Phil glared out the window and wanted to tell Chip to shut up, but didn't. They drove off, following the taxi, with Chip whistling a stupid love tune. The trees were heavy with leaves and only the white birch trunks gave relief to the green forest bordering the road. When they passed by the road leading to Erich's place, Phil asked, "Henri still upset about living there?"

"He hated it while he was there. Finally made it back to his cabin on Lake Damant."

"You fly him in?"

He smiled. "Funny thing. Everyone seemed glad Henri got out of town, including his girlfriend, Leah. He kept taking out his frustration on her. In the end, even Sergeant Michael seemed glad to be rid of him. 'Course that doesn't mean he sanctioned Henri's going into the backcountry. Still, it makes life quieter in Fort Smith."

"So you did everyone a favor by getting him back to his cabin."

"I just eased everyone's pain."

"You like doing that, don't you?" Phil said.

"What?"

"You like to find people's soft spot and pick at it."

"You're a little prickly today, aren't you?"

"Getting the lay of the land. Have you been in touch with your friend Gilbert Tupper?"

Chip nodded. "He's been around, poking his nose here and there. There's stuff happening with the diamond mines hiring and sending explorations up the Thelon. They're not scared off by uranium stories."

"Henri seemed steamed about both. How about you?" Phil asked.

"There isn't a person in Fort Smith that hasn't taken a side on the exploitation of the area surrounding the Thelon Sanctuary. Watch out. If you or the others step on Henri's toes, I don't want to be the one to pick up the pieces."

"Thanks for the warning, but this is a peaceful wildlife expedition."

"Sure it is. That's why Sergeant Michael interviewed all of you. When are you going to tell that gal, Laura, what's going on? She'll find out, 'cuz everyone else in town knows the three of you dudes were here with Erich Mann during Operation *Morning Light.*"

"We haven't made a secret of that." Phil gritted his teeth. "What are you getting at?"

"Look, I'm no fool, and it's obvious Laura isn't either. Why don't you come clean?"

"Laura knows as much as she needs to know."

"Maybe so, but Tupper thinks there's more to this little foray than you're making out. He can make your life sweet or bitter."

"I'll be off in the wilderness. What Gilbert Tupper writes is none of my business."

Chip chortled. "Hey, I thought Grant would've told you. Tupper's a wily fellow. He'll be in your face every day, cuz he's going on Grant's trip with you."

Chapter 16

That night the group walked to the McDuffys' home for a welcome dinner. Phil reflected on the complications of the trip: Laura's cool response to him, Boris's romantic interest in her, the Mounties' inquiries upon their arrival, Deirdre's presence and influence on Cal, Tupper's interference. Nothing seemed to bode well for the mission. Would the authorities intervene and delay or cancel the trip? Phil's shoulders and neck ached from nerves tweaked too tight.

When Karen greeted them at her door, she was as vivacious and friendly as Phil remembered. Grant however seemed morose and aloof. Karen and Grant showed them into the dining area where the light of the Arctic summer's evening filtered through a wide window and spread across the cream-colored tablecloth laden with blue floral china. Obviously, Karen had brought out her best wares for the occasion.

"Please sit down," Karen said, smiling. "You know, the usual drill, alternate boy, girl. Grant and I sit here." She pointed to places at either end of the table then hurried to the kitchen, returning with a large teak salad bowl laden with greens and bright red tomato chunks.

Like obedient children on their first day of school, the guests selected their places. Phil scowled when Boris took the seat next to Laura. Cal held out the chair next to Boris for Deirdre, then took his place next to her while Phil sat next to Karen with Nancy to Grant's right.

Standing at the head of the table Grant carved a pork roast. "This is a little like the Last Supper. Trip meals won't be as sumptuous, but you'll have Karen's great cooking."

"You're going along?" Laura asked Karen as she passed the salad. "That's wonderful."

"Thank you. I can't always go along, but I look forward to them. That's how I met him."

"The meals are better now." Grant directed a smile toward his wife.

"I've taken your vegetarian diets into account, Laura and Nancy." Karen looked at each one in turn. "Tonight I prepared cheddar cheese-filled potatoes." Karen pointed to the other dishes on the table. "There's a green bean casserole and a salad. Will that be enough?"

"Plenty," Nancy assured her as she served herself from one of the platters and passed it along to Phil.

"I brought along some food supplements so I should be fine," Laura said.

"Not eating any meat on the trip can be difficult," Grant said. "Perhaps you'll eat fish." "I'll eat fish," Nancy said. "No point in making life more difficult than necessary."

"Sorry, I don't believe in killing." Laura looked at Nancy. "What prompted you to become a pseudo vegetarian?"

Nancy's brown eyes glinted with humor ignoring Laura's dig. "I thought a healthy lifestyle for a change might eradicate my demons."

"Did it?" Cal asked.

"A few," Nancy said, then chuckled. "But I've got a long way to go."

"Don't we all," Karen said, as she shook the saltshaker vigorously over her food.

"I've been a true vegetarian for three years, and the diet is definitely healthier," Laura said, and after a slight hesitation, added, "Salt can cause high blood pressure."

"But it makes food taste better," Boris said. "I use wine in sauces, but I still like a hint of salt."

Laura nodded to Boris. "He hasn't succumbed to vegetarianism yet, but I'm working on him."

"Don't worry, Karen," Boris said. "For this trip, I'm a carnivore."

"Glad to hear it," Grant said. "The Inuit people would have died if they'd been vegetarians. Surviving in the tundra without eating meat or fish is impossible." Grant frowned, as he continued to carve. "It's difficult to transport extra provisions for special diets into the backcountry, but Karen will see to it." He passed the carved meat platter down the table and put the empty dish on the teak buffet behind him. "As I wrote you, all your things will be put into special duffle bags I furnish. I'll hand them and paddles out after dinner. Tents will be stowed on the plane and given out the first night. I hope all of you followed my clothing instructions."

Everyone nodded, although after an uncomfortable glance from Cal, Deirdre said, "Dressing all in beige seems a bit over the top. I mean, what does it matter?" Deirdre scanned the table obviously hoping for support.

"My advice for clothing is consistent with what I've learned from traveling in the backcountry over twenty years," Grant said. "This time of year blackflies and mosquitoes can be particularly insidious, especially to those who aren't used to them. Beige doesn't attract insects; dark colors like navy blue do. If you haven't prepared yourself in the proper manner, the trip can be difficult." He tossed an unctuous smile at Deirdre. "Perhaps tomorrow you can spend some of your free time buying items better suited for the trip, if you feel you've made some mistakes."

"I read Edgar Christians' *Death in the Barren Ground,*" Boris said, glancing at the others. "It's a wonderful account of John Hornby's 1926 adventure that tells about the caribou in the Thelon Game Sanctuary."

Phil noticed the look of admiration on Laura's face. *Why did he rate that look? So he read a book. Big deal.*

"Tell them the outcome of Hornby's adventure," Grant said.

Boris gave a halfhearted smile. "Don't want to put a damper on the party. The caribou didn't show that year and all three died."

"We'll be visiting Hornby's grave and cabin," Grant said.

"I thought the herds follow the same migration path every year," Laura said.

"The herds are not computerized," Grant said. "The mass migration surges out onto the tundra in the spring, then back to the taiga in the fall. The best time to observe them on a daily basis is now since the herds are widely dispersed along the tree line and adjacent tundra. Sometimes in July I've seen tens of thousands of animals traveling together. This trip is timed to intercept the Beverly Caribou Herd. However, there's no guarantee of a sighting."

"Muskoxen are my favorite," Karen added, looking at her guests, "so prehistoric. Did you know that's the reason the Thelon Sanctuary was set aside, to protect the muskoxen? And of course, the wolves. Grant's specialty."

Grant walked around the table to pour his guests a glass of red wine. Laura and Nancy demurred. Phil watched Laura as she ate meticulously, savoring each bite. She never pounced on her food, but stared at it as if waiting to be introduced. He'd noticed ever since Nancy gave up drinking and cut back on her smoking, she relished every morsel.

"About your gear." Grant's voice interrupted Phil's thoughts.

"Each of you will get a plastic liner for your bags in case of capsizing, although that seldom happens. Leave things you don't need on the trip here at our house."

"Tomorrow you'll have a free day," Karen said. "I suggest you visit Wood Buffalo National Park."

"What a good idea," Laura said.

"You can rent a car by the hour. That's probably your best bet. You don't need a guide," Karen added. "Anyone else interested?"

"Maybe." Deirdre stole a glance at Cal. "I think I have a little shopping to do."

"I'd like to visit the park," Boris said. "How about the rest of you?"

"We'll shop," Cal said, "then go to the park."

"I'm meeting with a business associate at noon," Nancy said, avoiding Phil's eyes.

"I've got some things to take care of, too, but it sounds like a fun excursion." Phil paused and turned to Grant. "We've learned you're taking a reporter on our trip. I think I speak for the others in protesting his accompanying us."

"Perhaps I should have let you know earlier, but it seemed unnecessary." Grant put down his fork. "Gilbert Tupper asked to go because of restrictions on entering the Barrens without an approved guide. He wants Canadians to understand the beauty of the Thelon River Sanctuary to invigorate the campaign against the misuse of this land. Other guides take people on the more heavily traveled Hanbury River, whereas my trip takes us through the most isolated part of the Thelon." His gray eyes darted from one person to the next. "It's important the natural habitat of the Thelon be publicized during these political times. Many of us worry outside interests are exploiting this land. That's why he's joining us."

Phil met Grant's eyes. "That well may be, but it's an intrusion on our privacy." He could tell he wouldn't change Grant's decision, but he had to make the effort, before he considered other options.

"I've had a talk with Sergeant Michael." Grant looked at each of the men in turn. "The sergeant felt I should know about my clients because of the recent scare about uranium and your past and present interest in that subject." Grant held up his hand before anyone could interrupt. "You three gentlemen were with Erich Mann during Operation *Morning Light*. Now, if this trip is something more than a nostalgic return to the past, I'd like to know."

There was silence, until Deirdre spoke, her blue eyes flickering with annoyance. "This trip is a memorial to their friend. Is there a problem with that?"

Phil rubbed his hands together under the table and cracked his knuckles as Nancy rerouted the conversation back to Gilbert Tupper.

"Under the circumstances," Nancy said with her English professor look, "I can understand your desire to give the Thelon area publicity. However, Gilbert Tupper will inhibit our privacy and our enjoyment. This is our trip. We're paying for it. Certainly, you can accommodate our request."

"You signed up to go along on my guided trip to see wildlife." Grant gave a stern look at Nancy and a quick glance at the others. "This is not 'your' trip, as you put it. It's my trip, and you're my paying clients. We'll be together for over two weeks. I don't want to start out with hard feelings, but Mr. Tupper is also a paying client. I cannot, nor do I wish to start a precedent of taking one client over another. If you wish to withdraw from the expedition, you're free to do so, with the usual penalty as stipulated in the contract you signed."

The room held an uncomfortable silence. Phil could think of no rational reason to further his argument against Tupper. There'd have to be another way to take care of him. When the time came, Grant wasn't going to be a pushover, but if Grant continued his authoritative manner, the group might turn to Phil for succor.

"If I count correctly, that gives us nine people," Boris said. "I thought you said only eight people on a trip. Are there other participants on the trip we aren't aware of?"

"No. Nine is all," Grant said. "I'll paddle solo."

Karen rose to clear the empty plates. "Dear," she said to Grant. "Perhaps you'd explain how you plan to divide up the paddling arrangements and settle the tent sharing matter."

Grant cleared his throat. "Some of you have little paddling experience," he nodded toward Nancy, Cal and Boris. "Although this is not a school for canoe strokes, Karen or I will instruct as we go along. There are only a few difficult rapids and a long portage south of the Clarke and Hanbury Rivers junction where there are magnificent falls. After that we'll have to line the canoes. The paddling days can be long. As I wrote you, this is no leisurely trip down a river. I believe you all understand that."

As Karen made a second trip from the kitchen, Laura asked her, "Can I help?"

"No thanks," Karen said, then nodded to Grant. "I think our guests want more information."

Grant gave his wife a weak smile. "We can change paddling partners as I see strengths and weaknesses of each pair. It's my understanding Boris and Phil would share a tent, and Laura and Nancy would share a tent."

Laura fiddled with her napkin, then looked up. "That won't do. No offense, Nancy, but I didn't know you were a smoker when I agreed to share a tent, and I imagine you'll want to smoke in the tent."

"Sweet of you to think of that." Nancy put on a smile, but Phil thought it was forced. "I agree. I'd like a single, too."

"That'll add to our weight," Grant said. "Perhaps Tupper could share a tent with Phil and Boris." Boris and Phil scowled. "I see. Very well, Tupper can take a single as well. You understand you set up your own tents, take care of your own packs, load and clean your canoes, wash your own dishes."

"We all help each other," Karen said, as she carried a tray of dessert plates full of sliced fresh fruit. "The trip is a group effort, but there must only be one leader, and Grant knows the backcountry."

Grant helped pass out the dessert. "I've never lost a client."

Soft laughter greeted Grant's attempted levity.

"Is it difficult to get fresh fruit here?" Laura asked Karen.

"Very." Karen slipped into her chair. "The salad greens came from our garden. The soil around Fort Smith is quite good, and we grow the hardier vegetables, but its a short growing season and most goods have to be brought in by plane or truck."

Phil was thankful for Laura and Karen's light banter, but listened halfheartedly.

"We appreciate your effort," Cal said. "Deirdre wondered what our food would be like."

Deirdre sent a hasty grimace in Cal's direction. "Speak for yourself, darling. Don't make me out to be a neophyte camper." She turned to Grant. "I've been on many camping trips and canoed with Laura in Costa Rica.

I'm a good stern paddler." She gave a soft nudge to Cal's forearm that rested on the table. "I know we'll be eating freeze-dried food."

"Mostly," Grant said. "We also pack in oranges and apples, tins of vegetables and sometimes catch trout or grayling to augment our supplies. I think you'll find the meals adequate."

"I'm sure they will be," Deirdre said.

"What about contact with Fort Smith?" Phil asked. "You wrote you carry a two-way radio."

"My radio is patched into the telephone system, so I can telephone anyone, anywhere. However, atmospheric conditions sometimes prevent radio communications. We have the option of ending the trip at several locations along the last ninety miles. This gives us a great deal of latitude depending on how fast we paddle and where we want to pause."

Phil suppressed the pleasure Grant's words gave him. *Perhaps it won't be as difficult to scout designated areas after all.*

"The various rendezvous sites are given to Chip at Loon Air Charter as well as the Mounted Police," Grant continued.

"You're very thorough," Boris said. "I brought along a GPS."

"I imagine you'll enjoy using it. I'll give you names of the maps you might want to buy. I believe you already picked up maps, didn't you, Phil?"

"Yes. I'll be glad to share, but you all might want your own copies." He made a point of nodding to Cal and Boris.

"Do you carry a gun with you on these trips?" Laura asked.

Phil knew her abhorrence of guns ever since her father had shot himself, and knew Deirdre and Cal understood this as well.

"No," Grant said. "I never take a gun, only a hunting knife. I've never been in a situation where I needed a gun. I'm very careful about how close we get to wildlife, and besides, the only animal that could hurt you is the grizzly. I've been chased only once and that was under unusual circumstances. Normally, a grizzly will only attack if you get between a she-bear and her cub. Wolves in the Sanctuary have had very little contact with people and occasionally are quite curious. Trapping isn't allowed inside the Sanctuary, but trappers work the edges." He smiled at Laura. "I assure you, there's nothing to fear in the Thelon except human error."

Grant rose from the table. "If everyone's finished dessert, we can go to the cellar, and I'll dole out the equipment."

Karen said, "If you wish, I could drive some of you to the inn with your gear."

"Hey, we've got two weeks of hard labor in front of us," Cal joked. "We should be able to haul a pack and a paddle to the inn." He peered out the window. "And it's still light out."

After they had their gear, Grant stood next to them in the front doorway. "The day after tomorrow, two cars will pick you and your gear up at seven in the morning. Please be ready. Keep your rain gear and head nets handy. Looks like rain at take off."

"Where do we leave from?" Boris asked.

"We'll be using seaplanes, a Twin Otter and a Cessna 185. Loon Charter flies out of a lake just outside of Fort Smith and we'll land on Lake Damant. Chip flew my canoes in two weeks ago." Grant looked around the group. "Any other questions?"

"When will Gilbert Tupper join us?" Phil asked.

"At takeoff." Grant waited for other questions.

Karen stood next to her husband. "If you should need anything between now and departure time, call."

The group walked toward the inn, each carrying a tan canvas pack and a long thin Canadian-style canoe paddle. Phil, Boris and Cal drifted next to each other while the women walked ahead, chatting about the coming expedition and how they were going to fit their clothes and personal items into the four foot duffles.

Phil noted the women's hips undulating in their khaki pants, particularly Laura's. With an effort, he pulled his thoughts back to the job at hand. "I'd like to meet to discuss certain aspects of our trip," he said, getting the men's attention.

"You certainly selected a bad ass for a leader." Boris tossed his canvas pack over his shoulder. "He's worse than a drill sergeant. 'My trip.' Give me a break. A real unsociable type, and we're stuck with him for two weeks."

Phil put his hand on Boris shoulder. "I understand your feelings and I think we all share them, but there isn't much we can do since Grant was and remains our only option."

"You said this newspaper fellow took our picture after our rescue in '78. What the hell are we going to do about him?" Cal asked in a hoarse whisper.

"A lot to discuss, including how we get Grant to stop at certain areas Erich noted in his journal," Phil said quietly.

"How about meeting at the bar later tonight?" Boris said.

"I couldn't get away without Deirdre wanting to go along," Cal said.

"Tomorrow, then," Phil said. "My room, two o'clock. That should give each of you time to buy maps."

"I plan to go to the Wood Buffalo Park with Laura," Boris said.

"Remember why you're here." Phil nibbled at his lower lip at the lack of focus his partners seemed to exhibit.

"If you'd given us more information before we'd come, we wouldn't have to do this last minute planning," Boris said. "I made a commitment, but I don't want my life turned topsy-turvy because of Erich's death."

"In case you hadn't noticed, old buddy," Cal said, "when we first got in that Kiowa helicopter accident with Erich back in '78, and found that miner, our lives spun into another orbit. You've gone along on the fruits of that ride, so don't start complaining now."

"Who's complaining?" Boris said. "All I said was that I want to go with Laura to the Park."

"You sure have fallen for her, haven't you?" Cal said. "Good to see it. She needs someone solid. She's had a tough time since her father's death and some asshole jilted her." He looked over Boris's head at Phil.

"Glad you approve." Boris gave a mock bow.

Phil stared at Boris for a moment and felt his face redden. He gazed at Laura striding along in front of them. *So Boris really had moved in on Laura.* Phil thought she might have been kidding just to spite him. *Jilted, my foot. I just didn't contact her after I got back from Costa Rica. My job comes first. Surely she'd understand that.* He consoled himself, knowing Boris and Laura couldn't be too involved since they had separate sleeping arrangements.

Phil's frustration leaked out. "For crying out loud, go to the damn park in the morning. We'll talk tomorrow afternoon at four o'clock. Okay?"

At the inn they went their separate ways and after depositing his gear in his room, Phil headed toward the Road End Bar, hoping to get information on anyone new in town. Nancy had remained closed-mouthed about her business associate and, short of following her tomorrow, he'd have to find out tonight what he could.

He was hoping to spot Chip among the noisy crowd, and he wasn't disappointed. In the far corner next to the pool tables tall lanky Chip stood above the others. After getting himself a frothy beer, Phil moved toward his prey.

When Chip noticed Phil, he waved nonchalantly. "Hey, how's the greenhorn crew coming along? All set for the backcountry do?"

"We'll do just fine." Phil glanced at Chip's friends, but none seemed to notice Phil's presence. "Thought I'd get a nightcap before turning in."

"You came to the right place. Gilbert Tupper was in earlier, talking about the trip. Have you seen him?"

Phil shook his head. "You keen on Gilbert going in with us?"

"I don't care one way or another." Chip took a sip of his beer. "Let's sit. My feet are about to give out, or maybe it's my knees." He dragged a chair against the wall away from the pool tables.

"Grant thinks Gilbert's writing a piece on the environmental beauty of the Thelon." Phil pulled up a chair next to Chip.

"You don't?"

Phil tilted his head to one side. "Maybe." He looked around the room. "You seem to know everyone. Any newcomers, other than my group?"

Chip eyed him, then took a swig of beer. "You're an interesting man. Always asking questions. Gilbert Tupper wants to know what you know. It sits in his craw that you might be up to something. Are you?"

"Of course. I'm retracing Erich's footsteps."

"It's the why of it, though. After you left, Gilbert kept asking me, 'why's that dude coming up here? Uranium? Why? Something to do with the past, but what?'" Chip's long thin face melted into squinting puzzlement.

Phil fiddled with his glass, running a finger down the sweating beer mug. "He's a newspaperman."

Chip shrugged. "Sometimes I think he'll get his backside whipped sticking it where it doesn't belong, but reporters are like that, aren't they?" Chip wiped his mouth with the back of his hand and lazily nodded in the direction of someone across the room. "See that dude? I flew him in a few days ago. Sergeant Michael questioned him for a long time."

"Problems?" Phil tried to spot the fellow Chip had pointed out, but lost sight of him in the crowd.

"How the hell do I know? I just fly you jocks up here and into the backcountry. Chip brushed his sandy hair back from his forehead in an absentminded gesture. "Doesn't seem the outdoor type. He's staying at Henri's in town."

"I thought Henri was in the backcountry."

"He is. Leah's given the guy room and board. Seems she knows him from some political shindig the Dene tribe had." Chip leaned back and put his boots up on the chair across from him. His frame relaxed like a sack molding itself to the seat. "If Henri knew some guy was shacking up in his house with Leah present, he'd have a fit. Hell, what Henri doesn't know won't hurt. But just between you and me, this guy's bad news. A Quebec separatist." He spit the words out. "When a guy like him sticks his nose into this town's business, he might get it bit off. I almost wish I hadn't taken his fare."

"He's from Quebec?"

"That what I just said."

A chill ran down Phil's spine. "What's the fellow's name?"

"Pierre Giraud."

Phil winced. *Giraud, the separatist and terrorist. Nancy's contact.*

Chapter 17

The Arctic dawn came too early for Phil as he dragged his body out of the warmth of the snarled bed linen and endured a cool shower. While shaving, he reflected on the complications that had sprung up even before the trip got underway. A heart-to-heart conversation seemed the only way to learn if Nancy was meeting Pierre Giraud. As to Gilbert Tupper, he thought an accident rendering the man incapable of paddling was the most expedient, but setting up the how of it was another matter. That would be on the agenda when he met with Boris and Cal. Boris!

"Shit!" He slammed down the razor on the side of the sink, dabbed at the nick on his chin, and went to get dressed. Out his bedroom window he could see chimney smoke in cloud-like plumes swirl into a clear sky. He spotted Nancy in her dull orange parka striding down the street. *Where's she going at this hour? To meet with Giraud?* He pulled a gray wool sweater over his denim shirt, donned his parka and hurried out.

In the lobby he bumped into Laura as she came through a side door, looking like a wood nymph risen from a dewy morn, fresh and damp: her cheeks flushed, her short blonde hair mussed.

"Hi," she greeted him. "I've been out for an early jog. Beautiful day."

Surprised and tongue-tied, he muttered, "Sure is." Before he could stop himself, he asked, "Boris with you?"

"Should he be?" she asked with arched brows.

"I was on my way for a walk."

"I passed Nancy. You joining her?"

"Ah…I didn't know she was out." He felt like a schoolboy caught in a lie.

"Oh, really." She dabbed at the perspiration on her brow with a tissue.

"Well, you said you were here with Boris." He wanted to grab and shake her into admitting Boris was a subterfuge to make him jealous.

"That's true. So you and I will be...friends." She held out her hand.

He took her hand and held it until she withdrew it. He wanted to plead his case, but instead, muttered, "Enjoy the Buffalo National Park."

"I intend to." Her words jabbed him like cactus barbs.

"I can't go, but...." His words trailed off as she turned and walked toward the stairs. There never seemed to be a good time to make things right. Laura and Boris? How did Boris hope to win her? With his intellect? Phil almost laughed out loud. He remembered how each new adventure stirred Laura's passion. It hadn't taken much—an evening paddle, a wild animal seen up close or a swim in a dark hidden lagoon. Laura's eyes would widen with delight, her smile, usually cautious, would etch across her face. She liked excitement, so how could she possibly settle for Boris's pedantic intellect? How exciting could he be to a woman who thrilled at the sight of wildlife and liked living on the edge?

He dispelled further thought, rushed out the door, and caught sight of Nancy in the distance. The smell of her cigarette smoke drifted back to him as he jogged toward her. She must have heard his footsteps, for she turned and waited. When he drew even with her, she began walking again, and they fell into step.

She inhaled deeply from her cigarette, then said, "I saw Laura, bouncing about like a tiger in heat."

"Your claws are showing."

Nancy shrugged. "I have trouble with nicey nice."

Phil was taken aback by her remark, but he had to admit Laura was nice, but not too nice as Nancy implied. This morning's brief meeting with Laura had jarred him. Before her temperament had always accommodated his; now she was abrupt, making him feel inadequate and bumbling.

Nancy took another drag. "The damn sun comes up so early that I couldn't sleep. It's a good thing there's no booze on this trip, or I might indulge." She paced on, silent for a while, apparently absorbed in her thoughts as she puffed on her cigarette, then tossed the butt into the gutter where it rolled, sputtering. She blurted out, "Don't you think Grant's a bit of a prick? 'It's my trip, not yours.'" She mimicked his speech. "Maybe he'll break his neck."

"Grant might be a little autocratic, but we need him."

"A little autocratic?" She grunted, then waved her hand in the air as if brushing away a fly. "Forget it. I'm in a foul mood."

They continued walking in silence. Inwardly he smiled, pleased the group had reservations about Grant's style. Those feeling did not perturb him, for he could use them to his advantage. After a time, he asked, "Where are you headed?"

Nancy stopped. "I don't know. Got any ideas?"

"Spotted a small coffee shop and bakery two streets over."

The Bell Bakery wasn't much to look at—just another square building with yellow linoleum floors and plastic chairs, but the aroma made up for the decor. After viewing the baked goodies, they settled on cinnamon buns and coffee and headed for a small table crammed against one of the double-paned windows overlooking the street.

"We'll probably think this place is paradise after we've been in the wilderness for a week," she said.

"No illusions about the romantic outdoors?" Phil munched on his cinnamon bun.

She ignored his teasing. "You should have shared your maps with me earlier, but I'll get my own when the stores open. I've read enough about Operation *Morning Light* to know that the biggest Cosmos debris finds were near Warden's Grove. That'll come late in the trip." She stared out the window for a while, then eyed him. "I can't get anyone to tell me exactly where Henri Deforte and Erich Mann were before Erich died. Do you know?"

"Not exactly. Henri claims Erich died at Helen Falls, but that's on the Hanbury River. Henri's place on Lake Damant is a long way from there."

"You don't believe his story?"

Phil shrugged. "Hard to tell. His story is too pat and the distance makes it improbable." His assessment of Henri and Erich's last camp differed greatly from the accepted theory, but then no one else had Erich's journal and papers, and he wasn't going to divulge that information.

"I'd ask the Mounties for their take on Henri, but they'd grill me with questions I don't want to answer." Nancy sipped her coffee.

"Sergeant Michael knows you're an environmental activist. Your clever story about cigarettes you told the others didn't wash."

She winked. "No need for everyone to know my business." After another silence, she leaned her head against the windowpane. "You know, maybe Gilbert Tupper going on this trip isn't such a bad idea."

Phil's satisfaction vanished. He leaned forward to protest, but before he could utter a word, she continued. "I want the world to know there still might be radioactive debris in the area. It's dangerous stuff. People can get hurt, like Erich Mann got hurt. I could turn Gilbert Tupper's entire story into," she spread her hands up and apart, "a headline that reads 'Uranium Debris Destroys Wilderness!'"

His pulse quickened. *God, if she ends up in collusion with Gilbert Tupper, there'll be hell to pay.* "What if we don't find anything?" He sipped his coffee, acting indifferent to her proposal.

"Even if nothing is found, I can turn his story into propaganda for my cause."

Phil studied her look of smug satisfaction. "I see. The old, if you can't beat 'em, join 'em theory. How are you going to get him to write a story about radiation? Feminine wiles?"

She laughed her deep-throated chortle. "I don't even know what the guy looks like."

"Not your type, a bit dull, short, not handsome, unless you like the acne-stippled look."

"Could you possibly be jealous?" When he didn't respond, she lifted her coffee cup and toasted him. "To using the enemy to my advantage."

"You're going to be a very busy gal. Even today you've planned a meeting." He continued in one breath. "Who with?"

"I think it's time I got back to the inn. After Grant's harangue on clothing, I have some repacking to do." Pushing her chair back, she began to rise.

Phil grabbed her hand. "You're meeting Pierre Giraud."

Nancy's smile froze, her lips narrowed, and she sat down. "How did you find out?"

"I was at the same bar he was last night." Phil's hard gaze forced her to look away. "You promised you'd wait to meet with him."

"I couldn't pass up this opportunity." She wiggled in her seat as if she were too warm. "He can help my organization with his contacts. He's meeting with the Dene tribe to help fund a separate province controlled by the natives."

"So how does that help *Cure the World*?"

Nancy's mouth hardened into a thin line. "We're all surrounded by governmental regulations. He knows how to strip power from those who have it."

"Through terrorism."

She took out a cigarette and rolled it round and round between her fingers as if it were a worry bead. "Look, I'm just talking to him. He was coming here, and I was coming here. Kismet."

"Disaster is more like it." He made no effort to quell his anger. "You're going to turn all your gains of public awareness into losses if you collaborate with him. In case you didn't know, the public doesn't like terrorism. What can he possibly do that we can't do for ourselves?"

"Money. Money is power." She sat up straighter, looking smug. Her black eyes danced with excitement of a future only she could view. "That's why he's here."

"You said he was working with the Dene tribe."

"I don't know the details, but the point is, he's willing to divert some funds to my...our organization."

"You know the axiom: you play in the gutter, you get dirty." He heard his words and realized they applied to him as much as to her. Hunching forward, he grasped his coffee mug, now cold as his mood.

"I know his game can get rough, but Pierre can help. I'm meeting him at Henri Deforte's at noon." She rose to leave. "I expect you *not* to be anywhere near there."

"Will you let me know the outcome?"

"Sure. You're on the board of *Cure the World*. I'll keep you informed."

He knew she was lying.

After they parted, he spent a miserable morning rereading details from Erich's notes and coordinating areas on his maps. He'd watched Laura, Deirdre, Boris and Cal drive off toward the National Park and their merry mood had irked him to such a degree that he found himself unable to concentrate. It would be at least two or three hours before they returned. To hell with it, he thought. He walked to the car rental office, got a car and set off in the direction of the park.

Traffic was essentially nonexistent, but when he approached the outskirts of town, a sedan hurtled toward him. As the car came abreast, he caught a blurred glimpse of Gilbert Tupper's pasty face. He drove on, thinking about Tupper's image and the problems surrounding the man's presence on the trip.

The air held a crisp edge, and he settled back to enjoy the scenery. When he passed the road to Henri Deforte's, he slowed, checking for cars.

A flash of orange in the forest caught his eye. Was that Nancy? He pulled over to the weed-choked shoulder and stopped. Nancy hadn't wanted him around when she met with Giraud, but something didn't seem right. He made a U-turn and stopped at the lane to the house. He rolled down his window and listened, but only heard muted bird songs, the whisper of swaying trees and buzzing insects.

He turned into the gravel road, driving slowly, peering into the woods. When he again spotted a smudge of orange at the edge of the forest, he stopped, got out and eased the door shut. When he reached the edge of the trees, he called out, "Nancy. Nancy, is that you? It's Phil."

Branches rustled and Nancy stepped forward. Leaves and twigs entwined in her tousled hair, and her eyes stared like a cornered wildcat. "Phil. Help me." She rushed toward him, slamming into his chest. "Get me out of here. Quick." She clung to him.

"Hey. What's going on?" He cradled her trembling body and stroked her head, trying to calm her.

"He's dead." She pulled back, looked up at him and shrieked. "He's dead."

"Who? Who's dead?" he asked, but she only sobbed into his chest. Standing at the edge of the forest with Nancy in his arms wasn't solving anything. With her stumbling along next to him, he led her to the car and opened the door. She sank into the seat and curled into a fetal position as he ran around the other side to get in.

"Drive," she pleaded. "Get me away from here."

He turned around and drove to the main road, found another gravel road some distance from Henri's and turned into it. After turning off the engine, he waited until her breathing steadied.

She sat up, looked around and with trembling hands brushed her tangled hair back from her face. "Thank God, you came by. I'm not sure I could have made it to town without being seen."

"Why would it matter if you were seen?"

She stared out the side window, shivering. "He's dead Murdered."

"Who's dead?"

As if she hadn't heard him, she spoke in a breathless outpouring of information. "I took a cab to the house. No one answered my knock, so I went around back." She swallowed, hesitated, then continued. "The door was open. I went in and called out. I went from room to room, wondering where Leah and Giraud were. The front door slammed, and I heard a car drive off. I walked into a room with furniture turned upside down." She paused and put her hand to her head. "I have this snapshot in my brain. I can see everything perfectly—the man lying face down on the floor, blood...blood pooling by the side of his head. He was dead. Skull smashed."

Phil pulled her quaking body toward him. "Who?"

She shook her head and put her hands to her temples. "I wasn't sure until I found his wallet." Nancy shuddered, then pulled away from him. "My God," she continued in a strange lucid voice, "my luck stinks. It was Pierre Giraud."

Chapter 18

In her room at the Pelican Inn Nancy shivered as she lay in bed, her hands cupped around a hot mug of tea. She spoke coherently, yet her eyes remained dilated, haunted.

Phil wondered how much of what she'd told him was the truth. His first instinct had been to return to the house and witness the scene, but realized if he got involved in a murder investigation, he could get stuck in Fort Smith. His duty as a law enforcement official and his private agenda were in conflict.

"You sure you didn't leave any fingerprints on anything?" he asked.

She shook her head. "I don't know. I looked at his wallet and put it back in his pocket."

"You went through his pockets?"

"Yes."

"That could be a problem if they get your fingerprints off of it. The back doorknob? Did you touch it?"

"No, the door was ajar. I don't think I closed it when I left the same way. I only touched his wallet."

"You said someone drove away. Did he leave by the front door? Was the car there when you arrived? Can you remember what the car looked like?"

"Why are you badgering me?" Her eyes swam with tears.

"Because this could jeopardize our trip and might give us a clue to the killer." He stood and paced. "If the body's found before we take off tomorrow morning and they link you to visiting Pierre, we could all be stuck in Fort Smith."

"A man's dead, and you're thinking of the trip?" She rubbed her lips. "God, I need a drink."

"No." He knelt in front of her. "The last thing you need is a drink. Now, more than ever, you need a clear head. Don't say anything to anyone about going to Henri's house."

"The cab driver knows." Her smeared lipstick made her look waif-like. "Besides, I didn't murder Pierre."

"The police don't know that. If we get out of town before they find out about your being there, the investigation might be wrapped up before we return." Even as he said this, he had his doubts. "What about the car? It must have been parked there when you arrived."

"There was a car." She frowned. "A two door or maybe a four door or…." Nancy put a tissue to her nose. "I don't know."

"A sedan," Phil said.

She nodded, sniffled and blew her nose.

"The only car that passed me on my way out of town was driven by Gilbert Tupper, driving fast. I wonder if he was involved?"

She stared at him. "Oh God. He's going on our trip. What if he thinks I saw him kill Pierre?"

He moved next to her and put an arm across her shoulders. "We're not certain it was Tupper, but we'll have to be cautious. I'll watch out for you, but keep your wits about you. If we learn it was Tupper, Grant can phone the Mounties."

Her body trembled under his arm and her red-rimmed eyes bespoke of a trust that caused him to squirm. His job was to stick with her and that included protecting her from Tupper or anyone else.

"I'll try to find out where Leah is," he said. "If she's out of town, the body might not be discovered for a few days. In the meantime, you've got to act normal."

She smiled. "I've *never* acted normal."

"Atta girl." He patted her hand. "Keep your sense of humor and you'll do fine. Stay in your room until you feel able to meet people, then go shopping. Let people see you acting like a tourist."

She nodded. "I suppose that's the best way." She took a sip of tea. Phil stood and moved toward the door. "I've got to make my day seem normal, too. I'm meeting with Boris and Cal to reminisce about the old days."

As he was about to leave, she muttered, "I wonder how much money Pierre would have diverted to *Cure the World?*"

He shook his head in disbelief as he closed the door behind him. Too bad her efforts couldn't be redirected toward more reasonable environmental endeavors, but she was proving to be resilient and right now that was more important.

Back in his room, he reflected on his divergent allegiances, the Bureau's and his. What good would it do if he found the diamond lode? He'd need a Canadian partner to establish ownership and help extract the diamonds. He was convinced the lode was outside the Thelon Sanctuary, otherwise it would be impossible to mine. A Canadian partner would have to be someone who disliked the big diamond mining companies, someone who had aspirations, someone who needed extra cash. Chip? How deep in debt was he?

Cal or Boris had a naive faith that Phil would handle all details then blithely share equally in the profit. Was it the excitement of the hunt that drew him or the money? The Bureau had promised excitement, but his present assignment was mundane and boring. How would Pierre Giraud's murder affect the search? Was Tupper the killer?

When Cal and Boris arrived, they talked about the wood bison they'd seen and the loons they'd heard. Phil's frustration grew. "Let's get down to business. We haven't much time."

Boris gave him a steady stare as if he saw something new in Phil. "Of course, let's keep things on a business footing."

Phil wondered what was eating Boris, but shrugged it off. "As you know I have Erich's journal and notes." He pointed to the items he'd left out on the table.

Boris fingered the map and pointed to Warden's Grove and the place where Hornby's Camp Garland had been. "I understand the commemorative plaque is still there. Grant said we'd have a look."

"I think we'll find what we came for before we reach that point." Phil noted several places farther south. "These are the places Erich mentioned in his journal that make sense geologically, and they're outside the Sanctuary. We've got to get Grant to camp in these areas so we can explore. If not, I'm willing to go off on my own." Neither of the two men seemed alarmed at his statement. "If that becomes necessary, I need to know you're with me."

"Grant will use his two-way radio and call in a rescue," Cal said.

"Not if he doesn't have his radio," Phil said.

"Now, wait a minute." Cal frowned. "That's too drastic. My wife's on this trip. I can't endanger her."

"I don't like your idea either," Boris said. "You've got to think of the others, something you don't do very often. Leave Grant his radio. It's a big area. We can find our own with my GPS."

Phil didn't mention he'd also carry a GPS as well as a radio. He studied his partners, trying to gauge their commitment. "If Grant's half the guide I think he is, he can get to any of his rendezvous points without maps. His radio is a secondary precaution. Besides, Chip and the Mounties have the route." He shrugged, as though he'd given in to them. "It may not come to that. It looks to me that this," he pointed to a place on the map, "is the most likely spot. If you remember when we had our accident in '78, it was here." He moved his finger to another mark. "According to Erich's calculations, the body of the prospector we found was here. Those two areas and the geological formations indicating diamonds are in the proximity. From what I can determine, that area is about eight to ten days into our paddling trip."

Boris studied the map. "Those areas don't jibe with Erich's death at Helen Falls on the Hanbury."

"I don't think he died at Helen Falls," Phil said. "I'm not convinced Erich died accidentally."

Cal and Boris stared at Phil in silence.

Boris paced away from the table with his hands in his corduroy pants pockets. His leather boots scraped on the wood floorboards, muffling his hushed voice. "I was afraid of that. Erich was no greenhorn. Falling and hitting his head seemed a bit odd. And the uranium traces.... Wonder what the Mounties made of it?"

Phil laid down his pencil. "I've had a cursory talk with one of the constables. They're swallowing Henri's story, probably because they have no other option, and it clears their books."

Cal asked, "How exactly do you figure things?"

"When I talked to Henri, he said it took him three or four days and nights to get Erich's body back to his camp. Even though Henri is a strong canoeist, he couldn't get back from Helen Falls in that time paddling against the current. Erich's last entry was here." He pointed to a spot on the map, and the others moved closer. "That's why I think we should start examining the area here." He tapped the spot.

"What about the uranium?" Boris asked. "Do you think he could have found debris?"

"I do." Phil was unsure how much information he should give them, but decided they needed to know. "Erich had traces of radiation on his clothes and gloves. He wore protective gloves when Henri buried him. Henri had burns on his hands and face, probably attributable to uranium. I think Henri knows a whole lot more about what Erich found and where he found it. If that's the case, where is it and what did he do with it?"

"So," Cal said, "how are we going to get him to tell us?"

"I don't think he'll tell us, but he might show us," Phil said.

"How do you intend for that to happen?" Boris settled into the only chair and crossed his arms over his broad chest.

Phil sat on the bed and looked from Cal, who leaned against the wall next to the window, to Boris, whose body language connoted hostility. For better or worse, they were his partners, they were smart, both in good physical condition, and he knew they could keep a secret. They'd done that for seventeen years.

"This is how I figure it. The wilderness is the most important thing in Henri's life. From what Karen McDuffy told me and from what I've learned from Erich through the years, Henri's tough and can be physically violent. He's obsessed with his wilderness and he's clever. Hell, if he's the best wolf trapper in the area, he's got to be clever. Grant said Henri will be at his cabin on Lake Damant when we land. In the short time we have there, we've got to make Henri believe we know what Erich found, where it might be, and that we plan to get it."

"But we don't know what he found and where it is," Boris said.

"Let him finish," Cal said.

"If we press him, he may follow us."

"Following isn't leading us." Boris's arms remained crossed.

"Will you let him finish?" Cal fiddled with the window shade. "Christ, you're fussing like an old woman."

Oddly, Boris glared at Phil not Cal as if it were Phil who had reprimanded him. Puzzled by Boris's reaction, Phil continued. "If Henri doesn't appear interested in our endeavor, I have a backup plan. We have an odd number on this trip. If one of the canoes became damaged, what would Grant do?"

"Make someone sit in the middle of one of the canoes." Cal emitted a disheartened laugh.

Phil shook his head. "We're hauling too much gear for that, besides, we can complain if he does."

"So, he gets another canoe," Boris said. "That means Chip flies back to Fort Smith and picks up another one. That might give us time to work on Henri."

"Or," Phil said, "Henri might suggest he goes along and use his canoe."

"Seems farfetched," Cal said. "What if none of that works?"

"Then we're back to using Erich's journal, which isn't all that bad," Phil said.

"I'd like to look at the journal," Boris said, pointing to it.

Phil hesitated. "Sure. I forgot you know German. His handwriting is in old German script. That's why Henri was so dumbfounded when he looked at it."

Boris chuckled. "Even Erich's handwriting in English would give anyone fits." He stared at the floor for a moment then looked up with a serious expression. "If it weren't for Erich's obsessive nature, we wouldn't be here now. I'm not sure I'm pleased or sad about that, but he was a friend and I owe him. If Henri killed him, I'd like to nab the bastard."

Cal moved away from the window. "We still have to deal with Gilbert Tupper."

"I think we're stuck with him," Phil said, "unless you can come up with a way to get rid of him before we leave."

"Short of murder you mean." Boris shot back.

"Ah, yeah, short of that," Phil said. Having a murderer who might know Nancy had been at the crime scene, made for a dicey situation. He pushed the thought aside and concentrated on the immediate plan. "Mark your maps to correlate with mine. Keep them in a safe, dry place."

Phil had sewn a special pocket in his vest to protect Erich's papers and a set of maps. He was loath to part with the journal even for a short time, but Boris had a right to study it. However, it had taken Phil months to decipher and draw conclusions from what he had read. The last entry corroborated data from Erich's previous notes. Phil rose from the bed, walked toward the table with the maps and journal and gave the latter to Boris. "Read it tonight and give it back to me in the morning."

"That doesn't give me much time," Boris said, reaching for the journal. "This is our last night in town. Laura and I thought we'd celebrate."

"What do you have to celebrate?" Phil's gut cramped.

"We plan to announce our engagement when we get back to California."

The pride in Boris's voice so infuriated Phil that he was unable to speak.

It was Cal who reached out a hand. "Congratulations. When did you decide this?"

"I've asked her before, but she put me off. All of a sudden today as we're walking in the park, she asked me. Isn't that something? I feel ten feet tall."

"Good for you," Cal said. "She's a great gal."

Phil erupted in anger. "You're jeopardizing this operation with a love tryst?"

"I'm not jeopardizing anything. This is none of your business." Boris moved toward Phil. "She told me today that she'd known you in Costa Rica."

Cal moved forward to stand shoulder to shoulder with Boris. "I knew you dumped her, Phil, but didn't want to say anything."

"I didn't dump her." Phil squared around to his attackers.

"She told me about your relationship. Laura's honest, unlike you. She's finished with you." Boris moved toward Phil. "I'm in on this deal. Finding the diamond lode and Erich's uranium debris and avenging his death, if it comes to that, but my personal life and Laura's is no concern of yours."

Chapter 19

Dressed in rain gear, Grant's group huddled under the overhang of Loon Charter's austere wood-framed office at the lake's edge behind a stubby pier stacked with red and yellow oil drums. In the steel-gray morning, two seaplanes, a navy-blue Otter with red tipped wings and a white Cessna, hugged the pier's sides like earthbound geese. The gear had been stowed aboard, but there was a delay without any explanation. Phil hoped this was not an omen of things to come.

"Feels like I'm back in the military." Cal fumed as he stood next to Deirdre and waved away mosquitoes. "Hurry up and wait. Why doesn't Grant tell us what's going on? What's the delay?"

"Rather than a what, I think it's a who," Boris said. "Perhaps Gilbert Tupper wants to make a grand entrance." Boris leaned against the building, his pack and Laura's camera bag at his feet. Heavy raindrops plunked onto the huge waterlily pads choking the lake's shoreline.

Not a good day for taking photos," Boris said to Laura, who snapped shots of the area.

"Actually, it is." She pointed to the waterlilies. "Their pink and white flowers contrast well against the murky water."

"I like the sound of the bull frogs." Deirdre pulled the collar of her green rain slicker tighter as she huddled next to the chocolate-colored building.

Through the office window, Phil saw Grant's head next to Chip's as they pushed charts back and forth. While he watched the two men, Nancy moved next to him and pulled at his sleeve.

"Gilbert Tupper's arrived," she whispered.

As Karen introduced the reporter to the others, Phil took Nancy's arm, and together they joined the group. "This is Nancy Plowright," Karen said, turning toward them. "And you said you knew Phil."

"Yes." Fiddling with the straps of his small personal pack, Gilbert acknowledged Nancy and Phil with a nod. "Is my gear on the plane?" he asked Karen.

"Grant stowed it aboard last night."

"You'd have been out of luck if you'd missed the flight," Phil said.

Gilbert ignored Phil and shifted his gaze from Cal to Boris. "You two haven't changed much. Seems you've kept in better shape than I have." Gilbert gave a dry laugh that no one else participated in. "Not an auspicious day to fly," he continued, "but can't let a little weather stop a brave entourage like this, can we?"

Karen rubbed her hands together as if warding off the chill that had settled with Gilbert's arrival. "Grant and Chip are having a last minute discussion about the route. We'll break into two groups. I'll go in the Cessna and Gilbert will ride with me. We need one other person in that plane. The rest will go in the Otter."

"I'll go with you," Phil offered, eyeing Gilbert.

Gilbert pulled out a cigar, but before he could lift it to his thick lips, Karen shook her head. "No smoking out here near the fuel." She pointed toward the drums.

Gilbert shoved his stogie back into his jacket pocket. "Smoking keeps the bugs at bay. Cigars should be standard issue." He glanced around, but received no response from the others. "How much longer will we be standing around?"

"We leave when the pilots are ready," Chip said, having overheard the question as he came out of the office. "The cloud cover is beginning to lift. Waiting on land is better than mucking up a flight because we didn't read the weather correctly." He strode out to his planes.

The group milled around, wondering if they should follow Chip or stay where they were?.

"Last call for the outhouse." Karen pointed towards a small shack back in the woods away from the lake. "It's about a three hour flight."

While some heeded Karen's warning, Phil strolled onto the pier next to Chip who was inspecting the Otter's cowling. "You were a little abrupt with Gilbert, weren't you?"

"Maybe." Chip rubbed his hand along the blue metal like a father patting his son on the head. "Guess the weather's got to me, and he isn't the most likable chap."

"Most would agree with you, but I figured you were close to Gilbert since I met him with you and Henri in the bar."

"Drinking and liking don't necessarily go together," Chip said.

Phil wondered if all Chip's friends were only drinking buddies. Since Chip seemed to know everyone in town, as well as their business, Phil thought the man would have many close friends. Now he reflected this might not be so. "You've got quite a fleet. Loon Charter must be doing very well." Phil traced the scars on the side of the plane. "Looks like you've had a few scrapes. How many planes do you own?"

Chip slapped the side of the Otter and grinned. "Me and the bank own three—these two and the one I fly in and out of the Fort Smith airport." Chip gazed up at the sky. "Looks like it's letting up. It's an intermittent low band of clouds at about 900 feet, but we'll be above them in no time." He glanced at Phil. "You ready to tackle Erich's route?"

Phil shrugged. "It'll be interesting what we find. He had varied interests in the backcountry. Geology was a hobby of his."

"Geology can lead to some fancy findings these days. I heard rumblings from Erich over the years. He liked all kinds of treasure. Problem is after you find it, you got to mine it and get it out and big corporations have that locked up." Chip stared at Phil with a bland expression. "Course it's not impossible if you know the right Canadian."

"My sentiments exactly." Phil knew he and Chip were speaking the same language. If he needed a pilot to remove anything from the backcountry, Chip was his man.

Grant called out. "We're all set."

Phil watched the group come forward. "I feel like a paratrooper making his first jump, but I don't much feel like yelling Geronimo," he said to Chip. "Do you carry parachutes?"

"Nope. Don't plan to lose an airplane or a passenger." Chip glanced at a swarthy-complexioned man coming out of the office. "Ready, Georgie?" In an aside to Phil, Chip said, "He's my extra pilot; he'll fly the Cessna. He likes flying so much that he takes unscheduled jobs like flying Henri in and out of the backcountry. Gives us some extra income without the authorities sticking their noses in our business." Then Chip called out, "Saddle up, folks."

The group moved onto the pier and took refuge from the spritzing rain under the wing of the Otter while they boarded. Phil he reached out and put his arm around Nancy's shoulders and said, "See you at ground zero."

She gave him a wan smile and murmured, "Be subtle if you ask Gilbert about yesterday."

"Don't think that subject will arise," he whispered, then pulled away. Laura gave him a searching look before she entered the Otter. Phil smiled and gave her a mock salute.

While Chip started the Otter's engine, Gilbert and Phil walked over to the Cessna and squeezed in behind Georgie and Karen. They watched the Otter take off and moments later their small plane rocked forward and began its taxi. Without a hint of separation from the water, the craft cleared the lake, soared over a grove of trees at the far shore and soared upward through the clouds. Phil watched the altimeter settle at 1,600 feet as Georgie leveled the plane.

Phil was content to watch the land below. The water came in different hues, emerald and aqua to navy blue, depending on the depth of the lakes and rivers. Rain pelted the plane off and on as it headed in a north by northeast direction.

Phil spotted a rainbow below them with the shadow of the plane within its circle. "Look," he shouted. "The Specter of Brocken."

"The what?" Gilbert asked.

"Specter of Brocken," Phil repeated.

"Never heard of such a thing." Gilbert stared out the window.

"It's the name for the phenomenon when a shadow is projected onto heavy clouds and a rainbow appears to encircle the image," Karen said, half-turning toward the two men so they could hear her. "I love rainbows. Some African tribes call them the 'bride of the rain.'"

Gilbert let out his breath, shook his head, and said, "Native Americans believe rainbows are the paths of the dead."

"They're too lovely for such a negative view," Karen said. "I've heard them referred to as a little window in the sky."

Phil would have continued the conversation, but yelling above the engine noise was too much effort. Instead, he continued to gaze at the terrain below. The esker sandbars stretched out in long undulating lines across the land. Tundra polygons generated by heaving frost spanned the region like cracks on dried clay. From the air, the earth looked cold and forbidding. He knew from the past just how unforgiving the Arctic land could be.

Everyone had acted out of sorts this morning. Before they'd taken off, Gilbert had been fidgety and anxious. Boris had returned Erich's diary with gruff thanks. Phil hoped that wasn't going to be his attitude the entire trip. Laura seemed in her own world, and except for that last look before takeoff, she'd avoided eye contact.

He leaned his head against the pack on his right and awoke some time later as the plane descended. Checking his watch, he was startled to see three hours had elapsed. Below was Lake Damant. Eagerly, he arched his neck to see if he could spot Henri's cabin. His palms pressed against the cold window.

A swoosh of water and soon Georgie taxied the plane to shore. They'd arrived after the Otter, and the others were already transferring gear to the land with Grant directing the effort. Henri helped Chip with the ropes Georgie tossed them.

When Phil reached the gravel beach, the bleakness of the area stunned him. The pristine land he'd flown over disappeared as he viewed Henri Deforte's place in the taiga. Moving from the shore to the calf-high juniper brush, he glimpsed tufts of wolf fur flapping from rusted wire strung between wood posts. One or two well-used traps leaned against the crude cabin, and rusted metal scraps, nails and screws lay scattered among chopped-off branches of jack pines. The tree's sap, coagulated into thin lines and lumps like blood. The squeak of the pink outhouse door, hanging off its hinges, added to the bizarre scene. How could Henri trash the land he claimed to love?

He shuddered and glanced at the disgusted expressions on people's faces as they stood temporarily paralyzed with disillusionment. Their boots crunched on the sand as they shifted restlessly. The sky had cleared, and the sun broke through the intermittent clouds. Rain gear and jackets were shed and stowed into personal packs.

"Keep your head nets handy," Karen advised.

"If you'd like to look around," Grant said, "the hill over there gives you a view of the Thelon. I'll see to the canoes and call when I need a hand."

Gilbert ignoring Grant's suggestion, went down to the shore and lit his cigar, while Karen and Grant walked toward a thicket of bushes where the canoes were stashed. Boris and Cal hiked up the hill with Nancy and Deirdre following.

Boris turned back toward Laura. "Coming?"

"I'll take some photos here," Laura said and waved for him to go on.

Although Phil wanted to talk with her, he had another agenda and went over to Henri. "I see you kept your promise."

Henri's broad hand scratched at his beard, and thick wrinkles appeared on his forehead. "My promise?"

"You told me in March. Mounties or not, you'd be here to greet us."

"Oh, *oui.*" Henri nodded toward Gilbert down on the beach smoking his cigar. "You brought him?"

"Gilbert was a late addition, not someone we chose," Phil said in a hushed tone. "Grant wanted him along. My friends and I only want to follow Erich's footsteps. His notebook was most instructive. It gives us an idea where he might have come across some interesting findings."

Henri looked down and gave an almost imperceptible sigh. *"Oui.* Erich always took notes." Henri's hands worked a knot in a rope, seemingly unconcerned with Phil or the others.

Phil knew Henri had to be played like a wily fish, but he didn't have much time to goad the man.

Suddenly a yell ripped the air. Phil and Henri looked up to see Grant gesturing. He bellowed, his voice full of anger. "Henri. Look what's happened. My canoe."

Henri's boots churned in the coarse gravel as he strode toward Grant. Phil followed and listened to the heated conversation between the two men. Karen moved back avoiding the confrontation, but Chip hurried forward to hear the exchange.

Grant's usual placid face reddened; his fingers flexed open and shut. "How could my canoe get crushed like this?" Grant said in a raised voice.

With his hands in his pant's pockets, Henri shrugged. "I saw bear tracks."

"This wasn't done by an animal. The hull's been stoved in," Grant said.

"You accuse me?" Henri's thick face grew darker.

Grant stared at Henri in helpless rage. "No. Why would you do such a thing?"

"Chip can take the canoe back and have it repaired," Karen said.

"We can't wait," Grant said.

"Mon ami," Henri said, "I'm sorry about this."

"What about Erich's canoe?" Grant asked. "It's still here, isn't it?"

"I sold it to a fellow trapper."

"How about your canoe, then?" Grant glared at Henri.

Henri hesitated. "If I go, my canoe can be used."

Grant slapped the sides of his khaki trousers with the end of a rope. He nodded. "We can't paddle three in a canoe." He gazed at Chip. "You'll have to take this one and get it repaired. We can set up a rendezvous four or five days out."

"Sounds logical," Chip said, "but I'll have to bill you."

"I know." Grant turned to Henri. "Could you paddle with us for four or five days? When the canoe's repaired, Chip can fly it in, and you can leave us."

Henri seemed to ponder this solution with a grave face as he stared down at the damaged canoe. *"Oui."* His broad shoulders hunched forward as he looked up at Grant. "Do not be angry with fate, *mon ami.* There's a reason for everything."

Henri's philosophizing gave Phil a slow, burning sensation of confusion. Henri appeared to be one step ahead of him.

Chapter 20

When Laura heard the tramp of boots, she looked up from her camera to see the others returning, looking like space aliens with head nets on.

"We heard someone yell," Cal said. "What happened?"

"One of the canoe's been damaged," Laura said.

"You're joking," Deirdre said. "We can't ride three in a canoe with our gear."

"Relax," Cal said. "I'm sure Grant will figure something out. After all, he's the I-know-everything captain."

"Let's hear the final verdict before we get riled." Boris moved to Laura's side to fan insects away from the mount as she changed the lens. She glanced at him and smiled. "Thanks. They get into everything."

"My God." Deirdre waved her hands in front of her face. "The mosquitoes are horrendous. Look at this welt." She stuck her hand out. "Cal, have you got the insect repellent?"

Cal reached into his shirt pocket and handed her a small green plastic bottle of Muskol. "You don't need much."

"Laura, you were smart to stay near shore." Nancy, keeping her hands in her pockets, nodded toward Gilbert, "He's got the right idea. I bet there isn't an insect within four feet of him and his smoke."

"I'm surprised you aren't down there with him," Deirdre said.

Nancy's response was slow in coming, but even through the head netting, Laura caught the woman's frown and raised eyebrows. "Honey," Nancy said, "I'm particular who I smoke with and I only brought a limited number of packs."

"Trying to quit is tough," Boris said. "I took the plunge over ten years ago, but I still remember the agony."

Laura turned toward him. "I didn't know you smoked."

"I don't now."

Deirdre interrupted. "Whatever caused the ruckus, his highness is about to explain, I hope."

A few snickered before Grant reached them. "We've had a mishap with one of the canoes," he said. "Henri will join us with his canoe until Chip can bring back the repaired one."

"How did it happen?" Cal asked.

"Don't know. The hull's smashed."

"What did Henri say?" Boris gazed at the row of canoes.

"He doesn't know." Grant started to turn away. "At any rate, Henri is helping out by joining us for a few days."

"Good of him." Cal gave a knowing nod to Boris.

Laura didn't understand the implication of Cal's nod, but she was disturbed that a man who not only despoiled the land around his cabin, but also killed wolves, was joining them. From the expressions on Deirdre and Nancy's faces, they, too, appeared uneasy at the turn of events.

"Let's hope neither of us has to paddle with Henri," Laura whispered under her breath to Deirdre as they followed Grant.

Gilbert, chomping on his cigar, joined them. When he heard Henri was going along, his shoulders sagged. Following Grant's meticulous instructions, they brought down the rest of the canoes and distributed the gear, cross-lashing it to the thwarts and gunwales.

Afterward Grant said, "I expect your canoes to be kept clean. Besides the painter lines, I've supplied a bailer and a sponge in the bow of each canoe. We can get two hours of paddling in before we camp." Grant turned as Henri strode down to the shore with a pack on his back, a rifle in one hand and three paddles in the other. His canoe had been set a little apart from the others. They watched silently as he placed his gear into his battered canoe and lashed his bags down. He wedged his rifle under the ropes with the butt facing the stern. The rifle's weathered wood stock spoke of years of use.

The sight of the weapon increased Laura's sense of foreboding. She winced at the flashback to her father's suicide. From the set of Phil's jaw, the frown on Boris's face and Cal's raised eyebrows, they were all uncomfortable with the gun. If Grant asked her to paddle with the man, she'd refuse.

Grant, apparently noting the consternation of the group, said, "As I told you before, I don't take a gun on these trips, but Henri has to return alone and feels more comfortable with a rifle. He's assured me, he'll keep it out of harm's way while he's with us and won't use it."

"Looks like a Winchester 94, .30-30 lever action," Phil said.

"Ah, you know guns?" Henri asked. "I use it when necessary. No one need fear."

"It's got an accuracy range of up to a 100 yards. Right?" Phil studied the rifle from afar. "You use a scope?"

Henri raised his hand, rubbing his thumb and first finger together. "Such gadgets for amateur hunter."

Phil's assessment of Henri's weapon did nothing to assuage Laura's concern, but Grant's instructions overrode her thoughts about the rifle.

"Karen will paddle in the stern in one canoe," Grant said. "Cal, since you don't have paddling experience, take the bow in Karen's canoe."

Cal picked up his paddle. "Glad to take orders from you, Karen."

She smiled and patted him on the shoulder. "It's not like that. The power should be in the bow. I'm the rudder. You've got to keep an eye out for jutting objects."

"Nancy, you'll paddle in the bow of my canoe," Grant said.

She pushed her head net onto her forehead, and chuckled softly as she walked over to Grant's beige-colored hull. "Strength in the front?" Her brown eyes twinkled.

Grant continued to set the order. "Deirdre and Phil will paddle together. You can choose who wants the stern. Laura, you take the stern and have Boris paddle in the bow."

"That leaves me with Henri," Gilbert said, picking up his personal pack. "Hey, Henri, you want a cigar?" He pulled one out of his jacket pocket.

Henri took the cigar and lit it.

"Since we're paddling together, you can explain all about your trips with Erich," Gilbert said. "Give me some good background. You know, details."

Henri glared at Gilbert. "I gave you story once. You forget?"

"Of course you did, but details make the story better."

"You want details, talk to others." He gave Gilbert a slight shove at the shoulder, sending the reporter toward the bow of the canoe. "Tie your gear down, get in, sit down and don't rock my canoe." Henri clenched the cigar between his teeth.

Chip walked over for a last minute conference with Grant about the coordinates of the rendezvous site. Phil leaned over the map and watched where Chip's pen marked an X. When Grant gave him an odd look, Phil said, "It pays to have more than one person know what's going on."

"I've been guiding trips for years and have never had my role questioned."

Phil marked the coordinates on his own map. "I like to know where I am and where I'm going."

"Exactly," Boris said. "I enjoy maps, and you told us we should each buy a set."

Laura thought, shouldn't we all know the route?

"Georgie and I'll shove off," Chip said. "Don't worry about the canoe. She's tied on tight, and I'll get her fixed and back to you so Henri can go back to his traps."

Chip backed away, gave a small salute to the group and walked past Henri. "Do you have a message for Leah?"

"Why? She does what she wants. I see her in winter," Henri said with a scowl.

"Hey, Georgie gave you a free ride, so I know you've seen her recently." Chip winked and swatted his baseball cap on his thigh. "Don't give these folks trouble, or I'll tell Leah. You've given her enough trouble to last a year."

"What more she want? I gave her house."

"If you don't know, I'm sure not going to spell it out." Chip walked on down the beach toward the planes. He waved to Georgie already seated in the Cessna's cockpit. Both pilots started their respective engines.

Laura shielded her eyes as the planes, one after the other, taxied on the water and lifted off. The hum of the engines became muted and the silence of the wilderness enveloped her. The connections with the outside world passed into the distance, and she felt abandoned.

They launched their canoes and with rhythmic stroking moved the small crafts out from shore, past the point, and into the Thelon River. They bantered back and forth with a few suggestions from one partner to the other to accommodate paddling sides or stroke speed. But for the most part, the canoeists were quiet as the taiga shoreline of straggly jack pines slipped by. The underbrush thinned, and spruce trees and a few white birches came into view.

The river moved snakelike, smooth and silky, at times a hundred feet across and sometimes twice that. Rounded rocks curried the shore, then stumpy cliffs appeared and naked tree roots hung in the air where the ground had eroded from under them.

The sun was warm, the air still, and Laura was thankful they paddled in the middle of the river avoiding the insects hovering near shore. Her camera bag, wrapped inside a waterproof bag, was tied to the portage yoke, but she had one camera at the ready under her seat in a clear plastic baggie. The water was calm, and she had no concern about it getting wet today. In front of her, Boris's back muscles rippled through his khaki shirt. The force of his stroke made steering easy.   The canoes began to space out as paddlers found a comfortable pace. Henri kept his canoe well to the rear as if understanding he was not completely welcome. Gilbert puffed on his cigar and scowled.

Laura noted that despite Grant's domineering style, he had a good eye for people's abilities. There was little disparity in canoe speeds. Grant paddled the point, giving Nancy the best view of the virgin horizon. Grant had the lean hard body of an outdoorsman and could have paddled solo and still maintained the lead. Laura didn't understand why he act like the captain of a runaway crew. Perhaps Karen's warmth would make up for his dogmatic attitude.

The sun's fierce ultraviolet rays streaked through the earlier cloud cover. The river reflected the sun, and the water changed from oily gray to a brilliant blue.

Grant had explained there'd be no rapids the first day, so they could practice their strokes. Although Laura was in good physical condition, her palms were soft and within the first hour she developed a blister on the inside of her thumb. Nancy and Deirdre wore gloves, but she'd packed hers in the duffle bag. She sat on the canoe seat, her legs splayed out in front of her with her boots nudged up against the tarp-wrapped gear. Sweat beaded her forehead and upper lip.

Perspiration darkened the back of Boris's shirt. He pushed his wide-brimmed hat back off his forehead. Occasionally, he swiveled around and gave her a thumbs up. He sat with one knee on the hull, and the other leg extended as a brace. For a big man, he was agile, and had a calm, zen-like nature.

As Karen and Cal's canoe came abreast, Cal nodded, his back ramrod straight, his thighs braced against the gunwales. Even in khakis and a canvas hat with his head net propped on top, he appeared dapper like a mannequin dressed for a safari. Even if his canoe capsized, it was even money his slicked back hair would never tousle.

Laura had hoped to see wildlife immediately, but after two hours, when Grant nosed his canoe into shore, she hadn't even seen a bird. It was as if they'd entered another planet. Clumps of stunted spruce surrounded a small meadow of stubby mixed grasses. The beach consisted of large cobblestones, rocks rounded and tossed shoreward by the winter ice heaves. They unloaded and hauled the canoes far above the rocky shoreline with Grant supervising every detail from their placement to their cleaning. Like a stream of ants, they picked up their gear and established a place for their tents.

Each tent had a space around it—a zone that made for good neighbors. Blackflies and mosquitoes buzzed about their new fodder. After setting up her tent, Laura opened the flap, tossed in her large duffle, sleeping bag and camera satchel, then sprayed inside the tent with the insect repellent Grant had provided, and quickly zipped it closed.

With a camera hanging around her neck, she began to reconnoiter the area. She noticed Nancy had yet to raise her tent and offered to help.

"Lordy, yes." Nancy looked out from under her head net. "I can't figure this part." Laura spread out the rain fly, and soon they had the tent staked and erected. "I tossed my stuff in and bombed the inside with the repellent," Laura said.

"Good idea." Nancy grabbed her can and blasted the inside of her tent. Afterward, they stood in front of the tent and listened to the buzzing insects in their death throes. "Do you think it'll be this buggy the entire trip?" Nancy asked. "I feel like I've got bugs in my hair even though I've got it tied back."

"That's why I keep mine short," Laura said. "I can't be bothered fussing with it when I'm on a shoot." Laura looked at Nancy's weary, smudged face. "You've got lovely hair. I don't blame you for keeping it long."

"Did I hear someone mention hair?" Phil asked as he came toward them. "I was going to help with your tent, Nancy, but I got hung up map reading with Boris."

Gilbert joined them, looking disheveled and tired. He slouched under his hat and clasped his arms across his chest. "Would you believe this place? I'm not so sure it's the paradise Grant talks about."

"Isn't that the point of your trip?" Laura asked. "You're going to let your readers know what a wonderful place the Thelon Sanctuary is, so it'll remain pristine and protected against big mining interests."

"Yeah, that's about it." Gilbert scratched the side of his head and flies flew upward. "Damn creatures!" He looked at Nancy. "No offense, but you look about as done in as I feel. You don't want to get chilled after the heavy paddling. Perhaps you should put on your orange parka."

Nancy peered at Gilbert as if he'd just asked her to jump into the river.

Ignoring her gaze, Gilbert continued in a chatty tone. "It's been a long day, especially after yesterday."

"Yesterday?" Nancy swayed and pushed at a lock of hair through the mesh of her head net. Phil stepped forward and put his arm around her shoulders.

Well, isn't he attentive, Laura thought..

"What about yesterday, Gilbert?" Phil asked. "Was yesterday a rough day for you?"

"What?" Gilbert took a step back. "I…ah…what do you mean?"

"You passed me on the road going into Fort Smith as if the devil was chasing you," Phil said. "What were you fleeing from?"

"I had to file a story before I left town, so I might have been speeding." Gilbert reached into his jacket pocket and pulled out a cigar. "I'm just trying to be friendly. You people seem to have it in for me. I'm here doing my job. No need for you to treat me like a pariah."

Boris joined them to stand next to Laura. "Gilbert, we're here to enjoy ourselves." Boris had a look of sour amusement on his broad face. "Grant told us you were coming along, but we expect you to honor our privacy."

"I'm paying my way and I have a job to do. None of you can stop me from finding out what you're up to. Tracing Erich Mann's path means you're after something, and I aim to find out what. You find anything, and I'll let the world know."

"Perhaps we should let Grant in on why you're really on this trip," Phil said.

Laura wondered why it mattered that Phil and the others wanted to follow Erich's trips. What could they possibly find that Gilbert would want to write about? Fed up with the men's squabbles, Laura turned to Nancy. "How about a stroll along the shore to get our land legs back?"

Nancy agreed, and they walked off side by side. Their khaki pants swished against scrubby bush branches and neither spoke for some time.

Finally Laura said, "Gilbert's a very disagreeable man, but perhaps we shouldn't be so unfriendly toward him."

"Perhaps."

So much for breaking the ice, Laura thought. "Isn't that a berry bush?" she asked, trying another tack. "I forget what they call them. A Norwegian relative used to serve them at Christmas time."

"Lingonberries, I think," Nancy said somewhat absentmindedly. "Some are still in flower."

"I'm surprised they grow here, but it's the right latitude," Laura said.

They continued walking close to shore and rounded a bend where the breeze ruffled the water. The opportunity to remove their head nets was a blessing and although a few mosquitoes persisted, the breeze rid them of most of the tormenting insects.

"It's heavenly not to wear this damn thing." Nancy glared at her head net.

"But a godsend when we need it," Laura said. "Can you imagine the early explorers? You could literally go mad from blackflies."

For a time the two women stood, silently drinking in the graying of the early evening. Again it was Laura who broke the silence. "I understand why the men came on this trip, and Deirdre had this bee in her bonnet about learning about Cal's past, but I don't understand why you've come along. You don't seem the outdoorsy type. Is it to be with Phil?"

"We're just friends."

"I didn't mean to pry."

Nancy's smile seemed to say, yes you did. "Let's be friends. Neither of us needs extra hassle." She picked up a rounded rock, then stared out across the Thelon. "I'm an English professor who's involved in an environmental movement. I care about what happens to the land, the destruction man brings upon the innocent earth, and I care about the corruption of governments that assuage big business in its mindset of growth at all costs. I want to make a difference." Nancy turned and faced Laura. "Don't you?"

Shocked by the abruptness of the question, Laura stammered, "Of course...I...ah...was appalled at how Henri let his place become a dump."

"It's not just the Henris of this world, it's people like us who don't say anything, who watch silently and allow men like him to continue their destruction." The passion and fierceness exploded from Nancy, wiping away her tired mask. "Henri believes this wilderness is his territory. Too many people believe the land belongs to them to do with it what they want. That's not true. The earth does not belong to us. We belong to it, and until we realize this, we will doom earth and ourselves."

Nancy's chest rose and fell rapidly. As if shaking herself from a trance, she smiled at Laura. "Be careful what you ask. I'm passionate about the environment."

"So you came here to view the wild or to do something about it?"

"Let's walk back, shall we?" Nancy took Laura's arm. "If there's something to be done here, I'll do it, but we don't know that yet, do we?"

Despite Nancy's double talk, there was something haunting behind her words. The woman remained a mystery, now more than before.

Chapter 21

Boris gazed at the sickle moon as it rode low across the horizon of the gray Arctic night. Reluctant to crawl into the tent he shared with Phil, he'd stayed by the shore after dinner. Under siege from blackflies and mosquitoes, conversation during the meal of chili and canned peaches had been brief. It dealt mostly with tomorrow's logistics, although he attributed the real reason for the sour mood of the camp to Gilbert and Henri's presence.

He'd tried to converse with Laura about the day, but she'd only smiled wistfully and appeared distracted. Perhaps she was tired, for her attitude conveyed no other message. Even though she'd agreed to marry him in the nebulous future, something told him it might never happen. Was she still in love with Phil? The question burned in his gut.

He squatted, balancing on the balls of his feet and dipped his hands into the river to scoop a brimful of cold water to his face. Day-old whiskers scrubbed his palms. Water dripped from his chin as he stared at the river with his forearms resting on his thighs. He thought of Phil's plans and about his belief that Henri was not guiltless in Erich's death. If Phil was correct, the danger was worse than Boris had originally thought. He surveyed the steel-blue river and sighed heavily.

"Even the wolves across the river hear you." Henri's voice came from behind him.

Boris half-turned and, in one fluid motion, stood and rubbed his wet hands on the sides of his pants. "It's been a long day." He peered at Henri in the fading light. "You and Erich must have had many days like today, paddling, hunting, talking." Boris paused and rubbed his chin as if deliberating about the past. "Erich was always a staunch ally, strong, ethical."

Henri approached Boris and nodded, but offered no words.

"It must have been difficult for you when he died."

"Oui."

"You miss him?"

"But of course. Most...I miss his harmonica playing."

Boris gave a noncommittal grunt. "Guess he picked that up after I knew him."

"We beat, how you say, around a bush," Henri said. "Do you want to know about Erich or about me?"

"Can I learn about one without the other?"

Henri cocked his head to one side and eyed Boris. "You interest me. You say you're Erich's friend, but you never wrote him, never saw him from the time you leave here."

This short, square man might not be an academician, but he was wily as the wolves he trapped. "A life-threatening event develops a strong bond," Boris said.

Henri scratched the side of his bearded face. "The old helicopter crash site has meaning for you, no? You want to visit the place?"

Boris stuck his hands in his pockets and thought a moment about Henri's not so innocent question. Did Henri know where they'd crashed in '78? "I'm not sure exactly where the crash site is. That was some time ago. Did Erich tell you?"

"No, but big mouth Gilbert might know. He's one big talker." He gave a low throaty snarl. "Bah, a no good one." He spit.

"Gilbert's a piece of work, all right." Boris toyed with a stone with the toe of his boot. "Now, take Erich. I don't remember him being much of a talker. Still and all, you two spent a lot of years together. Must have been times when he reminisced."

The little Frenchman pursed his lips. "The past...." He shrugged. "Not so important to us." Henri chose a large boulder to sit on. "Erich's crazy idea, you know, the Russian spy satellite...always the extra gear and his silly lead box." Henri paused, then asked, "Do you think you find it?"

"Find it? What do you mean?" Boris looked down at Henri's relaxed body.

"I'm no fool, *monsieur.*" Henri's hands cupped his knees, and his squinty eyes searched Boris's face. "You may hunt for more, but uranium is the *it.*"

"The Mounties don't believe there's anything to find. That should be good enough."

Henri chuckled and shook his head. "Is it?"

Boris sat on the gravel a mere three feet from Henri, but he faced the river and not his opponent. It was an interesting cat and mouse game, but who was the cat and who was the mouse? "What happened to Erich's lead box?"

Henri shrugged. "At the bottom of the river. I towed Erich's canoe against the river flow. Extra stuff, I toss."

"Must have been tough hauling him and his stuff. How long did it take?"

"One day led to another." Henri rocked back and forth on the rock. "A few days can seem like many, and many can seem like few."

"You okay now? Radiation burns can make you darn sick. How do you think you got them?" Out of the corner of his eye he watched Henri's reaction.

"Erich and I trekked many places." Henri laced gravel through his rough hands. "That crash in '78—spring, no? Gilbert said you brought back a body, an old prospector someone had shot. He mined for gold and diamonds, like De Beers now."

Boris paused before replying. He might have to give a little info to gain some. "We were downy-faced boys back in then. Erich was the oldest, the Canadian sergeant, our leader. Unlike Erich, we were untrained in the wilderness. We were technicians brought in for the cleanup job. Pilot of the chopper was killed, radio out, weather set in. Damn cold even in April." Boris glanced at Henri. "'Course, you know all about the weather here, but we didn't. Our supplies were in the drink along with the chopper. We hiked along the river, thinking our guys would spot us from the air. Before we were found and hauled out, we came across the old miner, half-buried. When we were rescued, we brought out the body."

"You tell a dull story. Most men make big to-do about such a thing. Talk on and on. Erich didn't."

"Maybe the experience wasn't any more memorable to him than it was to me."

Henri dropped the pebbles and dusted off his hands. "How did you know the man was a prospector?"

"We didn't. Headquarters told us later." *Little man, you interest me. Why do you want to know about a dead prospector? And how did you know he was shot? The newspapers reported he sustained a crushing wound to the head.* "I didn't realize it was common knowledge that the miner was shot."

"People talk."

"You've been hunting wolves for a long time in these parts?"

Henri nodded. "Before '78. This land," he motioned out across the river, "is my home since I got tossed out on my own. I learned from hardship; I learned from the wolves. No man taught me what I know; no book teach what I know. It's here." He pointed to his heart and then his head. "This land and me, we are one." He put his stubby hands together as if in prayer. "No one take it from me; no one know its secrets like me and no one gonna take from this land what belongs to it."

"You take wolves from the land."

"No, *mon ami*, you're wrong. The wolves give themselves to me, so I live. They kill the caribou, so they live. I live with nature. I don't desecrate the land."

You're a frigging liar. "Are you sure you're seeing yourself clearly? What I saw at Lake Damant didn't impress me that you cared for the land."

Henri's eyes narrowed as he brushed the back of his hand across his cracked lips. "Housekeeping is woman's work." He rose from the boulder. "I think you and your friends are here to cause trouble for my land. No owner allows theft."

Boris remained seated, stared across the Thelon, refusing to look at Henri. He remembered a saying his Iowa family had, when you deal with a high-strung animal, you've got to leave him a way out. "The thieving's being done by everyone who ever set foot here. Each has taken something even if it's a picture. Grant and people like him promote the place, and more will come to see the beauty. That's what Gilbert's supposed to do. Write how beautiful the area is. That's what Erich did when he wrote his notes. You can't stop it, Henri. No one can. You can...." Boris heard the crunch of gravel, turned and saw Henri's retreating figure.

He continued to sit by the river, thinking about what had been said, and more to the point, what hadn't been said. He rose and walked back into the meadow where the tents stood in a jagged indiscriminate formation. No one else seemed to be up, but a light came from Laura's tent. He hesitated, then strode up to the zippered flap, crouched and softly called her name.

"Boris? Is anything wrong?" she asked.

"No." He felt foolish, kneeling there like a besotted lover. "Just taking in the evening air. A few more nights and it'll be dark enough to see the aurora borealis." The rustling of the sleeping bag told him she'd moved toward him. He caught a glimpse of her sitting with a book in her hand and a sweater wrapped about her shoulders as her flashlight beam lit the tent's interior.

"I couldn't suffer the insects any longer," she said. "Up until a while ago, they were bumping against the outside of the tent. How can you stand them?"

"They weren't bad down by the river with the breeze along the shore. Don't let them ruin your trip. Try a different mindset. Concentrate on other things, like you do when you meditate." Through the tent mesh, her sweet breath brushed over him. "Now that the air has cooled, the insects have settled."

"Wait a minute. I'll get dressed and walk down to the river with you."

He stood and soon she crawled out of her tent and zipped it closed. Looking up at the sky, she drew her fingers through her hair, ruffling it. "I can make out a star or two." She stretched and breathed deeply. "The air is crisp and fresh, but there's not even a scent from the scrub pines."

"Hadn't noticed, but you're right." They walked side by side down to the river. "With darker nights, we'll be able to see more stars." When she was about to sit on the same boulder Henri had used earlier, he took her arm and guided her farther upstream where the land angled steeply toward the water. There they sat together on the hard cold gravel. With the calm night, the silent moving river and Laura at his side, Boris felt at ease despite his worries about Henri. Far away the muted call of a wolf echoed across the river.

"I wonder if we'll see wolves tomorrow," Laura said.

"Henri mentioned a wolf, but I thought he meant it metaphorically." He laughed. "That'd be way too esoteric for him."

Laura ran her tongue across her lips and shook her head. "I don't like him."

"He's a loner. Wonder how Erich put up with him? The talk in town was they fought all the time."

"You were all very fond of Erich."

"He kept us from freaking out when we got lost."

"If Erich was such an upstanding fellow, he and Henri must have been an odd couple."

Boris felt her eyes studying his face. "That's for sure."

She continued, "Henri's only part of the reason I feel uncomfortable."

"I know his rifle rattled you, but—"

"It's not that. The trip has a peculiar vibe, a mysterious undercurrent." She linked her hands around his arm. "I need to talk to you about what's going on. Am I the only one who's not in on some secret?"

He wanted to take her in his arms and comfort her, but how could he explain, when their plans had to be secret? If they found the diamond lode, then what? "It's Gilbert and Henri," he said, patting her hand. "They've got everyone upset. There isn't going to be any uranium find. We all know that. They're troublemakers."

"Nancy believes there might be uranium. At least I think that's what she thinks."

"I thought she came along to be with Phil."

She shook her head. "I did too, but now I'm not so sure. She's involved with an environmental group and she's passionate about the land. She plans to do…something."

He could hear her frustration and felt the imperceptible droop of her shoulders. "Nancy seems nice enough, although a little high strung." Boris bit his lower lip, puzzled over Laura's observation about Nancy. "She's not the outdoor type, is she?"

"That's just the point. She's here for a different reason. Could you talk to Phil about her?"

"I suppose. I'll see what he says, but I think she's here to be with him." Laura's chin rose, her eyes narrowed. *Damn. If Laura's jealous of Nancy, it can only mean she still cares for Phil.*

They continued to sit quietly together, but Boris felt a small rift between them. She said, "Thanks for getting me out of my tent. I was really mopey."

"After a good night's sleep, we'll all see things differently." He hoped to mend whatever had upset her and put his arm around her shoulders.

"I'm glad you're here, Boris," she whispered.

Her drew her to him and kissed her. Afterward, she pulled away and rubbed her lips. "Those are some whiskers you've developed."

"Sorry."

"Boris, don't always say you're sorry. In a few days you'll have a soft beard to keep you warm, and I'll look like hell with a swollen face from sun exposure, and you'll wonder what you ever saw in me."

"Never!"

After leaving Laura at her tent, he walked around the camp perimeter as if he were back in the military. A faint odor of tobacco wafted from Nancy's darkened tent. Off in the distance, he heard deep angry voices. He moved forward, picking his way over the stunted spruce and clumps of fescue.

"You stick your nose in my business. I cut it off." Henri's voice curled with venom.

Gilbert's nasal twang was no less angry. "My paper sent me here to do a story. You can't interfere with the press."

"Stay out of my gear. I give you no second chance."

"You've got a radio transmitter. Does Grant know?"

"In the wilderness, a radio always good."

"Where was your radio when Erich died?"

Boris heard an animal-like growl and knew it must have come from Henri. "Beware what you say or you may not get back to write your story."

"Don't get upset. I didn't mean anything." Gilbert whined like a dog backing down from a fight.

"You talk too much. You think too much. Perhaps you saw too much," Henri said. "Watch out. The wilderness can be cruel."

Henri's shadowy stout figure walked off; Gilbert remained behind in the shadows. Soon Boris smelled the pungent odor of urine. He turned away and retreated through the camp and heard things he wished he hadn't.

"You insisted on coming," Cal's voice drifted into the night. "You said you could take it. There's no turning back now."

"It's the bugs," Deirdre whimpered. "They're awful. I only wanted to see what you'd been through. I thought this trip would be good for us."

Boris heard sniffling and quickly moved on. At his own tent, he crawled inside and found Phil reading Erich's journal by flashlight.

"You've been out on the town." Phil let the notebook fall into his lap.

Boris took off his boots and placed them outside the tent under the rain flap. "I heard Henri and Gilbert in a fierce argument," he said in a hushed voice. "Earlier, I had an interesting chat with Henri," he said as he removed his clothes. "He's keen to know about the prospector we found and knew he'd been shot."

"Interesting," Phil said, putting down the journal. "We knew that, but were told to say nothing."

"Yeah. It got me to thinking. Henri claimed he'd heard about it."

"That's possible."

"I'm not sure Henri knows the site of our helicopter crash." Boris looked at Erich's journal. "I didn't have much time to read that. Did Erich mark where we found the prospector?" He squirmed into his sleeping bag, stretched out with a comfortable groan and laced his hands behind his head.

"Yes." Phil swung the beam of his flashlight onto the journal. "About five kilometers north of the first eastern tributary after Eyeberry Lake. He also gives the coordinates of our crash, but you know those."

"Gilbert might know those coordinates, too. I wish I knew if Henri knows." Boris turned to gaze at Phil.

"Henri knows the land and doesn't need Erich's coordinates." Phil put the journal down between them, laid back and clicked off the light. "Henri knows where Erich died, and it wasn't at Helen Falls. If he knows where we crashed in '78, then he's got a good idea about the places we want to search."

"He mentioned Erich had a lead box," Boris said. "That might be significant?"

"I hadn't heard about that."

"Henri claims he ditched it in the river." Boris was silent for a moment, then continued. "He doesn't seem like the kind of guy who would toss away something of value."

"Hell," Phil said, "he tossed all kinds of things away around his cabin."

"Right, but they weren't of value. If we find anything, Henri will try to prevent us from taking it out, even if it's information." Boris couldn't see how to avoid the dangers of the trip. "We'll have to think about the women. Laura and Deirdre are here for pleasure. What about Nancy?"

Phil didn't answer. Boris heard him breathing, but knew he wasn't asleep. "She told Laura she's with an environmental group. It sounded to Laura like Nancy was up to something."

"Nancy wants what Erich wanted—the uranium debris. Only she wants to let the world know it's deadly. Blame the Canadian and U.S. governments for hiding their ineptitude over the cleanup. She'll use Gilbert's news story to get a scandal brewing that'll throw the public into a tizzy and probably make the area politically dangerous to allow mining of any kind."

Boris heard the hard edge to Phil's voice, but he recognized something else in Phil's tone. "You care for her, don't you?"

"Of course." Phil rolled over and pounded his jacket with his fist as if to make himself comfortable. "Hell, I've been a friend of hers for a couple of years, but damn it, she goes off on these toots instead of sticking to being an English professor. Her forays into skullduggery drive me nuts."

Boris smiled to himself, pleased at what he'd just learned. "Women do that."

"Do what?" Phil asked in a crabby voice.

"Drive us nuts."

"Oh, shut up."

After a moment Boris asked, "What do we do about Henri?"

"Watch him like a hawk and try to stay a step ahead of him."

"That won't be easy. He knows where Erich died and we don't."

"Exactly. Wherever he doesn't want us to go, we go and…" there was a long pause, "we search every area I've marked on our maps. We know the last place Erich found showed geological signs of the possible existence of diamonds."

"Seems like a thin plan," Boris said.

"You got a better one?"

"Let's attack rather than react," Boris said. "Shake Henri's composure. Push on every point, the lead box, Erich's death, the time it took Henri to paddle back, all the discrepancies in his story. I did a little foray into that already tonight."

"We might even question him on how he knew the miner was shot." Phil's breathing quickened. "I asked him about Erich's notes, but you're right. We'll show Grant exactly where we want to stop. That should goad Henri."

Chapter 22

The following day a light breeze scuffed the river as the canoes moved through blue water. While paddling, Grant reflected on how each year his tours became more difficult, yet this one surpassed the others. Last season Karen had suggested he stop guiding, but her teacher's pay wouldn't support them and besides, he was too young. What else could he do? Teach? He'd go crazy. Like Henri he thrived in the wilderness. Grant's knuckles whitened as he gripped his paddle tighter. This tour could have paid off the loan on his equipment, but the repairs to the damaged canoe, plus the cost of Chip's second flight, made this trip a break-even proposition. But it was more than the expenses that bothered him. Something was amiss with this group. Clients usually followed his lead without question, but these men had their own agenda and a fondness for secrecy. Phil had lied to him, but why and for what purpose?

Sure, Gilbert's presence grated. Whenever the man entered a discussion, a palpable chill descended. Had he made a mistake including him? It had been his prerogative to take Gilbert. His articles might help save the Thelon area from exploitation.

As for the others, what harm was there in their reenactment of Erich's journey? Still, he understood that Cosmos 954 was uppermost in their minds. Did they really believe there were pieces of uranium in the area? Last year the doctor's diagnosis that Henri's blisters could have been caused by radiation exposure had riled the press and the local populace, but since then things had calmed down.

Henri's addition might be an asset. Despite the women's negative reaction to the Frenchman, Henri could help mark Erich's trail. Grant decided if Phil's route changes were within reason, he'd agree.

Focus on the people, Grant told himself. Deirdre was most affected by the pestering blackflies and mosquitoes and today, due to the lack of wind, the insects swirled unmercifully. To Grant, a still wind, calm waters and a bright sky created a mystical union on the Thelon. Looking back on the trailing canoes, he noted with satisfaction the group's steady pace. He dipped one hand into the cool river and splashed his face, letting the droplets trace down his cheeks. He studied Nancy, who paddled in the bow of his canoe. For a first time paddler, she learned quickly and even though she wasn't the outdoor type, she had a good attitude.

Pristine water gurgled into bubbles as he thrust his paddle down and through the river's blue water. As he stroked, he watched the water ahead and reflected on the other women. Deirdre appeared competent, yet behind her smile dwelt a hidden sorrow and a certain selfishness. Laura was the type of woman he was accustomed to seeing on his trips, outdoorsy, strong-willed, a team player with a sense of humor. Yet, she saw everything through the narrow lens of her camera and missed the overall oneness of the wilderness. He heard the swish of another canoe approaching and turned to see Karen.

"We need a rest stop," she reminded him.

He sighed. "Already?" He caught the glint in her light blue eyes. "Right. Niceties will be observed. A pit stop coming up."

Heading into a gravel bar jutting out from an esker, he stood in his canoe, pondering the landing and looking for wildlife signs. Nancy stopped paddling and looked back at him with a frown. Standing, Grant stirred his paddle in the shallows, moving his craft forward. When the bow grounded, he nursed the canoe sideways to the shore and stepped onto dry sand, then held the canoe steady for Nancy to climb out. He watched as the other canoes docked bow first, forcing them to wade in shallow water. Only Henri and Karen followed his docking ritual. Grant said nothing, believing people should learn from observation.

"Girls to the left, boys to the right," Karen called out after all the canoes were beached. She looked at Grant and added, "Ten minutes."

When people returned, Karen passed out dried fruit and trail mix, and while everyone milled about nibbling on the morsels, Grant strode inland through the brush and up a small knoll. He returned a short time later shaking his head. "A few caribou tracks, two or three days old. I don't expect to meet the main herd for at least a week, but we'll be seeing stray calves and lone males."

"What happens to the strays?" Nancy asked.

"Once the young get separated from their mothers, they die from star-vation if the wolves don't get them first. A female caribou won't accept a calf that isn't hers." Grant glanced at Henri, who sat on the beach oblivious to the blackflies and mosquitoes. "See anything I haven't?"

Henri shook his shaggy head. "Not even trout or pike. Up ahead may-be moose."

"Good thought." Grant hesitated, then abruptly said, "Maybe you'd like to come along for the entire trip. You're not trapping now anyway."

Henri rose and stretched. "You pay?"

"We can talk about it." Grant ignored the women's scowls, thinking if he could call off a second flight by Chip, he might make a profit after all even with a small payment to Henri. "We'd better get going." Grant wiped his hands on his khaki trousers. "Everyone ready?"

"Might as well." Deirdre picked up her jacket she'd tossed on a nearby rock. She'd applied lipstick during the break, and her red lips seemed out of place. As she strolled by Grant, she said, "At least out on the river, the blackflies aren't as bad."

"You get used to it," Karen said, as she readied to push off with Cal already in its bow.

Phil held his paddle in one hand and pulled the canoe sideways to shore. "I'll take the stern for a while if you don't mind," he said to Deirdre.

"I don't care at this point." She walked to the bow.

"Hey, Deirdre," Laura called out from her canoe. "Where's your sense of adventure? You can handle this stuff. Costa Rica had mosquitoes, remember."

"Do I." Deirdre called back. "And heat, but not these damn blackflies."

Phil waited for Deirdre to settle in her seat, then pushed off, sat and dug his paddle into the sandy bottom, allowing the canoe to sideslip into deeper water.

The flotilla paddled until they spied a moose, munching sedge grass in the shoals on the left bank. The big bull ignored them as they paddled to within thirty feet. When they edged closer, he lifted his immense head. Greenish-brown plants dangled from his massive jaw. The sun sparkled from the drizzle of water dripping from the animal's muzzle onto the dark blue river.

Laura twisted her telephoto into the bayonet mount and clicked off several shots.

Boris half-turned to her. "You're going to have incredible pictures." He maneuvered the canoe with a cross draw from the bow so she could get the best angle.

"Can we get closer?" Her eye remained glued to the viewfinder.

When Boris paddled to within ten feet of the bull, the animal's eyes rolled, showing white. The moose turned and with an awkward jarring gait lumbered to shore and into the vegetation beyond.

Like a tour bus seeking its next site, the canoes headed back into the main current. Near noon Grant pulled into a landing, choosing a rocky point. After hauling their canoes out of the water, they convened around Karen, who laid out different cheese and meat spreads, bread, crackers, nuts and dried fruit.

"There's a wolf den around the next bend," Grant said as he opened a can of sardines and lanced a piece with a fork. "After lunch, we'll land and hike to it."

As they stood eating and facing what little breeze blew off the river, Cal quipped, "We're like horses with our heads into the wind." He raised his head net, took a bite, then replaced it while he chewed.

"I've given up picking the buggers out of my food." Boris stood next to Cal. "Hell, I just eat the damn things."

Phil shook his head. "I don't mind eating the blackflies, but the mosquitoes' long legs get to me."

"Ugh!" Deirdre said. "You're all disgusting."

"That kind of meat I can do without." Nancy said from her perch on a large rock.

Laura went closer to the water, leaned down and scooped something up with her hand. "What's this stuff floating at the shore? Feels like straw. I've noticed more of it as we've paddled."

"Caribou fur." Henri squatted on his heels away from the group. "From herds crossing up north." He motioned with his hand.

Nancy joined Laura and knelt to inspect the fur. "Do the caribou have to find shallow places to cross?"

Henri shook his head. "Caribou swim good."

"Their coats give them buoyancy, and their hooves are broad and hollow," Karen said. "Makes it easy for them to swim."

"You'll see them soon enough," Grant promised. "It's an amazing sight—heads held high, backs and shoulders out of the water, and stubby white tails standing straight up."

"Easy to shoot," Henri said. "Right through their back." He held out his arms as if he held a rifle. "Hit spinal cord. Pow."

"You're revolting." Laura turned her back on him.

Henri wiped his mouth with the back of his hand and rose. "How you think Inuits did it? Caribou mean life. Only they killed with short lances. Much harder."

Grant watched the group eye Henri with disdain. Truth is not what people want to hear, he thought.

After a miserable lunch fighting insects, they eagerly launched the canoes. At the next landfall, they pulled down their head nets and hurried after Grant to the wolf den.

While tramping up a sandy draw, Nancy paused and pointed to the brow of a hill on her right. "What's that up there?"

Everyone stopped and stared where she pointed.

"Good eye," Grant said. "It's a stone cairn piled to look like a man."

"Inuksuit," Henri said, squinting into the sun.

Grant nodded. "That's the native's word. It means, resembling a person." He pointed to another on the opposing hill. "In the old days the natives used the figures to scare the caribou herd into believing enemies were on both ridges. It helped them drive the herds through the gap."

"Amazing." Nancy's eyes kindled with excitement. "We're truly in the land of the past."

Standing behind Nancy, Boris said, "I thought the vastness drove men crazy, so that's why they erected those cairns. They made them feel less alone."

"Maybe." Henri stood apart from the others. "For me, I like the, how do you say...?" He groped for the word, "vastness. Cairns show distance."

Grant shrugged. "There are many different ideas about their uses. We'll be seeing more."

Single file they followed behind Henri and Grant. Soon the brush thinned and they spotted the wolf den on a small sandy mound. Grant cupped his hands to his mouth and let out one piercing howl after another. A wolf's far off response howled eerily through the tundra.

Grant motioned for them to wait as he and Henri circled the area. When they returned, Grant said, "Site's abandoned. Last year they were here." He turned to Henri, who stood to one side. "Any idea what happened?"

Henri folded his arms across his chest and pursed his lips. "Wolves follow the caribou. The alpha male smart, big. Never catch him. He stay inside Sanctuary."

After they returned to the canoes, Grant pulled out his map, and Phil moved next to him. "I've been wanting to talk to you about the route," he said.

"I know." Grant pointed out their location on the map as the others looked on. "Right now, I have another immediate concern. There's a rapid ahead, class II. We'll pull in before we get to it, climb a ridge and scout before we run it." He glanced at the sky. "Better get going. Weather's coming in."

"How can you tell?" Cal peered at the cloudless sky.

"You smell it," Henri said and headed toward his canoe.

"He's joking, right?" Cal said to Grant and glanced at Karen.

"The only thing I smell is Henri," Gilbert said with a guarded laugh and followed Henri to the canoe.

"Some talk from a guy who stinks of cigar smoke," Deirdre muttered.

Back on the river, they soon heard the roar of rapids. Pulling into the bank, they climbed a conglomerate and granite outcrop and peered down at their first set of rapids. Beyond the curling foam, the sinuous river ran seamlessly. All but Henri crowded around Grant as he pointed out how they would run the rapids.

"See that V and the rock to the right? Stay to the left of the rock, then cut hard to the right. That should set you up to shoot through the next V." He glanced from one person to the next, trying to read their reaction. "I'll go first, Karen second." He nodded to Laura and then Phil. "Henri last. Don't get too close to the canoe in front of you. Got it?"

After a murmur of assent, they descended to the canoes.

"How do you feel about my paddling stern through this rapid?" Phil asked Deirdre.

"If you take this one, I take the next one," she said, tucking her shirt neatly inside her belt.

"Deal," he said with a steady gaze.

As each canoe moved into the river, the interval between them grew. Grant's canoe hit the churning water and maneuvered through the chop, shot through the V, made a turn after the rock and hit the next V in the middle. After the rapids, he turned his canoe sideways in an eddy to watch each canoe come through the narrow gap. He could always tell a great deal about people and their abilities after the first test.

Grant watched Cal's posture and face as Karen adroitly paddled through the rapids, and then drew next to them in the eddy. A boyish grin spread across Cal's tan features.

Boris and Laura were next. She had trouble getting the nose of the canoe around after the rock, but Boris helped with a firm draw stroke, and they slid into the next V in perfect style. When they arrived at the eddy, they were laughing. "You saved us," Laura said. "We would have rammed the next rock if you hadn't pulled the bow around."

"Great fun, wasn't it?" He had a twinkle in his eyes.

"You made it look easy," Cal said. "Think I'd like to learn how to paddle in the stern. Maybe paddle with Deirdre for a while first." He looked up. "Here comes they."

Although Phil had the canoe on line, Deirdre attempted a draw anyway, sending the canoe's bow too far around. Phil desperately used a pry stroke to right them, but Deirdre had pulled her paddle too close to the gunwale, got her blade stuck up against a submerged rock and under the hull and the canoe tipped, spilling them into the river.

"Oh God," Cal yelled and started to stand.

Karen shouted, "Sit down! Don't worry. We'll come alongside and let her hang onto our gunwale. She'll be all right."

Although Phil had a grasp of the stern of the overturned canoe, Grant and Nancy paddled out into the river to help him tow the canoe to shore. Laura and Boris picked up Deirdre's paddle, while Karen and Cal pulled alongside of Deirdre, so she could grab hold of their gunwale.

As they pulled into shore, Deirdre staggered to her feet. "God damn it!" She stood shaking, her eyes wide. Her well-manicured nails glistened in the sunlight as she pulled wet strands of tangled hair from her face. "Did you see that oaf?" She strode out of the water, her features twisted in anger. "He tipped us." She pointed at Phil. "You're a lousy stern paddler," she yelled at him as Grant and Nancy towed him and the canoe ashore.

Phil stood in the shallows with water dripping from his clothes. For a moment he stared in bewilderment at Deirdre, then turned away and righted the canoe, spilling out the water.

Henri's canoe arrived and Gilbert unable to hide his glee, said, "A bit of a mishap, I see."

Deirdre whirled on him, her face bright red, "Mishap my foot. Phil's incompetent," she screamed, focusing on Phil. "I'm not paddling with you." She stood with her feet planted wide apart, her eyes daring anyone to disagree with her.

Ignoring Deirdre's outbursts, the rest of the party went about helping. While Cal went to comfort his wife, Laura moved toward Phil. "It was her fault, but she's embarrassed. Don't be upset with her."

Phil grimaced. "She makes it difficult to be pleasant to her."

As if torn between loyalties, Laura hesitated, then hurried to Deirdre. "Come on, it's not that bad. You'll be the only two clean people. We'll get you into some dry clothes."

"It didn't happen to you." Deirdre sputtered, as she twisted her hair to wring it out.

"It could have if Boris hadn't been such a good paddler."

"See." Momentarily, she brightened. "Phil's stupid." Deirdre glared at Phil who continued to work on the canoe and its cargo. "I don't know where my bag is." Deirdre wailed and waved at the blackflies surrounding her exposed face.

Cal tried to put his arm around her, but she shrugged it off. He stood helplessly with a foolish expression of confusion, then turned away. "I'll find your bag." He sorted through the gear and pulled out Deirdre's day pack. Laura and Karen walked up the rocky slope with her, looking for a place for her to change.

Grant inspected the gravel bar where the canoes were strewn as haphazardly as match sticks. They had to move on. Deirdre's reaction to her own mistake disturbed him. He couldn't allow one woman's hysteria to undermine the trip. He kicked at a rock by his foot, then approached Phil who had stripped off his shirt, put his vest back on and donned his windbreaker. "Going to change your pants?" Grant asked.

Phil looked at his sodden khakis. "It's not cold. They'll dry quick enough if we get moving."

Grant patted him on the shoulder. "Good man. You kept your cool." He nodded in Deirdre's direction. "Too bad she didn't."

Phil shrugged and cocked his head as if assessing Grant's words. "We've just started, but I've been worried about her from the start."

"I heard that." Cal rose from where he'd been kneeling by his pack. "She's doing fine considering this godforsaken country. This'll probably be a wild goose chase. I don't need the money. You can take the d—"

"Shut up!" Boris's broad face hardened as he clasped Cal's arm. "We're all in this together. No need to get excited. A capsize here and there isn't so bad." He glanced at Grant, then turned back to Cal. "We'll talk about this later, right?"

Cal reddened. "Right." He shrugged out of Boris's grip and turned toward Phil and Grant. "Lay off Deirdre."

Grant stared at Cal, then looked at Phil. What had Cal meant about money and what was he about to say when Boris interrupted?

Deirdre came down the slope with her chin held high, her wet clothes slung over one arm, and joined her husband by the packs. The group moved in quiet hesitation, fussing with this or that, avoiding eye contact with the Sterlings.

Grant surveyed the scene and asked, "Ready to push on?"

"I will not paddle with him." Deirdre directed a smoldering stare at Phil. "The least you can do is apologize."

"Deirdre, you aren't hurt," Laura said. "It was an accident. It wasn't Phil's fault. Look at the funny side."

"Fun for all of you to laugh at me. Don't take your old boyfriend's side." Deirdre's eyes danced with anger.

Grant noticed Karen motioning to him, and he took her cue.

"Deirdre, perhaps you'd paddle with me for a while. Nancy can paddle with Phil."

Nancy nodded. "Sure." She walked up to Phil and patted him on the arm. "I haven't had my bath today, but I'd like to wait until after dinner."

"You're on." Phil bowed low in mock obedience and escorted her to the bow.

The group remained quiet as the crafts spread out across the river. For a while Grant watched as Deirdre stroked at a defiant pace. Finally he said, "I like to keep the group together. You're a strong paddler. Slow down so the others can catch up." She didn't answer, but slowed her stroke.

When they stopped for the night, they carted the canoes above the high water mark, sponged the interiors clean and set up their tents. An uncomfortable aura hovered over the camp. They talked in hushed tones as they ate dinner and headed to bed early. The group was now divided and functioning as a unit would be difficult.

Chapter 23

A cold misty rain set in before dawn. The river took on a gloomy fuscous color with rivulets dribbling down the hulls of the overturned canoes. Low clouds obscured hills that only yesterday could be seen rolling into infinite space.

With his rain hat shielding his brow, Phil hunched low, gripped his plastic coffee mug and watched the steam rise. In the gray morning, his plans seemed absurd. Yesterday's event made him wonder if they'd ever find Erich's trove of uranium pieces or the source of the old prospector's diamonds.

Deirdre's unwarranted temper tantrum and Cal's big mouth could have upset the entire endeavor. Even his feelings toward Laura were scattered like autumn leaves, and the feeling of impending doom hung heavy on his mind.

He gazed at Nancy, crouched, spooning oatmeal into a plastic bowl. Her tousled hair made her look younger. She'd surprised him with her humor and spunk. Now her brown eyes skewered him, and a mischievous, quirky smile played on her lips. He looked away and studied the outlines of the tents.

"Good mornings" were spoken grudgingly as they gathered near the makeshift kitchen of a tarpaulin lean-to, strung between scrawny trees and anchored at the back by two paddles.

Phil waited impatiently until Grant finished pouring his coffee. "I'd like to show you spots we'd like to visit—places Erich wrote about in his journal."

Grant took a sip of his brew, rose and balanced his cup on a nearby rock. "Sorry we couldn't have gotten to it earlier. Let's have a look." He walked under the tarpaulin and pulled out his map. Phil, Cal and Boris crowded around while the others watched from a distance.

Henri lowered his coffee mug from his lips and peered out from under his battered canvas hat. "Ask me," he said, moving closer. "I know where Erich went."

"You're staying?" Phil asked.

Grant looked up. "I'm contacting Chip this morning before we leave to tell him we won't need the other canoe. Weather's not too good for transmitting, but I should be able to get through from that knoll." He pointed above the tents.

"Henri," Boris said. "Let us know if we've chosen the right places."

Henri stuck his head between Phil and Grant's shoulders and stared at the map, while Phil pointed out various locations.

"I don't have any trouble with your choices," Grant said. "They're on the route I'd planned, except this one." He marked a spot up a side tributary. "It's not too far, but it's out of the way and out of the Sanctuary. If we camp here," he pointed to the far end of Eyeberry Lake, "you can take a side journey of an hour or two up to that point, look around and return the same day." He glanced at Henri. "There are wolf dens there. Might get a good sighting."

"Wolves gone," Henri said. "I told you last year."

"They must have returned," Grant said. "When I scouted this spring, I saw tracks of a large pack. Must have had a good litter."

Henri shrugged. "Maybe. I was stuck in Fort Smith." His eyes narrowed as he focused on something in the distance.

Grant scrutinized Henri. "It's outside the Sanctuary, so I know you can trap there. If we reconnoiter and find a pack, will you promise you won't trap there this year?"

"That's much to ask." Henri shifted his gaze to Grant and hesitated, stroking his grizzled chin. "*Oui*. Agreed."

"Are these places where you and Erich stopped?" Boris asked Henri as he indicated the notations on Phil's map.

Henri gripped one side of the map with his thick dark hand. The Frenchman's index finger with its bitten nails traced the river and stopped at each mark. "Bah! I know the terrain. Maps not necessary. This place up the tributary too far. No good. You make mistake. Other places. I show you." He shoved the map at Phil. "I always know where I am."

Phil smoothed out his map. "How long will it take to paddle to the tributary?" he asked Grant.

"Four days at the rate we paddled yesterday," Grant said. "Longer, if we stop more often. Depends on the weather when we cross Lake Eyeberry. The crossing can be tricky." He turned briefly to stare at Deirdre, who sat hunched over, staring at the ground, away from the others. "We all have to do our share. No slackers."

"I'll paddle with Deirdre," Cal said. "We'll keep up. You'll see."

A flush swept across Grant's usually passive face. "We'll see how the two of you manage. You can paddle together today."

"Well, thanks a lot, chief." Cal stormed off toward Deirdre.

Boris said, "Cal's a bit edgy, but he'll calm down."

Phil nodded with a frown. "Hope so," he said and turned to Grant. "Then we agree on the route?"

Grant folded his map and inserted it back into a thick plastic cover. "As long as we keep to a reasonable schedule, I have no objections. Ursus Island is our first good spot for Chip to pick us up after the portage, although we can paddle farther."

"Speaking of schedules." Karen looked at her watch. "I'm about finished packing up the food."

"Give me a minute to show our route and stopping places to the others," Phil said, beckoning the others to gather. Henri skulked down to his canoe, while Grant retrieved his radio and hiked to the top of the rise.

Nancy jotted the locations with a red pen on her map. As she turned to leave, she brushed up next to Phil. "Interesting locations. Have you been holding out on me?"

"You know as much as I do. My interests and yours are the same."

Gilbert moved next to them with a leer on his acne-marked face. "What're you two conspiring about?"

Nancy's dark eyes flashed. "What's it to you?"

He took a step back. "I was just trying to be friendly."

"That's what you always say," Nancy said. "If you want to get along on this trip, you might try to be less intrusive."

He recoiled like a snake before its final strike. "Careful, lady." His eyes narrowed. "You're in the wilderness, not Boston. Anything can happen out here."

"Is that a threat?" Nancy glared at him. "As a reporter, you should have researched the Cosmos and checked on the mining companies. Then maybe you'd know more than you seem to about what's happening to your Canadian wilderness. Isn't that what you're supposed to be writing about? The beauty that will be destroyed by mining interests?"

"My assignment's no affair of yours." He sniffed and brought out a well-used handkerchief to wipe raindrops from his face.

"You've made it our affair by your presence. So start acting pleasant, or have you got your head on your problems in Fort Smith?"

Gilbert's head jerked up, and he eyed Henri, who was only a few yards away. He turned back to Nancy and said in a hushed voice, "Maybe you and I should have a private talk."

Nancy's voice rose. "When we get back to Fort Smith, you might have to do a lot of talking but not to me." She faced him with her legs planted apart and her head net pushed high on her forehead, ignoring the flying insects. Her nostrils flared. Although she was shorter than Gilbert, he retreated when she stepped toward him.

"Okay." He put up his hands. "I'll stay out of your way, but remember we've got a long way to go, and enemies aren't good on a trip like this."

"We both know the reason you're my enemy," she said, but he had already turned his back and walked away. Only Phil and Henri caught her words.

Phil had wanted to intervene, but decided anything he said would only cause more trouble. Instead, he stuck his hands in his pockets and followed her to her tent. "Do you think that was wise?"

"I don't care." She refused to look at him and began to dismantle her tent. "If he killed Giraud, he doesn't deserve to be treated kindly, and if he didn't, then he should be doing his job, not making life miserable for everyone."

"If he killed Giraud, he's dangerous." He helped roll up her tent and stuff it in its bag.

Finally, she looked up at him with sparkles of tears edging her eyes. "What do you expect me to do? I can't avoid him. He's constantly in my face making insinuations. Thank God, he's paddling with Henri. They deserve one another." She dumped the tent bag next to her large duffel and stared in Gilbert's direction. "He really gets under my skin. Am I the only one?" She sighed and rested her head on his chest.

Phil put his arms awkwardly around her shoulders. "He's no prize, and you've got a reason to fear him." They stood together, neither speaking, and Phil found he didn't mind at all.

After a moment she pulled back. "The problem is, I can't picture him as a murderer. He's the type who'd use a gun, not hit someone. It just doesn't fit his...his slimy personality."

"He does seem weak and sniveling, but occasionally his claws come out." He gazed at her pensively. "But if not him, who?"

She moved away and fiddled with the tie on her duffle. "Maybe it's someone we don't even know. I keep running my mental tape of everything I saw and heard while I was in and around that house. Something's eluding me, but I don't know what." She brushed the hair out of her eyes and pulled it back into a ponytail, fastening it with a band. "Henri knows more than he's telling about the Cosmos debris. I can sense it."

"I'm not one to go against a woman's intuition," Phil said. "We're pushing him as hard as we can. If he gets angry, get out of the way. When it comes to anger, he's no lightweight. I heard he knocked his girlfriend around."

"Did she file charges?"

"I have no idea, but I doubt it."

Grant strode down off the hill with a deep frown. He called the group to gather around and announced, "I've canceled the rendezvous with Chip, but there's bad news. There was a murder in Fort Smith. Happened before we left." He looked at Henri. "At your house, Henri."

"Leah?" Henri asked, but his face showed nothing. A mask descended, and his eyes closed. "Is she okay?"

"Yes, she's fine. It was a man named Pierre Giraud. Know him?"

"No." Henri set his arms akimbo, and scowling. "Why was he in my house?"

"I don't know," Grant said. "When we get back, Sergeant Michael wants to talk to each of us."

"Ridiculous," Gilbert said. "None of us had anything to do with something that happened in Henri's house." He stared at Henri.

"Don't look at me. I was at my cabin." Henri turned his back on the group.

"Chip said Georgie flew you back recently," Phil said, before realizing the implication.

Henri stopped and swiveled around toward Phil. "Earlier in the month."

Phil shrugged. "I'm glad Leah's all right."

Henri averted his eyes. "Leah okay. That's important."

Without further discussion, the party prepared for the day. After some confusion about how and where the loads would be stowed, they pushed off. Since Deirdre and Cal insisted upon paddling together, Nancy paddled with Grant, and Phil took the bow in Karen's canoe.

Chapter 24

During the next few days, the weather continuously changed within the span of six hours from hot to cold. They sighted muskoxen far away on the hills in ones or twos. A molting merganser, unable to fly, paddled away from them. A fox dipped in and out of the blooming baked apple plants on an embankment. Patches of fireweed plants with their lilac flowers speared skyward, sunbathing in a last gasp before the onset of winter.

Early one morning they disturbed a grizzly fishing on the riverbank. He raised his head, snout high in the air. Although his beady eyes captured little but shapes, his sense of smell caught every nuance of the humans. His mighty jaw glistened with river water. Before Laura had a chance to bring her camera to her eye, the beast reared, whirled and slashed his way into the bush covering the bank. A collective gasp overrode the silence, and paddles froze in midair at the speed and size of the grizzly.

The canoes drifted with the river as they searched the landscape for more wildlife. Grant began to paddle, and the canoes moved on. The clouds evaporated, and the sun spun its golden web across the river.

The following day the Thelon flowed into Lake Eyeberry. The weather had changed overnight with strong gusty winds, grounding the blackflies and mosquitoes. They'd broken camp extra early, paddled for an hour and now huddled along a protected sandy spit of land to view the large lake. Clouds streamed past, rolling like spun cotton across the vast sky. The lake's shorelines faded into the distance.

"How far to the other side?" Phil asked.

"About four miles," Grant said. "We'll keep a mile out from the west shore. Much of it's marshland, so I don't want to get too close. With the wind coming from east to west, we could get stuck there. We'll camp another three miles beyond the far side of the lake."

Phil looked off to the east and pointed. "Looks like whitewater over there." He glanced down at his map and noted a river fed into the lake.

"The lake seems as wide as it is long," Boris said.

"Six, seven kilometers widest point," Henri offered. "Whitecaps always on lake. Water is devil in the wind."

It was Grant's call. By now the man had a good handle on the ability of the group. Each person had become physically stronger, but less communicative. Meals had been spent coping with insects, and tents had become welcome sanctuaries, leaving little time to bond or mend hurt feelings.

Grant surveyed the lake and sky as the group waited for him to decide. Henri nonchalantly leaned back in his bobbing canoe, while Gilbert paced nervously on the sandy shore, licking his lips.

"The wind will make waves, but we'll keep close together. No one lags behind." Grant stared at Deirdre and Cal.

There was a wordless acquiescence to the chore of the crossing. Phil got into the bow of Karen's boat and Nancy eased into Grant's. Phil bit his lower lip knowing that Boris and Laura had become an extremely proficient paddling duo.

Paddles rattled against hulls as they pushed off. When they entered the lake, a gust caught the bows, and the stern paddlers veered the canoe at a forty-five degree angle to the wind. Phil's arm and back muscles coiled and uncoiled with each stroke. He whipped off his rain hat and jammed it inside the front of his rain jacket. Immediately, his exposed bare head lowered his body temperature. Water splashed over the gunwales, and he was glad their load was lighter than earlier. His glasses, fogged, occasionally obscuring his vision. Henri's canoe danced like a stallion on the water with Henri's sure strokes. Gilbert's eyes widened, and his knuckles shone white against the paddle handle.

"Where's the bailer?" Cal called out to Deirdre.

"In front of your feet," she answered. "Paddle harder."

"Christ!" Cal missed a stroke and splashed water.

Phil could see Cal and Deirdre were falling behind, yet he was amazed at the expression on Deirdre's face. Like a Valkyrie, she faced the wind, head high, auburn hair streaming, eyes gleaming. It was as if she might sing out in a glorious voice as her canoe rode the waves. Had he misjudged her? Or was her joy for thrills? Apparently, the dumping earlier had been only a blow to her ego and not lessened her zest for adventure. Too bad she couldn't accept her own failings.

Grant glanced to the rear. "Keep up," he yelled back. "Make each stroke count."

Karen nodded to her husband between strokes. The stern paddlers had difficulty keeping the canoes on course against heavy cross wind gusts. The power had to come from the bow strokers. Phil's respect for Grant grew, for the man always stayed in the lead no matter who paddled in the bow.

The canoes crawled across the body of surging water. No rain fell, but waves cracking over the hulls soaked them. Water sloshed at Phil's feet rose. He bailed and when he straightened up, a heavy gust caught him in the chest. He bent to paddle and bailed intermittently—a futile task. A wave washed over the bow as the canoe dipped into a trough. Karen changed the canoe's heading. Phil bailed and paddled. The canoes spread out.

Grant yelled, "Close up, close up. Now!"

Gradually the boats responded. The wind's buffeting increased. Muscles strained, faces flattened, mouths hardened, eyes narrowed. Cal and Deirdre lagged, but by less.

Her elated expression seemed frozen in place. Several times Cal braced with his paddle so they wouldn't overturn. He'd learned a lot.

Grant glanced back. The canoes were floundering against the heavy surf. "Lash up!" The wind swept his words away, and he yelled again. "Two canoes lash together." His wiry body twisted back and forth as he watched the canoes respond.

Karen steered her canoe next to Laura's. "We're going to create a catamaran," Karen shouted, leaning forward to pass the extra paddle to Phil. "Use this as a pole. You and Boris lash it to each of the front thwarts. One of you always keeps paddling."

Phil fumbled with the painter line to secure the paddle handle to the thwart directly behind him. Finished, he nodded to Boris to lash the other end. The canoes began to drift off course, scuttled by the wind. Phil glanced over his shoulder between strokes. Karen struggled to prevent the boats from broaching, while Laura, her face a study of determination, tied her end of the extra paddle to the rear thwart.

"Move the bows a little closer together," Karen yelled to Boris. "Toed in more than the stern. That'll keep waves from piling up in a backwash between our hulls."

Boris grunted, wiped water from his eyes, and made the gap shorter. Phil stroked hard, moving the craft forward. Out of the corner of his eye, he saw Grant lash his canoe to Deirdre's. Henri, left to his own devices, paddled in the lee of the lashed canoes. The Frenchman's battered hat, pulled down over his brow hid his face. Gilbert's face was as white as the lake's frothy caps. His dead cigar hung in shreds from his gritting teeth. Phil heard a retching sound and glanced over as Cal threw up over the side of the canoe, yet he continued to paddle. After they'd lashed the canoes together, the threat of overturning eased, and they concentrated on paddling. Steadily, they made progress, but the wind never ceased howling.

At last they reached the headwaters of the river, and the bank cut the abrasive wind. The tightness in Phil's stomach eased.

"We can separate now," Grant ordered.

While the two catamarans again became four canoes, Henri and Gilbert paddled ahead. An hour later Phil spotted the two men on shore where ice heaves had created a steep bank set back from a cobblestone beach. At first Phil thought the two men were waving to them, then realized they were arguing. By the time Phil and the others docked, the two men had separated.

That night all but Cal and Gilbert enjoyed the pasta dinner. Still feeling the effects of the crossing, Cal lay in his tent. Gilbert pushed pieces of food around on his plate. The wind continued and the temperature dropped.

After dinner as Phil and Boris washed their plates in the shallows of the cold river, Boris said, "Looks like thunderheads building up in the northwest."

"Glad we're off the lake." Phil shook his head. "Poor Cal. He sure was seasick." He paused, contemplating how he should phrase his thoughts. "You and Laura paddle well together."

"Is that a backhanded way of saying you approve of my courting her?"

"Only you would put it that way," Phil said. "You're a gallant fool."

"I should take offense at the 'fool' remark, but I can't. Too damn tired."

"Me too." Phil hesitated, then said, "You handled Cal well a few days ago. I thought he was going to crack."

"He was protecting his wife's name. Instinctive response." Boris looked at Phil. "You've never felt that way, have you? No offense, but you're a loner. You think like a loner. I know, because I was one. Maybe that's why finding Erich's stash means more to you than to Cal and me."

"When or if we find the lode, it will mean as much to both of you. Stop fooling yourself. Why else would you have come?"

Boris rubbed the side of his nose as he stared hard at Phil. "Why indeed?" He turned and walked up the embankment toward the tents, threading his way between the black and green lichen-spotted rocks.

Phil blinked at the raw barrenness around him. Across the river, seven caribou trailed south and then disappeared. An Arctic loon's mournful call sounded like interrupted laughter. He strolled over to Grant and Karen who were cleaning up after the meal. "The group did well today," Phil said.

Grant nodded. "Followed orders like they should."

"Don't be so harsh," Karen said. "It was very rough out there, but everyone did wonderfully well. Deirdre and Cal have improved tremendously."

"I agree." Phil smiled at her compassion. On the rim of the hill where the tents were, he noticed Henri's plodding figure. Phil returned his gaze to Grant. "What's going on between Henri and Gilbert? Looked like they were sparring before we arrived."

Grant closed the cooking stove he'd been cleaning and stowed it under a tarp. "Henri can't stand a whiner, and Gilbert looked pea green out there on the lake."

"He pulled his weight," Phil countered. "Gilbert slunk off after dinner as if he were scared."

Grant shrugged. "Henri can be mean, but he knows his outdoor stuff. Gilbert's out of his element, but doing a good enough job as far as I'm concerned. I hope he writes great articles about this area. Maybe then the public will get interested in saving this land."

Phil stuck his hands in his pockets. "Thought the Thelon Sanctuary was off limits for development."

"Supposed to be." Grant wiped his hands on his plaid shirt. "You can't trust the government when it comes to getting money."

Phil chuckled and shook his head. "You sound like Nancy."

"She told me a little about her interests." Grant checked that everything had been stowed away properly. "The canoes are stashed high and have been cleaned." He turned to Karen. "Ready to call it a day?"

She walked over and put her arm around her husband's waist. "Absolutely." She glanced at Phil. "Good job today, partner."

Phil smiled. "It was a little hairy out there, but we all pulled together. See you in the morning."

Night closed down and with it came a terrifying lightning and thunderstorm. Phil lay in his sleeping bag as the crackle of lightning came closer. The storm spread over the encampment. He and Boris looked at each other.

"Should we check on the women?" Boris sat up and began pulling on his trousers.

"Always the knight in shining armor," Phil said, watching him. "Careful, it might be your undoing."

Boris ignored Phil's remark. "I'm checking on Laura." A lightning bolt hit not a thousand yards away. "Are you checking on Nancy or shall I?"

Phil gave him a quick look. "I will." He began to dress and when Boris unzipped the tent's fly, Phil said through gritted teeth, "Don't stay out too long."

Chapter 25

Phil had been awake long before the storm passed at dawn and looked out at the scene before him. Crystal drops hung like opals on the low trailing arctic willows and a soft breeze tugged at tent rain flaps. A lemming dashed into a tuft of grass. Although a cloudless sky bode well for the coming day, he felt lethargic and depressed. Boris had stayed out all night.

Phil wandered down for breakfast and stood next to the small propane stove to dish spoonfuls of honeyed oatmeal into his bowl. When Boris and Laura walked hand in hand down the incline of jumbled rocks, the mush stuck in his throat. He knew he'd lost her.

Karen and Grant working companionably side by side drove home his loneliness. Did they know how fortunate they were to have such a relationship? When Laura passed him, she neither glanced nor spoke to him, indifferent to his presence. He'd been egotistical to think she'd come back to him.

Nancy sat on a boulder smoking a cigarette and sipping coffee. She'd been husbanding her smokes. His ears still burned from her rejection when he'd gone to her tent last night and asked her if she wanted company on such a scary night.

She'd said, "My teeth chatter every time the thunder booms and the lightning pierces my eardrums, but other than that I'm okay." He'd mistook her words as a desire for company, unzipped her tent and moved inside, smiling. Had it been a lecherous smile? "We can drown out the storm. Two bodies entwined," he'd said.

"My, suddenly you're Romeo." Her long hair fell around her face.

He'd reached out to touch a strand, but she'd pushed it away. "I often wondered what your approach would be. Timing is everything, and for the record, yours stinks. I don't take another woman's scraps."

He'd left her tent, cowed and embarrassed. In the past she'd thrown herself at him, now he desired her, but she was no longer receptive. Had he changed or had she? Despite last night's meeting, she'd greeted him cheerfully this morning.

"Morning," Laura said to Nancy. "Beautiful day after last night's rain."

Nancy nodded, snuffed out her cigarette, pocketing the remaining butt and received a thankful smile from Laura.

Deirdre sat on her rain jacket a few yards away. "Some storm. I thought I'd get zapped. Scared me to death." She giggled. "It was exciting, but my boots got wet, and I'll have to wear my sneakers until they dry out." She waved her hand as an insect flew around her. "If only the flies would go away."

Boris clapped Cal on the back. "How're you doing?"

Cal sipped his coffee and forced a wan smile. "Seen better days. Can't understand why I got seasick. Never happened to me before."

Phil pondered Cal and Deirdre's teeter-totter emotional cycles. When one was doing well, the other floundered. Had their relationship always spun this way, or was this something new? Interpersonal relationships could doom a mission. That thought got his attention, and he realized he'd have to say something to Boris about Laura. He couldn't allow an undercurrent of bad feelings to continue. He'd like to believe Laura fell for Boris on the rebound, but knew that was a crock.

Unlike previous mornings, Gilbert hovered close to the group. "How about changing canoe partners?" He sent a darting glance in Henri's direction. "I mean, it's good to shift around so everyone gets to know everyone else."

Grant looked up from his cereal. "I don't mind." His spoon hung in the air as he searched faces. "Anyone want to change?"

An awkward silence followed. "I guess we'll stay as is." Grant turned to Henri, who sat Indian style off to one side. "That okay with you, Henri?"

The Frenchman nodded as he tossed the remnants of his black coffee onto the ground and ran his palm over his bristly beard. "Hey, *mon ami.* Gilbert paddles good, strong." He rose, walked over to Gilbert and rapped him on the shoulder, ignoring Gilbert's cringing posture. "We get along fine. No?"

Gilbert moved away to add more coffee to his already full cup. Phil wondered what had happened yesterday between the two men. Gilbert had lost his bravado, yet Henri was all smiles.

"We should make good time today," Grant said, seemingly unperturbed by the men's interactions. "We'll be entering the Sanctuary in two days, and you'll notice an increase in wildlife and wolf dens." He packed up the stove and other kitchen items and began to hum.

"The way you talk, you'd think the animals know they're protected in the Sanctuary," Karen said.

"Maybe they do." Grant looked at the group. "Let's get going. There's wildlife to see and a schedule to keep if Phil and others are to visit the wolf dens off the tributary."

As if Grant had thrown a switch, they cleaned their dishes, handed them to Karen and scrambled up the incline toward their tents. Rocks rolled from under their eager steps, and the cascading scree echoed around the encampment.

Phil and Boris took down their tent, working quickly and silently. After they slid the rolled tent into its bag, Phil said, "If you and Laura want to use this double, I'll switch to the single."

Boris hesitated and rubbed his hands along his pant legs. "I'll check with her." Before lifting his pack, he scanned Phil's face. "I know how you felt about her." Without another word, he held out his broad hand to Phil.

Phil's tension eased when he grabbed Boris's outstretched hand. "If I thought I still had a chance, my attitude might be different, but it's obvious how Laura feels."

Boris's face cracked into a wide grin. "I'm a damn lucky fellow." He shouldered his pack, turned and walked toward Laura's tent.

Phil sighed, carried his gear to the canoes and stowed it as others straggled down the incline in ones and twos. They were getting close to the important sites. If Phil's hunch was right about the Cosmos debris and the diamond lode, Henri would make his move soon.

Although Cal's color had returned, his mouth remained in a tight grimace as if he hurt. Was he physically sick or was it nerves? Fear could do strange things to a man.

Gilbert stood next to Henri's canoe with an unlit cigar clenched in his teeth. Henri strapped the packs in the boat and tucked his Winchester under the rope. The gun muzzle pointed forward. Gilbert shoved the barrel to the side.

"Hey." Henri pushed Gilbert's hand away. "What you do?"

"I don't want that fucking barrel facing my back," Gilbert said.

"It always faced that way."

"Well, I don't like it."

"Okay." Henri slanted the rifle crosswise. "Make you happy? All is okay. Give me a cigar, and we make peace."

Gilbert turned his back on Henri and stuck a new cigar in his upper pocket. "Haven't any left."

That's a tentative alliance gone sour, Phil thought. Before he could assess the argument further, the group set out on the river.

The glassy water reflected the images of the canoes. Neither a ripple on the water, nor a cloud in the sky disturbed the still atmosphere until a flock of geese flew overhead, and an arctic tern danced above the river.

Later in the day Grant raised his arm and pointed at a far hill. "Muskoxen."

"Looks like a blob of ink," Deirdre said. "Will we see them closer?"

"Absolutely," Karen said as her canoe joined the middle of the flotilla. "By the time you're through, you should have some close encounters with muskoxen."

"Muskoxen up close is fine," Deirdre said. "But after seeing the size and speed of that grizzly, I'll be glad not to have close encounters with them."

They'd been paddling for over two hours without a rest stop. Phil's knees and back were stiff, signs of yesterday's hard paddle across the Eyeberry. He looked back and noticed Henri and Gilbert lagged farther behind than usual. "Should we wait?" he asked Karen, nodding back to Henri's canoe.

"Henri can catch up any time he wants," she said. "I'll check with Grant."

"We need a stop." Deirdre's sharp voice came across the water.

Before Karen could utter her usual words, they all chorused in unison, "He forgets the rest of us are human."

Karen laughed, and Grant turned to look back.

"Potty stop," she called to him.

Within fifteen minutes Grant pulled to shore, and the others followed in his wake. Henri's canoe had caught up, and he alighted from the canoe with agile grace. Gilbert remained edgy and chomped harder on his cigar. Brown spittle ran down his chin.

While the group stretched, Grant stood in scrub brush on a hill from the esker's beach, binoculars to his eyes. He ran down the slope and said in a hushed voice, "Muskoxen herd on the far side of the hill. If we move quietly up the ravine, we should be able to get close. Leave your extra gear. Keep low and keep quiet."

They scrambled for head nets and binoculars, doffed their jackets and threw items helter-skelter into the canoes. Laura retrieved her camera bag. Despite the heat, Phil continued to wear his vest with its pocket for maps and Erich's journal. Bent low, they followed Grant. Mosquitoes buzzed around their heads and landed on exposed hands.

When they reached a sand dune, Grant sprawled on the ground, bellied up to the dune's crest and waved them to mimic him. A herd of forty muskoxen spread out before them. A large bull, the herd's leader, glared in their direction and moved forward a few paces. His long glossy coat shimmered in the sun, but his pelage was molting, leaving his underfur visible in places. He was over four and a half feet tall at the shoulders, weighed around six hundred pounds and his horns curved downward near his cheeks before hooking out and up. The bull displayed nervousness as he stared in their direction, then retreated, turning to face his herd. A few young bulls cavorted on a side knoll, testing one another with feints and charges, while young calves with cinnamon-colored fur stood near their mothers.

Phil's temples pounded from the race to the dune and the exhilaration of being close to such prehistoric-looking animals. The primordial smell of the muskoxen mixed with the odor of his own sweat. Grains of sand clung to his hands. Laura's camera clicks sounded like cannon fire in the quiet as she spun off pictures in hurried succession. The bull turned toward them again and pawed the ground as if preparing to charge, then moved back among his herd.

Laura's cool detachment, while she witnessed things through her camera lens, annoyed Phil. She seemed to want to experience everything only through her camera. Nancy lay prone next to him, her eyes glowing with excitement as she reached out and squeezed his hand.

Phil looked down the line of intense faces focused on the herd, their bodies taut, and he realized Henri and Gilbert were missing. Muskoxen might be a common sight for Henri, but Gilbert's absence bothered him. Thinking he should check on Gilbert, he started to inch down the dune, but the bull snorted and Phil stopped. The herd milled about and moved hesitantly toward them, as if scouting the dune to determine what enemy lay hidden there. Closer and closer they came until the bull spun around.

The herd followed in a thunderous explosion of hooves on the sandy esker. Grant stood and sprinted forward, followed by Phil, Boris and Cal. Karen ran to the right of the dune toward a far clearing, and the women followed her. After a dash over the uneven ground, they found the herd milling in a meadow surrounded by jack pines. The muskoxen held their ground and glared at the gaping humans. Then as if given a signal, the herd wheeled as one and galloped away.

"Fantastic and exciting," Deirdre exclaimed. "Did you get some good photos, Laura?"

"Think so." Laura grinned and turned to Cal. "Even your magazine will want these."

"You're probably right, and I expect first look." From under his head net, Cal's face glistened with sweat. "Perhaps the worst is behind us."

The group spread out and inspected the area, hoping to see more wild-life. Boris said, "This damn mosquito can't get a grip on my slick rain pants and is sliding like he's skating. Poor thing."

"Oh sure, poor things." Deirdre stepped closer to look. "I'd like to drop a bomb of pest control on the entire region."

"Then the area would be overrun with humans," Laura said. "The blackflies and mosquitoes help save the area from complete destruction by humans."

"Now, you're talking like a true environmentalist," Nancy said. "After this trip you should get in touch with me."

Phil shook his head. "Always proselytizing."

"It's important," she said defensively, then realized he was teasing. "I'll get back at you later."

"I'm sure you will," Phil said and smiled.

They ambled along, discussing what they'd seen. As they fanned away insects and sweated under the intense sun, Deirdre said, "I can't stand the bugs." She ran ahead and yelled back, "See you at the canoes."

Karen shook her head. "If she'd relax, she wouldn't be so bothered by them."

"The insects are a real pain," Nancy said, "but—"

A scream broke through her words.

"Deirdre," Cal yelled and vaulted forward through the brush, thrusting aside Grant as he ran past.

The group followed on his heels. Stepping onto the sandy beach, they saw Deirdre crouched by her canoe. Cal ran to her side. She lifted up a torn blouse then searched the ground for her belongings.

Duffel bags sagged in disarray, pieces of clothing, pans and food lay strewn on the sand and in the river shallows. They moved among the canoes, shocked by the chaos.

Grant searched through his pack. "Damn! Both radios are gone."

"Why?" Karen asked. "Why?"

The others wandered from canoe to canoe in a trancelike state, picking up clothing and other objects. Everyone's gear had been rifled. Phil hurried to his pack, only to throw it down in disgust. He muttered, "My radio's gone."

Grant looked at him. "I didn't know you carried one."

"It doesn't matter now, does it?" Phil said. "Henri's gone."

"Gilbert, too," Boris said.

Phil turned to Boris. "You still have your GPS?"

Boris shook his head. "The bastards cleaned me out, GPS, maps, everything. How the hell did they know what we had stored away?"

"We weren't exactly closed-mouthed about our equipment," Cal said. "And both those guys have been snooping ever since we started."

"I had my maps with me." Grant waved the plastic packet in his hand.

Phil was glad he'd had the foresight to tuck Erich's journal and maps in his vest.

"They left my extra camera and film." Laura clasped her pack to her chest.

"Look at the mess they made." Deirdre threw down a blouse in utter confusion as she knelt beside a small bag. "My lipstick, my shampoo and soap. They have sand in them."

"Give me a break." Nancy said. "We have more trouble than your lipstick."

Deirdre stood with her chin jutting out. "You don't have to be nasty."

"Take it easy," Laura said. "Nancy's right. We've got big time problems."

Grant strode from canoe to canoe, checking the gear. "Why in the hell did they do this?"

"They hardly seemed like cohorts." Boris's heavy brow furrowed.

"I don't think they were partners." Phil walked down the beach, staring at the sand as he went. "There was a scuffle." He reached down and picked up a chewed cigar, then raised his hand to ward off the others. "Wait a minute." He spotted a faint line across the sand leading into the brush. He followed the trail and at the edge of the sedge grass, trampled yellow flowers and crushed cotton grass gave away the hiding place. He pushed aside the dwarf shrubbery.

Although he'd expected it, he recoiled at the sight. Gilbert's body lay twisted, his skull staved in on the right side. Phil leaned down, fanned away the flies and, although knowing it was a futile gesture, felt for a pulse of the carotid artery jugular vein. Nothing. The body was still warm. He closed Gilbert's eyelids. From the cuts on his hands, he'd put up a struggle. The memory of another who'd died in a similar fashion came to mind. The coroner's report on Erich stated that the contusion to his head had also been on the right side. If facing an opponent, the blow would come from a left-handed person.

The bushes rustled, and Grant moved next to him. As they stood over the body, Grant said, "I can't believe Henri would do this. God, what a mess."

"The body says it all," Phil said. "Is Henri left-handed?"

Grant stared at Phil, then the body. "I see what you're getting at. Yeah, he's left-handed."

"Erich had the same type of head trauma." Phil stared at Gilbert's lifeless body. He couldn't tell Grant that the separatist Pierre Giraud had been killed with a blow to the side of the head, too.

Grant said, "I'll tell the others. We'll wrap him in a tarp and bury him deep in the esker. The Mounties can come for him later. We need to press on."

They stood around Gilbert's grave, and Phil wondered if the others understood the risks they faced. He knew where Henri was headed, but could he convince Grant without explaining too much? Henri had a good head start, and getting this group to hurry would not be easy.

"Shouldn't we get going?" Phil urged.

Grant stared across the fresh dug earth at Phil. "We must make our rendezvous. If Chip doesn't hear from me, he'll come looking."

"That's a long time from now," Deirdre said. "Another week?"

"Ten days," Grant replied.

"How will we make it? Do you know the way?" Deirdre's voice hung close to hysteria as she gripped Cal's arm.

"I know the way," Grant reassured her.

"We should go after Henri," Phil said. "We have no choice."

"Now wait a minute," Cal said. "This," he nodded toward Gilbert's grave, "changes everything. What we were looking for doesn't matter now. Survival does."

"I know where Henri is headed," Phil said. "It's on our way, but we've got to hurry."

Cal's eyes narrowed. "What makes you all-knowing?"

Everyone stared at Phil. "It's clear. Henri and Erich were partners. Erich was looking for remnants of Cosmos 954. Erich was killed the same way Gilbert was. Henri turned up with uranium burns. It doesn't take a genius to put the pieces together. Erich found parts of Cosmos 954. Henri knows we want to visit a place he doesn't want us to go—the wolf dens off the tributary. I think he hid the Cosmos debris there and is on his way to get rid of it."

"Why would he do that?" Grant asked.

Phil shrugged. "Maybe to protect his precious land. The point is, the longer we stay here, the easier it is for him to get away."

"Our job is to get out of this wilderness safely." Cal waved at the area around him.

"You're absolutely right," Phil said. "But on the way, we are going to get Henri and possibly find what Erich found."

Nancy nodded. "I'm with Phil. That's why I came. I'm not running back with my tail between my legs while Henri gets away with murder and hiding hazardous material."

Nancy's acceptance of his ideas heartened him. He was about to insist they get moving when Grant stepped in front of him.

"We are not splitting up," Grant declared. "We'll stay together and head toward the wolf dens, but if we're pressed for time, we'll go on toward the rendezvous site and forget Henri."

"If we find Henri," Boris said, searching Phil's face for corroboration, "we find the radios." He gave Laura a reassuring glance, took her hand and walked down the hill.

Before Phil reached the canoes, Nancy came up to him and grabbed his arm. "You omitted one thing back there. Why did Henri kill Gilbert?"

"You told me Pierre's head was bashed in. Do you remember which side?"

Nancy thought and Phil could see she was running the old scene through her mind. "The body was face down. Hmm. The right side."

"That's what I thought. A blow caused from a left-handed man when facing his opponent. Remember when you were arguing with Gilbert? Henri overheard that spat. Gilbert was at the scene of the crime all right, and I'll lay odds he saw Henri kill Pierre. When Gilbert realized Henri knew he'd been at the house and had seen him, he knew he was in danger from Henri."

"When did you figure out Henri killed Pierre?" Nancy asked. "He denied being in town during that time."

"True, but Chip said his copilot had taken Henri back and forth to Fort Smith. Although Henri claimed his trip was much earlier, I think he was lying."

"I remember. Back at the dock. I overheard Chip say something about extra flights with Henri." Her eyes searched Phil's face. "Do you think we'll catch him?"

"We can try. But remember, Henri might know you were at the house, too. If we find him, be very careful about what you do and say around him."

Nancy studied him with a crooked smile. "You really are sweet, and very bright about solving crimes. I wonder if I really know all there is to know about Phil West."

Chapter 26

Henri dipped his paddle in and out of the swirling water with a smooth J stroke that steered the canoe on a fixed course. His bowels churned, but he ignored his needs. He rode his canoe like a man on a horse, at one with his canoe and with his world. His knees splayed out against the sides of the gunwales, and his hips, pressed against the seat bar, swiveled easily with each stroke.

Three radios and a GPS rolled around at his feet. Shoving them forward with a whack of his paddle, he watched them skitter under Gilbert's pack. After dealing with Gilbert, he'd felt elated. Once he'd realized Gilbert had seen him at the house, he had no choice. And what about Nancy? He liked her better than the other women. She shared his passion for the land, but if she could place him at the scene of the crime…. He shrugged.

If they found Gilbert's body, they'd bury it and he'd have a good head start. If they didn't find the body, his lead would be cut.

He stopped paddling and scratched his groin. Studying the shoreline, he picked his spot and maneuvered his canoe into shore. Stepping out, he pulled his canoe up and went into the brush. When he returned, he pawed through Gilbert's pack. There wasn't much he wanted or needed. He stuffed the cigars into his shirt pocket and tossed the candy bars onto the floor of his canoe. He hesitated over the spiral notebook. Grant had wanted Gilbert to write about the Thelon River, yet all Henri's troubles had started with Erich's journal. He put the notebook into Gilbert's pack, filled it with rocks and hurled it into the water.

Back on the river he took bites of a candy bar as he thought of Phil. "*Mon Dieu,* but he's a devil. Erich's journal. *Merde.* Leah caused all this." He muttered, arguing with himself as he paddled. "Evil world. *Sacré bleu.*" He stared ahead at the bright water with the sun playing across its ripples.

How would they know about the diamonds? Erich's damn journal and the old prospector. When he'd killed the man, he thought a search for diamonds would end. Henri had no need of diamonds. These men had been with Erich during the helicopter crash and Gilbert said they'd brought out the prospector's body. These men look for the stuff that make men crazy—diamonds. He couldn't allow them to succeed.

They were troublemakers. Even Nancy, who loved the land but wanted to find the uranium. Get the government into things, cause trouble. He should have caved in their canoes, but there'd been no time. They all had to die, even Grant and his wife. No one must survive.

When Chip comes, I'll meet him—alone. Such a sad tale I'll tell.

He dumped the radios and the GPS over the side and watched the gurgling bubbles as they sank. Shifting his weight, he paddled on. He had his radio. As he came upon the campsite Grant would choose, he grinned with anticipation. They would come here, and here they would remain.

With the coming of evening, the cloudless sky began to lose its sparkle. Phil paddled harder in the bow of Karen's canoe. "Come on," he urged Boris and Laura, then turned on Cal and Deirdre. "We've got to get there before he gets set."

"What's that supposed to mean?" Deirdre said from across the water. Her paddle swung up and forward, matching Cal's cadence.

"He thinks Henri will try to kill us," Cal said over his shoulder, "He's right. Another reason not to go to the wolf dens."

Boris glared over at Cal across the bow of Grant's canoe, which glided smoothly by. "You want him to get away with killing Erich and Gilbert?"

"Hell, no," Cal said. "All we have to do is head for the rendezvous and tell our story to the Mounties when we get back."

"With what proof?" Phil demanded. Hadn't Cal understood the location of the wolf dens was also near where they'd found the prospector and where Erich's journal noted geological formations conducive to diamonds?

Nancy had been staring straight ahead, but now she glanced at Cal. "We need to get that uranium. It isn't safe to leave it out here. Who knows what Henri will do with it. Talk about an environmental disaster waiting to happen."

"It's been out here for seventeen years, it can stay another seventeen," Deirdre said.

"That's what the world's been saying about all kinds of hazardous waste and look what's happened." Nancy's face reddened as she began her emotional lecture about the environment.

"Give me a break," Deirdre muttered.

Phil didn't care who won the argument as long as their anger kept them paddling at a fast pace. Grant had said little since he'd made his pronouncement that the group would not split up. It was time Phil gave Grant a reality check. He paddled harder to come abreast of Grant. "Henri knows where we'd planned to camp," Phil said quietly. "Shouldn't we alter the location?"

Grant frowned and seemed to mull over Phil's question. "I can't believe he'd harm us."

"He killed Gilbert and probably Erich and Pierre and…."

"Okay, okay. I get it." Grant shook his head. "I've known him for years. He has a temper, sure, but…."

"Forget what you can't believe and start thinking the worst." Phil leaned forward over his gunwale toward Grant. "If we want to get this group home safe, we have to be prepared for the worst."

"He's got a rifle," Laura said. "We're no match for that."

"There's only one decent campsite in the area," Grant finally said. "We'll go in slow. Phil and I will take the first canoe in and reconnoiter. If it's safe, we'll signal, but come in one at a time and don't bunch up."

"Right," Boris said. "Then we can set up a perimeter and take shifts on guard through the night."

Phil decided that while everyone slept, he'd head to the wolf dens. He'd let Boris and Grant in on his plans, but the others didn't need to know.

When Grant signaled that the campsite was just around the river bend, Phil and Nancy exchanged places in their respective canoes in midstream, so Phil could paddle with Grant. Sunlight edged low on the horizon, giving the water a grayish cast. While Grant and Phil paddled on, the others headed for an eddy in a small inlet.

After Phil and Grant rounded the bend, they studied the exposed shoreline. Gray rocks made the steep embankment look naked and the drab greenish brown of cotton grass and tufts of saxifrage with its small purple flower gave no hint of being disturbed. It was a serene scene, but Henri was too clever to make anything appear out of place. Rivulets of sweat slid down Phil's back.

Grant propelled the canoe sideways to the shore, bumping the hull against the rocks. Glancing at one another, they pulled the canoe out of the water up the slight incline. The rocky shoreline ran four hundred yards before being claimed by brush. Since the land sloped up from the river, Henri could be hiding just over the rise.

"I'll go left," Grant said. "You go right."

Bent low, they walked along the shoreline in opposite directions, then circled inland. A ptarmigan squawked and flew skyward. A bullet ricocheted off a nearby rock as Phil stumbled into a depression and landed on his back. He squirmed around, clawing at rocks to dig a deeper hole, as another shot spattered the sand in front of him.

Grant ran a zigzag pattern toward him, keeping low. "I'm okay," Phil yelled. "Get down."

Grant dove headfirst toward a small outcrop just as a bullet splattered rocks. The two men were twenty yards apart.

Grant called over to Phil. "I can't spot him. What do you think?"

"I think we're in deep shit." Phil glanced at the canoe behind him. "We can't make a run for it. Too far, but he'll have to show himself to get at us. His rifle has six bullets and accurate to a hundred yards. Doesn't give us much hope." Phil scanned the area for a sight of Henri. "If he moves toward us, we'll have to rush him. Throw rocks as we go."

"Not much of a chance," Grant said.

Suddenly Henri showed himself and aimed his rifle, not at them, but at the canoe. He put two bullets through the hull, turned and jogged back into the taiga.

They got to their knees, staring after him. "We don't stand a chance against him in the open." Grant said. "He did what he wanted to do."

"Not quite." Phil felt a nervous tic in his eye as they backed toward the canoe in a crouch. "If it hadn't been for that bird, I'd be dead."

"I wonder why he didn't fire when we beached? We were sitting ducks."

"Maybe out of range for an accurate shot. He wants a sure thing." Phil studied the damaged canoe. "Can you fix it?"

"Patching it will take time."

"This area is too exposed for us to camp. How about the next place?" Phil asked.

"The entire area this side of the tributary is like this." Grant hauled his daypack out of the canoe. "We've got to get back to the others."

"They would've heard the shots," Phil said. "Henri's through for the moment. They could paddle in."

Grant shook his head. "Can't take the chance, Let's walk back to the river bend and hail them. Then we're heading on to the rendezvous point. Forget the wolf dens."

Phil grabbed his arm. "Are you crazy? Do you think Henri's going to let you catch that plane back to Fort Smith? We've got to get him before he gets us."

Grant shouldered his pack and lifted one of the duffel bags. "I'm heading back along the shoreline. I don't want them landing here."

"Henri's probably upriver, paddling for the wolf dens. Let's take the gear and leave it down there." He pointed downstream where the brush hid the bank's sharp turn and offered some protection. "After that I'll come back and carry this canoe there. We can divide the gear between the other boats, and sling this one across two of the bows."

Grant nodded. "Good idea. It'll be snug with three in two canoes. Let's get going."

After they carried the gear to the river bend, Grant continued along the shore to contact the group, while Phil retrieved the damaged canoe. Henri's bullets had sliced through the hull below waterline and penetrated both sides, two shots had created four holes. Phil rocked the canoe up onto his thigh then lifted it over his head, settling the center thwart across his shoulders. If Henri was still around, he'd be an easy target, and only when he arrived at the river's bend did he relax. He knelt in the bushes and waited for the others.

The canoes nosed into the shore with the group subdued, faces grim. They redistributed the gear amongst the remaining canoes and Laura wedged herself into Cal and Deirdre's canoe. The damaged canoe was balanced across the center of the canoe Grant would paddle with Boris, while Karen paddled in the stern of the other canoe with Nancy in the middle and Phil in the bow. Silently they eased out into the river.

Grant insisted they stay on the Thelon River and camp north of the tributary and, under the circumstances, Phil couldn't object. The campsite Grant chose had a buffer of stunted spruce. They were on the opposite side of the esker where the wolf dens were located. A ridge line divided the areas, and the map indicated two miles to the dens, but according to Grant, the terrain was difficult to cross. They secured the campsite, then huddled around Grant's map debating their next move.

Cal pointed to a spot farther up the Thelon. "That's familiar territory, isn't it, Phil?"

It was the location Erich had mentioned in his geological report. The diamond lode had to be near. If events had gone differently, Phil would have searched there, but right now, taking care of Henri was more important. "Can you lead me to the dens?" Phil asked Grant.

"Yes, but what will that get you?" Grant's pencil followed an invisible line from their campsite to the dens. "Henri has his gun."

"What we need is a feint." Boris pondered the map.

Cal crossed his arms over his chest. "This isn't one of your fencing matches."

"Yes, it is." Boris looked at the others. "It's somewhat like one. A short jab here, he parries, and we counter." He pointed to the spot where they thought Henri would disembark off the tributary to head toward the dens. "If we attack from the water and the land, we should be able to disarm him."

"We'd be sitting ducks on the river and him on shore taking shots at us," Cal said. "I vote we continue on toward the rendezvous, forget Henri."

Deirdre drew nearer to Cal. "We aren't involved with him," she said.

"You're dreaming," Phil said. "He knows we know he killed Gilbert."

"But we'd tell him we won't say anything," Deirdre said.

"Oh, sure." Nancy glared at Deirdre. "As if he would believe that. The man's a killer. I saw what he did to Pierre."

Everyone stared at her, frowning. Phil reached out and touched Nancy's shoulder. "We don't need to go into that now."

"Yes, we do," Deirdre said. "If she's involved with the murder—"

"I found the body. I didn't see Henri do it," Nancy said.

Phil thrust his way into the middle of the group. "We haven't got time to argue about what happened. If we don't go after Henri, he'll come after us. We've got to take the offensive, or he'll pick us off one by one." Phil ignored the chorus of protests. "Boris has a good idea. Grant said we need to stick together, and he's right, but we must move in a coordinated way." He looked at the map again. "I propose some go in canoes and—"

"Hold it," Grant interrupted. "My job is to see you come through this wilderness expedition. No one is going to paddle off while Henri has a rifle.

Cal's right, we'd be sitting ducks on the water even with a feint from the land. It would be too risky." He scrutinized the group. "I realize we're in a predicament. I don't want to split up, but under the circumstances, I don't think there's much choice. Phil and I will try to ambush Henri from the rear by going over the top of the ridge. He probably thinks we'll come from the river, if we'd come at all."

"I'll go too," Boris said.

Grant hesitated, "Okay, but everyone else stays here." His eyes softened as he looked at Karen. "Karen will be in charge here until I get back. If something happens to us, she has my maps and knows the route to the rendezvous. Don't wait past tomorrow noon, then paddled for the rendezvous and wait for Chip."

Grant darted a look at Phil as if expecting an argument, but Phil knew Grant was right. If they didn't succeed, the race to the rendezvous point would be the only option.

The three men grabbed their daypacks and stuffed them with parkas, rain gear and some dried food. Phil checked his vest pocket to be sure Erich's journal was secure, but transferred the maps to his pack. Grant strapped his large hunting knife to his belt. Phil withdrew, so Grant and Karen could talk privately, then watched as Laura hugged Boris.

Phil nodded to Nancy, and she gave him a warm smile. "Don't be too much of a hero."

"Good luck." Cal reached out to shake the men's hands as they passed him.

"You take care of these gals," Boris said with a wink and a wag of his finger. "And no funny business."

"Hey," Cal grinned. "Not to worry. I'm a married man."

Turning their backs on the camp, the men set off to cross the esker. When they reached the top of the rise above the camp, a wolf howl pierced the air.

Chapter 27

Sand sucked at their boots, insects swarmed, and the disc of the sun fell low on the horizon, creating deep gray light. At this time of year and at this latitude, complete darkness came for only one swift hour. Phil seethed with questions but found no answers. Would Henri be waiting for them? Maybe, but he'd be on guard facing the water, wouldn't he?

Grant stopped and held up his hand. "Grizzly," he whispered.

Phil and Boris strained to see where the bear was, but saw nothing. Grant pointed to the ground. Large fresh paw prints were imbedded in the sand and next to them were smaller ones. "Sow and cub, the worst combination," Grant's hushed tone was barely audible.

"Should we go back and warn the others?" Boris knelt in the sand next to the prints.

"They'll stay close to camp, so they should be okay," Grant said. "As long as we don't get between the sow and her cub, we'll be all right, too."

"Yeah, but how can we tell?" Phil peered into the brush.

Grant pointed to his left. "It'll take longer, but we'll circle away from the direction of their prints." He studied the trail, then led Phil and Boris higher onto the ridge away from their original route.

After stashing his canoe amongst trailing willows, Henri hiked inland to the wolf dens. He was angry with himself. Something had held him back from killing Phil and Grant when he had the chance. Only slowing them down made no sense. After he'd killed Gilbert, there was no turning back.

Despite the cool onset of evening, sweat trickled into his eyes, and he wiped his forehead with the sleeve of his brown plaid shirt. As he jogged over the soft earth, his wolf-hide vest flapped against his sides. His stocky bowed legs carried him up and down hilly pockets, through sedge grasses and across small ravines. He held his loaded Winchester loosely in his right hand.

This area was where he'd come across the prospector; where Erich must have found the rock with the diamond flecks and written Phil about it. Odd that it was so close to Erich's find of the Cosmos debris. *I had no choice. Erich had to die.* He'd been so sure no one would ever find the lead-lined box, but Erich's journal had changed that. In case he couldn't get rid of Grant and the others, he had to hide the box elsewhere.

A wolf howl pierced his thoughts, and he stopped in mid-stride. *So, my babies, you know I'm near.* He continued on, pleased with himself.

When he neared the den, he paused, his nostrils flaring at the smell of wolf. A large white female trotted away from the den, stopped, looked back, hesitated, then moved on. The babysitter of the den always tried to lure the enemy away. This brave act meant the adult wolves were out hunting, and only pups remained. This late in the season the pups would be about three to four months old, an age when they were cute and not difficult to catch. Today he wasn't hunting wolves.

He raised his head above a tangled mass of shrubs and moved silently behind a dwarf spruce. The flowers around the den had gone to seed, but the remnants of alpine foxtail, Jacob's ladder, and forget-me-nots lay in sharp contrast with the skeletal remains of a caribou strewn in a sandy depression.

Scanning the burrows of the den, he tried to remember which entrance he'd chosen to hide the box. *"Merde."* He froze and let out a guttural gasp, unable to believe what he saw. The box lay just outside the entrance to the burrow. The lines through the sand and the scars across the grassy slope told the story. The wolves had pushed the alien box out of their den.

Henri moved forward. Two dun-colored pups dashed out of a burrow, snarled and retreated. "One day you will be bigger, and your snarl will mean something, but so will your fine fur," Henri said as he watched the scampering pups.

He shouldered his rifle, lifted the box, grunting and walked away from the den. Knowing that the journey back to his canoe with such a burden would be an arduous one, he put his load aside, sat under a jack pine and took out a piece of jerky. He reflected on the next burial place. It must be so deep in the tundra that no one would ever find it.

Laura watched the men stride over the hill and felt a stab of apprehension. A wolf howl shattered the quiet and made her shiver. Deirdre and Cal had begun to set up their tent and looked up when they heard the howl. Karen and Nancy stood together near the shore as if seeking solace in nearness. Nancy fiddled with a cigarette, but didn't light it. Laura threw her duffel bag to the ground, as a surge of frustration swept over her. "What are we doing standing around? We should be helping them."

"I intend to follow Grant's orders," Cal said.

Laura fumed at his seeming indifference to the situation. "I can't just sit here waiting."

Cal turned his back, ignoring the harsh accusation in her voice. Deirdre paused with one flap of the tent in her hand and looked at her friend. "Grant knows what he's doing. They'll get Henri, and we can be on our way." She dropped the flap and walked over to Laura. "This whole trip has been a giant fiasco, and I'm sorry I talked you into it, but we'll be home soon. All this will be forgotten, and you and Boris will be together."

"Don't you get it?" Laura stared at her friend. "They might not get Henri. He's got a high-powered rifle. They don't. If things go haywire, they're in jeopardy and so are we."

"I know how you feel about guns, but you're exaggerating," Cal said. "Those fellows know what to do. Hell, Phil's with the Bureau and well trained."

Nancy walked over and stood next to Laura. "What do you mean, Phil's with the Bureau? You mean the FBI?"

Cal reddened and stumbled on a rock as he shifted his weight to pick up a bag. Recovering his balance, he faced the searching glances of the women. "Well, I'm not sure, but from everything I know, I assume he's with them."

"He's an agent?" Nancy's voice came out gravelly and slow.

"Yeah. I mean, I think so. This trip doesn't have anything to do with his job. Everyone knew Erich had been searching for Cosmos 954 debris. Phil kept in contact with him for reasons…." He hung his head and refused to go on.

"There's more to it, isn't there?" Nancy pressed, stepping closer.

Cal looked up. "It was a little thing on the side."

"A little thing on the side," Nancy repeated. "Out here in the middle of nowhere, you had something else going on. Like what?"

Cal looked from one woman to the next, his eyes pleading for under-standing. "It started a long time ago when we first came to the Arctic." He hesitated, but Nancy's glare cowed him. "Since we're all in this mess together, you might as well know," he continued. "We've been hoping to find a diamond lode." He glanced nervously at Deirdre. "That's why I final-ly decided to come back to this godforsaken country. The lode should be near here. Erich's journal noted a geological formation a little farther up the Thelon." He pointed north. "Over the other side of those rock formations north of the esker." Cal bit his lower lip and drew his hands through his dark hair.

"That's so exciting," Deirdre said. "It puts a different light on this trip. What if we found it?"

Cal brightened. "That was the idea. Erich wrote the information in that journal Phil keeps secreted away. Hey, we've got some extra time. This might be a good time to investigate. The spot's near here. We could hike up that ridge and head north along the river."

Nancy turned away with slumped shoulders, muttering to herself and Laura followed her. She was dumbfounded at the Sterlings' reaction. How could Deirdre jump for joy over Cal's confession? We're in trouble, while Cal's divulging secrets and thinking about treasure. "You all right?" Laura asked, putting a hand on Nancy's arm.

"I've just been told a guy I trusted is a spy by a man who doesn't under-stand that we might be shot by a crazy Frenchman." Her eyes smoldering with rage, laced with tears. "Why wouldn't I be fine?"

"Phil might be an agent, but not a spy," Laura suggested.

"Agent to you, spy to me." Nancy threw off Laura's hand, strode toward the water's edge and let out a scream, then whirled around. "I've been in the FBI's sights for years because of my environmental work. And who's been feeding them information about me? Phil! My trusted friend and compatriot. What a jerk I've been. I knew there was a traitor in my organi-zation, but I was too blind to see it was Phil."

Karen, who had stood aside listening, hurried to her side. "I don't like what I'm hearing, and I don't like what's happening, but right now, we've got to think about our immediate situation." Karen pursed her lips, and her blue eyes flared. "Grant said to stay put. Normally I do what he says in the wilderness, but not this time. I'm going to canoe back upstream and around the peninsula to the tributary to see what's happening."

"I'll go with you." Laura joined Karen to carry a canoe down to the water.

Cal ran down the incline toward them. "Wait a minute. You can't do that. I insist you stay here. It's the right thing to do."

Karen put down the canoe to face him. "Cal, you and Deirdre guard the camp. I'm going to help my husband."

He grabbed her arm. "We've got to stay together."

She pulled away from his grasp. "I'm in charge. You go after your damn diamonds. I'm going after my husband." Karen clutched her paddle as if it were a weapon, and Cal backed off.

Nancy, who'd been watching the confrontation from a distance, came forward. "I'm not going to stay here while you two go off like wonder women."

"I thought you were furious with Phil," Laura said.

"I am mad as hell, but I want to tell the bastard in person." She looked at Karen with an imploring expression. "Can we take two canoes?"

Karen grinned. "You bet. You and Laura paddle one. I'll paddle solo."

"You're crazy, Laura," Deirdre yelled. "Stay here and be safe. We'll find the diamond lode while they're gone."

Laura had forgotten how shallow her friend could be. Instead of screaming at Deirdre's selfish attitude, she turned her back and helped Nancy carry the other canoe to the river's edge.

Cal stood on the shore, glowering, but as they were about to launch the canoes, he moved next to Karen. "Okay, go, but listen. Henri's rifle shoots accurately up to a hundred yards, but that doesn't mean he can't shoot it farther. Stay at least two hundred yards off shore until you have some idea of what's going on. If he comes out after you, paddle like hell back here and hide."

Karen patted his arm. "We'll be careful."

As they paddled out, Laura looked back at Deirdre and Cal looking lonely on the shore. She was sorry their parting was acrimonious, but there'd be time later to make amends.

The three men hiked below a sandy ridge, and Grant pointed ahead, mouthing the words, wolf dens. They spread out and approached from different directions. Grant was in the center with Phil on his left and Boris on his right. They bent forward as they jogged, searching for Henri. In the dim twilight Phil saw Boris gesture. They stopped.

Three hundred yards ahead, Henri stooped, shouldered a large box and began to walk away from the dens, his rifle in his right hand. Phil picked up a rock and motioned the others to do the same, then they hurried forward. Phil's mouth was dry, his heart raced and sweat soaked his shirt as his daypack slapped against his back with each jarring step. He leaped over a trailing willow, landed on his hands and knees, got up and scrambled on. How close could they get before Henri saw them and opened fire?

Two hundred yards and closing. They had a chance. The heavy box slowed Henri's pace. Phil's breathing rasped as adrenaline spurted through him, and fear mixed with rage pushed him to move faster.

One hundred yards and closing. Phil focused on Henri, creating tunnel vision—the wrong reflex. His feet felt like they were in quicksand. The scene played out in slow motion. Henri turned toward them, dipped to one side, and slid the box off his shoulder. It hit the ground with a thud. Henri brought his rifle up, aiming to Phil's right and fired. A yell. The gun swung toward Phil. The dull metal barrel loomed large with Henri's face tucked behind it. No chance, but he kept running. A rock struck Henri's arm. A bullet buried itself in the sand at Phil's feet.

Boris and Phil hit Henri simultaneously, breaking Henri's grip on the rifle. The Winchester stuck barrel down in wet sand. The little Frenchman scrambled to his feet before Boris and Phil could disentangle themselves. Henri grabbed the rifle and swung it like a club, catching Boris across the ribs. Boris grunted, his knees buckled, and he collapsed.

Phil charged under Henri's next swing, dislodging the rifle. When Henri gripped Phil around the chest in a bear hug, he smelled the Frenchman's rancid sweat and sour breath. He clawed at Henri's eyes, and grabbed a handful of Henri's thick coarse hair and yanked it back. Henri's eyes bulged, but he maintained his deathlike vise around Phil's chest. A stream of French curses scorched the air. Phil's vision blurred. Sweat dripped into his eyes. He jammed his thumbs into the pressure points near the carotid artery below Henri's ears, forcing Henri's arms to weaken. Phil leaped away. The two men faced each other, gasping.

"You fuckin' bastard," Phil spat. "You killed Erich." Phil hurled himself at Henri, but the man stepped back, turned and fled. Stunned, Phil lay sprawled on the ground. Boris grabbed the rifle and aimed at the retreating

Frenchman. Phil reached over, slapping the rifle away as Boris pulled the trigger. The gun barrel, jammed with sand, exploded backward.

Boris grabbed his bruised chin. "Goddamn." He stared numbly at the gun. "It could have been my eyes."

Phil gawked at the empty dunes where Henri had disappeared. "He's going for his canoe."

"We gotta go after him."

"I don't think I can catch him," Phil said with his hands on his knees, trying to get his breath. "How about you?"

"Hell, I think my ribs are broken." Boris hunched over, holding his ribcage, grimacing. His usual ruddy complexion had turned pale with sand plastering his bruised face.

"We got his gun." Phil nudged the damaged rifle with his foot. "Where's Grant? I heard a yell, but I didn't see him fall."

Slowly, they retraced their steps. "If that bastard got Grant, I swear I'll kill him." Phil said.

"He needs killing anyway you look at it," Boris said between gasps.

"Over here," Grant called out in a strained and thready voice.

They found him sitting on the ground, blood seeping through his trouser leg at the thigh. He'd tried to stop the bleeding using his shirtsleeve as a tourniquet. Flies swarmed over him and his bloodied leg. Phil fanned away the insects, knelt and took his first aid kit out of his pack.

"I've got the bleeding under control." Grant clenched his teeth. "Didn't hit the main artery. Think it went right through the muscle."

Boris eased down awkwardly next to Grant and pulled his canteen off his belt. "Have a drink."

"Thanks. Used mine on the wound." Grant put the canteen to his lips, then glanced at Boris. "God, you look awful."

"Tangled with Frenchie," Boris said.

"Did you get him?"

Boris shook his head. "Bastard ran off."

Phil checked the tourniquet around Grant's leg as the blood continued to ooze. How would they get Grant to camp?

Chapter 28

When the rifle shots echoed over the river, Laura flinched and Nancy jerked almost tipping them over. Laura glanced at Karen, paddling on her starboard side. "What do you think?" she asked in a hushed voice, as if somehow the sound of her voice might trigger more shots.

Karen's face paled, her paddle stopped in midair. "We're almost there. Head for shore."

The women dug their paddles into the tributary's brown swirling water. A third shot roared from deep inland. "Oh God, please," Laura prayed aloud and paddled harder.

The canoes landed fast and hard, and the three women quickly exited. Karen carried the stern of each canoe on either side of her, while Laura carried the bow of one and Nancy the other. When Nancy and Laura slowed to set down the canoes, Karen said, "Keep going. Hide them in that thicket just ahead."

After setting the canoes into a hollow, Laura was about to walk onto the beach when she caught a movement down the shoreline. "Henri," she whispered, and grabbed Nancy's hand as they gaped at the figure trotting to the river's edge, dragging his canoe behind him.

Karen pulled them behind a screen of sedge grass.

Henri paddled toward the Thelon and turned downstream in the direction of their camp.

"What'll we do?" Laura asked, hoping Karen had an idea.

Nancy stared at Henri's disappearing canoe. "I didn't see the rifle, did you?"

Laura shook her head, but wondered if she'd missed it.

"He's paddling fast. The guys are probably right behind him," Karen reasoned. "Let's follow Henri's trail inland. It might lead us to the men." Her words left a lot unsaid.

While they searched for Henri's tracks back into the brush, Laura trailed behind. She couldn't lose Boris. She'd lost everyone else.

"Here," Karen called out. "The grass has been trampled." She moved on with Nancy and Laura close behind.

"Footprints. See? Over there." Nancy pointed at a sandy hummock.

They continued, then Laura ran ahead, her stride lengthening, her boots sending showers of sand behind her. Foot falls had crushed the underbrush ahead of her showing the way. Her running mode kicked in, and the earth passed quickly under her. In the murky evening light she spotted movement, then the top of Boris's shaggy head loomed above a dwarf spruce. Her heart leaped. "Boris," she yelled.

"Hey." Boris waved. She reached out to hug him. "Easy does it," he said, holding her away from him. "I've got a few sore ribs."

She recoiled. "Honey, your face." She reached up to touch him, but thought better of it. "Are you in pain?"

"A little. Is my mug messed up?" Boris held her hand.

"It'll heal," Phil said from his position next to Grant. "You never were an Adonis."

Laura darted a look at Phil. "He is, too." She stroked Boris's shoulder, then noticed Grant's bloodied leg. "My God, you're hurt, too."

Before anyone could explain, Karen arrived. "Grant." She knelt beside him, looking into his face, then to his wound and back to his face. "How bad is it?"

"The bullet passed through the thigh muscle without hitting bone or the main artery." Grant stroked his wife's hair. Tears welled up in her eyes as she gripped his hand. "I'll be okay," Grant reassured her.

Nancy, out of breath, joined the group. "Is everyone all right?"

"A few problems," Phil said. "You came from the river side. You canoed over?"

"Two canoes, enough to get us all back," Karen said.

"You were told to stay in camp," Phil said.

"Lucky for Grant we didn't," Karen said, as she tore Grant's pant leg to get a better look at the wound. She took out an antibiotic cream from Phil's first aid kit, smeared it on and then began to bandage his leg.

"You took a beating, Boris," Nancy said, ignoring Phil. "We spotted Henri paddling toward our campsite. Does he still have his gun? I didn't see it."

"We accomplished that much," Phil said. "The rifle's no longer usable."

Boris looked at Phil. "Thanks to you, I still have eyes and a face." He explained what had happened with the rifle.

"We're even," Phil said. "You saved me by throwing that rock."

"What do you mean?" Laura asked.

"Henri hit Grant with his first shot," Phil said. "Boris and I continued to rush him, but I was next in his crosshairs. Boris threw a rock at him before he fired. If he hadn't, I'd be dead."

Laura smiled at Phil and hugged Boris's arm tighter.

"We've got to get you to the canoes," Phil said to Grant.

Karen glanced at Phil. "He can't walk."

"I can with a little help." Grant flinched and paled as he tried to stand. "We've to get back to camp quickly. Who knows what Henri will do next."

"Henri won't stop at our campsite, will he?" Laura asked. "Cal and Deirdre are there. They'll catch him now that he doesn't have a gun."

"Henri's tough," Phil said. "I'm not sure Cal can handle him. God knows, I couldn't."   Nancy planted her feet apart with her arms folded across her chest. "My, my, with all your FBI training, and you couldn't stop Henri."

Phil blanched and drew himself up straighter, then turned his attention to Grant. "Let me help you stand?"

With one arm around Phil's shoulder and the other around Karen's, Grant managed to stand. Sweat dripped down his temples, and his eyes clouded.

"If Laura and Karen can help you to the canoes, I'll get the box Henri dropped." Phil said.

Laura looked at Boris, wondering if he'd be all right without her support. Boris gave her a reassuring nudge and she took Phil's place next to Grant.

"Boris, let's get that rifle. It might come in handy even if it isn't usable." Phil turned toward Nancy. "Want to see what's inside the box?"

"We all do," Boris said. "We've gone through a lot to find it."

With Grant hobbling between his wife and Laura, they walked to the box and watched Phil wrestle the rectangular box right side up. Sliding the bolt out of its hasp, he opened the lid. Boris let out a long whistle.

"What exactly are we looking at?" Laura asked.

"Fragments of Cosmos 954." Phil pointed to the various pieces. "Looks like parts of a beryllium rod. That cylinder could be from the satellite's powered reactor and would contain uranium 235, highly hazardous. No wonder Henri had blisters."

Nancy's brown eyes flashed, and a grin spread across her face. "The jackpot. You won't be able to keep me from telling the world about this, Phil. I'll slam the government's cover-up of Operation *Morning Light.*" She stood with her chin high and her eyes glued on Phil as if she were waiting for him to berate her.

Phil sighed, closed the lid and slid the lock home. "We can discuss that later. Right now, we'd better head to camp."

Boris bent down and picked up the damaged rifle. "I'm a lucky son of a gun." He examined the Winchester and expelled the remaining bullets into his hand. He glanced at Phil and the box at his feet. "That looks damn heavy, seventy to eighty pounds, I bet. About one foot wide by one and a half feet deep and two feet long with lead."

"Don't give me numbers," Phil said. "I might not be able to lift it." Grunting, he hoisted the box to his shoulder and staggered under its weight. "Lead the way to the canoes, ladies."

The canoes rode low in the water with Grant and Boris in one with Laura and Karen paddling. Nancy paddled in the bow of Phil's boat with the lead-lined box in the center. Phil's head reeled with the knowledge that Cal had divulged Phil's profession. Although he'd never told Boris or Cal about his association with the Bureau, Cal often dropped remarks that led Phil to believe he knew. When Nancy had burst out with the news, Boris hadn't seemed surprised either.

Would Nancy ever forgive him? He'd always thought he'd be able to fade out of her life without her knowing of his Bureau affiliation. If he'd found the diamond lode, he could have left the Bureau and started a new career. That scheme's blown to hell. At least we've recovered the Cosmos fragments. *You can rest easy, Erich, and soon I'll take care of Henri.*

He studied the lead-lined box, an icon to modern man's achievements. Its weight would make the upcoming two-mile portage south of the Hanbury and Clarke rivers' junction extremely difficult. With Grant out of commission and Boris hurting, the rest of them would have extra work to get to the rendezvous site.

As they approached their campsite, a canoe darted into the water. Henri. Grabbing his binoculars from his daypack, Phil surveyed their camp and his heart sank. "Christ. He's ravaged the camp." He put down his binoculars and picked up his paddle.

"I don't see Cal or Deirdre." Laura said.

"That son-of-a-bitch," Boris cursed.

Faces grim, they paddled landward. There was no movement save the flap of a loose tarp and bobbing debris in the water along the shore.

"Cal. Deirdre." Laura yelled into the eerie silence.

After they beached the canoes, Phil and the women jumped out and ran to the campsite, dreading what they might find. There was no sign of Cal or Deirdre. After viewing their slashed sleeping bags, tarps, tents and duffel bags, they drifted to the water's edge. Boris held Phil's binoculars with his left hand and scanned the ridge above the campsite.

"What'll we do?" Laura moved closer to him.

Boris clasped her hand. "One thing at a time. We'll get camp shaped up, then hunt for them."

"First, drag the canoes above the waterline," Phil said.

While Nancy helped Phil with the canoes, Karen and Laura assisted Grant to what remained of their camp and eased him onto a torn tarp. Boris began picking up remnants of a tent and erected it near Grant, then they began the depressing task of taking inventory. Apparently, Henri hadn't had enough time to destroy the canoe left behind, although he'd dented it. Most of their food supplies had been tossed into the river.

Boris and the women retrieved what they could, while Phil hiked the perimeter of the camp trying to determine what had happened to Cal and Deirdre. Above the camp, he found their tracks leading northwest into the esker. The same way he, Boris and Grant had gone earlier. Instead of following the tracks, he walked back. "Let me have your hunting knife," he said to Grant.

With a questioning look, Grant fumbled for his knife and handed the sheath and the knife over. "They went inland?" he asked.

"Yeah." Phil looked over where the others were working. "Explain to them where I went. I'll be back after I learn something."

"Take Boris with you."

Phil shook his head. "He's having trouble moving. I think his ribs are broken."

"Karen?"

"She's needed here to organize whatever we can save."

Grant's eyelids fluttered. "At least let them know where you're going."

"Right." Phil went and explained the situation. "I'm not sure what I'll find. Perhaps they bolted when they saw Henri and got lost."

Nancy sighed, gazing at a soggy bag of flour she held in her hand. "They were talking about finding the diamonds. You know, the lode you, Cal, and Boris were going to divvy up between you."

"I'd hardly put it that way," Boris said, his face red. "We wanted to learn about Erich—"

Nancy waved him off and dropped the bag back into the water. "They're probably digging in the soil this very minute. Bet they've forgotten all about us." She hesitated and stared at Phil. "Damned if I know why I trust you, Phil, after all I've learned." She released a heavy sigh. "Let's go."

"What do you mean? I'm going alone. Everyone stays here."

"Not on your life." Nancy picked up her jacket and moved toward the hill beyond the campsite.

Phil followed and grabbed her arm. "It's dangerous up there. We found bear tracks, a she-bear and her cub."

She pulled her arm away and faced him. "Look, Phil, you might be with the FBI, but at this point I don't give a damn. I am not letting you go off looking for those two alone. If they found your precious diamond lode, I want to know it. I'm not going to allow this wilderness to be destroyed by you and your friends gouging the earth to get rich."

"That's not what it's all about." He felt his face and neck grow hot. "I admit that's how it looks," he said, feeling her disgust. "Diamonds are only one of the reasons we're here."

"Let's go!" The crack of her voice sounded like his mother's when she was exasperated with him.

He stepped in front of her. "Remember, you insisted on coming." He walked to the top of the knoll and stopped. "Stay close behind me, and if I tell you to do something, do it...for a change."

He followed Cal and Deirdre's prints inland, scanned the bushes and moved with caution. "I hope you're right, and we find them up to their asses in diamonds."

"I hope no one ever finds any diamonds." Nancy stepped over a fallen tree stump. "Haven't you heard what the big mining companies are doing up here?"

Phil stopped and turned on her. "I know you're angry with me. You have a right to be. I had a job to do, and I did it."

"Are you happy being a spy?"

"Are you happy hurting innocent people and blowing up power stations?"

"I don't do that."

"Some of your people did. My job was to see you didn't break the law. I protected you from doing that until you joined Pierre Giraud's terrorist group."

"That was an exploratory talk."

Phil turned away and started walking, angry with himself and with her. The light dimmed further as the first phase of the summer's Arctic darkness cloaked them in drab gray. He checked his watch. Midnight. "They wouldn't have stayed away from camp this long."

Nancy gazed at the darkening sky. "Maybe they got lost."

"Maybe." Phil continued following the footprints, but stopped when bear prints crossed Cal and Deirdre's trail. Tensing, he searched the short foliage. Nothing moved. He pulled out the long hunting knife, feeling foolish. What hope did he have against a grizzly with a knife? "If a grizzly attacks, run like hell, and I'll do what I can to slow her down."

"I thought you were supposed to be still and curl up into a ball."

"Right, but if she charges, run."

Phil felt Nancy's hand on his back as they continued. Cream-colored rock formations spread out to their right as the esker ended. Prints became harder to detect, as the landscape turned to boulders with scattered brush.

Nancy grabbed the back of his vest. "There's something on the ground to the side of that rock. See? Where that tree snag is."

Cautiously, they moved forward. In the darkened sky, it was difficult to distinguish objects.

"Clothes," Nancy said.

When they drew nearer, Phil shuddered and ordered, "Stay here."

"No way. I'm keeping close to you," she said, clinging to his vest.

Something was wrong. The air was too still. No, that wasn't it. The smell. The buzzing. Flies. "Jesus!" He exhaled. Warily, he stepped forward.

Nancy peered from behind him. "Oh, my God!" She stumbled sideways and threw up.

He left her and moved toward what was left of Cal. His shredded clothes were soaked with blood and his limbs lay askew. Flies throbbed over his body like a separate creature. Bile surged into Phil's mouth. He gritted his teeth and swallowed. He closed his eyes, trying to steady his nerves, but the smell of death chiseled through him. Shaking, he backed away. He had nothing to cover the body and wondered where Deirdre was. Scanning the brush, he spotted crushed branches. He glanced toward Nancy and knew he didn't need to order her to stay put. Willing himself forward, he found Deirdre.

One swipe of the she-bear's paw was all it had taken. Deirdre's severed head lay yards from her torso.

Chapter 29

At three in the morning a rim of light on the eastern horizon brought some comfort to Nancy and Phil as they hiked back to camp. Phil's mouth was sour and dry. Not taking a water bottle with them had been stupid. Several times Nancy had stumbled, and he'd reached out to support her. Neither spoke. She seemed dazed and disoriented either from shock or exhaustion, he wasn't sure. Phil surveyed the surrounding brush, fearing the sow might still be in the area. Although drained from lack of sleep, it was the gruesome vision of Cal and Deirdre that haunted him. He could still smell the fetid odor of death.

On the top of the ridge their encampment below seemed like an oasis amidst a landscape strewn with death. They staggered down to the two tents sitting like little monuments to hope. Soft snores came from the larger tent.

Karen poked her head out of the smaller tent. "I thought I heard footsteps. I was getting worried. You didn't find them?"

Nancy sagged onto the sand next to the tent without saying a word, while Phil dropped to his knees in front of Karen and said softly, "We found them." He paused, not sure how she'd take the news. "There's no easy way to say it. They must have gotten between a she-bear and her cub. The grizzly attacked them. We...ah, we couldn't bury them."

Karen stifled a cry, then crawled out of the tent and cradled Nancy in her arms, rocking her back and forth. Nancy's tears spilled down her cheeks, yet she made no sound.

Phil felt like an interloper as he viewed Nancy's emotional state. He didn't blame her. If he could have snuggled into someone's arms, he'd have welcomed it, but he needed to suppress his feelings. "I'll go back tomorrow and bury them. Maybe there's a tarp or something that I can wrap them in." His voice seemed to come from outside of himself as if he were two people, one watching, the other speaking. "The wolves might get there before I do, but I can't go back tonight."

"No, you can't," Karen said. "We'll talk about it in the morning. You both need to get a few hours of sleep."

"Water," Phil said. "Do you have any handy?"

Karen nodded toward the bottles stored next to the tent. Phil took one and passed another to Nancy.

Nancy pulled away from Karen's arms, wiped her eyes and accepted the bottle. "Thanks for the shoulder. I'm usually not so…. God, it was awful."

"You handled it well," Phil said.

"Oh sure. I threw up." After taking a long drink of water, Nancy gave him a wan smile. "I never thought I'd see anything like that. This trip was supposed to be a coup of environmental discovery, not a death march."

"Yeah, well, the wilderness has its own laws." Phil glanced about. "What about the other tents?"

"These are all we could salvage," Karen said. "Grant has a fever. He and I have this two-man tent, and we thought the four of you could manage in the other one. Boris thought when you returned that the guys could sleep outside, but we set up four places inside with pieces of sleeping bags."

"What a mess." Phil looked around at the piles of goods stacked near the tents. "I'll sleep outside in case Henri comes back. Climb in the tent, Nancy, and hand me some bedding." He turned to Karen. "Go back to sleep. There's nothing we can do tonight. We'll make decisions tomorrow."

The following morning Grant remained in the tent with a fever while the others gathered around the gas stove, drinking coffee and discussing Cal and Deirdre. Boris wrapped his arms protectively around Laura as they sat on the sand. Laura attempted unsuccessfully to hold back tears and said, "Deirdre always enjoyed excitement. She liked the adventure trips. They made her forget the loss of her child." Laura looked at the river and sniffed. "This trip seemed perfect. She wanted to know about Cal's past, thought it would bring them closer. He never would talk to her about the Arctic. Now we know why." She shuddered. "How could the trip go so wrong?" Laura stared at Phil and leaned forward, pulling away from Boris. "Phil, you knew from the beginning this wasn't a simple paddle on the Thelon. You should have stopped her from coming with Cal. You knew this was dangerous." She glared at Phil, then pounded her fist in the sand. "She shouldn't have died."

Phil, caught off guard by her vehemence, was too tired to argue and in a way he did blame himself.

"I knew and so did Cal." Boris reached for Laura's hand. "This was the only way we could learn the truth about Erich's death and what he might have found. Sure, the diamonds were part of the incentive, but it's Henri who's to blame."

Laura turned to Boris and buried her face in his chest, oblivious to the pain that flashed across his face.

"Karma," Nancy muttered.

A hush coated the campsite. Phil glanced at the rich sky, full of cumulus clouds on the horizon. A dull ache throbbed across his brow, and he swallowed hard, then cleared his throat. "I'll go back with one of the tarps and bury them, then we'll paddle on."

"I'll go with you," Boris said.

Phil shook his head. "You wouldn't be able to help with your damaged ribs. Besides, someone has to guard the camp in case Henri shows up. He doesn't know you're injured or that the rifle is inoperable. We need to protect the remaining canoes."

Nancy's chin came up. "I'll go and help."

"You don't have to," Phil said, not meaning it, for he desperately needed help. Wrapping up the bodies was one thing, but transporting them out of the rocky area back to an esker would take hours if he had to do it alone.

"Yes, I do." Nancy stared at the sand in front of her.

"The four of us will go," Karen said, nodding to Laura, Nancy and Phil. "Boris can look after Grant. I can't do much for him except give him liquids." She rose to her feet and slapped sand off her khaki pants.

"Grant's a lucky guy to have you," Phil said and went to search for enough tarp to bury the Sterlings.

After performing their gruesome burial chore, they returned to camp late in the afternoon. Phil had protected the women from viewing Deirdre by wrapping her in a tarp while the women did the same for Cal. Afterward, they'd carried the remains to a sandy spot and buried them in a common grave, then stood in silence unable to offer a prayer.

Back in camp Phil knew they needed to get organized so they could move on, but a malaise gripped him. The group remained lethargic, fumbling rudimentary tasks. What they'd seen had drained their stamina and will.

It was up to Phil to set the tone, but apathy pulled at him. How could he lead when he felt depressed and guilt-ridden? Staring at the churning Thelon, he spotted an otter playing with a piece of wood, rolling it over and over in a ludicrous replay of Sisyphus pushing the rolling stone. He began to laugh and had an idea. He leaped up, ran to the water, stripped to the buff and plunged into the icy river. "Boris, you slacker," he yelled. "Get in here and heal your ribs."

The group on shore stared as if Phil had gone mad. After a slight hesitation, Boris grinned, walked to the water's edge and stripped. Unable to dive, he walked gingerly into the river until his shoulders were immersed. "The Ganges, only colder." He ducked his broad curly haired head under the water.

On shore the women gaped at the crazy men. Nancy cocked her head to one side. "Phil, you're one crazy fool," she muttered, got a towel and ran to the water. "What the hell." She stripped quickly before the flies could consume her body and dove in. Water flicked off her thin arms as she swam with neat strokes.

Hesitantly, Laura and Karen followed, turning their backs to the men when they stripped. Hurrying into the water, they laughed like young girls as the cold river lapped around their naked bodies.

Like frenzied fish, they thrashed in the water, splashing and yelling, innocent of their nakedness, completely and utterly drunk with the joy of living. The tension eased from Phil's body as he watched the cavorting group. If they had inhaled pot, they couldn't have been higher. He dove for the bottom, the cold penetrated his bones, but the numbness soothed him like a blanket. When he resurfaced, he felt empowered, purified.

"We are nymphs arising from the sea, immortal," Nancy shouted and lifted her arms above her head and pirouetted as if in a water ballet.

"I'm an oread, watching over the hills." Laura laughed, then coughed from inhaling water. Her blonde head bobbed, while she grinned, intoxicated with being alive.

"We are naiads, watching over the sea," Nancy countered in a singsong cadence as she and Karen joined hands above the water.

"I am Moses and will part the waters and leave you high and dry."
Boris laughed wickedly until he grabbed his ribs surrendering to pain. "Oh
damn, it hurts to laugh."

"What's going on?" Grant's weak yell from shore brought them back to
reality. He stood by the tent staring at them then began to stagger toward
the shore.

"Stay put," Karen yelled and waded out of the water, grabbed her
clothes and rushed to his side.

While Karen reassured Grant they weren't all insane, Nancy and Laura
swam to shore, leaving Boris and Phil waiting while the women donned
their clothes.

"A crazy idea." Boris winked at Phil.

"I feel much better. How about you?"

"Frozen solid but feeling damn good despite my ribs."

The men waded to shore and dressed hurriedly before their warmed
bodies attracted the ever-present flies. As Phil buttoned his shirt, he watched
the women dry their hair. The atmosphere had changed, and despite their
predicament, he felt a ray of hope. Tomorrow they'd paddle on, but tonight
they had to plan how to meet Henri's next move. For he would try to kill
them. Of that Phil was positive.

After a skimpy dinner of canned sardines, baked beans, biscuits and
half a candy bar, Phil asked Karen, "How much food do we have?"

She sat next to Grant, who reclined against a pile of cutup packs. Karen
pulled a crumpled piece of paper from her jacket pocket. "One jar of jam,
one peanut butter, six meat and fish tins, eight packets of oatmeal, two tins
of biscuits, and five freeze-dried dinners. Coffee, no sugar or powdered
cream."

"Too bad you didn't catch a fish while you were in the water," Grant
said.

Phil caught Grant's grin and realized their taciturn guide had some
humor. "I'll catch one by the tail next time." Phil made a grabbing motion
with his hand. "The food supply isn't too bad. We have what, seven or eight
days left of paddling?"

"It's a hell of a way to lose weight," Nancy said. "What about you,
Laura? I noticed you didn't eat the canned fish tonight. Are you going to
continue to be a vegetarian under the circumstances?"

"I hadn't thought about it," she said, looking confused.

"There's peanut butter and jam," Karen said, "but we should share everything rather than one person eating only one thing."

Laura squirmed as all eyes fastened on her. "I won't take more than my share of anything."

Boris took her arm firmly. "You can't starve yourself."

"He's right," Phil said. "Each of us must stay as strong and alert as possible. This is no time for martyrdom or diet restriction." He ignored defiant Laura. "Doling out the food is up to you, Karen."

Phil glanced at Grant, wondering if their leader noticed he'd taken charge. Since Grant didn't react, he continued his survey. "Laura, do you have a handle on the gear?"

"Two tents. We've cobbled enough bedding, and there are three large duffels. We each have our own daypacks."

"I suggest we continue to wear our packs at all time. Keep essentials in them just in case," Phil said.

Boris stretched out his legs and grimaced. "The third canoe's got a skewed bow, but could be used to tow things."

"It can haul the box," Phil said.

"We're taking it with us?" Karen looked toward her husband.

"We should leave it," Grant said. "When we get out, the Mounties can come get it."

Boris smoothed out the sand in front him, picked it up and let it stream through his fingers. "I'd like to take it with us." Without looking up, he continued, "The box is proof Erich's discovery might have led to Henri killing him. Who knows what might happen to the box if we leave it behind?"

"I agree." Phil looked at Nancy, who nodded in agreement.

"It'll make the two-mile portage very difficult," Grant said. "And," he looked at the others, "that's where Henri will hit us. It's the most likely spot to set a trap."

Phil pulled out his rumpled map from his vest pocket and unfolded it, laying it out on the sand. "I think you're right. He'll probably try to take us one by one. We must stick together, at least in twos and threes. He doesn't know Boris and Grant are injured, so we have a slight advantage there."

"We can't take all the supplies and the canoes across the portage in one load," Grant said. "There's no other way around the falls. That'll leave us vulnerable at either end."

"Then we won't take all the equipment," Phil said. "How far is it from the portage to the rendezvous site?"

"Normally a two-day paddle if the wind doesn't kick up," Grant said. "If Chip doesn't hear from us, he'll start looking along the river."

"If we get Henri's radio, we'll be able to contact Chip," Boris said.

"We can't count on getting the radio," Nancy said. "Is there any chance of repairing the rifle?"

"It would take tools we don't have, and besides there are only three bullets," Boris said.

"Henri doesn't know the rifle is inoperable," Nancy persisted. "We can bluff. If he sees the flash of the rifle, he'll stay away."

"I'd hate to play poker with you," Phil said.

"I think you have for the past few years." Nancy's eyes flashed. "I just didn't know we were playing."

"There's another element to consider," Grant said. "Nature itself can be a killer, especially if you're distracted."

"You're referring to Cal and Deirdre," Laura said. Even in the dim evening light, Phil could see her drawn face and tight lips.

Grant frowned. "I'm referring to us. Be aware of your surroundings. Out here nature dictates what happens. Forget that and you're in trouble."

After more discussion of their options, the conversation waned. Wearily, Nancy said, "I'm beat and ready to call it a day. Should we post a guard?"

"I doubt if he'll come back tonight," Phil said. "But to be safe, we should post one. How about switching every two hours?"

"I'll take the first watch," Laura said. "I couldn't sleep right now anyway."

Boris gazed at her with a wistful expression. "We can do the shifts in pairs. Easier to keep awake and not as lonely."

"Are you up to it, Grant?" Phil asked.

"Yes, my fever's down."

"Two hour shifts." Phil agreed. "Nancy and I'll take the second shift. We ought to get started early in the morning. Say six."

Phil felt uneasy in the tent with Nancy when so much had been left unsaid between them. He knelt as she fiddled with her pack in the corner of the tent. "Thanks for being so solid. It hasn't been easy," he said.

From the dark shadows of the tent, she said, "It's been a long journey. I'm almost out of cigarettes."

He chuckled. "Your last bad habit?"

"What about your bad habits?" For a moment she didn't say anything else, and he waited for on of her vehement her lectures. "You came here with ulterior motives," she finally said, sitting cross-legged at the back of the tent.

"So did you," he said.

"Mine were altruistic. The debris in the box proves my theory that there's still hazardous waste in the Arctic."

"It doesn't prove the government tried to cover it up." He smoothed out his bedding. "God knows, we tried to find every last bit of stuff from that satellite. You can't make every mistake, every accident, into a conspiracy."

"What was the government doing to me?" She leaned forward, her eyes locked onto his. "I set up *Cure the World*, and the government starts infiltrating my organization as if it were subversive."

"Some of your people were terrorists," he said, taking up her challenge. "You were headed deeper in that direction when you planned to meet with Pierre."

"Okay, that was a mistake, but what about you and your diamond mine? Did you plan to extract the diamonds without a permit?"

In the silence that followed, he thought about her question as he stretched out. Yes. That's exactly what he'd planned. For years he'd been consumed, just as Erich had been, with finding the diamond lode. Would they really have mined it illegally or would they have filed a claim and gone through the paperwork to get the mine operating? Either way, he knew the land would have been despoiled and they would be not better than the big mining companies. So what did that make him?

"I think of Chief Seattle," she said quietly as if talking to herself. "I used to have my students memorize his letter to President Fillmore when Fillmore asked to buy the land where Chief Seattle's people lived. 'How can you buy or sell the sky?' he wrote, 'If we do not own the freshness of the air and the sparkle of the water, how can you buy them?'"

She stared at Phil. "He goes on about how he wants the land preserved for everyone, for all children, and he wants the white man to revere the land as his people do. 'This we know: the earth does not belong to man, man belongs to the earth.... Man did not weave the web of life, he is merely a strand in it. Whatever he does to the web, he does to himself.'" She paused. "I think I forgot the meaning of his words."

Phil's chest tightened, and he rubbed his eyes. Nancy had never shown this side of her character, always leading with an iron fist, no give, no softness. Had her strident view of environmental causes strangled this other side? Even her humor had glazed over this other philosophical Nancy.

He rose on one elbow and gazed at her, seeing who she really was for the first time. "You never talked like that before."

"I've never faced a life-threatening situation before." She relaxed on her side, facing him. "It's made me think about what I've done and what I should be doing."

He reached out and momentarily held her hand, then released it. "Perhaps we both have some learning to do." Lying on his back, he studied the top of the tent with his hands behind his head.

"Is there a chance for us, Phil?" she whispered.

"We'll make it."

"That's not what I meant."

"I know," he said. They were like icebergs chaffing against each other, neither fully trusting the other.

Chapter 30

In the morning they gathered the remaining gear and set out, trying to forget what had occurred and what might still happen. Soon after leaving their campsite, they paddled into the Thelon Sanctuary. Despite their safety concerns, they marveled at the sighting of two red foxes and later a long-tailed jaeger flew overhead. Each night as they huddled in the two remaining tents or stood guard, they heard the primeval howl of wolves. During the short spurts of darkness of the summer Arctic, the aurora borealis flickered in frost-white beams and multi-hues of green and orange across the distant skyline. The moon carved a white-etched sickle in the short hours of blue-black nights.

For three days they saw no sign of Henri, but sightings of caribou increased. A small herd of forty crossed the river behind them, and clusters of caribou fur drifted to the water's edge. A river otter splashed in playful delight in the shadow of a cliff. A pair of whistling swans broke the skin of the water as they landed ponderously on the opposite side of the river. Floating majestically, the swans surveyed the passing canoes with regal disdain, and the river played like an accordion, narrowing and widening.

Grant remained weak, so Karen and Nancy paddled the canoe with him as passenger along with half the gear. Laura and Phil were in the other canoe with Boris wedged in with their meager supplies. The dented canoe containing the lead-lined box was tethered to Phil's canoe and it yawed from side to side, unwieldy as an anchor.

Meals were skimpy. Before they set out on the morning of the third day, Nancy smoked her last cigarette. Phil watched her inhale. "You're now entering smokers anonymous," he said, feeling ridiculously righteous.

Nancy sighed, field stripped the butt and strewed the remains on the ground by the canoe. "Thanks for your sympathy."

"My dad always told me sympathy could be found in the dictionary between sex and syphilis." He laughed, thinking of his dad and not of Nancy's discomfort.

"And you have a nice day, too." She turned her back and picked up her paddle.

Boris gave Phil a scornful look as he eased himself into the canoe. "You do have a way with women, don't you?"

"Trying for humor," Phil said.

"Trying, ain't succeeding," Boris said wearily.

The day wore on, and the wind picked up. Head nets hung around their necks, at the ready against the pesky flies. They labored under their cumbersome daypacks strapped to their backs. Laura kept half her camera equipment in her pack and half in a bag tied to the center thwart of her canoe behind Boris.

The river slithered through the land like a snake, preventing a view of what might lie ahead. As the river curved around each bend, they edged toward the middle, always fearful of a trap by Henri. Each day nerves frayed further, conversations became curt and arguments erupted about hauling the box.

The canoes separated more than usual, for the tug of the extra canoe had become a heavy burden. In the lead canoe, Grant raised his hand and signaled toward shore. Phil thought he might have spotted Henri and called out, "What is it?"

Grant put his forefinger to his lips, then cupped his ear. Laura stopped paddling and their canoe lagged even farther behind. "What's he hear?" Laura asked.

"Hush," Boris said and sat straighter, wincing with the effort.

Around the bend, Grant pointed toward the far shore and waved. Nothing had prepared Phil for the sight of the shimmering, throbbing horde of caribou milling at the edge of the riverbank. The gray brownish creatures covered the earth like a mantle far back into the tundra.

"The main herd of the migrating Barrenground caribou," Grant called out.

Henri stalked the rear of the caribou herd with his wolf hide vest under his arm. The caribou were pressed from behind as more gathered at the river. When the canoes rounded the bend, he flapped his jacket, and the caribou exploded forward.

The caribou at the river's edge leaped into the water. Like a mass of lemmings, the herd moved in one massive surge into the river, necks high, antlers swaying.

Phil now realized that Grant had been trying to tell them that they were in the herd's path. Their canoes would collapse like matchsticks in front of the onslaught. "Paddle!" he yelled. From his position in the bow, Phil flung a look back. Laura had her camera to her eye. "For God's sake paddle." Phil implored.

"I'm getting a picture." Her voice rose with excitement, while she kept her eye glued to her lens piece. "It'll be a minute."

"Take a picture later." Boris stared at the oncoming herd.

"I'll get great close ups." She snapped pictures as the herd drew ever nearer. "Laura," Boris's voice boomed. "Paddle."

In the bow, Phil paddled hard but knew it was hopeless as the first caribous with their magnificent and deadly antlers swirled toward them. "Laura, pull in the line of the tethered canoe," Phil ordered. "Get it in front of us. They're going to hit us broadside."

Waves from the herd's churning hoofs and heavy bodies rocked their canoe. Startled, Laura finally realized the danger. Her camera dangled from her neck as she handed the line to Boris and he in turn passed it to Phil. Phil yanked the rope, grabbed the craft's gunwale and he and Boris forced the extra canoe between them and the herd. Although the caribou split apart instead of crashing directly into the canoes, their antlers scraped both ends, tossing the boats back and forth. The water roiled. The heavy box sitting deep in the hull kept the battered canoe upright. As the backwash sloshed toward their canoe, Phil tried to lean into the roll. Laura sprawled forward onto Boris with her camera strap around her throat.

"My camera strap's caught under the thwart," she yelled.

Boris pulled the strap off her neck. The camera skid around the bottom of the canoe and she tried to grab it. Boris grasped the gunwales on either side to steady the rocking. As if a rug had been pulled out from under the hull, the canoe began to capsize.

"My camera," Laura wailed.

As they rolled, Phil yelled, "Stay close to the canoes." He held onto his paddle as they keeled over.

Water closed over Phil's head as his daypack tugged at his shoulders, pulling him under. The wheeling legs and hooves of the caribou thrashed near him. Terrified, he surfaced like a breaching whale, then ducked down again to swim under their craft and resurface between the two canoes. He tossed his paddle into the upright canoe with the box and clung to its gunwale with one hand and reached out with the other to grasp the hull of the capsized canoe. He looked about frantically. "Boris, Laura."

"Here," came Boris's bass voice.

"Swim under and get between the canoes."

Boris and Laura popped up next to him. "Keep hold of both canoes to keep them apart," Phil shouted.

"Our canoe's sinking," Boris yelled. "Cut the lashing around the equipment."

"No," Laura screamed. "My camera bag."

Phil reached for Grant's knife strapped to his belt. Their good canoe sank farther. It would be only a matter of time before a hoof pierced its hull. He slipped under the water and severed the line holding the equipment, allowing the canoe to bob upward.

"Get it at right angles to the other canoe," he shouted above the din of snorting, bleating caribou. He pushed and heaved the hull around. "Push the nose on top of the other one, like a T."

They huddled under the T, drifting with the current while the primordial herd driven by migratory instincts, churned past. Phil glanced at his watch. What had seemed like an hour had taken only minutes. He shivered in the cold water. The caribou jostled and pushed their makeshift raft from all sides. It took all three of them sculling and kicking to keep their raft at right angles to the wild horde.

Wave after wave of bodies with huge brown eyes wheezed, grunted and splashed—a living flood, streaming across the river. A dank odor permeated the air as a band of massive bulls swam by; their antlers stretched skyward like a moving forest.

Phil's hands and feet grew numb from the cold. Boris and Laura's faces paled, their lips blue. The effort to keep their barrier at right angles to the herd weakened as the buffeting continued.

"Keep moving, kicking," Phil hollered. "It'll end soon." *But when?* Each time he thought the surge of caribou had passed another group thrashed by. A few lone calves bleated plaintively for their mothers. Phil hauled himself high enough over the canoes to view the shore. Except for a few strays, the main herd had crossed. Now, thousands of hooves striking land echoed from the opposite riverbank.

"We've got to get out of the water." Phil tried to flip their good canoe off the battered one.

Boris's attempts to help were feeble. An ashen-faced Laura reached up with one limp arm.

"We'll turn it over on the count of three," Phil said. With a unified effort, they flipped the canoe upright, slid it off the other one and eased it into the water. "I'll get in and help you up. Laura, swim to the other side to steady it." He kicked hard as he grabbed both gunwales and hauled himself into the canoe, landing like a floundering fish. Sitting up right, he helped Laura ease into the bow of the boat, where she sat shivering.

"Okay, Boris." Phil reached a hand down to him.

"Not sure I can make it with my ribs." Boris tilted his face upward. Phil saw the dull sheen in his eyes. "Paddle to shore and drag me along until then."

"You need to get out of the water, now," Phil urged.

"Whitewater." Laura shrieked. "Whitewater. We're nearing rapids."

"Boris, get in." Phil grabbed Boris's arm. "Come on."

"I can't. Too painful."

"God damn it, man." Phil yelled at him. "Work through the pain."

"Please, Boris," Laura begged.

As Boris struggled, Phil latched onto Boris's belt and yanked upward. An ugly scream pierced the air, as Boris hung over the side of the canoe. "You got it made," Phil said and pulled his legs up and over the gunwale.

When Boris lay quivering like a jellyfish, Phil looked up to see frothy water along the width of the river. The canoes bounced heavily as they hit the first riffles. He settled in the stern and hauled in the line attached to the other canoe, grabbed his paddle from its hull and released the line again. "Laura, paddle."

"I lost it." Her eyes shone with terror.

"Hold tight." From his place in the stern, he searched for the widest V in the river and paddled toward it. Blindly, they entered the first part of the rapids. The battered canoe, lashed to the stern, acted like a wayward missile. He reached behind him and tugged at the line. Like a stubborn ass, it balked. Between using paddling strokes and prying, he drew in the line. When he thought he had the canoe well in hand, it careened toward their hull. He grabbed for its bow, but missed. It smashed into his canoe, mashing his hand between the two hulls. White-hot pain seared through him. He lost focus. Fought off fainting. Dropped his paddle onto the floor of the canoe. Grasping the line tight with his right hand, he lashed it around his left boot, bringing the extra canoe snug so both canoes reacted in unison.

Water splashed aboard, blinding him. Frantically, he swiped at his glasses, thankful he had them attached with Croakies. He picked up his paddle with his right hand and used the heel of his left on the nub of the handle. Pain spun through his spine and shot to his head.

Laura screamed. "Watch out. On the left."

He managed a cross pry stroke by holding the paddle handle to his chest with his left arm. Steering as best he could, he kept the canoe on line through the rapids. The hull scraped and grated over rocks. As though disgorged from a pinball machine, their canoes darted out of the rapids and drifted into calmer water.

Phil shuddered and doubled over from pain as water sloshed at his feet. The line remained tied around his foot, and the nose of the tethered canoe clicked against their hull.

"Good job," Boris said from his position facing Phil. "I thought we'd bought it. Your hand doesn't look good."

Phil gazed at his throbbing hand as if it didn't belong to him.

"Give your paddle to Laura," Boris said.

Phil's vision blurred, and the pinprick of light vanished.

Henri crouched in a rocky formation past the rapids, his canoe hidden behind boulders and brush. He waited patiently, certain nature would handle his enemies. The crossing of the massed herd was a beautiful sight, but not if you were in its path. He smoked a cigar and exhaled softly, watching the smoke curl around him.

Through his binoculars, he watched an upside down canoe careen through the rapids, drifting past his hideout. One survivor swam toward shore. Alone. She wouldn't last long. The others had obviously drowned. He pulled out a hunk of pemmican and chewed, salivating. With a light heart, he dragged his canoe out of hiding. A high-pitched shout startled him. He looked up to see two canoes flush out of the rapids. Grabbing his binoculars, he cursed. "The box."

The canoe landed, and the woman on shore ran to meet them. He'd wait for nature to kill them; if not, he would.

Chapter 31

Phil woke as the canoe nudged the shore, and someone helped him stumble out and stagger up a rocky shoreline.

"Help me get his pack off," a voice said.

He tried to help, but sank into darkness. When he awoke again, the pain in his hand had subsided into a hard, dull throb. Afraid to look at his injured hand, he concentrated instead on the blue sky above him. How long had he been unconscious? He turned his head to the right and found himself snuggled against rocks, warmed by the sun. What warmed him on the other side?

"How're you feeling?"

He turned his face toward the voice. Nancy's soft body gave him warmth.

"Okay," he said in a hoarse whisper. He noticed her scraped and bleeding face. "What happened to you?"

"Had a battle with a rock." She didn't elaborate.

"Are you okay otherwise? I mean, no broken bones or anything?" He lifted his head and shifted his body to rest against the rock, his mangled hand inert in his lap. A light wind tugged at his damp shirt and vest. "The rock windbreak's a good idea. Where is everyone?"

"Laura and Boris are behind another rocky outcrop. They're okay. Cold and wet like us." She hesitated. "I told them I'd call when you woke up."

"Let them rest. Nothing they can do."

"If you look over my shoulder," Nancy said, "you'll see the canoes and the box. Boris thinks a storm's coming in and thought we could use the canoes for shelter."

"Where are Grant and Karen?"

"I don't know. We capsized. I couldn't hold on to the canoe. Maybe they stayed with it."

He leaned his head back, trying to absorb that news. Surely, those pros made it through the rapids. "They're probably holed up licking their wounds just like us." Phil sank back behind the rock shelter. Their jackets had been spread out in the sun to dry with rocks holding them down against the wind. "We'll make it. I promise."

"Don't make promises." Nancy's voice trembled. "We're in bad shape. Our food's gone, we have one paddle, and your hand isn't usable."

He stole a glance at his throbbing hand that was was swollen and red like a sunburned blowfish. He was sure some bones were broken, but the skin was only abraded.

"I didn't know if I should bandage it or leave it alone," she said. "The metacarpal bones look broken."

"Mashed." He didn't dare move his fingers. "When did you go to medical school?"

"You pick up useful information when you're around a university. I tried to find something to use as a cast, but there isn't much available."

"You're hurting too." He inspected her bruised face. "A cold compress might help. Soak a cloth in the river."

"I didn't want to leave you until you woke up. Besides, I'm too cold."

"My pack?" He fumbled around and found it above his head. "Help me get my stuff out. I've got a first aid kit, candy bars and a wool sweater. Even wet, it'll help keep you warm."

Nancy got to her knees and grabbed his bag while Phil struggled to sit up and pawed with his good hand through his pack. He pulled out the sweater and two candy bars, handing one to Nancy. "Binoculars are okay and my first aid kit is still sealed."

She took the kit from him and opened it. "Tape, gauze, antiseptic cream and a few ibuprofen pills."

"I gave Boris most of them."

She looked at him. "Do you want one?"

"Damn right. Three." He reached out, then hesitated. "How about you?" He held out the plastic bottle. "That scrape looks nasty. The cream might help."

She nodded and took two pills with a sip from a water bottle. "From my pack," she said, handing the bottle to him.

"Where's your pack?" he asked.

She pointed to the gear and clothes spread out on rocks. "Trying to dry them out before the storm hits. I have a few bags of peanuts and a granola bar, but I didn't want to eat them yet. We should check with Boris and Laura. I'm not sure what they have."

"We can pool our resources later, but now we need energy, so enjoy." He tore off the wrapper with his teeth and took a large bite. While he chewed, he watched her eat. "Like a picnic and no pesky flies. Which reminds me…." He searched through his bag and came up with a T-shirt, a bandana and a wool hat. "Here," he said, holding out the bandana. "Use this for a compress for your face. Soak it in the river." He saw her shiver. "You need to get your circulation going. Jump up and down or run back and forth. I'd do that, but I'd probably faint. Afterward, I can put some of that cream on your face."

She tilted her head. "You're being sympathetic."

"So?"

"I thought you only found it in the dictionary between sex and syphilis."

He looked at her, puzzled, then sighed. "I'm a real ass at times."

"Yes, you are." She smiled, stood and jogged to the river, pulling her hair back in a pony tail as she went.

While she was gone, he studied his hand. He'd have to immobilize it. He thought of the vest he wore and Erich's notebook stashed there. "Perfect," he mumbled. Struggling out of his vest, he unzipped the pocket and removed the notebook. He left it in its plastic wrapper and let his damaged hand rest on it. He tied his hand to the notebook with the gauze, using his teeth to secure the knot. When he tightened it, he winced in pain.

"Nice casting job for a one-armed man." Nancy knelt next to him. "You had to bandage it by yourself, didn't you?" She shook her head and used pieces of tape to re-enforce the bandage. "That should help."

Phil pulled on his wool hat and felt warmer.

Nancy cradled the wet bandana against the side of her face. He handed her the antiseptic cream and she applied the cream to her cuts, then re-capped the tube. "I must look like hell."

"We both do, but we're alive. Let's keep it that way." He pulled on the wool sweater. "Come on in."

"I hate the smell of wet wool." She snuggled against his side, careful not to touch his damaged hand. After a time, she asked, "Do you think Henri's nearby?"

"Unfortunately, yes."

"Will he come after us if he knows how vulnerable we are?"

"Not sure. If he saw what happened, he might think nature will kill us without his intervention. On the other hand, he might want to finish us off." He shut his eyes for a moment. "Karen and Grant could be anywhere, this side or across the river. Did Laura and Boris look for them?"

"They searched this side, but they were too tired and cold to walk far, and they didn't want to leave us alone. Boris's ribs are painful. I think they're broken."

"Pulling him into the canoe probably made them worse, but we had no choice." Phil tried to think what they should do next. Holing up temporarily, at least until the wind abated, seemed practical. Paddling against the wind would be futile and besides, they only had one paddle. "Let's get the other two and set up a more permanent shelter for the night."

Henri watched through his binoculars, undecided on his next move. Four left, and Grant was not one of them. Was he out in the tundra? If Grant was alive, he had the experience to survive in the wild. Henri shrugged off any sense of guilt.

He rubbed his bearded chin and thought about the remaining four. Would they make it? They had two canoes and the box. As he often did, he traced the river's topography in his head: the upcoming waterfalls—sandstone rocks stacked like plates with water rushing over their edges, steep drop after steep drop, a panorama of giant stepping stones, beautiful and deadly. Creamy white cliffs jutted upward through stubby growth clinging to the sides.

What would be the condition of the four survivors when they got to the portage site, if they got there? The two-day paddle to the falls with no food, no shelter, no extra clothing would leave them weak, but they still might be able to manage the portage. Henri pounded his fist into his palm. They must perish before they got past the Clarke and Hanbury junction, otherwise, canoe tours coming off the Hanbury and heading for Baker Lake might find them. He'd get them and the box at the portage. Afterward, he'd paddle upstream and bury the box in a remote spot. This time no one would be there to record the event and his wilderness would be safe. When they didn't show at the rendezvous spot, Chip would search for them. Henri would be there, shocked that Grant and his party had disappeared without a trace. The government would consider the area around the Thelon too dangerous for adventure travelers, too dangerous for anyone, except trappers like himself.

He stuck one of Gilbert's cigars in his mouth and lit it.

After a night of thunder and lightning, but little rain, the sun shone with fluffy clouds lolling in the northern sky. A soft breeze kept the flies at bay as Laura and Nancy took turns paddling in the stern of the one worthy canoe, dragging the other one behind them. The men could offer little assistance. Boris sat in the middle of the first canoe and Phil agreed to be relegated to the trailing canoe with the lead-lined box. He sat in the stern, using a withered spruce branch as a rudder. His effort did little to aid the steering, but it made him feel useful.

At first light they attempted an upstream ferry to reach the opposite shore to search for Karen and Grant, but with only one paddle it had proved perilous. The river's current carried them backward and sideways. They called out and listened, but after several hours they headed the canoes downriver. Phil scanned the shoreline through his binoculars, holding them somewhat unsteadily with one hand.

"Hey," he shouted. "Over there. Paddle toward the right shore." Laura turned the craft toward a small inlet. As they got closer, they spotted an overturned hull bobbing in the water like a lifeless whale.

"Maybe they're close by," Nancy said. "Grant. Karen," she called, only to be rewarded by silence.

When they came alongside the canoe, they saw a gouged hole in its side. Nancy slumped. "Could they have survived?"

"The ropes are still tied to the thwarts. Let's pull it to shore." Phil grabbed the bowline with his good hand while Laura paddled toward a rocky beach. In the shallows Phil and Nancy got out into ankle-deep water, tugged the hull to shore and turned it upright. One duffel bag and a paddle remained lashed to the canoe.

"That paddle will help," Boris said, as Nancy slid it out from under the rope.

Phil cut the bag loose and helped Nancy haul it to shore. Like an eager child searching for treats, Nancy fell upon it.

"Damn. Wrong bag," Nancy said as she pulled out sodden sleeping bags, a tent and a few pans. "The other bag had the food." Her shoulders slumped. "Grant and Karen couldn't be...."

"They're somewhere out there." Phil nodded in the direction of the far land. When we get to the rendezvous, Chip can set up a search and rescue." He spoke with more bravado than he felt, but believing their guides were alive would energize them to make the rendezvous point at Ursus Island.

Boris nodded. "We got another paddle and a tent. It'll be a piece of cake. Let's get going."

"Easy for you to say," Laura said with a half-smile. "Nancy and I are doing the paddling."

"Women's lib is a grand thing." Boris settled back in the canoe.

"The day after tomorrow should bring us to the falls and the portage point." Phil waded out to the second canoe. He looked at the box and wondered, how the hell they were going to get it over a two-mile portage?

Chapter 32

After days with little food, pictures of hamburgers and beer swirled through Phil's mind and Nancy and Laura paddled slower and slower. He helped haul the canoes and set up camp, and Boris could do even less, yet the women never complained.

The current increased, and the riverbanks changed from low shorelines with open tundra beyond, to steep, dun-colored cliffs of stratified shale and slate. The muffled thunder of falls reverberated over the river. Hugging the right shoreline, they searched for a landing site and spotted a small flat shelf at the base of a cliff. The river sliced through the stratified rock as if a knife had cut a layered cake.

They landed and surveyed the steep slope that ran some thirty feet to the top of the ridge, where tips of trees jutted like pins toward the blue sky. A chiseled path to the top traversed the hill. The beginning angled gently upward, but the last ten yards rose sharply. This had to be the beginning of the portage, for farther along, the shoreline disappeared as the rock cliff disappeared into swirling water.

Phil stood with his legs planted far apart, trying to appear stronger than he felt. "We've got to watch out for Henri. He won't give up. He'll try to kill us."

"You're a big comfort." Nancy, disheveled and pale, perched on a rock. "I looked forward to getting here, but now it gives me the creeps. That's a tough climb."

Laura studied the blisters on her hand. "At least we'll be walking instead of paddling."

"Climbing is more like it," Nancy said.

Boris took Laura's hand and beckoned her to sit next to him. "You've done a grand job." He nodded to Nancy. "Both of you." He gazed up at the incline as if taking its measure. "If we stay together, we should be okay."

Phil didn't like the odds or the climb and knew a difficult choice had to be made. "We've done well till now, but unless someone's been holding back, we're out of food." He looked up, squinting into the sun. "We've got water, so we can last a long time, but we're weaker. Grant said there was good fishing on the other side of the river junctions." He hesitated. "Once we're on top of that plateau, we need to find the portage path. That means we have to reconnoiter the area and we can't do that with the canoes in tow, but we can't leave them unattended."

"Let's leave the canoe with the box behind," Laura said. "Hide it. The Mounties can get it later."

"If we leave it, I stay with it," Nancy's chin came up.

"We can't lose the evidence." Phil held up his hand before Laura responded. "I know you and Nancy have been doing the hard work, but we can't allow Henri to bury it again."

Boris shrugged. "We've come this far with it, we might as well go all the way." He looked at Laura. "How about it?"

Laura slapped her hands against her sides and grimaced. "Looks like I'm outvoted."

"Splitting up isn't a good idea," Boris said.

"If you've got a better one, I'm listening." Phil picked up a stone with his right hand and pumped his hand up and down as if weighing it. "I've got the knife. I can go up and search the path."

"You've got only one good hand," Nancy said. "You can't take on Henri in your condition."

"Can any of us take him on alone?" Phil asked.

Nancy stood. "I hate to tell you this, fellas, but Laura and I are in better shape than you. Between the two of us, we should be able to handle Henri." She pointed to the paddles. "They make good weapons, especially if we attack at the same time."

"Kipling was right," Boris said and gave a husky chuckle. "The female of the species is more deadly than the male."

"I bet you know the entire poem by heart." Laura's tired dirt-smeared face smiled fondly at him.

"Well, yes."

"I think we better split you Amazons up." Phil smiled as he looked from Laura to Nancy. "After all, both Boris and I need protection. Walking is tough for Boris. Laura, you're a stronger hiker than Nancy, so you and I should scout ahead." He looked at Boris and Nancy. "All right?"

Laura stood and scuffed a rock with her boot. "Okay. I think that's the way to go. Leave one paddle with Nancy and Boris. You've got the knife, and I'll take the other paddle."

"Right. Let's get on with it," Phil said. "I don't want to hike overland at dusk if Henri's lurking about." As he and Laura started up the path from the river, he turned. "Keep an eye on those boulders behind you and give a holler if you hear or see anything."

"You do the same," Boris said.

"Good luck," Nancy said. "Remember you're a one-armed bandit."

"I'll protect him." Laura patted Phil on the shoulder.

"I hope Henri knows Kipling's poem and believes it," Nancy said.

Phil and Laura hiked up the grade. He tucked his bandaged left hand inside his half-zipped vest and held the knife in his right hand. They climbed at a steady even pace, but Phil felt the strain. He heard the click of Laura's paddle as she thrust it on the ground with each step. At the top of the ridge, they caught their breath and scanned the area. Grant had spoken of this area as the Thelon Oasis. Extensive stands of dwarf spruce and willow at least chest high dominated the region. If Henri attacked, it would be here.

Laura turned to him. "Do you want me to lead?"

"Take your time. Head along the cliffs first, but not too close. If we don't pick up a path, we'll turn inland."

"I don't like the look of the terrain out there." Laura walked along the rocky surface of the top of the cliffs. "Henri could be in that mini forest, and we'd never spot him."

He took a deep breath, nodded, but said nothing. They wove back and forth through heavy brush and came onto a small clearing. "This must be the campsite," Laura said. "It's perfect. High and clear and look at that view." She walked closer to the edge of the cliff, and after looking over his shoulder, he joined her.

"We can bring the canoes up here and camp," he said. "There isn't another path from below, and we're bound to find the portage path. Up here we can see what's coming at us from the forest."

A ptarmigan blasted from a thicket into the air, screeching. Laura grabbed Phil's arm. "That spooked me," she said.

"More important, who or what spooked it? A ptarmigan's warning can be a blessing." He moved toward the dwarfed trees. "Henri has to be out there somewhere, waiting, watching. "

"Phil, don't," Laura said with a catch in her voice.

Phil ignored her plea and walked cautiously toward the tree from which the bird had flown. *He's here, moving like a wolf.* Phil stalked through the area with his knife at the ready, but found nothing, not even an imprint or a crushed plant. Wending his way back to Laura, he said, "Perhaps we're too skittish." He didn't believe his words.

They retraced their steps down the path to the landing. "Looks clear, but I'm not certain." Phil turned to Laura. "What do you think?"

"We didn't see anything." She shrugged. "What choice do we have?"

"We should transport one canoe at a time to the top," Boris said. "Two carrying and two scouting for Henri."

"We can't leave one canoe unguarded." Phil pursed his lips. "Laura and Nancy, can you haul the canoe with the box in it?"

"We can try." Laura looked at Nancy.

Nancy gazed up the slope. "That uppermost part's steep, but if you're already on top, you can help us pull it the last few yards."

"Help me get the other canoe up on my shoulders, then I can carry it. Boris, you take the tent and scout ahead of me." Phil studied the others. "I have a feeling Henri's up there, watching, so keep a sharp eye."

Laura hefted the paddle she'd carried earlier. "I can use this in more ways than a walking stick."

"If I spot Henri and he has food, he'd better watch out," Nancy said. "Not having cigarettes is bad enough. I don't know which is worse, my headache or my stomachache."

Phil nodded to Boris. "Go ahead." He turned to Nancy and Laura. "Okay, help me become a beast of burden."

The women hoisted the canoe so the center thwart rested across Phil's shoulders. "Follow at a reasonable distance." With his head buried in the canoe's hull, his voice resounded as if he were in a cave.

They began to wrestle the canoes up the incline. Sweat dripped down Phil's back. He slipped several times, and each time his instinct was to reach out with his left hand to keep his balance. Instead, he concentrated on resting his bad hand against the outside of the hull. The throbbing pain from the pressure made him queasy. His calves strained and his thighs ached with each step. The thwart dug into his shoulders.

Behind him, the women grunted and groaned as they heaved and pulled the heavily laden canoe up the incline. This was when they were the most vulnerable, and Phil could only hope that with Boris giving them cover, Henri wouldn't attack. When he reached the top, his knees were shaking. He sighed and, like a mule trying to rid itself of cargo, he started to slip the canoe off on his right side.

Boris shouted, "Phil, watch out!"

Phil heard a thud as if a melon had been dropped. From under the hull, Phil spotted bowed legs running at him. He dropped to his knees and flipped the canoe toward the onrushing Frenchman. Henri rammed the canoe from the side, sending it and Phil to the edge of the cliff. The hull screeched across the shale like fingernails on a chalkboard. Phil scrambled to get hold of something, anything, to stop his momentum. His injured left hand flailed in the air as he gripped a bush with his right and flattened his body against the rough ground. Like a hat caught by the wind, the canoe slid over him, teetered on the edge, and fell into the river below. Phil rolled away from the precipice and staggered to his feet.

To his left, Boris sprawled on the ground, his face and chest bloodied. Henri disappeared over the lip of the path with his knife drawn. He heard screams from Laura and Nancy.

Boris struggled to rise and yelled at Phil. "For God's sake, help them."

Phil reached the top of the path as Laura dropped her end of the canoe. Henri slashed at her with his knife. She swung her paddle, catching the Frenchman on the right side of his chest. Henri spun, momentarily off balance, his face contorted in surprise. Phil scrambled down the path and leaped, clipping Henri from the back. They both fell, getting entangled by a thick mound of brush off the side of the path. Henri recovered first and stood, snarling. Laura swung her paddle again, but this time Henri grabbed it with one hand and swiped at her with the knife he held in his other hand. Trying to avoid the knife, she stumbled, grabbed a jutting rock and found a purchase for her feet. Phil pushed Henri from the back, sending him into the canoe. Nancy let go of her end of the canoe. A startled expression flashed across Henri's face as the boat slithered sideways.

Gravity did the rest. Henri grabbed the gunwale, his knife still clutched in one hand. Like a surfer, he rode the canoe as it slid down the path past

Nancy. The canoe tilted over the edge and skied down the slope, landing upright in the water. The river grabbed the craft, spinning it into the riffles away from shore.

Phil and Nancy helped Laura from the cliff's edge back onto the path. Laura clung to him, shaking, then pulled away. She wiped her hands on her pants, then she and Nancy hugged each other fiercely.

"We were awesome, weren't we?" Nancy said.

Below them Henri frantically looked toward shore, then at the falls. The craft headed toward the swirling rapids, bouncing and fluttering in its headlong run into whitewater. Without a paddle, he was at the mercy of the river.

"His only chance is to swim for it," Phil said as the three of them walked up the path.

Laura hurried to Boris who stood in wobbly stance. "Boris, your head's bleeding." She untied her bandana she wore around her neck and held it to the side of his head.

"He blind-sided me with a rock. I'll be okay. Thank God, you're all right. Lordy, but you're an avenging angel. Help me to the cliff edge, so I can see what's happening."

"The box." Nancy said. "If the box splits open, it'll contaminate the river."

They stood mesmerized by the unfolding drama below, their eyes riveted on Henri and the canoe.

"Can we do something?" Nancy glanced at Phil who shook his head at Henri's predicament.

Henri jumped into the water, pulled the painter line behind him as he swam toward the bank. An odd sense of loss came over Phil, and he found himself cheering the trapper on, hoping he'd make it.

"He's belaying the line around a rock mid river," Boris said. "Damn, if he isn't going to save himself and the bloody box."

But Henri was stuck. Swimming to shore was impossible, given the speed of the current. Only the shore below gave any hope of a landing and that was too far upstream. Henri climbed into the canoe, sat next to the box and waved to them.

"I'll be damned," Boris said. "What a fiend. He tried to kill us and now he's waving at us."

"There's not a thing we can do," Nancy said. "We haven't got a canoe."

Phil stared at Nancy. "Yes, we do." He watched the trapper gesticulate. "He's not waving at us. He's trying to tell us where his canoe is. It must be stashed along the river."

"He's pointing upstream," Laura said. "Even if we find it, what can we do?"

"If he's got enough rope on board, we can line the canoe out to him," Phil said.

"After he tried to kill us?" Laura voice strained with incredulity.

"The box," Nancy said. "We've got to get it, save it, save the river. Henri knows that. He loves the land."

"Let's search for his canoe." Phil started down the steep incline with Nancy behind him. When he got to the bottom, he looked upstream along the shore for a hiding place. Wriggling out of his daypack, he pulled out his binoculars and scanned the shoreline. "I can't see anything. I'll wade along the shore."

Nancy took off her pack, dropped it next to Phil's and pointed at the rocks above them. "Maybe I can spot it from above."

They started off in different paths over the rough terrain. In ankle freezing water, Phil struggled over slippery rocks, glanced up and saw Nancy covering ground faster than he was.

"Hey," she called. "I see it. Go another twelve feet. I think I can get to it from here if you can't." She skidded off a rock, caught herself and climbed from one boulder to the next. Phil, standing knee deep in water, waited. "I'll slide it down to you," she said, gasping as she lifted and pushed the laden canoe toward the water.

Phil grabbed the painter line with his good hand when the nose of the canoe jutted over a rock above the water. "Give it one more shove. I've got its line."

With a swoosh, the canoe splashed into the water. Nancy peered over a ledge and grinned. "Wait up. I'll help you haul the line to the landing."

When they had the canoe at the small inlet, Laura stood there waiting. "Boris stayed on top. He's in no condition to help. What now?"

"Rope." Phil began tossing Henri's bags onto shore.

Nancy rummaged through the gear. "Look, beef jerky." She hugged the package to her chest, then proffered it to Phil and Nancy.

"Rope." Phil yelled. "We need rope, now."

She dug farther and pulled out a packet of cigars. "Oh," she cried out. "A smoke."

"Damn it. Try the other duffle bag," Phil yelled.

"Okay, okay." Nancy rummaged through the other bag and pulled out a coil of line.

"It might be enough." Phil glanced at the downstream shoreline. "We can line the canoe down this bank closer to Henri, then belay one end of the rope to a rock or…maybe that root sticking out." He pointed. "See? With the line around the canoe's stern ring, it'll be safe for me to paddle the canoe out to him."

After they emptied the rest of the gear from the canoe, Laura took the bow line and crept forward along the base of the cliff. With Phil instructing her, Nancy held the stern line taut, letting it play out a little at a time as she followed Laura. Phil brought up the rear with the coil of rope around his shoulder.

"You realize you can't paddle," Nancy shouted over the river's roar as she concentrated on her footing.

"I'll have to."

"God, but you're egotistical. Don't you think anyone else can do anything?" She flung her words at him over her shoulder.

He didn't answer, but inched forward toward Laura, who stood on the last foothold where the cliff met the water. Out on the river about twenty feet away, Henri sat on his precarious rocky perch with the cold churning water beating against his legs. Phil began to tie one end of the rope to the canoe's stern line, but had a difficult time doing it with one hand, and Laura took over and finished the job.

"If you can't even tie a knot, how do you expect to paddle?" Laura asked as she tightened the knot.

"He's not, I am," Nancy said.

"Like hell." Phil was furious at himself, at the situation, knowing he really couldn't manage it with his damaged hand. He stared at Laura, hoping she'd offer since she was the better paddler, but Laura ignored him. "It's too dangerous for you, Nancy," he said.

"Look around," Nancy said. "That root you wanted to belay the rope around is useless. You're the only one strong enough to pull me back in and you'll probably need Laura's help to do it."

"You don't have enough experience." Phil looked at the coiled rope as if it were a snake.

"I've come too far to let that box smash up in the river. It's the only way and you know it. Everything I've ever taught, ever believed in is riding on this." She climbed into the rocking canoe and settled in the stern, her paddle poised.

Laura stared at her. "What about Henri? You can't trust him. Look how many people he's killed."

"I have no choice."

Phil held fast to the gunwale as the canoe dipped and bobbed in the water like a steer waiting to go out the rodeo gate. His mouth was close to Nancy's ear. He could smell her essence, her excitement, her fear. "When you get close, have Henri tie his painter line to your bowline. Make him get in the other canoe, not yours. Insist on it. If he doesn't comply, back off and we'll tow you back. Understand?"

"Got it." Nancy gripped the paddle tight, gritted her teeth and her dark brown eyes flashed.

"Paddle upstream like you were going to ferry across," Laura instructed, enunciating each word loudly with her hand on Nancy's tense shoulder. "When you can't paddle any farther and you start to slip back, turn the nose of the canoe downstream and stroke like hell into the middle of the river. That way you should sideslip toward Henri."

"Gotcha," Nancy said.

"You can do it," Phil called out as he gave her a mighty push with his good hand. A surge of helplessness enveloped him, and his heart pounded. He watched her maneuver the canoe upstream. She stroked pure and true into the churning water, sending the buoyant canoe's bow into the current. As if she'd canoed all her life, Nancy turned the nose downstream. Laura played out the rope, while Phil anchored himself to pull the rope back in. He belayed one end of the rope around his waist, waited and prayed.

"She's going to make it." Laura glanced at the amount of rope left to be played out. "She's there."

Henri reached out for the bow of Nancy's canoe. As he'd watched her paddle through the whitewater, he felt a rising pride in her accomplishment. *How odd, I cheer for my enemy. Here is the woman who ties me to Pierre's death, but this woman shares my dream for a pure wilderness. This is my place, my home. If this is what I must do, I do it.*

He caught the bow, looked up and smiled at a white-faced Nancy. "Courage. You did well, *mon Cherie,*" he shouted to be heard above the rush of water and the pounding falls. The canoe bucked under his firm grip. 'Take care. Keep canoe straight with the current. Makes your return better, so no capsize."

"Tie the painter lines together," Nancy yelled.

"Oui." Henri leaned over his canoe and plaited the two lines together before unraveling his line from around the rock. Instead of remaining in the canoe, he crawled onto the rock and hugged it between his short legs. Water spilled over his feet and gushed up his legs. "Now, sit in the bow of your canoe," he ordered Nancy.

She didn't move. Henri thought she hadn't heard him. He yelled louder. "Move to bow."

"No." She pointed at him. "You get into the other canoe first."

"Aha." *Crazy woman. She thinks I harm her.* "There's no return for me. Save my land. Go back with box." He gesticulated wildly, but she shook her head.

"Mon Dieu." His frustration grew. He was cold and tired, knowing his end was near. When he'd failed to kill them on the cliff, all was lost. The one act left for him was to save the river from the debris in Erich's box. "Listen, sit in bow. Face stern. Paddle from bow or you spin canoe and overturn."

Nancy's eyes searched his face. "You killed Erich, Pierre, Gilbert. How can I trust you?"

He shook his head. "I am fini."

Her body shivered, but she refused to move, fighting to keep the canoe in line with the current. It began to drift.

"Keep on line," he screamed and tugged the bow hard. The canoe rocked dangerously and she clutched the gunwales for support. *"Oui.* I kill all. You knew that. Anger a curse. I thought Leah and Pierre…." He shrugged. "Jealousy cruel, but I…. For my wilderness, I beg you, move to bow."

Unsteadily, Nancy rose from the stern and moved toward Henri. The canoe teetered. She clung to a gunwale with one hand, the paddle in the other. Henri's voice soothed and coaxed, as she continued toward him. At last she sat in the bow and faced the stern, opposite from the way she'd paddled before.

"Get in the other boat," she commanded.

Her back was now to Henri. For a split second, he thought of shoving her overboard, but instead took a deep breath, drew close to her and shouted in her ear.

"Too late for me. Go with God. Go, like eagle on wings. Save my land." He pushed the canoe hard. "Paddle."

And she did.

Henri waved for Phil to pull the canoes to shore. Phil leaned back and pulled the rope. *"En avant!"* he yelled as he hugged the rock amid the rapids and watched the canoes head toward shore and safety.

For the first time in years, Henri felt at peace. He scanned the cliffs and looked upward at the tissue paper clouds, then turned to view the great Thelon as it hurtled over the rock shelves. The awe and love he felt for the land burned within him, and he was not afraid. The river traveled through the wilderness, emptied into the ocean and became part of all that made up the world.

"Adieu," he whispered to the wind and slipped into the cold waters of the Thelon.

Chapter 33

Without a word, Laura and Phil pulled the canoes along the shore toward the rocky inlet. After securing them, Nancy got out and Laura hugged her. "Good job."

"Good, hell. It was fantastic," Phil said.

"Henri was brave in the end," Nancy said. "The roar of the falls is his elegy."

"After all he did, you're way too kind," Laura said.

"We'd better get everything topside," Phil said. They made two trips up the incline and then began to inventory Henri's supplies. A breeze fluttered Nancy's hair as she pawed through the packs and pulled out candy bars, pemmican and two cigars. "A treasure trove." She passed out the candy, then sat back on her heels munching while she studied a cigar lying by the toe of her boot.

"You're not going to smoke it, are you?" Laura asked.

Nancy shrugged.

Phil found Henri's two-way radio and tried to get a signal. Static crackled until a voice broke through—Chip's.

Phil grinned and nodded to the others. "Phil West here. Over."

"You're checking in early. Problems? Over."

"Yes. We need a pick up right away. We're at the portage campsite on the cliffs before the Clarke and Hanbury junction. Four dead. Two missing and two injured. Over."

"Jesus! Who's with you? Over."

Phil clicked off their names, feeling as if each of them were blessed.

"How bad arc the injured? Over."

"Not life-threatening. We can walk. Over."

"Can't pick you up at the portage. Can you make Ursus Island? Over."

"It'll be difficult. Only a little food left. Grant and Karen missing near last rapids. Over."

"I'll notify the Mounties. They'll start a search. No helicopters available for four or five days. All diverted to a disaster at Lac de Gras. Over."

Phil looked at the grim faces raised in anticipation. "We'll strike out for Ursus. Leaving the lead box with debris from Cosmos at portage campsite. Can Mounties pick up when helicopter available? Over."

"Understood. Will explain to them. Over."

"Isn't Lac de Gras the headwater of the Coppermine River? I thought mining interests wanted to drain it to mine for diamonds. Over."

"They had a cave-in. If you start the portage tomorrow, it should take two or three days to Ursus. Weather looks good. Some wind might slow you down. Check in tomorrow at 1600 hours. Good luck. Over."

"Thanks. Till tomorrow. Over." He clicked off the radio and stared at his companions. "You heard?" They nodded as he sank to the ground next to them.

"I thought our problems were over." Laura heaved a sigh as she held Boris's hand. "It's endless. Boris needs a doctor and so do you, Phil."

"I'll be okay," Boris said. "It's only a few more days. By the time we get picked up my ribs should be better and my head won't ache."

Phil gave a halfhearted smile. "Sure. You'll heal while the women do the work."

"You'd think we planned it." Despite his wounds, Boris had a twinkle in his eyes.

Phil turned to Nancy. "What's the food supply like?"

"Uninteresting, but edible. Pemmican, six freeze dried meals, powdered juice and coffee, hardtack biscuits and two cooking pans."

"I saw fishing gear," Laura said.

"Food's a little lean, but should be able to last us three days," Nancy said and smiled at Laura. "You and I are getting to be good paddle partners."

"Paddling out to Henri was heroic," Laura said.

Nancy gazed at the landscape and quietly said, "I feel bad about him."

"There wasn't anything you could have done," Phil said. "He was doomed from the moment he killed Pierre."

"I know." Nancy sighed. "He loved the land too much, but, damn, we need people with a passion for the earth."

"We wouldn't be in this predicament if it weren't for Henri." Laura's voice rose. "Deirdre and Cal would still be alive, and Karen and Grant. I'm glad Henri's dead." She paused and her eyes widened. "God, could he have survived the falls?"

"Not likely." Boris patted her hand. "It's over, honey. He paid for his crimes."

Laura hugged Boris gently, and Phil knew the two of them would be all right. There was an awkward silence, and he averted his eyes.

Nancy picked up the cigar, toyed with it, then stuck it between her teeth. She paled, removed the cigar and spat. "Yuck."

Phil threw his head back and laughed. "You might be cured of smoking."

"Hell of a way to do it." Nancy threw the cigar at him and stood. "When do we start hauling our gear across the portage?"

Phil glanced at Boris. "Walking two miles might be a bit much right now, and we're not sure what's on the other side for a campsite. Let's camp here tonight and set out at first light."

That night Boris and Laura used Henri's tent, while Nancy and Phil shared the sleeping bag outside. With the sun setting, the wind died, and the chill of night settled over them. Tucking extra netting from Henri's equipment around them, they watched the night deepen. On the horizon the thin red line of sunlight blinked out.

With her arms under her head, Nancy gazed heavenward. "What're you going to do after this, Phil?"

He turned his head toward her. "I'll stick with the Bureau. Ask for a transfer."

"You've become a good teacher. You can make a difference in people's lives teaching."

He pursed his lips. "That's why I joined the Bureau, to make a difference."

"Have you?"

"I think so. There are too many people who thwart our laws."

She turned to look at him. "Meaning me?"

"What're you going to do about *Cure the World*?"

"I still believe in our cause. Maybe I did take a wrong turn with the organization, but that doesn't mean its principles aren't worthwhile. Henri did a lot of evil for what he perceived as a just cause."

"He believed the end justified the means," Phil said.

"And you?"

He was about to argue, when she continued. "I don't want to debate. Not now, after all we've been through." She looked at him and traced the back of her fingers across his whiskered jaw. "I don't want my organization to cause evil, but I'll continue to protest against things that harm the environment. I'll keep a steady hand on the tiller, keep the boat upright, even in rough water." She smiled at her metaphor. "I've become a good paddler, don't you think?"

"In many ways, you're on course. I'm glad. Makes it easier for me to move on."

"We are what we are." Nancy hesitated. "Always be my friend, Phil. Let's not lose that."

"You've got a deal."

She began to laugh. "It's ironic. I finally get you in bed and I'm asking you to be my friend."

Phil smiled, leaned over and kissed her on the cheek. "To friendship."

Three days later, the portage and the falls were behind them and Ursus Island came into view. They beached the canoes and waited for Chip's seaplane to wing its way across the far plateau, bank up the river and glide toward their sandy beach. He was late, and the little band of survivors worried. Phil tried the radio to no avail. They sat on the beach, waiting and discussing their options if he didn't come. Time ticked by.

Late in the afternoon the soft drone of an engine slid through the air. They stood and waved with excitement and relief when they spotted the seaplane. After a clean landing followed by a docking near the shoreline, Chip's lean frame appeared in the fuselage door. He waved with a wide grin on his face, threw a line to Laura, who caught it deftly, and then he leaped ashore, giving both women a bear hug.

Chip glanced at Phil's left hand as he grabbed his right hand in a hearty shake. "Guess you won't be needing a partner after all, but what the heck, you got out alive." He pulled Phil's head onto his skinny shoulder and thumped his back.

"Don't grab me," Boris said, backing away. "My ribs are cracked."

Chip put his arm around Boris's shoulders in gentle camaraderie. "You're too ugly to hug. You were prettier when I dropped you off. What in the hell happened to your face?"

"Henri took a couple chunks out of me."

"That old hunter must have hung a tin can to your tails. I'm really sorry. Glad to see your bright faces. You gave the Mounties and me a real scare. I'm sure you're eager to leave."

"That's an understatement," Laura said.

"Before we pack you into the plane and tie on the canoes, I've got a surprise for you." He turned toward his plane and hollered. "Come on and show 'em how tough we Canadians are."

The thin, bedraggled figures of Karen and Grant appeared in the open doorway. Phil and the others hurried forward to the couple risen from the Thelon River.

During the emotional meeting, Chip stood aside. "Found them this morning when I gave another look-see on the river's western bank. Had to make a fancy maneuver to land, but I took a shot and it panned out."

With the six survivors on board, Chip's plane sped across the sky above the Northwest Territory. Cloud shadows spread across the earth below. The raw beauty of the land pulled at Phil as he mulled over all that had transpired. *Seventeen years is a long time to harbor an obsession. I wanted riches from this land, expected it, dreamed about it. Now, all I want is peace for me and this land.*

Perhaps Henri had won after all.

JUN 0 3 2023

CPSIA information can be obtained
at www.ICGtesting.com
Printed in the USA
FSOW03n0825151015
12053FS

9 781593 308407